Dear Reader:

Is it possible for a man to truly change? Can he go from being selfish and immature, to being responsible and compassionate? In *A Cold Piece of Work*, Solomon Singletary becomes that man. Curtis Bunn has penned an honest portrayal of a man who initially believes that women are fit for only one purpose but realizes that without one true love, nothing else really matters.

A man can have a thousand lovers but, at the end of the day, he might very well have absolutely nothing to show for it. Once he comprehends that he has allowed Mrs. Right to slip through his fingers, Solomon becomes determined to make amends for his previous actions. It is not easy but he forges on, hell bent on rekindling a flame that has long ago been extinguished and trying to make up the time he has lost with the one person who should be the most important element in his life.

A Cold Piece of Work is both a masterpiece and a conversation piece. It is refreshing to see a male writer write so candidly about men, instead of trying to sugarcoat the truth or portray them in a perfect, positive light. Everyone is flawed but everyone can also be redeemed.

As the Founder of The National Book Club Conference and an *Essence* Bestselling Author, Bunn knows what readers expect from a powerful book, and he delivers expertly.

As always, thanks for supporting myself and the Strebor Books family. We strive to bring you cutting-edge literature that cannot be found anyplace else. For more information on our titles, please visit Zanestore.com. My personal web site is Eroticanoir. com and my online social network is PlanetZane.org.

Blessings,

Zane

Publisher
Strebor Books
www.simonandschuster.com/streborbooks

A
COLD
PIECE
OF
WORK

A NOVEL

ZANE PRESENTS

A COLD PIECE OF PIECE OF WORK

A NOVEL

CURTIS BUNN

SBI

STREBOR BOOKS

NEW YORK LONDON TORONTO SYDNEY

SBI

Strebor Books
P.O. Box 6505
Largo, MD 20792
http://www.streborbooks.com

ISBN 978-1-59309-376-1
ISBN 978-1-4516-1716-0 (e-book)
LCCN 2011927933

First Strebor Books trade paperback edition July 2011

Cover design: www.mariondesigns.com
Cover photograph: © Keith Saunders/Marion Designs

10 9 8 7 6 5 4 3 2 1

Manufactured in the United States of America

For information regarding special discounts for bulk purchases,
please contact Simon & Schuster Special Sales at 1-866-506-1949
or business@simonandschuster.com

The Simon & Schuster Speakers Bureau can bring authors to your
live event. For more information or to book an event, contact the
Simon & Schuster Speakers Bureau at 1-866-248-3049 or visit our
website at www.simonspeakers.com.

To my son, Curtis Jr., daughter, Gwendolyn (Bunny)
and my nephew, Gordon, who is like a son.
You warm my heart, even on the coldest days.

ACKNOWLEDGMENTS

God, the Almighty, is the beginning and the end for me. He carried me not only through the journey of writing this book, but also through my daily challenges. As with everything in my life, He deserves all the praise.

Family is everything, and mine makes me whole, starting with my late father, Edward Bunn Sr. His memory lives through us, his family. My mom, Julia Bunn, is the best and most giving. My brothers, Billy and Eddie, and my sister, Tammy, mean the world to me. My grandmother, Nettie Royster, is our spiritual foundation.

Curtis Jr. and Gwendolyn (Bunny) are my children and lifeblood. My nephew, Gordon, is essentially my second son. And my niece, Tamayah (Bink Bink), and nephew, Eddie Jr., are blessings. My cousins, Greg Agnew and Warren Eggleston, are like my brothers. And I am grateful for cousin Carolyn Keener and uncle Al and aunts Thelma and Barbara.

Najah Aziz is special to me and is fodder for a future book—a love story.

So much love and respect go to Zane, Charmaine Roberts Parker and the entire Strebor Books family for the confidence to make this book a joyful reality. I'm proud to be a part of the Strebor family.

My support is vast and I am grateful (there are not enough pages to document everyone by name) for the people who mean something to me. Here are some: Trevor Nigel Lawrence, Wayne Ferguson, Kerry Muldrow, Keith Gibson, Randy Brown, Sam Myers, Tony Hall, Tony Starks, Darryl (DJ) Johnson, Rick Eley, Denise Bethea, Betty Roby, Tara Ford Payne, Diana Joseph, Marc Davenport, Greg Willis, Ronnie Bagley, Brian White, Ronnie Akers, Jacques Walden, Dennis Wade, Julian Jackson, Mark Webb, Kelvin Lloyd, Frank Nelson, Mark Bartlett, Marvin Burch, Shelia Bryant, George Hughes, Serena Knight, Marty McNeal, Tamitrice Mitchell, Edward (Bat) Lewis, Kathy Brown, Darryl K. Washington, Shelia Harrison, Patricia Easley, Lateefah Aziz, Kent Davis, Jeff Stevenson, Derrick Muldrow, Lyle V. Harris, Brad Corbin, J.B. Hill, William Mitchell, Carmen Carter, Lesley Hanesworth, Gina Dorsey, Mary Knatt, Sonya Perry, E. Franklin Dudley, Skip Grimes, Denise Taylor, Bob White, Jeri Byrom, Hadjii Hand, Laurie Hunt, Monya Bunch, Karen Shepherd, Clifford Benton, Rob Parker, Cliff Brown, Stephen A. Smith, D. Orlando Ledbetter, Michele Ship, Leslie LeGrande Pitt, Francine McCarley, Emma Harris, Garry Howard, Len Burnett, Venus Chapman, D.L. Cummings, Jay Nichols, Ralph Howard, Paul Spencer, Jai Wilson, Garry Raines, Glen Robinson, Dwayne Gray, Jessica Ferguson, Carolyn Glover, David R. Squires, Mike Dean, Veda McNeal,

Alvin Whitney, Avis Easley, Kimberly Yeager, Penny Payne, Tawana Turner-Green, Sonji Robinson, Vonda Henderson, Mark Lassiter, Shauna Tisdale, Tony Carter, Tamaira Thompson, Sharon Foster, LaToya Williams, Claire Batiste, Olivia Alston, Brenda O'Bryant, Sheryl Williams Jones, Leticia McCoy, Dorothy (Dot) Harrell, Bruce Lee, Elaine Richardson, Aggie Nteta, Danny Anderson, Val Guilford, Luther Clark, Leon H. Carter, Bruce Lee, Curtis West, Zack Withers, Ramona Palmer, Andre Aldridge, Marilyn Bibby, Brad Turner, Desyre Morgan, Billy Robinson, Denise Thomas, D.D. Turner, Judith Greer, David A. Brown, Linda Vestal, Sharon Foster, Anita Wilson, Derek T. Dingle, Tim Lewis, Carrie Haley, Demetress Graves, Dexter Santos, Ron Thomas, April Tarver, Karen Faddis, Michelle Lemon, Regina Collins, Michelle Hixon, Jay Nichols, Regina Troy, Karen Turner, Quimonder Jones, Dr. Yvonne Sanders-Butler, Toni Tyrell, Tanecia Raphael, Tracie Andrews, Sheila Powe, Tammy Grier, Sid Tutani, Mike Christian, Carla Griffin and The Osagyefuo Amoatia Ofori Panin, King of Akyem Abuakwa Eastern Region of Ghana, West Africa.

Special thanks and love to my great alma mater, Norfolk State University (Class of 1983); the brothers of Alpha Phi Alpha (especially the Notorious E Pi of Norfolk State); Ballou High School (Class of '79), Washington, D.C.; the lovely ladies of Like The River The Salon in Atlanta, the Aziz family and ALL of Southeast Washington, D.C.

I am also grateful to all the book clubs that have supported this work and to my literary friends Nathan McCall, Kimberla Lawson Roby, Carol Mackey, Linda Duggins, Karen Hunter, Troy Johnson of www.aalbc.com and Terrie Williams.

I'm sure I left off some names; I ask your forgiveness. If you know me, you know I appreciate and I am grateful for you.

Peace and blessings,

CURTIS

CHAPTER 1
LOVE TO LOVE YOU

The force of his thrusts pushed her to the edge of the four-poster bed. She was lathered as much in satisfaction as she was in sweat, exhilarated and weary—and unable to hold herself atop the mattress against his unrelenting strikes. A different kind of man would have postponed the passion; at least long enough to pull up her naked, vulnerable body.

But Solomon Singletary was hardly one to subscribe to conventional thinking or deeds. He always had a point to prove and always was committed to proving it—with actions, not words.

And so, Solomon thrust on…and on, until they, as one, careened onto the carpet together, she cushioning his fall from beneath him. So paralyzed in pleasure was she that she never felt the impact of the tumble. Rather, she found humor that they made love clean across the bed and onto the floor, and she found delight that the fall did not disengage them.

Solomon lost neither his connection to her nor his cadence, and stroked her on the carpet just as he had on the sheets—purposefully, unrelentingly, deeply.

"What are you trying to do?" she asked. "Make love to me? Or make me love you?"

Solomon did not answer—not with words. He continued to speak the language of passion, rotating his hips forward, as one would a hula-hoop. Her shapely, chocolate legs were airborne and his knees were carpet-burned raw, but hardly did he temper his pace.

His answer: Both.

She finally spoke the words that slowed Solomon. "Okay, okay," she said. "Okay." She gave in, and that pleased Solomon. She would have said the words earlier— before they tumbled off the bed—but he never allowed her to catch her breath. All she could make were indecipherable sounds.

"I mean, damn," she said, panting. "We're good together…Damn."

Solomon kissed her on her left shoulder and rolled off her and onto the floor, on his wide, strong back. He looked up toward the dark ceiling illuminated by the single candle on the nightstand, so pleased with himself that a smile formed on his face.

Then he dozed off right there on the floor. She didn't bother to wake him. Instead, she reached up and pulled the comforter off the bed and over both of them. She nestled her head on his hairy chest, smiled to herself and drifted off to sleep with him, right there on the floor.

That was the last time she saw Solomon Singletary. And he only saw her a few times, but only in dreams that did not make much sense.

"I wish I knew what the hell it meant," he said to his closest friend, Raymond. He and Ray became tight five years earlier, when they got paired together during a round of golf at Mystery Valley in Lithonia, just east of Atlanta. They had a good time, exchanged numbers and ended up becoming not only golf buddies, but also great friends.

Ray was very much the opposite of Solomon. He was not as tall but just as handsome, and he was charismatic and likeable, in a different way. Solomon was sort of regal to some, arrogant to others. Ray was more every man. He had a wife of seven years, Cynthia, and a six-year-old son, Ray-Ray. He was stable.

Solomon knew a lot of people, but only liked some and trusted only a few. He really only tolerated most; especially the various women who ran in and out of his life like some nagging virus. "In the end," he told Ray, "the one person you can trust is yourself. And even with that, how many times have you lied to yourself?"

Ray figured there was something deep inside Solomon that would bring him to such feelings, and he figured if Solomon wanted him to know, he would have told him. So he never asked. Ray and Solomon coveted each other's friendship and had a certain trust. And they shared most everything with each other.

Ray's way was to provide levity when possible, which, for him, was practically all the time. His upbeat disposition seldom changed. If the Falcons lost a football game, he'd show disgust and disappointment for a while, but he'd let it go.

Solomon Singletary was not that way. He could be solemn at times, even-tempered at others and occasionally aggressive. Above all, he was quite adept at pulling people close to him. He had a unique ability to be open but remain private. He could be disinterested but still engaging. And those unique qualities made people open up to him; especially women.

"You're so interesting," Michele told him that last night together. "We've dated for six months. You try to act like you don't love me, but you do; I can tell by how we make love. Why won't you say you love me?"

"Come here." Michele came over to him, to the edge of her bed. "Don't get caught up on what I say to you or don't say," he said. "Worry about what I do to you; how I make you feel."

"Is everything about sex with you?"

"See, I wasn't even talking about sex. I was talking about how you feel inside, when we're together, when you think of me," Solomon said. "That's more important than what I say. Right?"

Before she could answer, he leaned over and kissed her on the lips softly and lovingly. "What does that kiss say?"

"It says you want to make love," Michele said sarcastically. "Some things can get lost in translation. That's why you should say it. Plus, sometimes it's just good to hear."

"Hear this." Solomon kissed Michele again. This time, it was not a peck, but a sustained coming together of lips and tongue and saliva. He leaned her back on the bed, and she watched as he pulled his tank top over his head, revealing his expansive chest and broad shoulders.

He smiled at her and she smiled back and the talk of saying "I love you" ceased.

"Whatever happened to that girl?" Ray asked Solomon. "You regret not having her now?"

"Regret? What's that? You make a decision and you stick to it. No looking back. But a few years ago, I saw a woman briefly who reminded me of her, and it made me think about calling her."

"You thought about it? Why didn't you call her?" Ray wanted to know.

"Hard to say. Young, dumb. Silly," Solomon answered. "What would've been the point? I got a job here with Coke and wasn't about to do the long distance thing. So what was the point?"

"Well, did you at least break up on good terms?" Ray asked.

"The last time I saw her, she was on the floor next to her bed, sleeping. I got up and put on my clothes and left. The next day, the movers came and I drove here, to Atlanta."

"Wait," Ray said, standing up. "She didn't know you were moving out of town?"

"Nah," Solomon said, looking off. "Nah."

"How can you just roll out on the girl like that?"

CHAPTER 2
DINERO

Solomon Singletary had a perfectly rhythmic name, a strong name, a Biblical name—a name that effortlessly rolled off the tongue, like a drop of rain down a windshield.

To say his full name was akin to singing the first notes of a song, a ballad about love lost and found or triumph over tragedy. Something that signified a happy ending.

And yet, on many occasions, when he was feeling especially ornery, he preferred to be called "Money." This was a rather parochial moniker for someone who was quite sophisticated, well-traveled, educated and un-assuming.

The irony was that his name was not about currency at all. Not really. It was more about confidence.

When he was twelve, playing basketball at Fort Stanton Park in Southeast Washington, D.C, an older guy who was respected in the neighborhood because he was an outstanding player—but mostly because he could whip anyone's ass—told a group of his peers one July after-noon his impressions of Solomon as a player.

"This one right here," Big George said, holding onto the back of Solomon's t-shirt. "This kid is a player. This kid is money."

Those thirteen words from Big George changed the way Solomon looked at himself. He became the most respected kid in the neighborhood just on Big George's word. He was money, literally. At least for Big George.

It was not until about three months later, when the weather broke for good and outdoor hoops was close to being shelved until spring, that Solomon learned Big George had been placing bets on his pickup games with other older guys. They bet on most everything and would even bet to see who could predict what time the Metro bus would come over the hill on Morris Road toward the park.

While handing him fifty dollars a week before Halloween, Big George said to Solomon: "Like I said a while ago, you are money. I bet on your teams to win and you did. So, here's your cut."

"Why didn't you tell me you were betting on my teams?" Solomon asked, and it was the right question.

"'Cause I didn't want you to be gambling. And I didn't want you to know," Big George said. "Sometimes, people start trying to do too much when they know someone's relying on them. I wanted you to do what you do, play like you play. And you were money."

"Why do you say that? Money?" Solomon asked.

"'Cause money is good," Big George said. "With money, you can do anything. I looked at you as a good player who could do anything on the court. You were good. You were reliable. I could see that in you."

"Oh, okay." Solomon looked at the fifty dollars.

"You ain't never had that much money before, huh?" Big George said.

Only twelve, Solomon recalled the hundred dollars his uncle from New York had given him one Christmas, but he had enough common sense to lie to Big George. *Why take away Big George's moment?* he thought, even at that young age. "No," Solomon said. "Thank you."

"Hide it from your parents; don't let them see it," Big George said. "They gonna think you did something bad to get it."

"Okay," Solomon said, and Big George rubbed him on his head and actually thanked Solomon.

"Kid, I appreciate you," he said. "See you later…Money."

Solomon walked away beaming and feeling he was full of promise. He had called himself "Money" ever since, to himself mostly. Growing up, "Money" was more of an internal flame than an outward appearance. He was shy and soft spoken—and scared of girls, even. But Big George instilled something in Solomon that never diminished.

He was proud to have grown up in Southeast Washington, D.C., a fact he proudly displayed on a tattoo on his left shoulder blade. Only if he took off his shirt could it be seen. It read, simply:

S.E. D.C.

He would move from home, but the tattoo was a way

of his city staying with him. "Southeast D.C.," he answered when someone asked where he was from. Never just "D.C." He was always specific.

"Just so they know," he said.

He was proud that he "escaped" the traps that too often crippled many he knew: crack, crime, craziness. His high school basketball coach—someone he at one point admired—was arrested for selling drugs…during the season. His good friend and neighbor stole the one girl he had interest in. Classmates were killed or strung out on drugs.

Ultimately, Solomon "Money" Singletary believed that the fewer people he called "friends," the fewer opportunities he would have to be disappointed.

"If I want to deal with drama," he told Ray most times when his friend tried to coax him into connecting with more people, "I'll create it for myself—not let someone else do it."

His mom and dad divorced when he was seventeen and about to graduate from Ballou High School. That was drama. "You couldn't wait another month to save me all this chaos?" he asked his parents, tears streaming down his hairless face. "Thanks a lot."

He had no siblings and was not mad about it. "Just another person close to you who would let you down," he said.

Kids he considered friends joked him about his dark complexion and pronounced ears. "The Fly," some kids called him. He grew into a handsome man, but the name-calling hurt him as a child. Worse, he gained an utter disdain for females. More accurately, he detested their potential to hurt his feelings.

All that around him, and he would not acquiesce to the elements that were pulling him toward trouble. And for all his parents provided—love, attention, guidance— it was Big George's confidence in him that held him together.

He never spoke to Big George again after that day he planted fifty dollars in his hands; a few months later, Big George was killed. The newspaper said it was a random shooting. Older guys in the neighborhood said it was a direct attack at Big George. They said, ironically enough, he owed some people some money.

Whatever the circumstances, Big George was gone, and Solomon felt almost an obligation to be "Money" as a way of honoring the guy who unwittingly gave him some self-esteem.

That self-esteem was prominent in how he slowly blossomed from a shy kid to a confident young man. Girls he once considered too cute for him eventually pursued *him*. He was smart, tall, handsome, funny, charming and, most significantly, Solomon knew how to harness his confidence in a way that exuded self-assuredness, not cockiness.

All those virtues attracted women almost nonstop and from all walks of life, so much so that he referred to them by their profession instead of their names.

There was "the CEO," "the nurse," "the project manager," "the collection agent," "the dancer" and "the bartender," among others. Those surnames spoke to his lack of regard for them. Solomon was wary of women. They say your childhood shapes who or what you become, and the way he was ostracized or disregarded by girls as a youth and then mistreated by them as a young man created a disdain and lack of trust in them as an adult that was hard to shake. He actually grew to find a mild level of satisfaction in disappointing them.

His pain came in a succession of events that turned him from an innocent teenager into a scorned revenge-seeker. Stephanie Morrison, the cutest girl in his neighborhood, became his first real girlfriend at fourteen. Everyone at Douglass Junior High School knew they were together.

So when he saw her kissing Doug Packer after school by the corner store, Solomon was crushed. He ran home, devastated. In high school the next year, Sandy Taylor was his first love. Three months into the relationship, he found out that she was also the first love of Mark Johnson. Solomon wondered if he was the problem.

But when, in college, he learned that girlfriend Lisa Maxie was the person who took his television, VCR, CDs, suits and jewelry from his apartment, he *knew* he was the problem. He had trusted women to do as right by him as he was by them. He thought they would appreciate that he was unlike other men. He didn't need to have two or three girls to feel fulfilled. He remembered Al Pacino, in the movie *Donnie Brasco*, saying, "One broad; that's enough for anyone."

But as the disappointments kept piling up, his bitterness turned into distrust and dislike.

Of all the friends and fraternity brothers—Alpha Phi Alpha—he made over the years, in Ray he confided the most. "I love women, but I don't know if I like them or believe in them," he said to Ray one day as they played a round of golf at Wolf Creek near the Atlanta airport. "You know what I mean?"

"I sure the hell don't," Ray answered.

"Well, women might not run the world," Solomon explained, "but they pretty much control relationships. The man has to do the chasing. If you don't look a certain way or do certain things, they aren't interested. It starts young, too. I had women do me wrong from when I was fourteen.

"When I got to high school, it wasn't any better. We had 'season girls'—when your season as an athlete was in, they were interested in you. In college I had women steal from me, cheat on me—basically dog me. I was the victim."

He stood there—a muscularly slender six-foot-two, two hundred fifteen pounds—and stared at Ray with those eyes that were dark and quiet, like nighttime in the woods.

"Here's the thing I believe in: I'm here to please." His voice was clear and there was no ambivalence. He said what he meant. "Some women simply need to be pleased. Not enough good men to go around, so I do a service."

Ray did not accept that. "And you connected with none of them? You're completely detached?" He was miffed at his friend. "Of all the women you know and you've dated, none of them made you believe she was there because she liked you as a person? None of them made you feel good about her? None of them? You still angry at women over things kids said to you?"

"Well, in a way, yeah," Solomon said. "It is what it is. And, for the record, there was one chick who was cool. But she would've been a disappointment, too. It's their way."

"You know what? It's sad you are this jaded. I never would've guessed it," Ray said. "Not by your actions. You're with beautiful women all the time.

"You've got issues," Ray added, which was a reason Solomon was close to him. Ray had no problem giving it to Solomon raw. There was no pretense in the relationship; no bullshit. "Let go of these issues with women. I don't know how, but—"

"I don't have any issues with women; I have *beliefs* about women," Solomon said. "But I'm not worried about women. I have that under control; believe me. How we get on women anyway?"

More important to Solomon was making an impact on kids the way Big George had impacted him. So he volunteered as a youth basketball coach at Gresham Park in Decatur, near Atlanta. His kids called him "Coach Money."

"Kids are safe," Solomon said. "I can hang with them, coach them, teach them some things and feel good about it. I don't have to worry about them wanting anything from me. They're innocent."

"Man, you sound like Michael Jackson," Ray said. "The late, great Michael Jackson."

"Whatever, fool. You know what I mean."

In his two years as a youth basketball coach, he became particularly attached to one kid who reminded him of himself: a seven-year-old named Gerald Williams. Gerald was somewhat quiet, but talented and tough. Brown skin, long arms and legs, round head with Martin Lawrence ears.

Gerald's mom would drop him off at the gym an hour before practice on her way to a part-time job as a jewelry store sales clerk at South DeKalb Mall. Solomon would arrive a little while later, giving the kid and the coach time to chat before the other kids arrived. And they would talk about everything.

"My momma said I can play basketball if I do my chores at home," Gerald said one evening.

"Your momma knows what she's talking about," Solomon responded. "I've been coaching you all season and I haven't met your mother yet. But she's teaching you responsibility. You know what that is?"

"Yes. It means to do what you're supposed to do," the kid said.

"Oh, so you're smart, too. Good," Solomon said. "Does your daddy give you chores, too?"

He was sorry he asked the question as soon as it came

out. He noticed that most of the kids who came to the center were picked up and dropped off by mothers, meaning the fathers were less involved than they should have been. Or not involved at all.

"My daddy is no good," little Gerald said.

"Why do you say that?" Solomon asked.

"That's what my momma says."

"Do you see your daddy?"

Gerald shook his head. "I never seen him," the kid said.

"Saw," Solomon said. "You should have said 'I never saw him.' Not 'seen,' okay?'

"Okay," Gerald said. "I never saw my daddy."

And in that instant, Solomon became sad—and more attached to the kid. He felt even more of a responsibility to impact his life, to give him guidance. He was fortunate to have had both parents growing up, and realized how much it meant to have his father around to help mold him into a man.

"Well, guess what? He doesn't know you and that's too bad for him because you are a special young man," Solomon told Gerald. "You remember that, okay?"

"Yes, sir," Gerald said.

After that day, Gerald became Solomon's feel-good project. The kid was the team's best player and his confidence grew as he took individual instruction from Solomon, who had been a basketball star at Ballou High School in D.C. and at Norfolk State University.

Their routine was set: Solomon would arrive at practice

to be greeted by young Gerald at the door—smiling and eager. The boy became the shining beacon in Solomon's life. There was Ray, his closest friend, some golf buddies and fraternity friends and a host of women he dealt with, but had no true connection to.

"You know what I noticed?" Ray said to Solomon one Saturday afternoon following the last game of the season. Solomon's team had won its fourth game in a row and little Gerald scored eleven points. They were standing by the team's bench and Gerald and his teammates were exiting the gym to meet their parents in the parking lot.

"Do I really want to know?" Solomon said. "Better than that: Do I really care?"

"Like I care if you care or not," Ray said, smirking. "Anyway, you smile when you're around that kid more than you do when you're with any of those women you run around with. Why's that?"

Solomon smiled at the thought. "You know what?" he said. "You have a point. I guess it's really because he's a good kid who I can see is coming out of his shell. He reminds me of me. I was shy and quiet growing up. I kind of grew out of it later in life.

"And guess what I called him today?"

"What?"

"Money," Solomon said, and he could not help from flashing a brilliant smile, a smile that made him look younger than his thirty-four years.

"What's that about?" Ray said.

"When I was a kid—but not as young as Gerald is now," he said, "I was unsure of myself about sports and girls, you know? Then this older guy that everyone considered cool told everybody I was 'money.' He thought I was the best player among my friends. Because it came from this guy—'Big George'—it boosted my confidence.

"So, I look at Gerald and think maybe I can do the same for him."

"That would mean he thinks you're so cool he'd be inspired by you, which is a leap," Ray said, laughing.

Solomon could not help but laugh. It, indeed, was presumptuous to think he could be a factor in Gerald's life. He could impact women; he'd done it much of his adult life, and with great ease. A kid? He wasn't sure. Then that confidence that engulfed him took over.

"Whatever, fool," Solomon said. "This kid never met his father and sounds like his mom is some bitter woman who hates the daddy. That's tough on a kid. If I can make him feel better about himself, what's wrong with that?"

"Oh, nothing wrong with it at all, Coach Money," Ray said sarcastically. "Seriously, though, that's a good thing. I've been talking about joining Big Brothers of Atlanta."

"Talking to who?" Solomon asked.

"Myself," Ray cracked.

"My bad—I forgot you're a mental patient. But anyway," Solomon said, "In essence, this is my Big Brothers project. And, to be honest, I need this for me as much as I need to do it for him."

On the way out of the gym, the youth league director, Jay Nichols, caught up to Solomon and Ray. "Coach Money," he said, "just want you to know the end-of-season banquet is here in two weeks. I need you to pick the award-winners for your team so I can get those trophies."

"I can give those names to you now," Solomon said. "I'm looking forward to it."

Immediately, Solomon began to plot on how to *really* make an impact on young Gerald. He was going make him the team's most outstanding player. He was going to tell all the players and parents about how much growth he had seen in Gerald, how he had grown as much as a young man as he had a terrific young basketball player.

How could that not make the kid feel good? Big George hardly had any pomp and circumstance with his declaration of Solomon as "money," and Solomon swore it changed his life.

This platform—at the banquet—was just the place to laud Gerald. No way he could leave feeling anything but pride and have a measure of confidence that would stretch as wide as his infectious grin.

So, when the banquet came, Solomon was particularly excited. He was dapper in a navy suit that draped off his fit body and a crisp white shirt with a dazzling multi-colored necktie. His shoes glistened as if waxed at a car wash.

He hung out behind the stage during the ceremony

until it was his time to deliver awards to his players. When he went to the bathroom, he ran into Gerald. "Hey, Gerald. How are you? Where's your mom?" he said.

"She's at the table, in there," he said.

"Okay, see you later."

The gymnasium at the rec center was packed, which pleased Solomon. He was comfortable in front of people and wanted as many people as possible to learn about Gerald.

So, when it was his turn to distribute awards, one-by-one, he not only delivered the trophies, he also offered insightful, humorous and encouraging remarks about each player.

Predictably, he saved Gerald for last.

"This young man has grown so much since the first practice," Solomon said. "He came here a little shy and uncertain of himself. By the time the season ended, he was our leader on the floor and a very productive player. Actually, he reminds me so much of me as a kid that it's scary.

"With that, I am proud to give our outstanding player award to…Gerald Williams."

The audience clapped as Solomon searched the crowd for Gerald. Finally, he spotted him at a front table near the front right, apparently with his mom, who Solomon could see was crying.

He motioned for Gerald to come forward to receive his award, but his mother clutched his arm. Solomon could not make out what the kid said to her, but his gesture indicated he was puzzled as to why she would not let him come forward.

Solomon was puzzled, too.

"Gerald," he said into the microphone, "come on up."

Most eyes turned to the kid and his mom, which prompted her to let him go. Finally. As Gerald made his way to the platform, Solomon zoomed in on the mother. She looked familiar, so much so that a feeling came over him as their eyes locked.

Tears flowed down her face, and Solomon could not look away. Gerald made it to the stage, but Solomon was transfixed on his mother. And as sudden as a thunderbolt, it hit him: Gerald Williams' mother was Michele Lynn—the woman he left sleeping on the floor next to her bed *eight years* earlier.

Solomon's heart raced. He was shocked, but he shook himself out of it long enough to greet Gerald.

"Uh, Money, congratulations," he said, shaking his hand and handing him his trophy. "I'm really proud of you."

Gerald clutched the award and raised it so his mother could see. She smiled through the tears and clapped for him.

Solomon and Gerald posed together for pictures taken by the hired photographer, Sid Tutani, and others. Gerald went back to his seat and Solomon stood there, watching, staring, trying to make sure his eyes were in tune with reality. It was her; a little heavier around the waist and face. But it was her.

"Oh, my God," he mumbled to himself. "Oh, my God."

CHAPTER 3
EIGHT
WAS ENOUGH

Solomon was as sure of himself as most anyone, especially with women, but he was uncertain how to deal with seeing Michele at the banquet. Her presence threw off his equilibrium. Suddenly, he was totally uncomfortable.

He had left her while she slept; moved from D.C. to Atlanta the next day and never looked back. Changed his cell number. Did not answer her e-mails. Totally cut her off—and with no explanation. Ever.

Now there she was, looking every bit as captivating as she did when they dated: flawless skin, save for a small mole on the left side of her face; fashionable short haircut that was longer but still nicely shaped her oval face; chic eyeglasses that magnified her intellect and gave her a more conservative look than she really was. The added pounds were noticeable but it was Michele.

To add to Solomon's drama, unbeknownst to him, he had gained affection for the son of a woman he'd abandoned.

He literally could feel sweat developing on his forehead.

Solomon wanted to talk to her, but was wary of how she would react to him. Plus, he was unsure of what explanation he had to offer if she were interested in what he had to say.

After they made eye contact, Michele would not look his way. And when the closing statements were done to wrap up the banquet, she grabbed Gerald's hand and they headed for the exit.

That's when Solomon acted like Solomon. He hurried behind them and caught up just before they departed the building.

"Hey, Gerald!" he yelled out. They stopped and turned toward Solomon. He hurriedly walked forward. "Is this your mother?"

He looked at Michele and there was an expression of anger in her eyes he had not seen.

"Coach Money," Gerald said excitedly.

It took all her might, but Michele composed herself. "So," she said, "*You* are Coach Money? I had been hearing about Coach Money for months. I had no idea. And now I finally get to meet you...Coach Money."

He extended his hand. Michele glanced down at her son, who seemed happy to see the two most important adults in his life chatting. She reluctantly shook it.

Touching her took him back to their time together. Solomon did not want her to leave. He wanted desperately to talk. "You all running off so soon? We did a lot to get some refreshments here. Have some."

"Gerald, go to the bathroom," Michele said.

"But I don't have to go," he answered.

"I don't care—*go*," she said sharply. Then she adjusted her tone; she was not mad at the kid. She leaned over to him and spoke in a reassuring way.

"Honey, go on, please. Sometimes you get in the car and have to go and then we have to find some place to stop. So just see if you need to go—just in case."

And off young Gerald went. She watched him bounce down the hall and then turned to Solomon.

"What, exactly, do you want?" she said. Her tone was aggressive and no-nonsense.

Solomon looked at her.

"Well?" she said.

Solomon surprised himself; he was tongue-tied. "Well, I, uh, I, you know—"

"No, I don't know," Michele said. "Wait—let me tell you what I know: The last time I saw you was eight years ago. The last time I heard from you was eight years ago. The last time I was hurt by you was eight years ago. Are you getting the point?

"Eight years is a long time, and it seems any talking we needed to do was then. Because, as you can see in Gerald, I've long since gotten over the fact that you vanished off the face of the earth."

"We should talk—" Solomon said.

"Too late for talking, don't you think?" Michele said. Her voice softened, but her rage showed through her eyes. They were teary and angry. "I wanted to talk eight years ago. I called you and e-mailed you. And I got nothing in return. I didn't even know you left town. What did I do to deserve that? So, Mr. Money, don't talk to me about wanting to talk. I tried that eight years ago and you were nowhere to be found. So it's fine with me if you vanish again."

Right on cue, Gerald emerged from the bathroom. Solomon and Michele stared into each other's eyes until Gerald came over and took his trophy from his mom.

"Let's go, honey," she said to Gerald while staring at Solomon.

"Ah, Gerald, congratulations, buddy," Solomon said. "I'm proud of you."

"Thanks," the boy said as his mother pulled him toward the exit.

Solomon stood there and watched them leave. A sheath of amazement covered his body, the way ice covers the ground on many a Minnesota winter night. He walked out the building in time to catch them pull out of the parking space and drive off. He was transfixed there, unable to decide what to do next.

Finally, he walked to his own car and sat in it for several minutes, thinking, wondering and admitting something he never thought he would: regret.

He called Ray, but did not get an answer on his cell phone. Then he called his home, and his wife, Cynthia, gave him some alarming news: "He said he was going to your banquet tonight. He's not there?"

Immediately, Solomon's instincts kicked in. "I saw him earlier, but then I didn't," he lied. "There are so many people here. I thought he might've left and gone back home. But he must still be inside. I'll find him."

He delivered it without any detection that he was covering for his boy. Once he hung up from Cynthia, he called Ray again on his cell phone. This time, he answered. "What's up? How'd it go?"

"Where are you?" Solomon said.

"Why?

"'Cause I called your house and spoke to your wife."

"What?"

"Yeah—and she said you said you were with me."

"Oh, man. Damn. I did tell her that. I had to tell her that because she's okay with me hanging with you. But one of my boys is in town—Dwight—and she can't stand him. So I had to use you as my out."

"Yo, don't you know that you need to tell me you're using me as an excuse?" Solomon said. "That's on page one or two of the man guide."

"My bad. We're at Atlantic Station, at the bar at the Twelve Hotel."

"Well, I'm surprised your wife hasn't called you yet."

"Shit. She's calling right now. Hold on."

A minute or so passed before Ray came back to Solomon.

"I'm good," Ray said. "I told her that I was in the office at the rec center, talking to the director about becoming a coach. That's why you didn't see me. She's cool. I hate to lie to her, but sometimes I feel like I don't have a choice."

"You have a choice; don't fool yourself into thinking you don't," Solomon said. "What you need are some balls."

"Very funny," Ray said. "What you call me for anyway?"

"Ray, you're not going to believe this," Solomon began. "The kid I was telling you about, Gerald?"

"Yeah? Don't tell me something happened to him," Ray said.

"No, nothing like that. But I found out who his mother is," Solomon said. "And I couldn't believe it."

"Who?"

"It's Michele Lynn."

"Who's that?"

"The chick I told you about in D.C., that I left hanging… Well, she's Gerald's mom."

"Come on, man. You can't be serious," Ray said. "We were talking about her the other day. Are you sure? You're positive?"

"Dude, I spoke to her. When I saw her, I couldn't believe it. My first reaction was shock. Then I was actually glad I saw her. But she wasn't happy to see me."

"What'd you expect?" Ray asked. "This is the one you left sleep on the floor and moved here the next day? And never talked to her again, right? I don't know about you, but I ain't surprised she wasn't happy to see you."

"Well, maybe she shouldn't be happy," Solomon responded. "But she was angry and bitter. I admit: It was wrong. But I wouldn't hold a grudge for eight years.

Listen, I had a great friend, Kim, who I sent $300 for two Continental Airline buddy passes back in the day. My girl kept my money and disappeared on me.

"I was furious at first. Then I was just surprised. And then I was disappointed. Then, over time, I got over it. I liked her as a friend—believe it or not—and I wanted to be her friend again. So, the bitterness wore off. But Michele seems very bitter after all this time."

"Maybe she's been holding in what she wanted to say to you for all these years and it just came out," Ray said. "Or maybe she's one of those women who can stay angry for a long time. I know a few of them."

"Well, we'll see what happens."

"What do you mean?"

"I've got to say what's on my mind to her," Solomon said. "I need to apologize and try to explain myself."

"That sounds like you want to talk to her to clear your conscience," Ray said. "And explain yourself? You don't have an explanation."

"That's why you're my boy. You pull no punches, which is the way a friend should be. And, I'll admit, you're right, to a degree. Knowing she is Gerald's mother and knowing how she was with me, it made me actually wish I didn't leave the way I did."

"So how you gonna make it right—if that's even possible?"

"I don't know," Solomon said, which was big. He always had an answer; a solution; a way of getting things resolved;

an idea. "A doer," he called himself. But this was different.

It was more than seeing Michele after eight years. It was more than the way he left. There was also the matter of her son, whom he had grown to really care for. Together, all that put Solomon in a quandary.

Bigger and more surprising than all that was that he actually felt something when he saw Michele. In an instant, he recalled the connection he developed with her over their six months together. He recalled the passion. He recalled the laughter. He recalled the friendship and conversations of substance. And then he did something he hardly ever did: He questioned himself.

"What was I thinking?" he said aloud in the car on the way home.

Through it all, he never allowed himself to question his abrupt and, ultimately, mindless decision to move to Atlanta without saying a word about it to Michele—and magnified it by never reaching out to her over eight years. Now he was face-to-face with his decision and he regretted it.

"A cold piece of work," Ray called him, and it was hardly flattering.

Solomon went straight home after seeing Michele, although he had plans to make a late-night visit to Marie, a forensic psychologist he "dated" from time-to-time. Translation: He fit her into his rotation of women whenever he desired being pampered—in and out of bed—in her fabulous home in the swank Buckhead section of Atlanta.

Around eleven, Marie called. "Honey, where are you?" she said. "I made chicken piccata, sautéed bok choy and Bananas Foster. I figured that food at the rec center wouldn't give you the proper energy you need to spend the night with me."

Solomon had been looking forward to all the sexy divorcee had to offer. But seeing Michele messed up his head. "I hope you can forgive me, but I can't make it, Marie," he said. "I had to come home and I'm really not up to making the drive up there; although I do want to see you."

"Want me to drive over to you?" she said, not getting the hint.

"I can't ask you to do that," he said. "I have some things going on I need to sort out. I promise I'll make it up to you."

The silence told of Marie's disappointment—and anger, too.

"You're mad at me, and you should be," Solomon said. "But you know me: I never cancel on you. And I wouldn't now if it wasn't important. I'll tell you about it eventually. But I've got to deal with this now. And believe me, I'll make it up to you."

"Solomon, I don't pressure you about time," she said. "I've accepted that I can't see you as much as I'd like. Really, I only see you when you have time for me. I don't complain about it. So, I was looking forward to tonight."

"If you want me to come over there right now, I'll get up and come," Solomon said. That was classic Solomon:

He understood the psychology of women. Volunteering to come despite what he said showed that was not can-celling their date to be with another woman, that he was willing to please, that he was willing to sacrifice. He knew Marie's mind and personality—and that she would not ask him to extend himself.

"No…No. It's okay," she said, and Solomon smiled to himself. He, again, had gotten a woman to say what he wanted her to say without asking her to say it. "I appre-ciate that you're willing to make the sacrifice. But it's okay. Do what you need to do to be all right. I will see you soon, right?"

"Definitely, baby. And thank you for understanding. That means a lot to me."

Marie was effectively out of the way, leaving Solomon to himself and his thoughts. And his thoughts ran long and deep and, in the end, left him confused about him-self but resolute: He wanted Michele Lynn Williams.

To get to that thought took some time. After talking to Marie, Solomon took off his suit and tie and lay on his bed upstairs in total darkness in his T-shirt and boxers, and revisited his history with Michele. He wanted to figure out how she, after all that time, now mattered to him.

They met one evening during the Congressional Black Caucus weekend in D.C. They were at a party at the Capital Hilton: Solomon was with a few golf buddies in the lobby; Michele was with her cousin, Sonya, a flight attendant who was visiting for the weekend from Atlanta.

Solomon noticed them walking into the ballroom. Michele was statuesque at five-foot-nine and clearly com-fortable with her height by the three-inch heels she wore and the confidence in which she maneuvered her shapely legs and wide hips. There was a grace about her, an elegant nature. Solomon detected that right away. But he needed confirmation.

So, he did not even excuse himself from his friends, who were engaged in idle chatter about one thing or another. He eased away from his boys and trailed Michele and Sonya into the ballroom. After he found them standing near the bar, he approached.

"Excuse me," he said to both ladies. "How are you? I'm Solomon. Solomon Singletary."

The ladies looked at each other and smiled. He extended his hand. "I'm Michele Lynn. This is my cousin, Sonya."

"I don't mean to bother you," he said, looking into Michele's brown eyes. "I really felt compelled to meet you. Can't say why, either, other than the fact that you look wonderful tonight."

"Really? Well, thank you...Solomon, right?" Michele said.

"Yes, that's right, Michele Lynn," he said.

"You're good with names, I see," Michele said.

"I pay attention to things that matter to me," he said.

Seeing where Solomon was going, Sonya excused her-self. "I'm going to get in this drink line," she said.

"I'm impressed, Sonya," Solomon said. "Most women

almost instinctively try to pull their friend away or block when they see a man is interested. But you are willing to give Michele room to converse—very commendable. I'm impressed."

"That's my cuz," Michele said. "Always trying to peddle me off."

The three of them laughed. "If you don't mind, I'll get your cocktails for you," he said. "You shouldn't have to do that."

"I could've sworn chivalry was dead," Michele said.

"Burned and buried," Sonya added.

"Well, I'm resurrecting it," Solomon said.

"I heard that," Sonya said.

Solomon took the drink orders, excused himself and returned a few minutes later with the cocktails. He had a hotel worker bring them on a platter.

"How about a toast?" he said, raising his Tanqueray and ginger ale. The ladies elevated their mojitos.

"To the beauty of meeting good people," he said.

They all tapped glasses and took a sip of their respective drinks. The three of them chatted for the next several minutes; light-hearted conversation that gave Michele a chance to get comfortable with Solomon, to embrace his charm and wit. And vice versa.

After about twenty minutes, he said: "Michele, I realize that you're with your cousin and she's visiting, so I really don't want to break up your bonding opportunity. But I'd love to meet you for lunch tomorrow. Both of you. I know of a little Latin place on 14th between G and H called Ceiba. Very good food—and far better mojitos than those, I'm sure."

"What do we have planned tomorrow?" Michele said to Sonya.

"Whatever it was, it just got changed," Sonya answered, and Solomon could not help but laugh.

"I like you," he said to Sonya. "You're too much."

He was well aware that getting the friend's endorsement was like winning Iowa in the Presidential primaries. Her seal of approval meant everything.

"Well, I guess we're available then," Michele said, smiling. She was interested but not anxious. And Solomon respected that. It showed that she was sure of herself. She gave no sense of desperation. Still, she was skillful enough to not discourage Solomon, either.

"Good," Solomon said. "And thank you."

"Thank you," the women said in unison.

He reached inside his suit pocket to pull out a card. He turned it over and wrote his cell phone number, the name of the restaurant and its location.

"Is one o'clock too late?" he asked. "I figure that should be enough time for you to sleep in a little, lay around and gossip and still make it to the restaurant."

"You've got it all figured out, huh?" Michele said.

"Pretty much," he answered without smiling, and Michele was then really intrigued.

He had a confidence that the men previous in her life lacked. They were either intimidated by her height and strong presence or insecure or lacking in chivalry or unaware of how to treat a woman or just plain uninteresting. Something.

Solomon walked outside the ballroom into the lobby with Michele and Sonya, where Solomon's boys were still hanging. "If I know my friends, they'll be over here in about fifteen seconds," he said to the women.

Before Sonya could get "really?" out of her mouth good, all four of them were in their space.

"Okay, okay, gentlemen," Solomon said. "Put your tongues back in your mouth."

"I'm checking to see if these ladies are all right," said Brad, Solomon's fraternity brother and golf partner. "You like to snatch purses."

Everyone laughed.

"You're right," Solomon said. "I did snatch your purse earlier."

Everyone burst into laughter again. And Michele instantly became more intrigued. *And he's funny, too*, she thought to herself.

Over the next thirty minutes or so, the seven of them ended up conversing about the CBC, the Redskins, Atlanta vs. D.C., the seemingly overabundance of black gay men and on and on.

When Solomon noticed Michele moving to Jay-Z's and Alicia Keys' song "Empire State of Mind," he sidled over to her. "How about we get a dance or two in?" he said into her ear. "I hate to let a good song go to waste."

"Same here," she said. "I'd love to."

They chatted and smiled at each other while they danced.

But even as he watched Michele, Solomon prospected the worse. *There's got to be something wrong with her*, he actually thought on the dance floor. *Why doesn't she have a man? Probably crazy.*

Michele's thoughts were different. *Could I be so lucky to actually find a man who has something between his ears? Who knows how to act? Who is tall enough?*

"This turned out much different than I expected," Michele said at her car; Solomon walked with her and Sonya at the end of the event. "I expected my feet to be hurting and to be ready to go home and to bed. But my feet feel fine and I'm wide awake."

Solomon laughed. "That's funny because my feet hurt."

"I couldn't see your shoes in there." Sonya glanced down. "Nice. You know you can tell a lot about a man through his feet?"

"His shoes or his feet?"

"Both," Sonya said.

"I'm not even going to ask you to explain what it means," Solomon said.

"Oh, I'll tell you," Sonya said.

"No, you won't," Michele interjected.

Solomon grinned. "I'm sure I have an idea."

Sonya winked. "You have on a nice pair of shoes."

"Thank you."

"What size do you wear, Solomon?"

"These are a 13—and they are a size small," he said, and they laughed.

"I heard *that*," Michele said.

"It was a pleasure; you ladies made my night," Solomon said.

Sonya extended her hand for him to shake.

"We've had drinks together, talked about everything under the sun, including the value of a man's shoe size... We've graduated beyond the hand-shaking stage," Solomon said.

Then he opened his arms and leaned in and hugged Sonya. "Goodnight," she said.

He turned to Michele. They hugged. With her in his arms, he said, "Thank you. Ah, and you smell good, even at the end of the night. I guess you aren't wearing Avon."

They laughed.

"Please call to let me know you all made it home," he said.

"The chivalry never ends, huh?" she asked.

"Why would it?" Solomon answered. "Why should it?"

That was their beginning. From there, they dated hard, but it was more than two months before they were intimate. He wanted her in bed long before then, but he was patient and unwilling to rush something with someone he felt so good about. After that first time, though, they were physically drawn to each other as if by magnets.

"Seems like the more I have of you, the more I need to have you," Michele said to him a month after they first slept together. "I realize that I used the word 'need' instead of 'want.' Being with you has become something I need to feel good physically and mentally. It's become a part of my life."

All that, and it did not prevent Solomon from leaving her with any notion he had accepted a marketing director position with Coca-Cola at its headquarters in Atlanta. And that thought—eight years later—haunted him.

"Damn," he said as he lay in darkness on his bed. "Damn."

CHAPTER 4
STORM
AFTER THE CALM

The serenity of a quiet morning brought no peace for Solomon. He woke up feeling cold on the outside and empty on the inside. So he lay there in bed, under the covers, unable to sleep, thinking, reminiscing. It was 5:24 a.m.

Solomon was ambivalent about mornings as it was. "Is it more the end of a good night or the beginning of a not-so-good day?" he liked to ask.

Uncomfortable physically and mentally, he still managed to come to a personal truth he never before pondered. It wasn't as if seeing Michele aroused feelings in him that he did not know existed. Seeing her *confirmed* a connection he had with her, one that he actually…feared.

He did not disappear on her because he believed she would disappoint him. He did so because he was afraid she could hurt him. And for Solomon, like most men, to feel vulnerable in a relationship with a woman was unbearable.

It also was undeniable. They were together only six months, but it was 182 days of fun, enlightenment, adventure, calm and even growth. In that time Solomon found himself doing things he had no interest in doing—and enjoying them.

Like cooking. Michele loved to eat and was stellar in the kitchen: "Ah, excuse me, but I prefer to be called chef," she said to Solomon after the first meal she prepared for him.

It was so delicious that Solomon accepted an invitation to cook the next meal with her, and ended up not only enjoying the process, but he eventually became an outstanding cook himself. "You don't have to call me a chef," he told Michele after he made stuffed trout, pesto risotto and sautéed peppers for her. "As long as you like it, you can call me Julia Child if you want."

He was enlightened and impressed that Michele had the courage to eschew a solid career as a lawyer to pursue a new business as a caterer. He, at first, thought it was a silly notion. Then he listened to her talk about the joy and reward she received in creating dishes in the kitchen and the satisfaction she gained from people enjoying her food.

"I can actually hear the passion and commitment in your voice," he said. "This is what makes you happy. There's a lot to be said for pursuing your passion."

Michele also influenced Solomon to skydive—something he never even pondered. She tried it once with a lawyer friend who regularly "jumped," and the thrill was addictive.

"If you're afraid," she said to Solomon, "I understand."

She knew what buttons to push with him. "It's not about being afraid," he said. "I'm not afraid of anything. It's just that I don't see the point."

"I think you're afraid," she insisted. "It's okay to be afraid; admit it. For me, I get a great thrill. It's the most liberating thing you can do. But if you're afraid…"

"Set it up," Solomon said, almost defiantly. "Let's do it."

And so, they drove to Chantilly, Virginia that following weekend and "jumped."

On the small plane, as it headed to the height of the flight, Solomon looked over at Michele. She was calm, smiling. "You okay, Solomon? You're going to love it. I promise."

"What if I don't? What do I get?"

"Whatever you want."

Solomon flashed a devilish smile.

A few minutes later, they were at the drop zone. "I'll go first!" she yelled. "Just do what you were taught to do! You'll be fine!" Then she jumped out of the airplane— and that daring was a turn-on for Solomon.

Fearless, he thought to himself. *Fearless.*

He, meanwhile, was fearful. In a matter of seconds, all the predictable questions surfaced: What if he panicked and forgot to pull the rip chord? What if the rip chord didn't come out? What if the parachute malfunctioned? How would it feel to crash to the earth?

Then another thought hit him: *Jump.*

And he pulled the goggles over his eyes, gave the jumper assistant the "thumbs-up" and they dropped through the hole in the plane.

All the training he had kicked in. He could see Michele just beneath him, arms and legs extended. She looked to be flying. He did the same and, after the initial stone-cold fear wore off, he took in the majesty of the view, and a sense of calm and exhilaration collided to create a once-in-a-lifetime stream of emotions.

The world was below him. Nothing mattered. He was at peace. Solomon waved to Michele and she waved back and, at thirteen thousand feet above the earth, he felt closer to her.

When the time came, he released his rip chord, the parachute came out and he shot up in the air. The breath in his body came out for a moment. He was no longer flying; he was floating.

Solomon was astonished at the feeling that came over him. He felt closer to God. He felt revived. Below him was a world that had no idea he was hovering above it. He felt free and more alive than ever.

When they careened onto the earth and pulled off their parachutes, Solomon hurried over to Michele. He didn't say a word. He ripped off his goggles and threw them to the ground. Then he embraced her and delivered the most passionate kiss he ever had shared. They fell onto the ground, and he continued to kiss her.

"Wow," Michele said, when their mouths finally parted.

"We should jump every day, if that's the reaction I'm going to get."

They were lying on their backs, panting, looking up at the sky. "Girl, that was...incredible. I mean, unbelievably incredible," he said. "My heart is still racing. But not really from fear. From excitement. Amazing... Amazing."

Usually, Solomon Singletary took women to amazing emotional heights, to where they were undaunted by the prospects of a significant fall. They just went with his flow.

Solomon realized through reminiscing that Michele Lynn Williams had taken him places he had not been before with a woman. And, he admitted, that he very much was afraid of falling from such a high place. Subconsciously, he knew there was something special about her. But his conscious mind also led him to think there was something scary about her, too.

So, intuitively, he ran. "Coward," he said as he rested on his back in bed. "Coward."

In his reality, his admission of fear was a monumental feat. A man's instinct is to project fearlessness. To be honest with himself about himself...well, it was rare. He could jump out of a plane from fifteen thousand feet above the earth, but he could not share his true feelings with a woman he cared for. That realization sickened him—and inspired him, too.

He sat up in bed and, in that moment, committed himself to making it up to Michele, making it up to himself. She was bitter and angry and wanted no part of him, but Solomon did not care. He had his way with women many times over, and it actually became less a thrill and more of a formality that no longer excited him.

Now, he was excited and motivated to truly do right by Michele. At the same time, he needed to prove to himself that he was capable of being a good man to a good woman. In the process, he thought maybe he could actually repair an eight-year-old wound.

Instead of the morning ending a good night, this new day offered something special for Solomon. Hope.

Hope that he could find it in himself to endure the rejection he believed Michele was sure to offer. Hope that he could dissolve her bitterness and gain a modicum of respect from her. Hope that she would allow him to mentor her son, Gerald. And hope that she could, some day, open up to reconnecting with him.

The other women in his life, while most were good women, did not hold him. They provided some level of satisfaction—in one area or another—but they were not magnetic enough to force him to focus solely on them.

He never felt that with Michele. For the six months they were together, he did not see other women, which was a first. It wasn't a conscious decision; he enjoyed her so much that he didn't much feel the need for others. He never told her that. In fact, he told her the opposite, that he *would* see other women. "We're just enjoying our time together," Solomon said, when Michele asked the predictable woman question, "So, what are we doing?"

"I'd like you to be less interested in who else I'm dating and more into us maximizing the time we spend together," he said.

Michele handled Solomon differently from other women. She refused to press him on the issue. She was not settling; her pride would not allow that. But she accepted his position for what it was and left herself open to dating other men if the opportunity arose.

This position confused Solomon and actually turned his behavior. "You're different," he said a few weeks later. "Most women press you for what they want. You haven't done that."

"Who said I wanted more than what you mentioned?" she replied. "Bottom line, as long as you treat me with respect, I'm okay with what we're doing right now. That might not always be the case, but that's how it is right now."

This hardly was the response he was used to receiving, and it threw him. It made him feel like he had to occupy her time to prevent someone else from doing so, which was exactly what women had attempted to do to him. Michele had effectively flipped the script on Solomon.

So, almost every weekend, they were together, and many nights during the week, too. As close as he grew to her, she grew equally close to him. But she was not afraid of how she felt.

"I love you," she said to Solomon one evening after dinner about five months into their courtship. She did it then so he would know it was not some proclamation in the throes of making love. During intense sex, she might say anything, and Solomon knew it.

Telling him as she stood in the kitchen washing dishes was hardly romantic. It was pure, genuine emotion, inspired only by her heart.

Clearly, Solomon was uncomfortable with Michele's expression. Their eyes locked for a few seconds before he looked away and finally said, "Really? Well, do you like me?"

"That's your response?" she said. She knew Solomon was crafty, that he was trying to avoid a direct response. "Okay, I'll play along: Yes, I like you, Solomon. Now what?"

"Well, I'm glad you do because that's where it all begins and ends," he said. "To me, you can't get to loving someone until you really like them. And I like you, too, Michele, very much. I have very strong feelings for you, too. I just don't throw around the 'I love you' thing recklessly. I—"

"Wait. Are you saying I'm being reckless?" Michele jumped in. "I know you're not telling me that when I have all these sharp objects at my fingertips."

"No, no, I'm not saying that at all," he quickly interjected with a smile. "I'm talking about me. I try to be responsible about that; if you don't mean it, it can be hurtful down the line. Liking you is more important than loving you; if we have a friendship and genuinely like each other, that's going to be our foundation that holds everything together. People fall in and out of love all the time. If you really like someone, that doesn't change—unless something really ugly happens.

"But to what you said, I know it's from the heart and real; that's the person you are. So, thank you for feeling as you do about me."

Once again, it was Solomon's wariness that prevented him from opening up to Michele. It wasn't that he could not love her; it was that he did not *want* to love her. To love her was to be susceptible to being hurt by her. So, he believed that as much as she opened up his life and as close as he felt to her, actually loving her would only complicate matters. And it would make things even worse if he told her that he loved her. He believed she would view it as a weakness in him that she could manipulate.

"Honey, that's so not right," his mother said when he shared his theory with her. "How many women have you introduced to me? Too many to count. Michele is the only woman who felt comfortable enough to be herself. I could see all the others trying to impress me to get me to say something good about them to you.

"You know what Michele said to me the first day I met her? You were in the bathroom. She said, 'Ms. Singletary, your son is a trip. I'm glad I got to meet you. I'm not sure you'll see me again.'

"I asked her why, and she said, 'He's a perfect gentleman. But he's spoiled. I know you spoiled him as an only child; that's what mothers do. Other women have, too. He's so macho that he thinks the world revolves around him and his decisions.' I was like, 'Oh, this is my kind of woman.' She wasn't trying to impress me. She was speaking her mind. That's the kind of woman I'd like my son to have. Not someone who placates him. How do you throw that away?"

The same day, Solomon drove to Sheridan Road in Northwest D.C. to see his father, whose advice was quite different.

"Son, you have the right idea," he said. "Always manage the relationship so that you're in control. They start thinking you're all head over heels and they'll turn you upside down. Keep them working toward pleasing you. You show them that you're all into them and they get comfortable. And then she becomes someone you don't like."

Eight years later, Solomon realized neither his mother nor his father got it quite right. Ultimately, it was about him and how he related to Michele. And reviewing his behavior with women in general, and Michele in particular, gave him a picture of himself that was hardly flattering.

It also gave him motivation to do something different.

CHAPTER 5

THE
CHASE

A man like Solomon got off as much on pursuing a woman as he did actually conquering her. The challenge was the thrill; making her expose herself and succumbing to his will. That was the turn-on.

Never before did he have a more intimidating challenge than that of reattaching himself to Michele Lynn Williams' heart. She was angry and bitter, and for good reason. But he was not scared.

So, after all the pondering and reminiscing and admission of regret, Solomon pulled himself out of bed. He lacked patience and was intent on making inroads with Michele. So, he was ready for the chase.

He knew where to find her; young Gerald talked often about his mom making him get up every Sunday for 10 a.m. service at Berean Christian Church, which was not far from Solomon's house.

He also had her phone number, e-mail address and home address from the team parent roster. So, he had means to reach her. Before he would, though, he had to give her a reason for his disappearance. And that was a problem, because nothing he said would make sense to her.

Finally, he decided on something he did not frequently do: he would tell Michele the truth. Even if it did not make her feel better, he would have done what was right, albeit many years too late.

Solomon was surprised that he was nervous as he approached the church. Confidence had been the foundation of his existence, be it at work or socially. But as he got to the front doors of Berean at 9:50, he began to doubt himself.

He decided he would take a seat in the back aisle of the center section, which would give him a vantage point to see Michele enter the sanctuary from any entrance. Before doubt took over, he spotted her.

She entered from the left side of the building, alone. It was like she was walking in slow motion. Solomon hoped Michele would be in a forgiving and jovial mood after church, making it an ideal time for him to make his initial move.

When the service ended, Solomon positioned himself outside the sanctuary door Michele would exit. The palms of his hands were sweaty and he suddenly felt a need to go to the bathroom. But leaving meant he might miss her, so he waited.

Just a minute or so later, Michele emerged from the doors. She was chatting with another woman, who noticed Solomon and smiled at him. "Hello," she said.

Michele turned to see Solomon, whose deep brown

and sometimes enchanting eyes where fixated on her. "Hi," he said.

"What are you doing in church?" Michele responded without hesitation. There was no detection of anger in her voice or how she looked at Solomon. She held it together beautifully. "Diana, you'd better step back. He could get struck by lightning at any moment."

"You know him?" Diana said.

"I thought I did—a long time ago," Michele answered. "Let's go."

Michele and Diana began to walk away from Solomon. He followed them. "Michele..."

She turned around. "Oh, you remember my name?"

"Can I speak to you for a moment, please? Just for a minute."

"I'm going to go ahead to my cousin's house for a cook-out," Diana said. "Call me later, okay?"

She left and Michele turned to Solomon. "Let's go outside. What I have to say probably shouldn't be said in church."

They stepped out into the perfect spring afternoon and Solomon pulled out his sunglasses. Michele reached in her purse and pulled out hers.

"I really need to apologize to you," Solomon started. He had rehearsed some of what he wanted to say to her, but he forgot it all.

"For what?"

Solomon took off his sunglasses. He wanted her to

see his eyes, hoping she could detect the sincerity and truth in what he was about to say.

"For being a coward with you. I can't explain it in any other way than that, Michele."

"But what does that mean? And why should it mean anything to me all this time later?"

"I can't say whether it should mean something to you or not," he said. "What I can say is that it means I had feelings for you back then that I was afraid of. And I didn't know how to handle them. So I ran away from them to avoid having to deal with them."

"You're right—that's what a coward would do," Michele said. "You don't do people like that. And you're claiming you had feelings for me? That's hard to believe, based on your actions."

"Listen, I couldn't sleep ever since seeing you last night, Michele. I had all kinds of emotions running through me. I was shocked to see you at first. Then I was embarrassed because of what I did. Then I was…I was glad to see you."

"I can understand being shocked; I was, too," Michele said. "And I can understand being embarrassed. But glad? Why?"

"For a few reasons. One, I really like your son—I've tried to be a mentor to him—and I was glad to know his mother is someone like you. Two, it meant I could finally man-up and apologize to you—and, to be honest—get rid of some of the guilt and regret I've been carrying with me. I tried to not think about it, but it would never go away. It just wouldn't."

"But you never tried to reach me, Solomon, even with this so-called regret."

"Yeah, I know. It was like, the longer I waited, the harder it was to do," he said. "I got here, got engulfed in the job and getting adjusted and convinced myself that I was doing the right thing. Not the right thing by you, but the right thing for me. I didn't know how to handle really caring about you."

"That sounds silly, Solomon," Michele said. Her arms were folded, which Solomon took to mean that she was not open to what he had to say. She was, in fact, closed and withdrawn. However, she listened to him and still responded, which meant she wanted to hear what he had to say.

"It sounds silly. But it's the truth... Listen, I'm not good with feeling vulnerable. I felt like eventually you would—"

"Eventually what?" she asked.

"Hurt me," he said, looking down. "Break my heart."

Michele dropped her arms to her sides and shook her head. "You know what? I've got to go pick up Gerald."

"Michele, I'm sorry. I know it was wrong. It was stupid. But that's the truth."

She took a deep breath and pulled off her sunglasses. "You cared about me but you planned to move out of town and didn't tell me about it. You didn't say, 'bye.'

Just left me on the floor sleeping. And you did this because you *thought* I *might* break your heart?

"First of all, you have to have a heart before it can be broken. And anyone who does what you did to me doesn't have a heart."

Solomon ignored the slight. "I never told you the third reason I was glad to see you last night," he said.

Michele did not respond.

"Because I knew instantly that I still have feelings for you."

She smiled, placed her right hand over her heart and feigned dizziness. "Oh, my. Solomon Singletary—The Invisible Man—has feelings for me. Well, forgive me for not being honored. And I guess that means I won't see you again, because according to you just now, you left me in D.C. because you had feelings for me.

"Listen, I'm getting angry, so I'm leaving. You said what you had to say; I gave you more than a minute. I listened to you. Now I'm leaving. Your conscience should be clear now. You can go on doing whatever you were doing."

She put her glasses back on and turned away from Solomon. Then she quickly turned back.

"Oh, and stay away from my son," she said. "He won't be returning to that team you coach. I don't want him around you."

And before Solomon could say anything, Michele turned and left him in front of the church.

Demoralized, he put his sunglasses back on and watched her make her way to her car. Demoralized, but not defeated. While he wanted a better reaction from Michele, he was not surprised by her position. In fact, he would have been surprised if she reacted any other way.

The key was that she got to hear what he had to say. There was no way around Michele not thinking about it and processing it. And maybe through that process she'd soften some. Whatever the case, Solomon was not done.

As he spoke to her, he sized her up. She had gained a noticeable few pounds, but her figure remained well proportioned. She had her hair colored and cut into a different style. She wore contact lenses instead of glasses, offering a direct view of her subtly intoxicating eyes. She did not wear a wedding or engagement ring, which meant she probably was not serious with another man—at least, that's what he hoped.

And when she smiled, even though it was a sarcastic reaction, it was like the sun got brighter. He had forgotten how warm her smile used to make him feel.

CHAPTER 6
BE CAREFUL
WHAT YOU ASK FOR

Michele made it to her car, tossed her supple dark brown purse that matched perfectly her beige and brown dress onto the passenger seat and put her hand over her mouth. She was relieved to get away from Solomon without breaking down.

She did not rest well the night before, either. Seeing Solomon mixed up a confluence of emotions that ran through her mind and heart like a virus run amok. How could *he* be the coach her son talked about with such admiration? She was mad at herself for not going through the paperwork the rec center sent home when she signed him up for basketball. Solomon's information would have been right there.

As it was, she was looking forward to giving "Coach Money" a hug and resounding "thank you" for being a positive influence on Gerald's life.

Michele noticed how much more responsible around the house and committed her son was about school. When she asked him about his vast improvement, Gerald said: "Coach Money told me that I had to be a man for you.

He said to be a good basketball player meant I had to be a good son. So I made sure I cleaned up my room and took out the trash and stuff. Coach Money said every day I should try to make you proud."

Before Solomon, Gerald did not have a male influence of any consequence in his life. Michele's father lived in Phoenix. Her brother was in the Army, stationed in Kentucky and serving a long stint in Iraq.

She seldom talked about the kid's father, even to close friends. He "was unwilling to man-up to his responsibility," she said of him. In her more frustrating moments, she told Gerald, "Your daddy is no good." She regretted the words; trashing him would do nothing to help Gerald. But sometimes the burden of raising a child alone—forget the money, just the assistance and teaching of life lessons from a man's view—caused a momentary lapse in judgment. But she'd always recover.

"It's just you and me, baby," she said. "And we're fine, right? We'll always be fine. Your daddy, well, I think he's just not feeling well. Sometimes when people don't feel well, it's best that they stay away and get better… Sometimes they get better, sometimes they don't."

It frustrated her that Solomon had such an impact on her son. Ever since he disappeared, all she wanted was to have bad thoughts about him. She wanted to hate him.

To learn that Solomon, of all people, brought something to Gerald's life, well, it freaked her out. There was a time she thought so highly of him, to where she even envisioned herself as his wife.

It was a presumptuous notion, knowing Solomon for just six months. But she had met enough men and been disappointed by enough of them to know that he brought something out of her and into her life that she had not experienced. Ironically enough, he was a comfort.

While he at times displayed how spoiled he was by other women and even his mother, as Michele determined, he treated her as a gentleman, with respect. He engaged her with thoughtful conversation and supported her on her dramatic career change when others thought she was misguided to abandon a promising career as an attorney. He made her feel protected and like a woman.

That's what made his disappearance so shocking and so devastating. She was comforted by him and had come to need his presence. On her way from church, she recounted that morning she woke up alone on the floor.

Solomon had left her while she slept early one morning once before, so she was not surprised to search her house and find that he was not there. She called him and left a message: "Ah, I thought I told you to not leave me again while I slept. You're so hard-headed. Call me later."

That call never came. By nightfall, Michele got worried and called Solomon again. His cell phone went straight to voice mail. She left another message: "Solomon, what's going on? Let me know you're okay."

She then sent him the same message in a text. After a late dinner, she drifted to sleep on the couch while watching repeats of *Entourage*. When she woke up, it was nearly 2 a.m. and she had heard nothing from Solomon.

That was not his modus operandi. He *always* called back. Somewhat panicked, Michele called his home number. It was disconnected. She became puzzled then, and anxious.

In the morning, she called him again, to no avail. Then she decided to drive to his house. She wasn't sure what to expect when she got there, but she surely did not fathom what she discovered: a For Sale sign in the front yard.

Michele looked around to see if she was at the right house. She knew she was, but it didn't make any sense that his house would be on the block. She walked up to the front door and looked through the curtain-less windows to the right. Inside was empty.

Her heart raced. He was gone. She sat on his front steps to compose herself; it did not help. Dozens of questions ran through her mind, but two more than others.

Why?

How?

She met his mother once, but that was out at dinner; she did not have a way to contact her. Maybe he was getting settled in a new place and wanted to surprise her. He was big on surprises, which was another reason she liked him.

But the only surprise Solomon had to offer was that he did not call her. Days went by, then weeks. Michele's emotions went from disappointment to anxiety to hurt to, finally, anger.

She spoke with conviction and bitterness about him to family and friends. "I don't care what he's doing or where he is. I just don't care," she said.

So she started dating as soon as she could muster enough tolerance to deal with men. The first guy to come along—Andrew, a blind date set up by her friend, Rhonda—was nice and respectful and was able to take her attention away from Solomon. But he wasn't Solomon. Solomon had branded her; any man after him would be compared to him. And most men could not stand up to the standards he set.

Still, she hated him—or wanted to hate him. "A low-life," she called him.

At the same time, there was an underlying feeling that was contrary to her public declarations, even as she and Andrew became close. Even in her anger, she always wanted to hear from him, to learn why he did what he did, to see him even.

Now that she had, she was uncertain how to feel. But she was surprised to feel relief and not outrage that he would offer such a lame excuse after nearly eight years. Why did she even give him a platform to talk? Why didn't she walk away from him? She wanted to, but couldn't.

After she picked up Gerald from her cousin Sonya's house and got him an early dinner and settled for the evening, she called Rhonda, who lived back in D.C.

"So, all of this happened since last night?" she said to Michele. "Wow. What are you going to do?"

"What am I going to do? I'm going to live my life," Michele said. "What else can I do?"

"You can do what your heart and your body are telling you to do," she said. "Chell, you know you're my girl. But I always thought that deep down, you wanted Solomon to come back, to explain himself and make everything right."

"Girl, are you crazy? Why would I want that?" Michele asked.

"Why? You know why," Rhonda said. "And because you loved him, that's why. If you didn't, answer this for me, and I've wanted to ask you this ever since you moved there almost two years ago: Of all the places to move to, why Atlanta?

"I mean, after you heard he moved there, I would think Atlanta would be the last place you'd want to relocate to. But there you are."

"Well…" Michele said.

"Well, what?" Rhonda said. "You don't have to admit it to me, Chell. As long as you don't lie to yourself."

"You're a trip," Michele said. "Why didn't you say something before now? I moved here because I always liked Atlanta and everything I read told me Atlanta was a great place for my business.

"Did I hear Solomon was here? Yes. But I didn't come here for us to get back together. And I didn't expect to see him. I knew there was a chance we could cross paths, but I didn't count on it or want it. The bottom line is that Atlanta was the best place for me and I wasn't going to *not* come here because Solomon was here."

She was lying to her friend. Despite all the pain he caused, he left an imprint on her that, even in her fury, she could not shake. That was the magnitude of Solomon's power as a man; he was like a tattoo or a brand, a permanent impression etched not in her skin, but in her very being.

Moving to Atlanta very much had something to do with Solomon. Not everything, but it mattered. She did not *expect* to reconnect with him, but the idea that she *could* run into him was exciting, hopeful.

However, after more than a year of going out to Atlanta's hottest and most popular spots and not "running into him," Michele gave up the idea of their paths crossing. It was far-fetched to think they could have a chance meeting in a metropolitan area of 1.3 million people. Then, when she least expected it, when she had no notion of ever seeing him, Saturday night happened, and then Sunday morning, leaving Michele utterly confused.

She could not get out of her head that Solomon vanished on her. But the connection he made with her—despite the time apart—still existed. So, when he reappeared, the two dynamics fought against each other.

Her pride would not allow her to offer him an overt inkling that she was relieved and even happy to see him. On one level, she was not into playing games. But he would devalue her as a woman if she immediately forgave him and carried on as if nothing happened. So she held back, which was the smart move, anyway. It was better, safer, to see where he *really* was coming from before putting herself out there. And even if he seemed sincere, he already showed he was capable of really hurting her.

She never questioned herself about reconnecting with him. All she ever contended was that seeing him would be enough, hearing from him. She needed some explanation from him to gain closure on the matter. Michele tried to fool herself that that would be enough.

The fact that he expressed an interest in her after all those years was more than she could have expected and added to her dilemma. But the dilemma was even more monumental because of two reasons: one, he made a connection with her son, Gerald. Two, she could not trust him.

She could not teach her boy how to be a man, and so Gerald's response to Solomon as his coach was important to her.

Michele soaked every measure of her heart and soul into her kid, and was almost paranoid about him being "soft" or a "Momma's Boy." The dad was not around and so she played mommy and daddy, mother and father. Never a big fan of sports, she learned the basics of football and basketball. If she were interested in it, Gerald would be, too.

The idea of her son actually playing football, though,

was too much for Michele. That's why she signed him up at Gresham Park for basketball.

"Daddy, football is too rough," she told her father. "I want him to be tough, a regular boy. But I don't want him with broken arms, either. If he gets one playing basketball, then I'll have to deal with it. But at least in basketball the idea is not to throw you to the ground, like football. With basketball, he can play with other boys and hopefully learn about being on a team and togetherness and all the stuff that sports brings out."

Gerald received all that—and the only consistent male figure in his life that instilled values in him that only a man could offer. Some husbands of her married girlfriends offered to help, but made only token efforts. The irony that it was Solomon who put in almost daily time with Gerald over the course of several months caused her serious trepidation.

She was thrilled when her son continually talked about "Coach Money" and took to heart his words of being responsible and making his mom proud. But knowing Solomon had the capability to walk away at any time was unsettling.

How could she possibly trust anything he said? Why wouldn't he walk away from a group of kids that included her son? Solomon might have remained in her blood stream like an IV drip for nearly eight years, but Gerald was her life's blood. Nothing or no one came before him. She would protect him at all costs.

"How can I allow G to be around that man?" Michele

asked her cousin, Sonya. "I know what he's capable of."

"I know," she responded. "But it also seems like he's capable of really being a male figure that could help Gerald. You said he responded to Solomon. I'm his godmother and I want to protect him, too. If a man can come along and pry him away from your paranoid arms and toughen him up, that can't be a bad thing.

"Listen, girl. I know from my girlfriend, Gina. Same thing happened to her. So-called boyfriend ran when she showed him the pregnancy test results. And ever since, her life mission has been to protect her son. But no amount of watching sports together and knocking him down and not babying him can replace what a man can share with a boy. The best mothers in the world— and you and her are right up there with the best of them— can't be the best daddies in the world.

"You feel me? So, I'm not saying let him play for Solomon. But I'm not saying don't let him play, either. That's your decision. There's no defending what he did to you. But the man has had an impact on Gerald. That should count for something."

It counted for a lot, actually. But how could she account for Solomon?

CHAPTER 7
CAN'T STOP, WON'T STOP

"She listened to me; that's the best I can say about it," Solomon told Ray that afternoon. "She didn't budge. She was composed, but furious. Kinda sexy, actually, that she could be so angry with me but hold it together like that."

"You find the weirdest stuff to get turned on by, I see," Ray said.

"Actually, it takes a lot to turn me on. I'm not conventional," Solomon said. "Like, for instance, most men prefer a woman just butt-naked."

"And? What's wrong with that?" Ray said.

"I didn't say anything was wrong with it," Solomon answered. "I'm just saying I prefer sexy, tasteful lingerie. That creates anticipation, an allure. It adds to the moment."

"So, Michele made you want her more because she cursed you out without cursing?"

"I wouldn't put it that way, but she did show me that she's poised, which is good," Solomon said. "But I already knew that. This is a chick who jumps out of planes, so she's not fearful of much."

"For your purposes, the fact that she took the time to talk to you means she's willing to talk, at least," Ray said.

"Yeah, well now it's time to see if she's willing to text me," Solomon said. "I looked at my team's parents contact list last night. Her cell number is on it. I'm going to hit her up and see what happens."

What he would text her, he was not sure. He spent hours trying to figure out the approach that would get a response from her. Solomon actually had to grow into text-messaging. He, at first, had no use for it. He considered it a passive means of communication. "If you have time to sit there pressing buttons, just call me," he said.

But he saw the benefits of it as time wore on and actually came to rely on it. "I'd rather do this than actually have to talk to some of these women," he said.

He preferred to speak to Michele, but he strategized that passive-aggressive would be the best route. So, after watching *Curb Your Enthusiasm* on HBO, Solomon changed into some lounge-wear, made himself comfortable on his couch in the den and started with his next phase of pursuing Michele.

"Hi Michele. This is Solomon," his first text read.

He waited ten minutes for a response and got none.

So he texted her again.

"What, u scared of me?" he wrote. It was a risk, but he concluded he needed to touch an emotion with her. Even if she responded angrily, he believed he could turn her. Anything to get her started.

Michele, dressed in a long pink cotton gown, rested in bed and flipped channels and actually was thinking of Solomon as her BlackBerry chimed, indicating she had a text message. Her heart fluttered when she read that it was from Solomon, but she decided to not respond.

Instead, she called Sonya, who was with her the night she met Solomon. "Girl, why not text him back?" Sonya said. "There's no harm seeing what he has to say."

"I figured you'd say that," Michele responded. "You always had a soft spot for him, even when he disappeared."

"If you knew I would say that, then why did you call me?" Sonya said.

"What you trying to say?" Michele answered.

"I'm saying you wanted me to say it's all right to text him back. "I know you. If you didn't, you would've called someone else."

"Maybe you're right—about knowing me," Michele said, laughing. "I'm not conceding anything else."

"Call me after you finish texting him," Sonya said. "Bye."

Of course, Sonya was right. Michele merely needed a confirmation from someone she trusted. She could have called any of her friends that she knew would tell her to ignore Solomon. She anticipated Sonya's response because she did like Solomon, but also because Sonya always had Michele's best interest at heart.

Michele knew that, as much as her girls loved her, misery, indeed, sought company. And her miserable, lonely girlfriends would hardly push for her to do something that might extract her from the miserable and lonely club.

So, Michele responded.

"Scared of u?" she wrote back. "I would have 2 care 2 be scared. And I don't care."

Solomon smiled and texted her right back.

"I'm sorry u don't care. But I care what u think about me."

It was on then.

"Really? I would never have known," Michele wrote back, reciting the words as she typed them into her phone.

Solomon: "I know. But it's the truth. U know, it's honorable 2 forgive."

Michele: "Yeah, but it's not mandatory."

Solomon: "Ur heart is 2 good 2 not forgive."

Michele: "U don't know my heart. My heart has been toughened up. Thanks to u."

Solomon: "I'm sorry, Michele. Let me make it up 2 u."

Michele: "U can't live long enough 2 make it up 2 me."

Solomon: "U should let me try. I'm betta than what I showed u. That was a long time ago."

Michele: "Seems like yesterday 2 me."

Solomon: "I'm not proud of what I did, Michele. I'm embarrassed. But I want to make it up 2 u. I can—if u give me the chance."

Michele: "I don't know of any reason to give u a chance. I don't even believe u want a chance. U just feel guilty."

Solomon: "I do feel guilty. But that's not y I want 2 make it up 2 u."

He set Michele up to ask him "why." And she knew it. So she didn't.

Michele: "Whatever ur reason, what's done is done. I have moved on. And I'm sure u have 2. I got over u. I got over being dogged by u. I'm happy with my life w/o u."

Solomon was disappointed Michele did not take his bait, but not deterred. He decided he'd stay on task, no matter what her responses were.

Solomon: "I've been happy w/o u 2. But I have not been whole. I felt whole with u, Michele. I did. I didn't know how 2 handle it. I was young and dumb—and scared. But I've grown up. I want 2 be more than happy. I want 2 be whole. U can make me whole."

Michele put the TV on mute. Solomon had gotten to her. She had actually told her cousin the exact same thing, using the same words, about how she felt with Solomon. "I can't say I've ever felt whole with a man," she said to Sonya. "This relationship, this man, makes me feel whole."

Of course, that was before Solomon vanished.

But her feelings for him remained; she could not believe all the emotions he conjured up in her were not real. Michele was an idealist, someone who wanted to believe the best in people. So, even in her borderline depression, she held on to what they shared, if only to *believe* it was possible.

When Gerald came along, she was able to focus her

attention and throw all her love and time into her little boy. With the father nowhere to be found, she did not get out of sync. She pressed on.

Michele contemplated so long how to respond to Solomon's text that he sent her another one. It read:

"???????"

She did not know what to write, so she decided to go with the truth. She was tired of playing coy.

"Solomon, that sounds great. But how do u expect me 2 believe u?"

"Just let me prove it to u," he wrote back. "I believe in action over words anyway. But I PROMISE u, I will not let u down. I have seen the light. ☺"

Michele: "Very funny."

Solomon: "I'm not joking. I just wanted u to smile. I'm very serious about this. I remember everything about our relationship."

Michele: "Oh, now it was a relationship? Back then u didn't want a title. U wouldn't even say u loved me. Now I'm supposed to believe after all this time that u did?"

Solomon: "I know how it sounds. But I can't do anything but tell u the truth now. And here's another truth: I feel closer to u thru ur son."

He struck another nerve with Michele, a very sensitive nerve. She was consumed with little Gerald. She tended to his every need. And he tended to hers without even knowing it. He was her "man" when there was no man around, which was most of the time. She hugged and kissed him not only because she loved him so much, but also because she had so much untapped affection in her.

But her affection had the potential to make him soft. That's why she got him into sports. And that's why she was so excited that "Coach Money" had a positive influence on him.

"Well," Michele texted back, "I was glad he had a male figure n his life."

Solomon: "What happened 2 his father, if u don't mind me asking?"

Michele: "I'd really rather not talk about it right now. Let's just say he was unwilling to step up to his responsibility. That's my stock answer. But maybe I'll give u the details 1 day."

Solomon was so happy with that response that he yelled out loud.

"Yeah!!!!!"

"One day" meant the future, which meant she expected to be in touch with him. This meant triumph to Solomon.

"OK," he typed back. "I wish u would let me coach him some more. He's a great kid. We talked a lot and I taught him a lot about basketball and life. He was my best player but also the kid I enjoyed the most. You've done an excellent job. U should be proud."

Michele: "I am proud. He's the light of my life. That's why I'm afraid 2 let him get connected 2 u more than he already is. I no u can disappear and not look back."

Solomon: "I deserve that. I do. But don't u know that

people grow & learn from their mistakes? Don't u know that? I'm trying 2 make up for what I did, if that's possible."

Michele: "I don't no if it's possible, and I don't want my son in the middle of it."

Solomon: "Before u knew 'Coach Money' was me, u said u were glad 'Coach Money' had an impact on him. I can still do that—whether u talk to me again or not. As far as this goes, this is not about u or me, really. It's about Gerald."

Michele: "Well, it's getting late and my fingers r tired. I will think about it."

Solomon: "While ur thinking about it, think about meeting me for lunch tomorrow. Please."

Michele: "Ur asking 4 a lot. I just saw u yesterday for the first time in 8 years. Don't u think we both need to back up a little?"

Solomon: "I will do whatever u say. But when I saw u Saturday, it was like my whole world opened up. I'm grateful to c u again."

Michele's mind and heart were in conflict. She wanted to hurt him for hurting her and, at the same time, she wanted to embrace him for their time together—and the possibilities now that he was back. That he could still matter after eight years spoke to what she felt back when they were together.

"Damn," she said aloud.

She did not know how to respond. Solomon had opened up to her in those text messages more than he had in their six months together. Maybe he had changed, or grown up, she thought. Why not give him the benefit of the doubt? After all, no man before or after him made her feel as he had.

Her mind told her to stay at a distance. Don't let him in—at least not too quickly. Bottom line: Solomon was not to be trusted. Maybe people could change, but maybe *he* had not.

"I don't think so," Michele texted him back. "Maybe another time. I don't think that's a good idea."

Solomon said aloud, "Damn." He was not surprised by her response, but he hoped it would be different. He knew Michele to be prideful and smart and any woman who was proud and bright would not jump to see him after what he did to her.

"I understand," he wrote back. "I hope it's OK 2 call u tomorrow evening."

Michele: "We'll see, Solomon."

CHAPTER 8
LET THE TRUTH BE TOLD

Solomon called on all the willpower he had to not call Michele the next day. Overnight he decided the best course of action would be to back off, to let her absorb all that had taken place on Saturday night at the banquet and Sunday at church and via text.

His boy, Ray, helped him get to that point.

"You can do what you want—you always do—but to me, you should not try to overwhelm the girl," Ray said. "Let her gather her thoughts; this is really not just about you. You want what you think you want. But she's got feelings involved, too. And a son.

"Look, if it's going to happen for you and her, it's going to happen. You can't *make* it happen. And out of respect for her, you should let her settle down and not pressure her."

Ray was so level-headed and persuasive that Solomon fought himself and did not reach out. Maybe she'd be disappointed that he didn't, he reasoned. Maybe she'd even call or text him.

A day went by, then two, and Solomon found himself falling into the mode of a political candidate who had to concede defeat on election night. He called Ray.

"At this point, I feel like it's not going to happen," he said. "I don't really know how to pursue a woman, anyway. I mean, I do, but I haven't done a lot of that. Haven't had to."

"Well, maybe that's the problem," Ray said. "You've gotten away with so much, including not pursuing women, that now when you want to—when you *need* to—you actually don't know how. What's wrong with that picture? Real talk: I changed my mind. If you want her, you're going to have to go get her. Clearly, she's not going to break unless you break her."

Ray's words again influenced Solomon.

"You know what?" he said to Ray. "This is the hard, cold reality—I want her."

"Then you have no dilemma. You understand what has to be done," Ray said. "And I know how to do it."

"Yeah, okay," Solomon said.

"I'm serious," Ray said.

"How?"

"Gerald," Ray answered. "That's your in."

Something sounded underhanded about that—but that's what also made it so intriguing.

"Yo, I didn't know you were that conniving," Solomon said to his friend. "Is that the right way to go about it, really?"

"You know why it's the right way to go about it? Because you already like the kid. You already wanted to help him. You told me that you called him 'Money' because he reminded you of you. You connected to the boy. So being a mentor to him is simply doing what you've already wanted to do—even before you realized who his mom was.

"And you also said Michele was happy that a man was influencing her son. She'll put her feelings aside to help her son. Watch."

Solomon nodded his head in agreement. He needed a pep talk to renew his pursuit. Ray delivered.

"Hello?" Michele answered into her cell phone.

"Hey. This is Solomon. Solomon Singletary. Remember me?"

"Can't say that I do," she answered. "Refresh my memory."

"I'm the guy you should let take your son to the Hawks' game on Thursday."

"Oh, I don't know about that." That was her first instinct. Even if Solomon did not have the history he created, Michele would have been guarded about letting Gerald go somewhere without her. With Solomon, she was doubly leery.

"I wouldn't let anything happen to him; except making sure he has a great time," Solomon said. "You have my cell number; you can call me at any time to check on him. I'll put him on the phone.

"It'll be a great experience for him. And I think I can arrange for him to meet Kobe Bryant."

Again, Solomon pushed a button with Michele. Kobe Bryant was her son's favorite player. Shoot, he was Michele's favorite player. She thought: *How could I deny my child a chance like that?*

"Solomon, I don't want to have to kill you. You know that's my baby. He—"

"I understand, I understand," he said, cutting her off. "I'm not ready to die, so I'll make sure he's good. I promise. It'll be fine."

"He's going to be so excited."

He gave her the details and she gave him directions to her house to pick up Gerald. In the three days before the game, Solomon did not contact Michele. He did not contact anyone—well, any women, anyway.

"I need to have my head clear," he told Ray. "Dealing with women never gives clarity. They only cloud a situation."

"Well, that's true," Ray said, and they laughed. "You're really serious about this woman. That's good. You need to settle down— although I'd have to see it to believe it."

"Yeah, me, too," Solomon said. "But people change, things change. I can change…I think. It's about being motivated."

When game day came, Solomon called Michele to tell her he would pick up her son at 5:30. "Why so early? The game isn't until 7:30, right?"

"I want him to have the full experience. If we get there early enough, we can eat dinner, get down on the floor so he can meet some players and get comfortable. I hate getting to anything late. That's a black folk affliction that I don't participate in."

Michele could not hold back her smile. She agreed with Solomon on that issue. It reminded her of one of their first dinner dates. She was late, unable to decide on an outfit or jewelry or a purse. Finally, when she arrived at Marvin's at 14th and U Streets, Solomon was on his second cocktail.

"You look great," he said to her when she arrived. "I see why you're a half-hour late." He smiled and her anxiety was eased. But she knew then that he took time-liness as a serious matter.

So she was hardly surprised when her doorbell rang at 5:29 p.m. "Can I get it, Mommy?" Solomon could hear young Gerald bellow through the door. "Can I get it?"

"Ask who it is first!" his mother yelled back. "You know the rules!"

Solomon smiled. He felt the mother-son connection through the door. They were tight. They doted on each other.

"Hi, Coach Money," little Gerald said when he opened the door. He wore a Kobe Bryant jersey and a wide smile.

"Gerald, good to see you, buddy," Solomon said. "You look good. You ready to go?"

Just then, Michele emerged from the kitchen. She did

not make eye contact with Solomon. Instead, she went straight to her son.

"Okay, listen to me, honey," she said while bending over and straightening Gerald's clothes. It was nervous energy—nervous about sending her child with Solomon and nervous about being in the same room with him.

"You do what Solomon—uh, Coach Money—says, okay? No running off."

"Okay, Mom. Okay."

"Hi, Michele," Solomon said.

"Hi," she responded without looking up.

Solomon smiled. "Okay, then. You ready, Money?" he said to Gerald.

Michele looked up at Solomon. "Why did you call him that?"

"Oh, well, he reminds me of myself when I was a kid. And this older guy used to call me that."

Michele gazed at him. There were a few awkward seconds of silence, with Gerald looking up at both of the adults. Finally, Solomon said, "Well, I guess we're going to head to the game."

Gerald headed for the door. "Ah, wait a minute, young man. Don't I get a hug?" Michele asked.

He ran back and hugged her, and tried to pull away. But she hugged him tighter, longer. "Mom, we have to go," he said.

"Okay...Solomon—"

"I know, Michele. We'll be fine and he'll be great," he said. "I'll call you when we're on our way back."

"Call me when you get there. Please."

Solomon left without answering. He and Gerald made their way to Philips Arena. When they got there, he gave the kid the tickets.

"I'm giving you the responsibility of taking care of these," he said. "You lose them and we have to go home."

"I won't lose them," Gerald said.

And he didn't. He was proud to be given such an important job. Their seats were in the club section of the arena, where there were several restaurants to choose from for a pregame meal. There was still an hour before tipoff, so they ate turkey sandwiches, fries and milkshakes.

"What are your grades like in school?" Solomon said.

"All A's," Gerald said eagerly, "and one B."

Solomon extended a clenched fist and Gerald put up his tiny fist and tapped Solomon's.

"I got the same grades when I was your age, too," he said. "And you know what? Once you get all A's, you can't get anything else."

"I'm not getting anything but A's," Gerald said.

"Okay, if you do, I'll make sure to get you a present. You get all A's, I'll take care of you. Cool?"

Gerald smiled. "Cool."

They got up from the table and headed for their seats, which were seven rows up from the floor, across from the Los Angeles Lakers' bench. There were still 45 minutes before tip off, and Solomon took Gerald as far down as they could get, which was right to the floor.

Just as they got there, Kobe Bryant emerged from the tunnel across the court. "Check this out," Solomon said to Gerald, pointing toward Kobe.

Gerald froze. He stared at the NBA superstar, uncertain of what to do or say. "You all right?" Solomon asked.

He didn't answer. Suddenly, a pass to Kobe went over his head, toward where Solomon or Gerald stood. Kobe turned to retrieve the ball, which had rolled under a chair right in front of Gerald.

"Get it," Solomon told him. Without looking up, Gerald squatted and squirmed underneath the chairs and picked up the ball. When he stood up, Kobe Bryant was standing over him, looking down, smiling.

"Hey, young fella," Kobe said.

Solomon pulled out his camera from his pocket. "Let's get a quick photo?" he said to Kobe.

"Let's do it," the player said. He turned around the stunned kid, put his arm around him and Solomon snapped the photo.

Kobe shook Gerald's hand and then he was gone.

"Oh my God," Gerald finally said. "I met Kobe Bryant. I can't believe it. I have to call my mom."

"Let's go to our seats and you can call her," Solomon said. He was happy for the kid and relieved; meeting and taking a photo with Kobe Bryant was bigger and better than watching any game.

"Mommy, guess what?" he said into the phone. "Guess… I met Kobe Bryant."

Solomon watched the kid's smile light up the arena. He was happy and proud that Gerald was happy, and it had to mean something for him in Michele's eyes, too. Still, in that moment, it was more important for Gerald to have a great experience than anything else. If Michele eased up on him, fine. But it was no longer about getting to her through Gerald.

He looked down at the boy as they departed the arena. "How was that?"

Gerald looked up at him with those bright, innocent eyes for a few seconds. "Awesome, Coach Money," he said, finally.

Solomon gave the kid the responsibility of finding the car in the crowded parking lot. "You sure it's this way?"

"It's over here. I remember," Gerald said.

And he was right. "You're good," Solomon said. "That's why I call you 'Money.'"

In the car, Solomon called Michele to tell her they were en route to her house. "I saw that the Lakers won." Her voice was pleasant; there was not a trace of discord. "How is he?"

"Great," Solomon said. "Happy. He's a great kid. I know you're proud. We had a great time."

When they arrived at Michele's house, she opened the door before Gerald could ring the doorbell. They hugged. "You had fun, huh?" she said.

Her son nodded his head. His grin said it all.

"Thanks for letting me take him," Solomon said as he

hugged Gerald goodnight. "Remember what I told you about school, okay? I'll see you later.

"Michele, as promised, he's back in one piece—and happy."

"He is." She paused and they stared at each other. Solomon detected a tear in her eye. "Thank you, Solomon."

He nodded his head.

"And thank you for letting him go with me," he said. "I enjoyed him."

He turned then and walked toward the car in her driveway. But he did not hear the door shut, meaning she was watching him walk away, meaning he had struck a chord.

When Solomon reached his car, he turned back toward the house. Michele was smiling.

"He had a good time, didn't he?" she said.

Solomon looked at her without answering.

"Thank you," she said again.

CHAPTER 9
THE BOOK
OF REVELATIONS

The ride home for Solomon was great. He enjoyed little Gerald and Michele was pleasant to him. It could not have gone any better. As was his way, he quickly shifted to the next move.

There was a fine line between being smart and being pushy. Solomon, as a marketing executive, understood the value of riding the momentum of a strong wave. And he recognized the value of planning ahead.

So, on the way home from the game, he gave Gerald an envelope. "Money, I want you to give this to your mom before you go to bed," he said. "You're going to remember to do that?"

"What is it?" Gerald asked.

"It's a gift for your mom for letting me take you to the game. I want it to be a surprise."

"Okay, Coach Money," he said, sticking the envelope in his pocket. "I won't forget."

It took Solomon about fifteen minutes to get home, and he figured that if Gerald did as planned, he had another fifteen minutes or so until Michele called to thank him for the present.

So, instead of taking a shower, he kicked off his shoes, made himself a margarita and got comfortable on the couch in anticipation of a call from Michele. After several minutes, he dozed off and woke up around midnight.

He looked at the time on the flat-screen television and was surprised his phone had not awakened him. He guessed that Gerald had forgotten to deliver his gift to Michele.

And just before he could ponder for long what to do, his cell phone chimed, indicating he had a text message. It was from Michele.

She had put Gerald to bed, tucked him in and said his prayers with him when he remembered what Solomon told him.

"Mommy," he said, as Michele was leaving his room, "I have something to give to you."

"You can give it to me in the morning, Gerald. It's time to go to sleep."

"But I'm supposed to give it to you now. I told Coach Money I wouldn't forget."

"Coach Money?"

"Yes, it's in my pants." Gerald got out of the bed and picked up his pants off the chair near his closet.

He handed the envelope over to her. "Here it is, Mommy."

Michele took it. "Okay, now it's time to get some sleep. Let's get you back in bed."

He jumped in and gave his mom another hug and kiss. Michele turned off the light in his room and took a seat at the bar outside her kitchen. She looked at the envelope, unable to figure what Solomon could have left for her. *It must be a note*, she thought.

There was no letter opener handy, so she grabbed a knife and used it to neatly but swiftly cut it open.

She unfolded the paper and received quite a surprise: a gift certificate from Thrill Planet in Marietta for a complimentary skydive. She could not suppress a smile from creasing her face.

Skydiving was one of her favorite activities. She had introduced Solomon to that adventure. But Michele had not "jumped" in years; the economic downturn impacted her catering business and she just could not pull herself to doing something she enjoyed over providing for Gerald.

She called Sonya. "Girl, guess what Solomon did? After he took Gerald to the Hawks game—"

"Wait," her cousin interrupted. "You let Solomon take Gerald to a game? When did this miracle happen?"

"Tonight. He asked me and I thought about it and let him go. He was so excited. And he had a great time, too. So, it worked out.

"But anyway, Solomon gave Gerald a gift to give to me."

"Really? What?"

"A gift certificate to skydive. Can you believe that?"

"Oh my goodness," Sonya said. "Weren't you talking about that the other day, that you wish you could afford to jump?"

"That's what I'm saying: This is right on time. How

could he know this is what I needed? Wait a minute—did you tell him?"

"What? No," Sonya said. "How could I tell him? I don't know how to reach him."

"Facebook; you love Facebook," Michele said.

"Girl, I don't even know if he's on Facebook. And if I did, knowing how you feel, you think I would contact him? And how do YOU know he has a Facebook page?"

"I don't know," she said. "Anyway, the point is, he gave me this gift. Now what do I do?"

"I know your mother and your daddy, so I know they taught you to say, 'thank you,'" Sonya said. "It's not that complicated."

"No, it is complicated because of who it came from, cousin," Michele said. "He took my son to the game and now he's giving me gifts. He's trying to lure me back to him."

"Well, what's wrong with that?" Sonya paused. "Listen, I'm not saying what he did wasn't wrong. But I do remember that you were happy with him. Now, all these years later, a lot has happened and here he is. So, do you ever forgive him for what happened—what, eight years ago?—or do you at least give the man a shot and see what's up?

"We talk every day, which means you don't have a lot to do. Here's a man you loved who's back in your life. And you know there's another very serious reason you should find out what the deal is. Don't do anything rash. Take your time and feel your way through it. Listen, he's here in Atlanta. He has his choice of many women; that's how it is here. He's trying to get with you. Shouldn't that mean something?"

Michele considered all her cousin had to say. "Everything you say is right," she said after a moment of contemplation. "But here's the thing: You've got to have trust. There's no way around that. He's working from a negative number—he's behind zero. So, it's hard knowing that he disappeared for eight years, Sonya. That's hard to get past."

"I'm sure it is. I can't imagine what it was like," she said. "But how about this: Just do the right thing and thank the man for the gift. You know you're not returning it because you love to skydive. So thank him. And just have an open mind. If he gets to be too much, tell him. But I'm not like most people. I believe people can change. Make that, people can grow up. If you are one way all your life, you might not be able to change. But if you were immature in some way, time allows you a chance to grow up. Maybe Solomon has grown up, realizes his mistake with you and wants to show you he's different. Isn't there a chance that could be it?"

"Anything's possible," Michele answered. "And I don't want to sound so pessimistic. But that's the best way for me to protect myself…I will call him—no, it's too late to call now. I'll text him and see if he's still up. I'll let you know what happened."

"You'd better," Sonya said. "Bye."

Michele hung up her home phone and picked up her cell. She texted Solomon: "Thank you for the gift. But why?"

Solomon responded: "Can I call you to explain?"

Instead of responding, Michele called Solomon. "Why waste another text when I could just call you?" she said when he answered.

"What are you doing up this late?" he said. "I thought my man forgot to give you the envelope."

"Almost," she said. "But he was so proud to do what you asked him to do. He told me that you let him hold the tickets and find the car in the parking lot. I really appreciate that. He likes when you give him responsibilities."

"I'm not just saying this, but that kid is a great kid. I see so much in him. I'm proud of him, so I know you are."

"I am. He's my heart."

"I can tell," Solomon said. "But listen, I'm really grateful that you're talking to me right now. I am. I got you the skydive certificate because I remember how much you loved it. And I'm sure you still do.

"So, for letting me take your son to the game, I wanted to give you something I knew you'd like… And, to be honest, I wanted you to know I remember and that I'm thoughtful—and that I'm sorry."

Michele was stuck. She didn't want to take too long to respond; it would give the impression of uncertainty. But she didn't want to answer so quickly, either; it would give the impression of surrender. She was somewhere in between, and that wasn't easy to convey.

After several seconds, she spoke. "Solomon, it's hard for me to not be straight up with you—and that's what I expect from you. Can I expect the truth, no matter what the answer to the question is?"

"Yes," Solomon said. He wasn't happy about having to answer that question, but he realized that he created doubt in Michele.

"Well, I actually want to trust you. I do," she said. "But I can't afford to get hurt. That's a part of life, but I can't set myself up for it. I loved you and you walked away from me. How could you do that?"

As smart as Solomon was and as much as he wanted to have a real conversation with Michele, he was not ready for that question. And, really, no amount of preparation could have made him ready. So, he dug down deep and gave her his truth.

"First, I gotta say I'm sorry again, Michele," he said. "I feel embarrassed and ashamed that I did that to you. At the time, it was not the thing to do, but I truly believed it was the right thing to do *for me*.

"Not because I didn't care about you—you know I did, I hope. But because…I have had a problem trusting people in general, but women in particular. My position has always been that a woman will eventually disappoint you. So, I told myself that before I got disappointed by you, I would leave."

"And you think that makes sense?"

"No, I don't," he answered. "All this time later, it sounds

stupid. But I'm a different person now. Well, maybe not even a different person, but definitely a more mature person. I thought I had it together back then, but I can see now—by the way I was thinking—that I didn't.

"I promise you, this has been a struggle for me, knowing I hurt you like that. You were nothing but great to me. Seeing you at the banquet…it made the light switch come on. I tried to block you out so I wouldn't have to think about what I did. But most of the time, it didn't work. To see you again brought all those feelings of being stupid and selfish, cowardly and shameful—I felt all that as soon as I realized it was you.

"But I also felt a sensation. It was like the sun was shining on me. Through all that shame and embarrassment, I felt good about seeing you. You know, excited. Hopeful."

"But is this about redeeming yourself with me or… well, what is it about?" Michele asked.

"I can't lie," Solomon said. "It definitely is about redeeming myself. You don't do that to people. It's hard to swallow that I let other women's actions change who I should've been. But here's the thing: If I didn't really care for you so much, redeeming myself wouldn't be as important—the true redemption, for me, comes with finding out if we still have that great connection."

"Solomon, are you telling me that here in Atlanta, where women are in overabundance, you don't have a girlfriend?"

"No, I don't," he said. "I date—well, I did date. But

since I saw you, I haven't had the urge to see another woman. And that's the truth. In fact, I had a date set for the night I saw you. After that, I cancelled it."

"Why?" Michele asked.

"Because it would've been a waste of time," Solomon answered. "I don't have a serious interest in anyone else. I have women I saw because I'm a man and I like women; we all need companionship. They are good women. But I don't really trust women, so I got only so close emotionally.

"But there was never that special something that we had. There were never moments like we had when I laughed till I cried. No moments when I would stare at someone while she slept, wondering what she was dreaming about."

"You did that?"

"I did, a few times," he said. "I think, Michele, the honest reality is that I was afraid of you. I wasn't ready for you. I was 25, 26 and just, you know, out there. Then you came along and I felt all connected to you. But I'm thinking, 'She's too good to be true. The shoe will drop.' And I'll be disappointed and hurt because that's what happened to me many times before."

"That's no way to live, Solomon."

"I know. I know that now. At the time, my mindset was effed up. It's hard for a man to admit this, but I'll be real with you. I was hurt several times by females, starting when I was a teenager. I came to believe that's what women will do to me, and I was scared of feeling that hurt and disappointment again. So, somewhere in my mind I decided to not get too close or care too much. Just get what I wanted out of it and leave. It was stupid, but it was a way to protect myself."

"So why didn't you try to reach me when you realized you messed up?"

"To say what? Sorry? Forgive me? I was sick in the head?"

"That's exactly what you're telling me now," Michele said. "The exact same thing."

"Yes, but it is the truth," Solomon said. "I never thought I'd see you again. But I never *hoped* I'd never see you again. I could go long stretches blocking all this out. Then one day I saw this woman on the opposite side from me at Lenox Square Mall. It looked like you so much. I tried to get a better look, but I lost her in the crowd.

"But it made me very curious. So I called your home number—I remembered it—but it was disconnected. I had changed phones about five times and somewhere in there I lost your cell number."

"So what do you want from me now?" Michele said.

"I want to hang out with you, have a cocktail or two, chat, enjoy the moment. And I want to sweep you off your feet so you can see how I grew up from back then. And anything in between.

"But right now, I want to take you to lunch next week."

Michele knew what she was going to do, but refused

to give in. "Well, I have to think about it, Solomon. Let's talk again in a few days."

"Fair enough. In a few days."

Those few days passed by slowly for both of them. Solomon's days were particularly mundane; he avoided the four-woman rotation he negotiated before Michele. Prior to their unlikely reconnection, Solomon went round and round between them, a carousel of meaningless and misleading sex.

But he needed the women for a number of reasons, reasons he did not truly contemplate until those days waiting to have lunch with Michele. The more Texas margaritas he consumed, the more honest he was with himself.

So, Solomon sipped cocktails and spewed truths. He confessed to himself that he juggled women because he did not like being alone—a hard reality for someone who claimed he did not care much for people; that despite the confidence he showed, there was an underlying insecurity that needed women to validate his worth; that he loved sexually pleasing women and being pleased, but only physically—not for an emotional charge because he could not put his emotions in a position to be influenced by women.

Above all, he surmised that there was something wrong with all that, something wrong with *him*.

By the fourth drink, he figured it out:

He did not have a soul.

That revelation saddened him, for a moment. He asked himself: Where did it go? *How* did it go? His spirits quickly changed when the next revelation arrived: Regaining Michele's love would be tantamount to regaining his soul.

And so his commitment was redoubled. If it were not 1:37 a.m., he would have called Michele right then. But considering the impact the liquor had on his mind, it was a good thing that he got to sleep it off and start fresh the next day.

If he had called, Michele would have answered. Unlike Solomon, who could not find his friend Ray to be a sounding board, Michele unloaded all her conflicting emotions on Sonya, who was a willing listener.

"So you think I should go out with him?" Michele asked Sonya. "Forget all about what he did to me?"

"In a word, 'yes,'" she answered. "What are you proving by going against your heart? You've been basically miserable for eight years. If you didn't have Gerald, you'd be crazy—and driving me crazy.

"Here's a man who is open about making a mistake and apologizing for it. Most guys won't even apologize for not opening the door for you. From what you have told me, Solomon has been almost overly apologetic.

"So I say, again, give him a chance. Because he did something years ago doesn't mean he'll do it again—or that you shouldn't forgive him. If you let your son go out with him, then why not you?"

Her cousin made perfect sense, but Michele learned something about herself: She was not a chance-taker.

"Honestly, the easy thing for me to do is to go on with my life," she said. "There's no risk in that—I know what that's like."

"Well, you can—and will—do what you want," Sonya said. "But to go on with your life when you're not happy with it…well, that doesn't show me a lot. Here's my last point and I'm done with it: There's something called risk-reward. The bigger the risk, the bigger the reward. Sometimes, that's what it comes down to in life. To me, there's something exciting about that. And whenever we can throw excitement into our lives, how can that be bad?"

Sonya then got up, hugged her cousin and left Michele in her home to deal with her dilemma. She was in a struggle with two sides of herself, and they were at a stalemate. When she finally pulled herself off the couch near 2 a.m., she stopped by Gerald's room to look in on him.

She stood in the doorway and watched him sleep soundly. Her existence was about providing and protecting Gerald. Michele threw herself into him partly so she would not have to deal with her loneliness.

The reality was that no man before or after Solomon even dented her sensibilities. She dated because it was, basically, a necessary evil. It had become so droll until it eventually became unimportant. Men bored her with talk of themselves or talk of nonsense; lack of chivalry or overly aggressive; so smart they were dumb in relating and so dumb they were intolerable.

The monotony and predictability of men changed her. She was audacious enough to jump out of an airplane, but scared to accept a date with the one man who actually moved her to emotional and intellectual heights.

The sadness of all that rushed to her brain as she looked at her son, and she shook her head. Her eyes watered—she loved little Gerald so much that she could become emotional about him in an instant. But the question she posed to herself was this: *Do I love myself enough to take a risk to get the reward I deserve?*

She had many girlfriends over the years that sabotaged their relationships because, in essence, they didn't believe they deserved the happiness they had. Michele deduced that she was doing the same thing to herself by hanging on to what Solomon did or *might* do as opposed to what he *would* do toward her happiness.

That thought allowed her to crawl into bed feeling differently about herself and the prospects of her life. If Solomon truly wanted her back, she was going to give him a chance to show it.

And that idea helped her to lay in bed with her eyes closed and her heart open.

CHAPTER 10
BABY STEPS

Solomon called Michele that next morning a little before nine. It was a Saturday. Michele answered after the first ring.

"Good morning," Solomon said. "I know it's breakfast time, but are you ready for lunch?"

Michele laughed. "Not right now, but I will be ready at one."

"Cool," Solomon said, relieved. "I'm thinking we could go to Arizona's out at The Mall at Stonecrest. I love the Pasta Sedona."

"I'm good with that," she said. "Actually, that's perfect; I can drop Gerald off at his friend's house in Conyers."

"Do you want to bring him to lunch?" Solomon asked. "I'd like to see him."

Michele felt good about that. But she wanted Solomon to herself. The conversation, she figured, would get too involved for Gerald's ears.

"Next time. I think he'd enjoy spending some time with you," she said.

"Okay, but I'm serious about next time," Solomon said. "He's a great kid."

"I appreciate you saying that," Michele said. "He likes you, too. He admires and respects you. And that's a great thing; I love it when a man can spend some time with him and impart things I just can't."

"My pleasure. So, we can figure out another time for me to connect with Gerald. I'd actually like to take him to the gym to work on his game. But we'll figure that out.

"In the meantime, I look forward to seeing you at one at Arizona's."

"Me, too, Solomon," she said before hanging up.

It was a date that generated actions Solomon rarely went through. That is, he tried on three outfits before deciding on designer jeans with a beautiful John Varvatos plum shirt and black Too Boot New York slip-on loafers. Stylish yet Saturday-afternoon-casual, he decided.

Michele went through an even more painstaking process. Jeans or skirt? Pullover blouse or button-up? Boots or heels? For ninety minutes she tried on combinations, seeking the attire that would not be overtly sexy but not shut down, either.

Finally, Gerald walked in her room as she was standing in front of the full-length mirror in the tenth outfit. "I like that, Mommy. You look good."

And her clothes for the lunch were decided right there, by Gerald: dark blue jeans with a crisp white button-up blouse and chocolate suede heels. Simple and elegant.

She smiled at the thought that a seven-year-old boy dressed her. Michele picked a pair of hoop earrings and a brown suede bag and she was ready. She wanted to wear a necklace, but decided it would draw attention to her cleavage, which had grown two cup sizes with the birth of her child. Even after so many years she still was, at times, uncomfortable with the growth. Besides, she would have to leave the top three buttons open to expose the necklace, which would expose too much and send the wrong message.

Solomon arrived early at the restaurant. He wanted to be there to watch Michele walk in. And she came in feeling and looking confident. She spent ample time applying makeup and lip gloss and styling her hair. She looked great, fresh.

The way he saw it, she was walking in slow motion as she entered Arizona's. Statuesque and radiant. The extra pounds she had put on did not faze him.

"Hi there," he said. Solomon was unsure if he should hug her or not—he told himself to be very careful about how to handle this first date—but he immediately discarded that idea and leaned in for a hug.

Michele leaned in, too, and they embraced. "Ah, you smell so good," Solomon said. "I see you're still into Avon."

She laughed loudly—that was one of his favorite things about her that he had forgotten: Michele laughed a full, throaty laugh that was infectious.

"I have you know this is Mary Kay," she joked, and they both laughed.

The hostess sat them in a booth near the front of the

dining room. "I think this is an occasion for a midday cocktail," Solomon said. "Some champagne?"

"Sounds great," Michele said, and Solomon ordered two glasses of Veuve Clicquot.

"What are we toasting to?" Michele asked.

"How about, to redemption and recapturing?" he said.

"And renewing," Michele added, and they tapped glasses.

Over the meal, they enjoyed small talk, caught up on each other's families and in general felt each other out.

The "elephant in the room" had been ignored for quite a while before Solomon said: "Thank you for being here, Michele. I don't even know if I deserve your forgiveness, but I've been asking for it for years, putting it out there in the universe because I didn't think I would see you again.

"But here you are and I'm grateful. I have a friend here, Ray, who I told that I don't live with regrets. But, really, that was crazy. Everyone does things they wish they hadn't, and at some point they regret them. I regret what I did to you."

Michele just looked at him; she didn't know what to say.

"Now, I'm trying to find my soul," he went on.

"Your soul?" Michele said.

"Yes, my soul," he said. "For me, my soul means my heart, conscience and rational mind. Those three together. And when I...never mind."

"What?"

"I'll leave it at that for now."

"Okay, I see," she said. "Well, thanks for asking me out

and being patient. My thing is I had to come down off the whole righteous indignation. I was hurt, but that's a part of life, relationships. It doesn't mean that it's okay or that I don't have my issues behind it because I do.

"And the main issue is trust."

"I understand that," Solomon said. "That's something, if you give me a chance, that I have to earn. That I can earn."

"Yes, but it's really more about me trusting myself," Michele said, "trusting my mind and my heart. And when they disagree, trusting that I can and will make the decision that makes the most sense.

"You may leave here today saying, 'She's gained some weight and she has a kid and she's crazy and I don't want to deal with her'—and disappear," she said. "That would be messed up, but I couldn't be afraid of that anymore. I had to go for what I believed in."

"And you believed in me? Wow," Solomon said.

"I believe in the *idea* of you," she answered. "And what's the idea of you? I'll hold that for another time."

They talked for another hour across the table after they finished their meal. The conversation ranged from living in Atlanta to the earthquake in Haiti to all the drama President Obama has had to deal with to Kobe vs. LeBron.

All the while, they were assessing each other and reaching the same conclusion: "We're good together."

Finally, Michele said she had to pick up Gerald at his friend's.

"Two things," Solomon said. "One, how does a kid born in 2002 have an old name like 'Gerald'? I'd think his name would be Hennessy or Escalade or Nuvo—something, uh, contemporary like that."

Michele laughed so loud other patrons turned toward their table. "You are crazy," she said. "But I was waiting for that question. I've heard that question a lot. Gerald actually was my dad's middle name."

"Your dad's middle name? Why didn't you just give him your dad's name?" Solomon said.

"Because I wasn't going to call my son Cleophaus," she said, and Solomon laughed as hard and loud as he had in who-knew-when.

"Oh, my God," he said. "Don't mean to laugh at your dad's name. I don't. But damn…"

"You can laugh at it; I don't care because it's funny," she said. "He didn't even go by it. Everyone called him 'O,' even my mom… But what's the second thing?"

"Oh, thanks for reminding me," Solomon said. "The second thing is this." He pulled out of his pocket a little pouch and handed it across the table to Michele.

"What's this?"

Solomon did not answer. In it was a David Yurman charm bracelet that he bought Michele for Valentine's Day of 2001. She wore it one time and left it at Solomon's house.

"Oh, wow," she said. "I thought I lost this… You kept this all this time?"

"I did," Solomon said. "Let me put it on you.

"Looks good. Just like I remember it," he added. "In fact, you look just as I remember you from back in the day. Your hair is different, a little longer."

"Yeah, well, there are some other *things* different, too," she said. "But anyway, you also look the same."

She wanted to add, "You look damn good, edible good," but that would've been her depraved body talking, which her conscious mind knew wouldn't have been right. So she left it at that.

Solomon got up from his seat and went to her side of the table and offered a hand to help her up. "I forgot you are Mr. Chivalry," she said. "Thank you. Trust me, it is much appreciated."

When she got to her feet, he hugged her again. This time, it was an extended hug, a more sensual hug. Michele tried to catch her breath; a man's body had not been pressed up against hers in quite some time. Solomon kissed her on the left side of her face.

"When can I see you again?" Solomon asked.

"When do you want to?"

"Tonight."

"Tonight?"

"Yeah, tonight," Solomon said. "I want to take you someplace where we can hear some music, be around people, have a few cocktails—"

"I'm sold. Let me call my cousin, Sonya, to see if she can keep Gerald. You remember Sonya?"

"Of course, I remember her," Solomon said. "I'm surprised I never ran into her. How is she?"

"She's great. Still flying. But she's here this weekend—and she's going to be my sitter tonight."

And so it was. Solomon picked up Michele at 7:30. She opened the door and the intoxicating scent of her perfume rushed to Solomon's nose. It was going to be a good night.

"You smell wonderful," he said. "And you look great."

"Thanks," she said. "I didn't know what to wear since you didn't tell me where we're going. So hopefully this is alright."

She wore an orange blouse that complemented her mocha skin color; a silk brown skirt that hung delicately above her knees.

"Perfect," he said, smiling and slowly nodding his head. "Perfect."

On the way to Craft restaurant in Buckhead, Michele called Sonya to check on Gerald.

"What do you want?" Sonya said when answering the phone. "Aren't you on a date? It's been a while, but I thought you'd remember how to act."

"Girl, I wanted to say goodnight to my son. What's wrong with that?"

"You already did," Sonya said. "We're busy. Go have a good time. Matter of fact, he's going to spend the night. That doesn't mean you need to make your date all night, though."

"Ah, I know that," Michele said. "You sure about that?"

"I'm sure," Sonya said. "He has clothes here. I have a toothbrush for him. He'll be fine."

"Okay, well, just tell my son I love him."

"Bye, Michele."

"You're not comfortable leaving him with anyone, are you?" Solomon said.

"He's in good hands, but he's my baby," Michele said.

Solomon did not respond; he kept driving—and thinking. He wanted to clear his conscience some more, tell her about everything: how he became cold enough to move away without telling her; how he came to regret that decision; who he has grown into; how having her back in his life would ignite his soul.

He just didn't know when to do it. The plan after dinner was to go to Drinkshop at the W Hotel downtown for cocktails. "Sounds good to me," Michele said. "I haven't been out in so long, we could go to Waffle House and I'd be good with it."

They made it to the restaurant and went to the bar as their table was being set up.

"Don't think because I'm here with you that everything is all great," Michele said. She was smiling but she was serious.

Solomon smiled back at her. "I understand," he said. "Everything takes time… Can I hug you?"

"You're something else," she said. "Looking for sympathy? From me?"

"Just a hug," he said.

They embraced. In her ear, Solomon whispered, "Thank you. Now let's have a drink."

"How about some water? We're getting drinks afterward, right?" Michele said. "I can't have but so many, so I'd rather wait until later."

"Cool. Water it is," Solomon said.

A few moments later, they were placed at a table at the window overlooking Peachtree Street.

"I read about this place but never really thought about coming here," Michele said. "Very nice."

"Why didn't you think about coming here?" Solomon asked.

"Well, everything costs money," she said. "And while my catering business is going okay—all my clients love what I provide—not enough people are using caterers right now for me to not have to work part-time to keep things going.

"Gerald's in private school—the Johnson Learning Center—which costs a pretty penny. So, I read about all the great restaurants here, but I don't get to go to many."

"We could change that. We *should* change that," Solomon said. "Maybe once a month pick a place and go experience it."

"You say that now," Michele said. "Let's see what the bill is tonight before committing to that."

They laughed. Finally, they scanned the menu and ordered.

When the bread arrived at the table, Solomon said,

"I've been trying to figure out when I should get into why I did what I did to you, and there's no time like the present, as they say."

"Is it going to spoil my appetite, spoil my mood?" Michele said. "I haven't had a really nice night like this since...well, I can't exactly recall when. I have a lot of emotions around what happened. Maybe we should talk about it tomorrow."

"I really don't think you'll get angry, Michele. Hopefully, you'll be enlightened," Solomon said. "You'll learn a lot about me."

"Maybe I *should* order a drink," Michele said sarcastically.

Solomon appreciated her attitude. She easily could have been contrary at best, ornery at worse. Her disposition helped his comfort level.

"This could really be a long talk, but I'm going to cut it down as much as I can," Solomon began. "I wasn't cold to you like that because I was born that way; something happened to grow that in me. A lot of things happened. I started off liking girls but not sure how to relate to them. So I did what was natural, which was be nice to them.

"My first real girlfriend came when I was in the eighth grade. I liked her so much that I used to have imaginary conversations with her. We were doing our thing—at least that's what I thought. Then one day I saw her kissing this guy I knew. My heart dropped. I was embarrassed and angry, but mostly disappointed.

"I got over it and the next year in high school, I had

another girlfriend. Of course, that turned out badly—she started dating someone else. I was hurt again. But I was angry this time because I had another girl, Sharon, who asked me to date her. I told her—and I'll never forget what I said— 'If I didn't have a girlfriend, I would date you. But I do, so I can't.' She was like, 'Wow, you are so different from other guys. Other guys would've tried to date both of us.'

"I felt good about doing the right thing. And then she does that to me? Yeah, I was angry. I went the rest of high school without a true girlfriend. But in college I met this really nice, sweet girl from North Carolina. Things were going great. Then one day, I came home to my apartment, and all my stuff was gone. TV, VCR, clothes, watches. It was crazy.

"After I called the police, I called her. She didn't answer. I couldn't find her, which was strange. Then I went over to her apartment and her roommate had this look on her face. I was like, 'What's wrong?' She said, 'Solomon, I'm sorry. But my girl stole your stuff. She's somewhere now trying to sell it.' Needless to say, I was dumbfounded.

"The police grabbed her—she had some guys with a truck take the stuff—but I couldn't find it in me to press charges. At first, I assumed that I was the reason for girls doing me wrong. But when I really thought about it, I realized that I hadn't done anything to make them act that way.

"The clincher came when I got older. I had dated this girl, Lauren, for almost a year. I was one of those 'I'll never get married' kind of guys, but I started thinking about it with her.

"So I come home one day from work and she's sitting in my living room with this guy who begged me to stay at my apartment for six months until he got on his feet. I was about twenty-three at the time. I didn't think much of it at first. But there was this awkwardness that I sensed after a few minutes.

"I stopped what I was doing and I just stood there. He was sitting in the single chair to my left. She was sitting on the couch in front of me. I looked at them carefully and they both seemed uncomfortable.

"I said, 'What's going on?' Neither of them said anything. Nothing. My heart started beating fast. 'What's up?' I said.

"When they looked at each other, I realized what was coming next.

"She burst into tears: 'I'm sorry, Solomon. I'm so sorry.' I was unmoved—I wanted to hear it come out of her mouth before I'd believe it.

"The guy started to speak. 'Hold on,' I said. 'I'm talking to Lauren. I'll get to you in a minute.' Then I turned back to her. I said, 'So what are you so upset about?'

"She looked at me with those eyes I used to think were innocent and said, 'We should talk. I don't know what happened. I like you. But...'

"She didn't finish her thought, but I did. 'But you've been messing around with this guy, right?'

"'It just happened,' she said. I was done. Another woman I cared about had disappointed me.

"And it happened a few more times—a disappointment of some sort. And, really, to be totally honest, it ate at my soul…until it was gone—or close to gone. I dealt with women without any trust and with a lot of bitterness. I became cold."

"I don't want to sound insensitive," Michele said. "But what you experienced—women being less than you expected them to be—is what millions of women have had to go through with men all our lives.

"That's what men do: hurt and disappoint women. Scar us. Take advantage of us. Use us. And, in the end, you wonder why we don't trust or why we're guarded? So, I understand about being disappointed and hurt.

"But the way you handled it with me…"

"I know," Solomon said. "I admit that in some ways women are stronger than men. Men have damaged women, but you—well, some of you—bounce back stronger. Some of you, a few of you, don't let it break you. I wasn't strong enough to bounce back. It broke me. I decided I wouldn't get close to anyone and that I'd leave her before she left me."

Michele fought getting angry. Solomon could tell by how she leaned back in her chair and folded her arms.

"I can look back on that now and see that it was wrong and I'm embarrassed by it," he said. "I had what I *thought* was a legitimate reason to do what I did to you. I liked you a lot, which equated to me thinking you were going to hurt me. The way to avoid it was to protect myself by running.

"Before you, I left a few women and I didn't look back. I was just cold like that.

"But with you, there always was the feeling inside me that made me wonder if our connection was as real as it seemed. It was hard for me to walk away from you. But I did it for one reason: I was scared. It almost was like I wanted embrace that time together and walk away from it rather than have you ruin it by doing like other women did me.

"It sounds crazy, but that's the truth. I wasn't trying to leave you at that time. The job here came up and I had no idea I would get it. When I did, I couldn't turn it down. And then I had to go."

Solomon's voice drifted off, almost as if he were falling asleep. It was the shame of it all. It ate at him.

Michele was proud of herself that she did not blurt out obscenities. The emotion of wanting Solomon to want her was greater than any residual anger remaining from him leaving her. Her reality was not complex: She desired not just a man, but Solomon Singletary. So she did not pounce on his excuses. She didn't like his reasons, but she understood based on what he explained.

For all those eight years, in her honest moments, she prayed for him to return to her.

"Well," she said, ending the silence, "I'm glad you told

me that. At least I know now that it wasn't me. That's something I lived with for a long time before I finally decided, 'This man is not going to make me think I did something wrong.' I knew I hadn't."

"Actually, you were great," Solomon said as their meals arrived.

The server placed their plates in front of them. "You were great," Solomon repeated.

"Looks delish," Michele said, studying her plate. A stellar "chef," she started her catering business only after completing culinary school. She wanted to learn all the intricacies of cooking, from food preparation to nutritional value to storage temperatures to presentation and on and on.

"You see how our dishes look? Looks good, right? That's an important part of the experience," she explained. "It must look appealing."

Michele ordered the swordfish with celery root, fennel, tangerine and oil-cured olives. Solomon had the hangar steak with potato puree and mixed vegetables.

"Can I say grace?" Solomon said. Michele smiled and nodded.

"Dear Lord, we thank You for this food we are about to receive for the nourishment of our bodies. And we thank You for our reconnection after so long. We know this is Your will. Bless the hands that prepared the food. Amen."

When Solomon opened his eyes, he could see that Michele was staring at him with a quizzical look.

"God's will?" she said, offering a smile.

"His will in His time," he answered. "I'm not the most religious guy, but I know us meeting as we did after all this time wasn't something we made happen. It was divine intervention."

"It *was* pretty incredible," Michele allowed. "I—"

She took her first bite of food. "O-M-G," she said. "Tastes as good as it looks."

"Mine, too," Solomon said, in between chomping down on his steak.

Michele took a few more bites and then completed her thought.

"I was saying that when I saw you walk up there at that banquet, I almost swallowed my tongue," she said. "I've never felt like that before: excited, angry, uncertain, happy, relieved, shocked—all at the same time. I was hoping all that wasn't showing up on my face. If it did, I looked like some creature."

"Oh, you played it off well," Solomon said. "All I saw was one emotion on your face: hostility. You were steaming. At the same time, I was like you, with all kinds of emotions running through me: shock, excitement, fear, surprise, regret.

"I was shocked not only to see you but to learn you were Gerald's mom; scared because I didn't know how you'd react to me; surprised at being excited to see you. I guess, in that very moment, all the denying went away and I admitted that I regretted leaving you like I did."

They stared at each other for a few seconds and then continued to eat.

"This is great, but from what I remember, you can create dishes like this—or better," Solomon said.

"I definitely think I've improved from when you last had something I prepared."

"Me, too," Solomon said. "I've improved my skills in the kitchen. And if you'll hang out with me again, I'd like to cook for you. Let you sit back and be served.

"I see you're still the same."

"The same?"

"The same. Charming."

CHAPTER 11

OH, WHAT A NIGHT

That dinner date with drinks afterward turned into their routine. For almost two months, they took on Atlanta's restaurant scene and grew closer and closer. Michele still had a trust issue with Solomon, but that sheath came down bit-by-bit.

Solomon, meanwhile, was catching heat from the rotation of four women he juggled before rediscovering Michele. He could not find it in himself to tell them he wanted nothing to do with them anymore. Instead, he used work and travel as an excuse to be unavailable.

Springtime came and his romance with Michele blossomed. However, they had not been intimate. One night, Solomon tried, but Michele rebuffed him.

"I remember how we were together," she said. "And please don't think I'm trying to tease you. But I think we should wait. For what, I don't know. But when the time is right, it will happen. It will feel right."

She was honest, but she also was imposing a test. If Solomon really wanted her, sex would not matter. Well, not that much. Besides, if he left her again, it would be easier to deal with without missing his intimate touch.

Still, her attraction to him was bubbling like volcano lava. It wasn't just the physical. It was more about how he made her feel in their talks and his manners and, significantly, how much he seemed to genuinely adore her son, Gerald.

He talked to Gerald several times a week, took him to movies and taught him basketball while Michele worked events she catered. He even picked up Gerald from school for her a couple of times.

"Coach Money, do you like my mommy?" he said one day as they sat in the square at Atlantic Station. Michele's business picked up and she was working a wedding reception.

"I do like your mom."

"Are you going to marry her?" Gerald asked.

"Marry her? Well, Gerald, I don't know about that. But I know this: I'm going to be around to hang out with you all the time. You're my buddy, right?"

Gerald nodded his head. "I like you, Coach Money."

"Give it up," Solomon said, holding out a clenched fist. Gerald tapped it with his tiny fist. "I like you, too, Gerald. A lot."

Gerald spent that night with Sonya. Michelle was tired from an afternoon wedding reception, but she summoned the energy to go out for drinks with Solomon at Café Circa on Edgewood Avenue, behind the famed Ebenezer Baptist Church.

He was surprised to run into his boy, Ray, there. "Yo,

what's up?" he said as they embraced. "Who you here with? Your wife?"

"Nah, one of my boys came in from out of town, so we swung through here," Ray said. "I'm about to take him back to his hotel now."

"Oh, cool. Listen," Solomon said, "this is Michele Williams."

"Oh, my goodness. So you really do exist? Nice to meet you," he said while shaking Michele's hand.

The three of them chatted for a while before Ray excused himself. "That's my boy right there, headed out the door," he said. "Chasing a woman, no doubt. Let me grab him so you can meet him. Be right back."

Ray headed for the door and Solomon and Michele headed for a table near the back, before the restrooms.

"What's it going to be tonight?" Solomon asked.

"I'm thinking something simple, but strong—those people worked my nerves today," she said. "I'm glad it was a noon wedding. Anyway, I'll have Grey Goose and cranberry. Can't get more simple than that."

It was so simple that Michele had three of them in an hour. "You okay?" Solomon asked. "That's a lot for you."

"I'm good. They are kinda weak, but good," she said.

"Your son, he's something else," Solomon said.

"Oh, boy, what did he do?"

"He didn't do anything," he said, "but he asked me today if I was going to marry you."

"No, he didn't. I guess he likes you, huh?"

"He told me that, too," Solomon said. "I've spent a lot of time with him and he's a special kid. Always a great attitude. A little spoiled—I wonder why—but not rotten."

"What was your answer to him?"

"I told him that until your mom gives me some booty, I'm not marrying her," he said, laughing.

Michele reached across the table and hit him on the arm. "Very funny," she said, laughing. "You'd better not talk to him like that."

"Nah, I told him that I wasn't sure about that," Solomon said. "But I told him that I'll be there for him. That's when he said, 'I like you, Coach Money.' We did a fist-bump and moved on."

Michele smiled for a moment and then a different look came over her.

"What's wrong?" he asked.

"I don't know," she said. "Well, I do know… Can I have one more drink?"

"Sure. You okay?"

The server made her way to their table and Solomon ordered one more round.

"Michele, you all right?"

"I'm really emotional about my son," she said, using the napkin under her glass to wipe away a tear. "I want him to be alright and I'm really glad you've been there for him like you have. He needs that in his life."

"You don't have to cry about that; I love that kid, so I'm going to be around—as long as you allow me to," Solomon said.

Michele shook her head and wiped her eyes. She looked down at the table, not into his eyes.

"Solomon…" She finally looked up. "Don't hate me for what I'm about to say."

"Hate you? Why would I hate you?" he asked. Then it hit him— Michele was about to end their courtship. Why else would he "hate" her? Another woman was going to disappoint him. Shit.

"Come on, don't tell me you're seeing someone else?" he said. Normally, Solomon would not even put himself out there like that. But he just didn't care. "I guess I'd deserve it, but please don't tell me that."

"Solomon, that's not it," she said. He was visibly relieved.

"Then nothing you can say would make me hate you."

"That's what you say now," Michele said.

"What is it?"

"Solomon…you…are…Gerald's…father."

He stared at her for several seconds without speaking. The expression on his face was blank. It was like he was frozen, like all the noise in the room went silent. Finally, he calmly stood up and went over to her side of the table.

Bending over to get closer to her ear, he said, "What?"

She did not look up at him. She looked straight ahead, across the table, where he had been sitting.

"Michele."

She looked up.

"Say that again. It's loud in here. Maybe I didn't hear you right," he said.

"It's true, Solomon."

He turned and walked to the small nearby bathroom. He was so rattled he had trouble locking the door behind him.

Solomon turned on the cold water, leaned on the vanity and looked into his eyes through the mirror. The thoughts in his head were jumbled. His emotions were crashing against each other.

He put some water in his hands and rubbed it on his face. With some paper towels, he wiped his face dry. With that, he settled some. But he still had a litany of questions.

Composed, at least outwardly, he returned to the table. Michele had broken down to where the server with the drinks and the couple at the adjacent table asked if she was okay.

"Michele," he said to her, calmly, "this is messing me up. How did this happen—didn't we use condoms? Are you sure he's my...son? Why are you just telling me this?"

"Let's leave—we shouldn't talk about this here," she said.

Before the server returned, Solomon calculated how much the drinks cost and put the money on the table. He stood up and extended his hand to help Michele from her chair, which gave her at least a little sense that he did not hate her enough to abandon the chivalry that was embedded in him.

He opened the car door for her, closed it behind her

and wiped his face as he made his way to the other side. When he got in, he shut the door and looked straight ahead. Neither of them said anything for about a minute.

"Solomon," Michele said, finally, "you've been living with what happened with us and I've been living with something hanging over me, too. I—"

"But why didn't you tell me?" Solomon said, turning to her.

"How could I tell you? You disappeared. When I found out I was pregnant, it was almost two months later. You hadn't answered my calls, e-mails, text messages. You were gone," she said. "I'm really not trying to make this about me, but you don't know what it's been like for me to raise him alone, to have people ask, 'Where's the daddy?' and for me to have to say things like, 'Girl, he's doing his own thing' or 'Getting himself together' or just plain 'I have no idea.' That's what it's been like for me. You know how embarrassing that is, how reckless it makes me appear?

"And think about the fact that I've had to answer my son's—our son's—questions about his father."

"Well, he told me what your answers were: 'He's no good,' etc.," Solomon said.

"I did say that, out of frustration because as much as I'd like to be, I can't be a man for him and that's what he needed," Michele said. "The few men I dated after I got myself together were not worth whatever they paid for their shoes."

"Okay, but we used condoms, Michele," Solomon said.

"Not that night, that last night we were together, the last night I saw you," she said. "You don't remember? We got caught up in the moment, I guess, which is stupid for mature adults. But I can't even imagine myself without Gerald, so…"

"I'm doing my best to not sound like I'm trying to run away from this, but I have to ask: How do you know it happened that night?" Solomon said.

"Because, for one, as you said, we used condoms every other time," Michele answered. "Two, I had not been with anyone other than you. Period."

"Oh, my God," he said. "I'm a father?"

"To be honest, that's why all those emotions I spoke about a while ago came up when I saw you. Do you know how amazing it was that Gerald was bragging about this 'Coach Money' and it turns out that 'Coach Money' is his father? The same man who disappeared on me? My heart practically jumped out of my chest when I saw you that night.

"More than for even myself, I wanted you for Gerald," she added. "Boys need men to help raise them, if at all possible. After I found out you were in Atlanta, I tried to get contact info for you, but there was none. So I was faced with the reality that I would have to do it alone.

"Okay, so now there you are, his father, at that banquet about three months ago. What was I to do then? I was angrier than I realized; I thought I had let that go after so many years, but seeing you brought it all back up. Then I had a big issue because Gerald liked you and he needed a man in his life. That's why we had to get out of there that night. I could hardly breathe."

"Unbelievable," Solomon said. "This is unbelievable. I love the kid, I can tell you that. When I first saw him, I told Ray that he reminded me of myself as a kid. There were even times when we were out together and people would say, 'You look just like your daddy.' He had to say, 'He's not my daddy. He's my coach.' Thinking about that now makes my stomach hurt.

"It's like, knowing this now, how could I have not figured it out? He's seven years old, with a birthday coming up. I last saw you eight years ago. And I recall you giving me really vague answers when I asked about his father. I—"

"I didn't know what to say, Solomon," Michele interjected. "I didn't know if I would *ever* tell you. That was something I've been struggling with for years. I thought, 'If I ever saw Solomon again, would I tell him he's a father?' Sonya told me that I should. But I thought that if you were married with kids, I wouldn't want to throw that into your family. But I also thought that's exactly what I should do; you deserved confusion and drama because that's what you caused me.

"In the end, Sonya made me realize that you gave me the most precious gift I could ever have. It wasn't intentional, but you did. So, having Gerald really is the main reason I even gave you a chance to be back in my life. It was more for him than for me."

"Well…I don't know what to say. I'm shocked and I'm scared and I'm a little excited, too," Solomon said. "I mean…damn! This is crazy. What do I say to Gerald? What do *you* say to him?

"He's about to be eight years old. I haven't been there for him. How do I explain that? How do I go from his coach to his daddy? I'm gonna have to discipline him at some point. How do I do that? When do we tell him?"

"Solomon, all your questions are valid. I don't have the answers to any of them, including when we should tell him. I mean, do you *want* to tell him?"

"Do I want to tell him? Damn, right," he said. "Look, if he's my son, I want to be a father to him."

And in that instant, a measure of pride came over Solomon. *He was a father.* The impact of it hit him and turned all his angst into something different.

"I don't know what it is I feel right now," he said. "But, while I didn't ever give being a father or having someone call me 'Dad' much thought, right now I feel like there is some power with that. I was trying to have an impact on Gerald. Now I *must* have an impact on him."

"I'm really glad and relieved to hear you say that," Michele said. "I didn't plan on telling you this tonight. It just came out—but it had to at some point… Now the big thing is, how do we tell him?"

"Well, we should do it together, I think; especially since you told the boy his daddy wasn't any good," Solomon said.

"That's not like me, but I was so frustrated at the time; I wish that I hadn't said those things. But you're here now and we're going to have to, together, explain everything to him," Michele said.

He stretched across the car and hugged Michele and kissed her on the side of her face.

"I'm a father. Unbelievable," he said. "Shoot, I also have to tell my parents. That's going to be interesting, but they'll be more excited than anything. But I know my mom; she's going to want me to take a DNA test. We had a cousin who found out when his daughter was sixteen that she wasn't his daughter. You talk about something devastating? It destroyed him."

"I don't have a problem with a DNA test. Solomon, I dated you for six months and didn't even think about touching another man," she said. "And after you left, I didn't date another man for more than a year. So, unless this was an Immaculate Conception, that's your son."

"I believe you, Michele… Oh my God, I'm a daddy, a father," Solomon said. "I'm not as shocked anymore— and I'm a little excited about it. We have to tell him tomorrow. I don't want to wait. I've missed almost eight years; I want it to be official, and it's not official until Gerald knows."

"Okay. Let's go to church and do it after that."

Solomon started the car. "Let's go to Sonya's house; I want to see him," he said.

"Solomon, he's sleep," Michele said.

"I know. I just want to look at him as my son."

Michele pulled out her cell phone and called her cousin. "I knew he'd be sleep, but we still want to come over," she said. "Why? Because Solomon wants to see his...son."

He could hear Sonya's scream fly out of Michele's cell phone. "Calm down, girl," Michele said. "Calm down... Yes... Yes. We're both happy... I'll tell you all about it later. We're on our way... Okay... Okay... Bye, girl."

"She handled that well, huh?" Solomon said.

"She's pumped and I am, too," Michele said as they drove up Moreland Avenue. "I was so nervous about all of this. It's such a relief to tell you."

Solomon did not respond. His attention was on the two young men standing at the corner of Moreland and Hosea Williams Drive. Several weeks earlier, a convenience store clerk was shot and killed a block from there. He remembered driving by and seeing the news trucks camped out one night and all the stuffed animals and flowers there the next night to honor the fallen man.

And before he could bring the site to Michele's attention, the two young men rushed the car, brandished guns and demanded Solomon open the locks on the door. They were being carjacked. Michele screamed.

"Oh, shit," Solomon said as he leaned away from the driver's side window.

He quickly looked to see if any other cars were approaching the red light; there were not any. For a nanosecond he considered speeding off. But just as quickly he pondered Michele getting shot. Or himself.

So he hit the locks release button and both "pants on the ground thugs" jumped in the backseat.

"You know what's up?" the one behind Solomon said while sticking the gun into his neck. "We taking this bitch."

He was talking about the car, but Michele thought he was referring to her, and she screamed again. "Shut the fuck up," the guy said in the seat behind Michele. "Don't you open your mouth again! But you can open your purse."

The robbers delighted in their morbid humor and laughed. They were in their late teens or early 20s. One wore a scarf on his head, the way Tupac did. The other wore a New York Yankees cap turned to the side. Clearly they were veterans of robbing and carjacking. Their comfort level and confidence were apparent.

"Turn right here into that parking lot and put the car in park," one said.

"Here, just take what you want. We're getting out," Solomon said.

"You ain't running shit; we running this," the guy with the gun at Michele's head said. "I should blast yo' ass."

"Wait—let's get the money first. Give me the wallet," the other guy said.

As he unbuckled his seatbelt to reach for his wallet, Solomon looked into Michele's eyes and saw tears and fear. And something came over him.

"Yo, this is real talk," he said. "Get that gun off of my neck. You don't want to shoot me and you don't need to. We're giving you what you want."

"You think we playin'?" the guy behind Solomon yelled. "Nigga, gimme your money. Then you'll see who's not gonna shoot somebody."

"Hey, man, I just learned I'm a father tonight," Solomon said.

"So what the fuck that mean to me?" the guy yelled back.

Solomon leaned away from the gun. "Look at me, man. You look like my cousin. We can't keep doing this to each other," he said. "Where's your father?"

"I ain't got no father," he said angrily.

"So you want to put my son in that position, too?" Solomon said.

"Man, fuck what he talking about," the other guy said.

"Yo, look at her," Solomon said to the guy behind Michele. "Doesn't she look like your sister or mother or aunt?"

"Hell, no!" he yelled back.

"Well, wait a minute," Solomon pleaded. "Wait a minute. She told me about thirty minutes ago that her son is my son. I just found this out. I need to be a father to this kid, man. Don't do this."

"Yo, shoot that nigga," he said to his partner in crime.

"Don't do it. You can take the car and the money. We ain't done nothing to y'all," Solomon said. "Why take another man's life? Why take us from our child? Man, you know that ain't necessary. We getting out the car and ya'll can go on. But you ain't shooting me and you ain't shooting this woman. I got to be a father to this kid, man."

The guy pulled the gun away from Solomon and they stared at each other for a few seconds. "Come on, man, let's go," he said to his partner.

"What? Man, we got to shoot these fools," the other guy said.

"No. Let's just dip," he said. To Solomon, he said, "Get the fuck out."

"Come on, Michele," Solomon said. "Come on. Open the door and get out."

She was so shaken she could not get her seatbelt loose. Solomon reached over and unfastened it for her, jumped out of the car and hurried around to her side to help her out. The robbers jumped in the car's front seats without even taking their money and sped away—the one guy pointing a gun at them as they drove off with Solomon's Saab 9.5 convertible.

Solomon hugged the crying Michele. "Oh, my God," she said. "Oh, my God."

He hugged her tightly, as much to comfort her as to conceal the tears that ran down his face. They were not tears of fear. They were tears of relief and anger. Neither of them said anything for a minute. They just embraced in the empty parking lot on Moreland Avenue and Hosea Williams Drive.

Solomon wiped his face. "You're okay, Michele," he said. "It's all right. It's all right."

He reached in his pocket, pulled out his cell phone and called 9-1-1. "I can't believe this shit," he said. "I'm glad I took my laptop out of my car. If my laptop was in there, they would've had to shoot me."

"Don't even play like that," Michele said. "I'm so scared. They might come back... Where's the police?"

A few seconds later, the cops arrived, lights flashing, sirens blaring. Michele sat in the police car and watched Solomon as he described what happened to the officers. He was poised, as if he were reporting stolen fruit from a stand and not a carjacking where two young men had guns to their heads.

She watched him closely. She rehashed the drama. She opened her heart. That was the moment. She loved Solomon Singletary again, but maybe even more this time. He saved her life twice in one night, first by accepting that he was Gerald's father and then by talking some criminals out of shooting them.

The officers waited with them until the taxi arrived to take them to Sonya's house. In the cab, Michele said, "I'm still shaking. I feel like I was this close to death. I can't believe you started lecturing them. That was incredible. You..."

"You know what?" Solomon jumped in, "somehow, even in my fear, the most important things came to me and I just hoped they would listen. I guess even the most evil person has a conscience that can be tapped into."

Michele reached over and grabbed Solomon's hand. It was not lost on them that they had endured a harrowing experience together. It cemented their bond.

"Some night, huh?" Solomon said. "I like excitement as much as the next guy. But this…"

"I know, right?" Michele said. "I needed to get out for a drink. It turned out to be one of the most important nights of my life in a lot of ways."

"Mine, too," Solomon said, as he handed the driver $30 for the fare. When they approached Sonya's door, she opened it.

"What took you so long?" she said. "And why are you in a cab? What's going on?"

Michele and Solomon looked at each other. "What's wrong?" Sonya asked. "I thought you all would be smiling and happy."

He extended his arms and hugged Sonya. "Good to see you; it's been a long time."

"Same here. Come on in. Will somebody tell me what's going on?"

"You have anything to drink?" Michele asked.

"Yeah, some juice and water," Sonya answered.

"No, some alcohol," Michele said.

"I thought you just came from having drinks. What's going on, Michele? Solomon?"

"Can I see…my son?" he answered. "Michele, please tell her what happened before her head explodes."

"Come this way, Solomon," Sonya said, leading him to her spare bedroom, where Gerald slept. "Michele, I'll be right back."

At the bedroom door, Sonya slowly opened it so as to

not awaken the child. "There's your boy." Her and Solomon's eyes met. He smiled and she went back to the living room.

Solomon stood in the doorway for a moment. He went from a single man responsible only for himself to a father of a soon-to-be eight-year-old...in an instant.

He left the door open so the hallway light could illuminate the room enough for him to see Gerald. All the obvious physical features he did not notice before were as blatant as a flashing neon sign then: his complexion, his nose, the shape of his lips. Even the way he slept—on his right side with a pillow between his knees—was the way Solomon often rested.

He was his son, all right, and to see him as such raised emotions in Solomon he never experienced. And pride, too. *That's my son*, he thought to himself. He leaned over and kissed Gerald on his forehead. Then he just stood there staring at him.

Meanwhile, Michele was giving Sonya the details of the evening. "So, you're telling me you had guns pointing at you and Solomon started talking about being a father to them?"

"That's what he did," Michele answered, sipping the vodka and cranberry her cousin quickly made for her. "I couldn't do anything but cry. I'm not being dramatic—they acted like they were going to kill us. It was like a dream. It's still a dream. The whole night is. But Solomon basically said he just learned he is a father and he wanted to see his child. Then he told them to look at me, that I represented their mother. You believe that? But I don't know how or why, but it worked.

"One guy acted like he didn't care; he wanted to shoot us. But the other one…something Solomon said registered with him. I don't know what, but after a while, he told us to get out of the car. And even then, I was so shaken I couldn't even undo the seatbelt. Solomon had to come around and let me out."

"Oh, my God," Sonya said. "I can't even believe this."

"Me, either," Michele said. "This has been a crazy night. A great night and a scary night all at the same time."

Solomon reentered the living room just then.

"I could use a drink, too," he said. "A big one."

CHAPTER 12

SONNY DAYS

Sonya had to go into her secret stash of liquor in the far reaches under her kitchen sink. She was so thrown by the events of the night that she started drinking, too, and they killed the half-empty bottle of Grey Goose.

"I have a question," Solomon said, his speech slightly slurred, his eyes reddening by the minute. "Who in their right mind hides liquor under the kitchen sink? That's some country stuff right there."

Sonya and Michele burst into laughter.

"And," he added, "who you hiding it from?"

"Forget you, Solomon," Sonya said, feigning anger. "I got that from my grandmother. She used to put her corn liquor under the sink, surrounded by mothballs. She said my late grandfather hated the smell of mothballs, so she knew he wouldn't go under there to look for the liquor."

"Okay, I get it. I mean," Solomon said, "I see why that worked for your grandmother. But your grandfather has passed on to glory, right? You expecting him to come back here?"

They all laughed again.

"Like I said, forget you, Solomon. I like it there. It's out of the way down there," she said.

The humor was a much-needed distraction—if only for a few minutes—from the serious matters that consumed them.

It was 1:50 a.m. "Cuz, we gonna have to stay here and drink all your liquor and take your car in the morning," Michele said. "I don't think we need to be on the road tonight smelling like a distillery."

"Hey," Solomon said rather loudly, alarming the women, "don't y'all get too loud and wake up my son."

The room went silent. The three of them looked at each other for what seemed like several moments, but, in reality, was about five seconds. Clearly, the liquor had kicked in with Solomon, who had a lot to say and the vodka made it come out easier.

"That's my son in there," he said, pointing toward the back of the house. His voice suddenly was low and serious, like he was revealing a long-kept secret. He spilled some of his drink on his shirt but did not bother to wipe it off.

"I feel like more of a man knowing I'm a father," he went on. "It probably doesn't make sense to you. And It probably doesn't make me more of a man, but it makes me feel like more of a man, like I have given more to the world—or that I had not given enough.

"I'm the same person, but it feels like—I don't know—

like I have a bigger purpose in life now. I grew up in the last eight years, Michele. I feel like I've got some more growing up to do, but I'm more motivated now to do that. I gotta figure out…*we* gotta figure out…how to tell Gerald that I'm his dad—and that I'm not 'no good' or some loser who didn't want to be his father."

"Solomon, I'm so glad to hear you say that," Sonya said. "Michele probably will get mad at me for saying this, but, hell, the rat's out of the bag now…"

"Damn, girl," Michele said, "I know you're drunk because you're messing up clichés."

"Wow, did I say 'rat'? I meant to say…'hat,'" Sonya responded.

"Hat is wrong, too," Michele said. "It's cat—let the cat out of the bag."

"Oh, is it? Well," Sonya said, "anyway, Solomon, since the cat's out of the thing, I can tell you that this is a dream come true for Michele."

"Sonya!" Michele jumped in.

"What? It's true, girl," Sonya shot back. "No need in trying to keep it a secret now."

"Well, can you be clear about what you're trying to say?" Michele said.

"Okay, okay," Sonya told her. "Solomon, what I was saying was about Gerald, not her. Having you back is not her dream come true. It's a dream come true for her that you know he's your son and that you're willing to be a father to him. She's been obsessed with that."

"No, I haven't been obsessed with it," Michele said. "But I always knew it would be better for my son if his father helped raise him. I knew that. I would always become jealous when I saw a father playing sports with his son or at the grocery store, the mall, wherever. And I would be sad about it, too…almost feel sorry for Gerald."

"Well, you can let all that go now," Solomon said. He wanted to ask her why she did not try harder to find him years before, if all that mattered so much. Why didn't she tell him the deal when they first saw each other at the banquet?

Women's intuition was as reliable as a wet tissue, but in this case, Michele could sense some angst in Solomon. So she tried to appease him before he asked.

"I wish this moment would've happened years ago, Solomon. I really do," she said. "Even if we weren't together, I wanted you to be in his life. I hope you can focus on what you can be to him now and not what could've happened."

"Honestly, I'm not good with how everything happened, but, in the end, it was my fault," he said. "So, if you're not mad at me, I'm not mad at you. Trust me, I'm focused on Gerald."

Pretty soon, they all drifted off in the living room. Deep into his sleep, Solomon had a dream that he was being chased by women of his past and present: Michele, Marie, Cathy, Dionne and Evelyn—the five women in his life. When he hurried inside and slammed the door behind him to keep them out, he turned around and was struck in the head with a golf club.

He jumped up from his sleep and decided then that he had to make peace with those women.

Marie, Evelyn, Cathy and Dionne were good women who were caught up in Solomon's web of indecision and selfishness. They accepted his terms, but they abandoned their pride and, in some cases, morals to do it. Solomon actually liked it when he broke a woman's will or made her succumb to his.

But those thoughts, while on his mind, were secondary. He had a son he had to get to know as a father. He had to tell his parents. He had to tell his friends, including Ray, who once told Solomon, "We'll know if God has a sense of humor if He allows you to have a kid."

Before he could gather himself and get off of the couch, little Gerald came sleepy-eyed into the living room. "Coach Money," he said to Solomon, who was taken aback.

Solomon was taken off guard. "Oh, hey buddy. What are you doing up?"

"I'm thirsty."

"Gerald, hi, honey," Michele said as she rose from the loveseat she had slept on. "Come here."

"I'm thirsty, Mommy. Can I have something to drink?"

"I'll get it for him," Solomon volunteered. "If that's all right."

Michele smiled at Solomon. "Sure."

"Come on, Gerald." Solomon put his arm around

Gerald and father and son walked together to the kitchen.

Michele's heart was full.

As Gerald downed the orange juice, Solomon told him: "It's five-thirty. I'm going to take you back to bed, okay? Then we're going to get together later today. I have some good news to tell you."

"What is it?" Gerald asked.

"I'll tell you later. We'll go to lunch. What's your favorite place?"

"Pizza Hut."

"Pizza Hut? Ah, man," Solomon said. "We'll find somewhere better than that."

"Okay," Gerald said.

"Come on. Let's go back to bed," he told the kid and walked him back to his bedroom.

When Solomon returned to the living room, Sonya and Michele stared at him.

"What?" he said.

"How do you feel?" Sonya said.

He smiled. "Great," he said. "A little awkward, too, though. I guess those were my first acts as a father with my son—or knowing I was a father."

"It was a sweet moment," Michele said. "Very sweet."

Solomon did not respond. He just lay back on the couch, with his arms folded behind his head.

Michele came over and kneeled down beside him. "I could've cried, seeing you and him together like that. It's going to work out. It's going to be great."

Then she leaned over and kissed him gently on the lips

and rested her head on his chest. He hugged her and rubbed her back.

"I need you to help me through this," he said. "I'm on board, no doubt. But we're talking about a complete lifestyle change for me—and him and you, too. For me, it's completely different. Everything changes."

"I know," Michele said, still lying on his chest. "I'm sorry this is happening like this. But I'll be there for you. It's going to take some time for you and Gerald to get comfortable with it, but it'll happen."

"What about you?" Solomon asked.

Michele pulled herself off his chest and looked into his eyes. "This has been a reality in my mind for seven years. This is all I ever wanted. So, I don't have to adjust. I've lived it every day for a long time, in my mind."

Solomon moved the cushions on the couch to the floor to make room for Michele. She pulled herself up and they hugged. They dozed off on the couch until close to 7 a.m.

When they awoke, they freshened up and took Sonya's car to Michele's. Solomon kept going to his house, where he showered and shaved. The plan was to meet back at Sonya's at noon. Then, they would take Gerald to lunch and tell him the news.

After showering and getting dressed, Solomon got comfortable and called his mom.

He followed the requisite small talk with the bombshell. "Ma, I've got to tell you something incredible," he started.

"Something good or bad, Solomon."

"Shocking, but good. You ready for this?"

He took a deep breath. "Ma, I told you that I reconnected with Michele a few months ago. I—"

"Don't tell me you're getting married already?" she jumped in.

"Ma, no. That's not it," he said. "Michele's son—"

"Oh, no. Don't tell me something happened to him," she jumped in again.

"Ma…" Solomon whined as if he were a kid. "Gerald is fine. The thing is, he's my son."

Nothing came back from the other end of the phone.

"Ma, did you hear me? You're a grandmother."

"Solomon, what are you talking about?" she said, finally. "Where are you getting this from?"

"I had a talk last night with Michelle," he explained. "She gave me the whole spiel on what happened. And it all adds up."

"Are you sure? You know what happened to your cousin, don't you?"

"I do, Ma. But this is a different case. Plus, I already told Michele we needed to do the parental testing or whatever it's called."

"My goodness, Solomon. My goodness," she said. "All this time you had your offspring out there? You had no idea? What's his name?"

"I didn't have any idea. But I know him; I was his basketball coach. Gerald, remember?"

"The one you said reminded you of you? That's your son?"

"Yes."

"How do you feel about all this?" she asked. "I don't know what to feel. It's not the same as knowing the child is coming and waiting for the birth. It's just all of a sudden he's here—and he's seven years old… My goodness."

"I know. It's strange for me, too, Ma," Solomon said. "I just found out last night. So I'm still dealing with the shock of it all. But, overall, I'm excited. The facts are the facts. He's my son and I have to be a father to him."

"I would expect nothing less from you," she said. "But you make sure you get that DNA test before you start getting attached to him."

"Ma…"

"I'm just saying," she said. "And I guess I could say 'congratulations,' too, huh? My son is a father? I always hoped that would be the case because I always wanted a grandchild to spoil. Now I have one that I don't even know."

"Well, we're going to change that, Ma," Solomon said. "I'm going to bring him up there for a visit sometime soon. He has an entire family that he has to meet."

"The good thing about children is that they adjust to things much quicker and better than adults," his mom said. "So he'll probably feel better about all this before I will. Or you."

"I hope so," he said.

Solomon did not tell his mother about the carjacking, figuring the news of Gerald was more than enough for one day. He next called his father.

"Son, you telling me I have a grandson?" his dad said. "There's a little you out there? Well, damn. All of a sudden I feel like I'm getting old."

"Dad, you're just as old as you were the second before I told you," Solomon said.

"I have a question for you," his father said. "Is he the only one out there?"

"The only what? Kid of mine?" Solomon asked. "Yeah, that's it—as far as I know. And I think I would know."

"You thought you didn't have any before yesterday," the father said.

"That's true," Solomon conceded. "Still, I'm pretty certain that's it."

"Well, son, I have this advice for you: Be a father to that boy," he said.

"Love him and spoil him, but discipline him. Make sure he respects you and understands authority. Make sure he's a Singletary."

"I will, Dad. I'll teach him what you taught me."

There were others Solomon had to share the news with, but only Ray was worthy of a call that Sunday morning.

"I guess God is a funny guy, huh?" was his response.

"Hilarious," Solomon said.

"So, how you gonna manage this?" Ray said. "You've intentionally gone out of your way to be non-committal. Now you have a son?"

"Non-committal to women," he said. "And even with that, it's been just me and Michele these last three months."

"You cut the other women? There had to be five of them," Ray said.

"There were four and they haven't been officially cut, but it's coming," he said. "I've just avoided them. But I've got to tell them what's up. And I will. In person. But I've got more pressing stuff to deal with now. Don't you think?"

"No doubt," Ray said. "You've got to turn that kid from your player to your son. Probably harder will be to turn his thinking from you as his coach to you as his father. It'll happen. But you've got to be patient; it probably won't be that easy."

"Well, easy or hard, it's got to be done," Solomon said. "I just want to get to the point where he calls me 'Daddy' and we're all comfortable and content with all this."

"So where is Michele in all this?" Ray said. "I mean, is this one big happy family now?"

"I wouldn't say that. I'd just say we're going to try to get Gerald through this together," Solomon said. "That's the big thing: making sure he's all right and understands all this. But Michele is happy; she's been dying to tell me and for me to be a part of Gerald's life.

"Still, I can't stop thinking one thing: This is crazy."

CHAPTER 13
DADDY'S HOME

Solomon arrived at Sonya's house before Michele, which did not surprise him. He knew how meticulous she was, which was a euphemism for saying she was slow. She would spend significant time in the mirror, toying with her hair and makeup and clothes to annoying lengths. Solomon cared about his appearance but was far more decisive.

When he got to Sonya's front door, Gerald was right there when Sonya let him in.

"Coach Money, what you doing here?" the kid said.

"I told you, your mom and I are taking you to lunch today. You don't remember that?" Solomon said.

"Oh, yeah, I forgot," he said. "Where's Mommy? Where we going? I'm hungry."

"Your mom should be here shortly," he said. "I think we're going to take a nice ride out to Alpharetta and go to a place called Kozmo. They have great food, and a great burger, which I'm sure you want, right?"

"I do want a burger," he said, flashing his bright smile. Solomon felt chills.

The boy looked like Solomon on his second-grade class photo. "I knew you wanted a burger," he said to Gerald.

"How did you know?" the kid asked.

"I was seven years old once. A burger was the best food in the world," Solomon answered.

He and Sonya laughed. "I'll be eight next year," Gerald said.

"I know. And we're going to really celebrate it with a big party," Solomon said.

"What's going on with your car?" Sonya asked.

"Gerald, you all set to go? Is your bed made up?" he said, looking down on his son. "You should get that together so we can go when your mom gets here."

That was Solomon's way of getting Gerald to leave the room. He didn't want the kid to know that his mom had been held at gunpoint. If Michele wanted him to know, he figured she should tell him.

"Thanks for letting me use your car," Solomon said to Sonya after Gerald disappeared into the other room. "Right now, nothing's happening with mine. I talked to someone on my way here. They haven't found it, but they believe they will. I don't know why, but the detective seems to think they would just joyride in it and ditch it somewhere since they didn't take our money. Maybe they'll take it to a chop shop. I don't know.

"My insurance company says I have to wait thirty days before I can get paid on it so I can get something else. I hope it doesn't come to that. I'm about finished paying that car off—three more payments. I ain't trying to start over with a new car note."

"I know that's right," Sonya said.

Just then, the doorbell rang. It was Michele.

"I was trying to beat you here," she said. "But I got in that shower and I couldn't get out—until the water got cold. Last night was too much. Sleeping on the couch didn't help, either. But I feel rejuvenated now."

Before she could ask, Sonya said, "He's in the back, making up his bed."

"How you know I was going to ask about Gerald?" Michele said.

"I know you, cousin," she answered. "And you don't go three minutes without asking about him."

Ignoring Sonya, Michele turned to Solomon. "How you feeling? You ready to do this?" she said.

"I will be when the time comes," Solomon answered.

"Mommy," Gerald said as he came from the back.

"Come here, honey," she said, and the kid hurried to her and hugged and kissed as if they hadn't seen each other in weeks. In a sense, that bothered Solomon. This was a different Gerald from when his mom was not around. He saw a softer kid cozying up to his mother. A momma's boy.

It wasn't jealousy, though. It was concern over his son being exactly what Michele said she didn't want him to be: overly reliant on her. Soft. A crybaby. A momma's boy. At that moment he realized that starting the job of father seven years late was going to be even harder than he imagined.

"I'm ready when you all are," he said, breaking out of his mini-trance.

"Where we going?" Michele asked Solomon, which made him feel good. It was like she was already starting the process of giving him authority as it related to Gerald.

"I was thinking this place called Kozmo Gastro Pub in Alpharetta," he said. "Black-owned, great food, great dining room—and a great burger."

"I want a big burger," Gerald said.

"This burger is nice and big," Solomon said.

"Okay," Gerald said.

"Well, have a great lunch," Sonya said. "I'm flying out tonight, so I won't see you all for a few days. But good luck with everything. Michele, call me."

Michele asked Solomon to drive her car, another act of putting him in the leadership role. He appreciated the gesture.

Gerald talked the entire way from the backseat, telling jokes he had learned at school, asking about summer plans and generally being the happy boy he was. Solomon's and Michele's eyes occasionally met during the ride, and they expressed both joy and anxiety.

"After we eat, honey, we have something really important to talk to you about," Michele said. She figured giving him a heads-up might take away some of the shock.

"About what, Mommy?" he said.

"About you and me and…" She looked at Solomon. She did not want to call him "Coach Money." Picking up on it, Solomon jumped in. "And me," he said.

"What?" Gerald said. "Are we going somewhere else?"

"We're not going anywhere else, not today. But it's going to be good; I promise you that," Solomon said.

They made it to Kozmo and gathered in a booth near the back of the restaurant, up against the window where the sunlight shone so brightly the adults had to pull out their sunglasses. They consumed their tasty burgers without much conversation. "You deserve a break today," he said to Michele. She laughed in recalling the old McDonald's commercial.

Finally, as Gerald sipped on his milkshake, Solomon and Michele began the hardest conversation of their lives.

"I'll start," he said to Michele, who nodded her approval. Solomon took off his sunglasses. He wanted Gerald to see his eyes.

"Gerald, I want you to really concentrate so you can understand what we're saying," he began. "As you get older, you'll learn that some things that happen in life don't make sense at first, but later they do. This is one of those cases."

Gerald looked back and forth between his parents. "Remember in the gym, when I asked you about your father that day?" Solomon continued. "You said you didn't know where he was.

"Well, that was because he didn't know you were his

son. If he had known that you were his son, he would've been with you every day. You know how I know this?"

"How?" Gerald answered.

"Because I'm your...father," Solomon said.

Gerald swallowed hard on a large intake of milkshake. "Huh?" he said.

"Yes, I'm your father," Solomon said. He waited for a reaction, but Gerald took another sip of his milkshake.

"You're my father?" he said. His look indicated he wanted to know more, but he didn't know how to express it. So Solomon went on.

"Yes, I'm your father. You see, eight years ago, your mom and I were friends when we lived in Washington, D.C.," he said. "It takes a man and a woman together to make a child."

Neither he nor Michele thought about having to tell Gerald *how* a baby was conceived. Solomon quickly decided he would hedge on the "birds and the bees" until Gerald was at least ten or eleven.

The kid seemed to understand this was a big deal, the more Solomon talked. An honor student, the inquisitive part of his character emerged.

"But how come you didn't know you're my father?" Gerald said.

"Well, I moved from Washington, D.C. to here and your mom didn't know where I was," he explained. "She tried to find me, but couldn't. So we didn't see each other until she came to your basketball banquet."

"Mommy," he said, turning to Michele, "you couldn't find Coach Money?"

"No, baby, I couldn't," she said. "But I always knew once he found you, he would love you and want to be your father."

Gerald turned back to Solomon. "You want to be my father?"

"I *am* your father, Gerald. And I'm happy that I am. I'm happy that we found each other," he said. "We found each other before your mom found me."

"So what do you think, honey?" Michele asked.

"The other boys in my class get picked up by their daddies sometimes," he said.

"And now your daddy will be picking you up, too," Michele said. "Are you happy about that?"

"Yes," Gerald replied.

"I have a question," Solomon said, looking at Gerald. "Do you want to call me Daddy? Or Coach Money?"

"Coach Money," he said. "You're my coach."

"Yes, but he's also your daddy," Michele said. "Your father."

"You said my father was no good," Gerald said.

"I know I did and I shouldn't have said that because it's not true," Michele responded. "I was angry at the time I said it."

"Why were you angry?" he asked.

"I didn't know where he was and I wanted him to be there for you," she answered. "I knew he would love you like I love you, but I was angry because I didn't know where he was.

"But now that we've found him, I'm not angry anymore. I'm happy now and I want you to be happy," she added. "You have your father—and he's also your basketball coach."

"You don't have to call me Daddy right now," Solomon jumped in. "Maybe one day you'll feel comfortable doing that. This is a lot for you. Call me whatever you're comfortable calling me. As long as you understand that I'm your father, that's the important thing…son."

Solomon looked at Michele, who was tearing up. "So, Gerald," he said, "Who's your daddy?"

"You're my daddy."

"And what is a daddy supposed to do?" Solomon asked his boy.

"Well, he's supposed to play with me and buy me things," Gerald said.

Solomon laughed. "And you know what else I'll do? I'll teach you things."

"Like a teacher?"

"Not exactly like a teacher. Like a parent. I'll teach you how to tie a necktie, how to be tough, how to look after your mother, how to be responsible, how to grow into a man. I'll teach you a lot about life. A whole lot."

"Oh, okay," he said.

"Honey, this is very new to you and it'll take you a while to get used to this," Michele said. "If you ever have any questions, just ask me or…your father."

"I have a question," Gerald said. "Where do you live?"

"Not too far from you and your mom," he said. "I have a question. Would you come and spend the weekend with me sometimes?"

"If Mommy says I can," Gerald said.

"Mom?" Solomon said, looking at Michele.

"Of course," Michele said. "I'll be lonely, but you should spend some time with your father."

"Well, I like to get to things," Solomon said. "Let's do it next weekend. We can go to the movies on Friday night and get up in the morning and cook breakfast—"

"I know how to make French toast," Gerald interjected.

"Really?" Solomon said. "But does it taste good?"

Gerald and Michele laughed. "Yeah, it's good. It's great," he said.

"Well, we'll see," Solomon said. "After breakfast, maybe we should go to Target to get some stuff to decorate your room. I'm going to make a room at my house your room."

"Can I put a Kobe Bryant poster on the wall?" Gerald asked.

"You can put anything you want up there; except naked women," Solomon answered.

"Solomon…" Michele said as Gerald laughed long and hard.

"So it's set," Solomon said. "Father/son weekend next Friday. Hey, uh, Gerald, listen: I'm really sorry I haven't been there for you all this time. But you know what? I'm going to make it up. It's going to take a lot of time, but I'm going to do it."

"I'm sorry, too, honey," Michele said, hugging her son. "But I'm so happy we have your father in your life. It's such a blessing."

The adults were quite mushy about the revelations. Gerald; not so much. "Can I have another milkshake?"

It was an innocent enough question, but one Solomon felt he should field—his first decision since revealing to Gerald that he was his son. It was his time to be tough, to let the kid know that he wasn't going to get his way all the time, that he was the boss.

"Of course you can, son," he said, and Michele's head snapped around as if on a swivel.

"Solomon," she said.

"Well, you can have a second milkshake *today*, because we're celebrating," he said. "Usually, one is enough."

"Okay, thanks," Gerald said, and he and Solomon bumped fists.

Michele said, "Uh, oh. I think I'm in trouble."

CHAPTER 14
FATHER KNOWS
NO REST

Solomon took his responsibilities as a father as if he could make up for seven years in a day. He doted on Gerald, picking him up from school, taking him to Hawks games, telling him about his childhood, introducing him to his friends, playing ball with him and generally trying his best to establish a strong bond.

It worked. They were practically inseparable. Each weekend Gerald would spend with his newly found dad. And when Solomon was not with Gerald, they talked on the phone before he went to sleep at night. Every night. They'd talk about each other's day and the days ahead.

"You've jumped right into this father thing, man," his close friend Ray said. "I guess I was wrong. I thought you were the last person who needed to be a father."

"So did I," Solomon said. "But you know what? When it's done, it's done. You have to do what you have to do. I think about what my life would be like if I didn't have my father the first seven years of my life. I probably would be a different person. I don't know, but I do know he was there for me, and that meant a lot.

"We used to go to Redskins games and he'd talked to me during the ride about being tough and being responsible. All kinds of stuff, at an early age, that built a bond that carried over all my life. It was my foundation of becoming a man."

Solomon enrolled Gerald in boxing lessons as a way of broadening his athletic interests. It was not easy, though; Michele vehemently objected at first. "He doesn't need someone punching him in the face," she said.

Solomon's retort: "Yes, he does, actually. It'll make him tougher and help him learn how to defend himself. Plus, I'll be there for every lesson."

Michele relented. "Okay, Solomon. That's my baby."

"Mine, too," he said, smiling.

Solomon's most rewarding moment came indirectly through boxing. After a strong showing against a kid two years older and a few pounds heavier at Hitsville Boxing gym in Atlanta, a trainer came over to Gerald when he left the ring.

"Good job, young man," he said. Solomon was nearby, listening with his chest stretched out with pride.

"Who're you here with?" the man said.

"I'm with my father," Gerald said. Then he turned and saw Solomon.

"That's my daddy right there," he said, pointing.

"Daddy," Gerald said, motioning for his father to come over.

It was the first time Gerald called Solomon "Daddy."

As much as he wanted to come forward, Solomon stood there savoring the moment. It had been three weeks since they had broken the news to Gerald. Solomon had never said a word about wanting to hear his son call him "Daddy." But the anticipation was there, like a wet sneeze at the tip of your nose.

And when it came, it ran through Solomon's body, through his bloodstream. Daddy. Father. It truly was official. They were father and son.

"Yes, this is my son," Solomon said to the boxing trainer, his arm draped over Gerald's shoulder. "This is my son."

Gerald looked up at his dad and Solomon looked down and they smiled at each other.

Leaving the gym, Gerald said it again, "Daddy, can we go to Waffle House?"

"You want Waffle House for dinner?" Solomon said. "You know what? Me, too."

So they drove to the Waffle House at Panola Road and Covington Highway in Lithonia. They sat at the counter and enjoyed their food. Midway through the meal, Michele called.

"Oh, man," Solomon said before answering. "I was supposed to call your mom."

"Hello," he answered. "How are you?"

"I'm good. What's going on with you guys?" she said.

Solomon covered the phone and said to Gerald, "She's gonna be mad at us. She cooked dinner." They laughed.

"Uh, we're actually sitting at the counter at Waffle House," he said.

"Waffle House?" Michele said. "Waffle House? Didn't I tell you that I was cooking tonight?"

She was disappointed and angry, too. It was obvious.

"I'm sorry; you did tell me," Solomon said. "But you don't understand. Can I explain it to you when we get there?"

"You can explain it now, Solomon," she said.

"No, I can't, not right now," he said. "You'll understand when I tell you."

"Solomon, you all are eating dinner at Waffle House, after I put together a wonderful meal," she said. "Why would you do that?"

"Hold on," he said to Michele. "Stay right here, Gerald. I'll be right back."

When he stepped out of the kid's hearing range, he said, "Listen, I'm sorry. I realized that you were cooking but this is where Gerald wanted to go and I couldn't deny him. Not tonight," he explained.

"Why not?" Michele asked. "What happened?"

"Because tonight, he called me 'Daddy.' He told a trainer that I was his father and then he called me 'Daddy'—more than once. It just happened. I don't know what triggered it. But it made me feel good. It made me feel like his father.

"I figured or was hoping one day it would happen. But to hear it... So when he said, 'Daddy, can we go to Waffle House?' I just couldn't say 'no.'"

Michele said, "Oh, wow. I understand that. I do. But you should've at least called me. And look at who is such a softie."

"I know and I'm sorry," Solomon said. "I'll make it up to you."

"Oh, you will? How?" Michele asked.

"I'll bring you a T-bone and eggs with scattered, smothered and covered hash browns."

Michele laughed her patented uproarious laugh. Then she added: "Don't forget an order of raisin toast," and they laughed again.

Solomon and Gerald, father and son, finished their meal and took Michele's takeout order with them. On the way to Michele's house, Solomon debated asking Gerald what made him go from "Coach Money" to "Daddy" that night.

Instead, he left it alone. He thought to himself, *It doesn't matter.*

At Michele's, she took her Waffle House dinner to the kitchen. "Thank you," she said. "At least I don't have to cook tomorrow."

"What did you make?" Solomon asked.

"You have to come back tomorrow to find out," Michele said as she walked over to Gerald. She asked him about his homework.

"I already did it and Daddy checked it," he said.

Michele's heart fluttered, and she *really* knew then what Solomon meant. Hearing Gerald say the word was different and powerful, even emotional.

"Great, honey," she said. "I'm going to eat my food,

since I was waiting on you all while you were eating. But you need to take a bath and get in the bed. It's almost nine o'clock."

Off Gerald went. "I'll tuck you in before I leave!" Solomon yelled out as his son headed down the hall.

"Okay, Daddy," he said without looking back.

Solomon and Michele looked at each other.

"What happened?" she said. "I can't believe it. I mean, I can, but it's so sudden. He didn't say anything about it?"

"Nah, he didn't," Solomon said. "I don't know what happened. He just said it and he hasn't stopped…I feel great."

"Me, too," Michele said. "It's all coming together like I wanted…except…"

"Except? Except what?" asked Solomon, who was sitting at the bar in the kitchen.

"The last three weeks have been great," she said. She pulled her Waffle House dinner out of the microwave and placed it on the counter, opposite Solomon.

"It's almost unreal that all this has come together," she added. "I don't want to sound like I'm bitching and moaning; I'm so happy right now that you and Gerald are father and son, together."

"What is it?" Solomon asked.

"Well, what about us?" Michele said. "I mean, it seems to me that you've been so focused on Gerald that you've let us go, sort of. We haven't done anything together since I told you about Gerald.

"Please trust me on this: I'm really grateful you've

taken on the responsibility of being a father to our son. That means everything to me. And now that it seems we're clearly headed in the right direction, I want to know what you think about you and me."

Solomon smiled because Michele was right. As soon as he had learned that he was a father, his entire focus was on *being* a father. He saw Gerald almost every day after the night that Michele had given him the news. He had talked to him the days they were not together.

He turned a guest room in his house into Gerald's bedroom so the kid could have a place there that felt like his. He cooked breakfast with his son, played basketball, went to the movies, introduced him to golf, battled him in videogames and just about everything else. Once in a while he included Michele in their activities.

"You know what, Michele?" Solomon started. "You're right. And I'm sorry. I've been consumed with Gerald and building a relationship with him. It's been great. I still can't believe it, really.

"And I guess I was too caught up in that. You're sweet and sexy and it's probably been a good thing I've been distracted. When I do think about you, a lot of times it's about making love to you."

Michele's body smiled. It had been aching for his touch for weeks; just his words made it blush. Those were the words she wanted to hear. It had been almost four months since they had reunited. Solomon had hinted at intimacy once in that time and Michele had balked, saying they both would know when the time was right.

That night was the right time, she decided. Actually, when Solomon saved her life twice in one night—by fending off carjackers and embracing the news that Gerald was his son—Michele's armor fell. She was his, if he wanted her.

It so happened that was the same time Solomon had become enthralled with learning that he was a father. And while he still wanted Michele, she had become a secondary concern.

"I've been thinking the same thing and for a long time," Michele said. "I'm a little shocked at how someone's life can turn around in a matter of months. Do you know I thank God every night for everything that has happened?"

"Trust me, I do, too," Solomon said.

"Come over here," Michele said in a way that Solomon had not seen or heard in years. She turned her head slightly to the right, squinted her eyes and pursed her lips. Instantly, Solomon was turned on.

He made his way around the counter to Michele's side. "Do you know you haven't kissed me; I mean, really kissed me?" she said.

"You haven't kissed me, either," he said, smiling. "But I'm here to change all that right now."

With that, he delicately placed his hands on either side of Michele's face. She looked up at him as if he were something edible. He looked at her the same way.

Slowly, he leaned in and pressed his moist lips against hers and closed his eyes. They kissed deeply, passionately; the kind of kiss that makes you light-headed with anticipation for more.

He moved his hands from her face to her shoulders, to her back and down to her waist. Every move was executed with a firm but caring touch, one that made Michele whimper in pleasure.

She pressed her body up against his to feel his rocket-like erection, and it was then that their mouths separated. Michele became breathless. "Oh, God, Solomon," she whispered. "Oh, God."

He did not respond; not with words. He held her even tighter and ran his hand through the hair on the back of her head. She elevated on her tiptoes and kissed him on his neck. The smell of his cologne added to her pleasure.

There was not a false move between them. Each touch made the other gasp. For Solomon, it was the only place he wanted to be. Michele had another place for him to consider, though.

"Please spend the night with me," she said. "I need to be with you."

Solomon did not answer, not with words. He leaned in and kissed Michele deeply again, and she understood what that meant.

"We've got to get Gerald situated," he said. "I should go check on him."

She looked down at his bulging crotch. "You might want to wait until some air deflates out of that tire in your pants, Daddy," she said.

They laughed. "You gonna pump some more air back into it?" he said, and they laughed again.

"Why don't you sit down and I'll go check on him," she said. "Here, have some water."

Solomon took the glass and downed half of it. Michele fixed her clothes and hair and checked on their son. After a few minutes, she came back to the living room with Gerald, who was wearing Redskins pajamas.

"Look at you," Solomon said. "Looking good."

Gerald smiled. "You like the Redskins?"

"Come on, now," he said. "I thought I told you. The Redskins are my favorite team. Maybe we can go see them play next season."

"Can I go, too?" Michele asked. "Ya'll always leaving me out."

"She can go, right?" Solomon said to Gerald.

"Yes, Mommy, you can go. It'll be fun."

"Okay, good, but right now," she said, "it's time for bed."

"You sleepy?" Solomon asked.

"A little bit," Gerald answered.

"Good," Solomon said, looking slyly at Michele. "Getting good rest is important."

Michele smiled and shook her head.

"Come on, son," Solomon said. "Let's get you tucked in."

Solomon listened to him say his prayers and was moved. At the end of "As I lay me down to sleep," Gerald said, "God bless Mommy. God bless Daddy. God bless the whole wide world. Amen."

"And God bless you, son," he said to Gerald. "God bless you."

"Thank you, Daddy. Goodnight."

Solomon kneeled down beside the bed and hugged his son and kissed him on the top of his head. "Goodnight."

He made his way back to the living room to find the lights out, TV off, a Teena Marie CD playing and candles burning. Michele was sitting on the couch with two glasses of wine in her hand, Chardonnay.

"This is nice," he said, sitting next to her and receiving the drink. "Is it okay for me to refer to times during our first time around?"

"Yes, it's all right; I'm over it. Living in the moment," she said. "That's what I keep telling myself."

"Good," he said. "You remember the time when we went to see Chuck Brown and Rare Essence at the Carter Barron?"

"Do I remember? That's when I learned I could dance on one leg," she said, laughing.

"What?"

"You don't remember? We were partying hard to Essence and it was crowded and this guy stepped on my big toe."

"Oh, yeah," Solomon said. "I was ready to punch him in the face."

"I know," Michele said. "My toe was throbbing. But you know how it is when you hear some good go-go music. You gotta dance. So I was up there shaking it while putting as little pressure as possible on that foot."

"Yeah, and you were shaking it pretty good, too," Solomon said. "You know what else I remember about that night?"

"What?"

"Before that dude stepped on your foot," he said, "I was coming back from the bathroom. You didn't see me. You had on this green and gold sundress with your back out. Your hair was darker then. The sun had not set yet, but it was getting dark. But it seemed like you were illuminated. I stood there and watched you for about a minute. I remember thinking to myself, 'Nice.'"

"Really? You never told me that before."

"That was one of those perfect dates we had. Other than the broken toe."

"It was a perfect night," she said. "You know what I remember? When we got to your place after the concert, you turned on some music, lit some candles and gave me a glass of wine.

"And you know how I remember it was that night? Because the music you put on was more go-go. You said, 'I can't get it out of my system.' And I was like, 'It's in my system, too, but the go-go gots to go. It doesn't work with wine and candlelight.'"

"You did say that," Solomon said. "Wow, I haven't thought about that night in years."

They talked and laughed and had a second and third glass of wine over the next hour. It was a conversation that did not include Gerald, which was unique for them.

"Do you realize this is the first time in three weeks when we talked about each other and things that did not involve Gerald?"

"True," Solomon said. "I'm still not used to this whole thing, but it's coming so much faster than I thought. Michele, we're going to be all right. The three of us."

She nodded her head. "Come with me," she said, grabbing Solomon by the wrist. He followed without issue. When they got to Michele's bedroom door, he stopped.

"If I think what's going to happen is going to happen, I need to go to CVS real quick."

"You're right. I actually had my tubes tied after delivery," Michele revealed. "But the responsible thing to do is to be responsible."

Solomon nodded his head in agreement. He did not like condoms—what man did? He found them unromantic, inhibiting, distracting and unnatural, too. But he understood their value.

"I'll be back in ten minutes," he said, turning away from Michele. She called his name.

When he turned around, she pulled him to her and they kissed. "Don't be long," she whispered.

Solomon did not answer. He smiled and walked away. In the car, he called his boy, Ray.

"It's going down," he said.

"What's going down?" Ray asked. "And why you calling me so late anyway? You're lucky I'm up watching *SportsCenter*."

"It's not even eleven o'clock; stop crying," Solomon

said. "Tonight's the night with Michele. I'm headed to CVS right now."

Ray said, "CVS? Oh... It's like that?"

"Yep, it is. She's been like my girl all this time, but this makes it official," Solomon said. "You know what it's taken to get to this point? Man, a lot."

"Well, wishing you good luck isn't the appropriate thing to do, huh?" Ray said, laughing. "Let's see: Break a leg? Nah, that doesn't work, either. How about 'have fun'? Or—"

"Yo, I'm outta here; you're crazy," Solomon said. "Call you tomorrow."

He found what he was seeking at CVS—Magnum condoms—but was embarrassed to go to the checkout line because there was an elderly lady standing there waiting to pay for her items. He didn't want her to see what he was buying.

So he piddled around the store, browsing magazines to bide time until she was gone. On that row were the greeting cards, which struck a notion for him to purchase one for Michele.

He ended up deciding on a card with a photo from behind of a man and a woman holding hands, walking down a beach at dusk. It was serene and romantic.

With the woman gone, he paid for his stuff and, in his rental car, pulled out a pen from the center console. He then wrote Michele a note inside the card.

Before he finished writing he received a text message

from Michele, letting him know that the front door was unlocked. When he got there, he locked the door behind him and headed through the living room to Michele's bedroom. On the way, he noticed that the door to Gerald's room was securely shut.

He could hear soft music the closer he got to Michele's room at the back of the house. The door was slightly ajar. When he slowly pushed it open, he saw Michele lying across the bed in a short white negligee, illuminated by scented candles on the nightstands that flanked the bed.

Solomon closed the door without turning around. He did not want to take his eyes off of Michele. He shook his head.

"What's wrong?" she asked.

"Everything is right," he answered, walking over to her and placing his bag on the floor beside the bed.

She rose to her hands and knees on the bed and he leaned over to kiss her again. "Beautiful," he said before pressing his lips against hers.

"Me?" she said wryly.

"You. This room. This *moment*," he said.

"I hate to go—"

"Go?"

"To the bathroom," Solomon finished. "Can I take a quick shower?"

"Oh, sure," Michele said. "Use my bathroom over here. Everything you need is in the linen closet. But don't make it a spa shower."

"Five minutes," he replied.

He was done in three. Solomon had never washed himself so quickly. As much as he lacked faith in women, he had always believed in romance. It was the seduction of women that he enjoyed, and it offset his distrust of them. So, he hurried because he did not want to blow the mood.

With a towel draped around his waist, he reentered the bedroom. Michele was sitting up with her back pressed against the leather headboard.

She smiled. "Welcome back."

"Sorry I had to go for a minute," he said. "But I feel refreshed."

She maneuvered across the bed and pulled the covers back. He pulled the knot from his towel and it fell to the floor, revealing his strong, lean, naked body.

"I remember all that," Michele said.

He climbed in the left side of the bed and under the luxurious six-hundred-count sheets. Neither of them played coy. Immediately, they embraced.

"You don't know how many times I've wanted to be right here with you," she said.

He didn't answer, not with words. Rather, Solomon kissed her on her neck and shoulders and she sighed with pleasure. He kissed her face and she turned toward him so their lips could meet.

She took in his body. It had been fourteen months since she had been with a man and even longer considering how uneventful that one-time encounter had been. Solomon was a committed lover. There was intense passion between them, even after so many years. So she anticipated the heat.

Caressing his shoulders and back and feeling his lips on her confirmed everything she had tried to suppress:

She loved Solomon Singletary.

In that moment, the pain of the past was so blurry and the pleasure of his presence and touch crystal clear. The reality was that she never stopped loving him.

Solomon's reality was that he loved her, too. He had never told her as much, not in words. He had always communicated his feelings to her through how he treated her and how he made love to her.

"I remember this, Michele," he said softly into her ear. "I remember how warm your body is and how soft it is. I've missed you close to me like this."

"Me, too," she said, reaching down and stroking the throbbing extension between Solomon's legs. "I've missed this."

That was her not-so-subtle hint that foreplay needed to be over. Always keen, Solomon got the hint and leaned over the side of the bed to pull the condoms from the bag.

As he did so, Michele grabbed his butt. "Still nice and tight."

He was so caught up in getting the condom out of the box and then out of the wrapper that he did not offer a retort. When he got it free of all the packaging, he lay on his back to apply it to his erection. Michele kissed him deeply as he did.

Once on, he pulled Michele on top of him and caressed

her back down to her hips and over her round and soft ass that he had first noticed that night in D.C. In one motion he rolled her over on her back and was on top of her, as a tiger would prey.

She spread her legs and he positioned himself between them to enter her. Just then, he remembered something important: Michele liked to do the honors of inserting him into her hot, wet, "good-good," as he called it. She said doing so gave her power.

And so, she did, and it was like an injection of life. She held Solomon back by his waist to prevent him from going in too deep too soon. But the sensation was unmistakable and it ricocheted through her body like a pinball.

"Baby, I feel you," she said. Her muscles began to loosen up and she went from holding Solomon back to pleading for deeper penetration.

"Oh, give it to me. Give to me, baby."

Solomon, meanwhile, was giving it to her. Her legs in the air and his arms locked inside her thighs keeping them there, he pumped up and down into her wetness, hitting it from angles and depths that made Michele scream.

Aware that Gerald was down the hall, Solomon tossed his pillow over Michele's face to smother her noise. And she had reason to be loud: She had not been so intensely screwed since Solomon had done the honors the night Gerald was conceived.

She pulled the pillow off her face. "Baby, you getting it. You getting it. Oh, damn. Damn! Keep doing that."

He kept doing that and doing that and doing that over

the next ten minutes or so. Suddenly, Michele's legs began to tremor. "Oh, oh, oh, oh…" she screamed.

She pulled Solomon down so that their chests met. "Owww, baby, do it, do it."

Solomon thought he *was* doing it, so he kept on stroking. Their body movements were synchronized. And her groans were in perfect rhythm to his thrusts.

Michele made sounds that she could only make in the throes of passion. "This is it, baby. Ohhhh, ohhh, awwwwwwwwwwwwwwwwww!!!!"

She climaxed with such a force that her body shook and all she could do was tightly hold on to Solomon. "Oh, my God… I can't stop…"

The heat that came from her and their passion got the best of Solomon, too. She would not loosen her clutch around his body, but he continued to pump inside her and as she came for the third time, Solomon exploded, too, breathing so heavily into the side of Michele's face that she had to turn away.

"Oh, my Lord," he said. "Michele…Michele."

He was sweating and struggling for air—and for the right words to describe how he felt.

She loosened her grip and they rested there for a minute or so, Solomon's large body crushing her. Michele's way was to please, so she did not say anything.

But Solomon knew. "I know you can hardly breathe," he said as he pulled up from her chest. He made sure the condom was still secure and slowly pulled out. This was one of the unromantic parts of using rubbers.

Michele took a deep breath. "Man, you know how to please me," she said.

He discarded the heavy condom in the plastic CVS bag and lay on his back. Michele rested her head on his chest and he put his arm around her. Neither of them said anything for a few minutes. They caught their breath and collected their thoughts.

Then Solomon felt something wet on his chest. It was Michele's tears.

"You all right, dear?" he asked with concern in his voice.

She nodded her head and wiped her face and his chest with her hand and kept her head down.

"I'm sorry to cry on you like that," she said. "I'm just... I...I don't know if I've ever been happier in my life than right now. Solomon, I love you. You probably don't want to hear that, but I do."

Solomon rubbed her arms and shoulders. "Can I give you something?"

She lifted her head. "You gave me plenty, but I'll take more."

He laughed. "You've got to turn on the light."

As she did, he reached over and picked up the card he had purchased from the drugstore.

"What's this?" she said as he handed it to her.

"It's yours."

She opened the envelope and then the card. It read:

"Michele, it is important for me to let you know that you have changed my life. I cannot go on without again apologizing

for my big mistake. But through fate and God, here we are.

"I believe we can/will be better than ever because I have grown and I see the light. And the light is you. I appreciate who you are as a woman, as a mother, as a friend, as MY woman. I am committed to you and to our son. Don't ever forget that.

"Above all, I love you, Michele.

"Yours, Solomon."

Michele's shoulders dropped and she raised her head toward the ceiling.

"I love you, too, Solomon," she turned to him and said. "Thank you for this. It means a lot."

She read the card again before placing it on the nightstand and turning off the light. Michele arranged the covers so that they were comfortable, kissed Solomon on his face and lay on his chest.

It was reminiscent of eight years previous, when Solomon had vanished. But this time, when she awoke the next morning, Solomon was there, holding her securely. Neither of them was going anywhere.

CHAPTER 15

THE POWER
OF (GOOD) SEX

That night of passion unleashed desires in both of them that had been distracted or untapped for eight years. And so, their sensual romps became nightly escapades.

Over the next three weeks, a routine was established. They would spend post-school with Gerald, helping with the mounds of homework, having dinner, talking, playing. By nine, like clockwork, the kid was exhausted and actually asking to go to bed.

It got to be that Solomon and Michele would look at each other with a devilish grin when Gerald started yawning. They knew their time was near.

The consistent, fulfilling sex changed Michele. She was perky and optimistic, smiling and energetic, jovial and spry. Spirited.

At her book club meeting one Saturday afternoon, she could not contain her glee—or desire to share the source of it to her five co-members. She did not go there planning to tell her business. But one conversation led her on a path of free speech.

"I enjoyed the book," said club member Renita, who hosted the meeting at her house in Southwest Atlanta, "but I don't know if it's realistic."

"How do you mean?" Michele asked.

"Well, the main female character let the guy get away with too much because the sex was good," Renita said. "No, I'm not having that. No way."

Michele laughed.

"What's so funny?" Renita said. "And why have you been so upbeat and happy lately anyway?"

"You noticed that, too?" Cassandra, another member, said. "When I called her last week, she could hardly stay on the phone with me. And I heard a man's voice in the background. Unless your son got old pretty fast, that was a man's voice I heard."

Michele hardly was one to expose her business to the masses. But her book club members were close friends and she could not hold back. Plus, she *wanted* them to know.

"Well," she started, "there is a man—the father of my son."

"No, wait a minute," Angie said. She was the audacious member who had a lot to say to everyone about everything. Every book club had an Angie. Diplomacy was not her forte.

"You telling me the guy who ran out on you all those years ago is back?" Angie said. "Since when?"

"It's a long story, but, yes, he is back," Michele said. "We've been working on things for about five months now."

"What?" Angie said. "And you held all this back because?"

"I wanted to see if it was real, where it was going," Michele said. "Here's what happened, and you're not going to believe this."

All the members closed their books and moved to the edge of their seats that were set up in a circle in the living room. No drama in a book was better than real-life drama; especially from someone they knew.

"My son played in this basketball league over at Gresham Park, and he kept talking about this 'Coach Money' that he loved. I never met the coach; when I signed him up, I signed him with the director of the program. And when I dropped him off at practices and games, I kept going.

"And when I got progress reports, it was from the director, not his coach. So, anyway, they had a banquet at the end of the season. I was excited because I could finally meet this 'Coach Money.'

"You know how obsessed I've been with Gerald having a male influence in his life and his coach was having an impact. So, we get to the banquet and it's 'Coach Money's' time to give out his awards.

"I look up on the stage and I can't believe my eyes. 'Coach Money' was actually Solomon Singletary, Gerald's father."

The women let out a series of expressions that told of their shock:

"Stop lying."

"Get outta here."

"Oh, my God."

"You can't be serious?"

"*What*?"

"For real. Solomon was coaching his son and neither of us realized it. Can you believe that? I was shocked, to say the least. When he saw me, he was shocked, too. Still, he didn't know Gerald was his son."

The women looked at each other, shaking their heads.

"So what happened, girl?" Angie pressed on.

"He apologized about what he had done and I gave him a hard time about it," Michele continued. "But the truth of the matter was I still had feelings for him, even after all that happened and all that time, even after what he had done. The problem was, I didn't trust him."

"How could you?" Angie said. "How can you?"

"He had to build it," Michele said. "If Gerald wasn't involved, I probably wouldn't have given him a chance. But it was always there that he was his father and should be in his life. That was always important to me.

"But I didn't tell Solomon about Gerald. I kinda-sorta got over the disappearing act he played on me. But it took a lot of time. I had to see what he was about before I told him about Gerald. I mean, it was eight years ago and we all grow up."

"Not all of us, honey," Angie said. "I know men who are the same jerks now as they were in their twenties. So…"

"Well, from what I've seen, Solomon has changed,"

Michele said. "He admitted a lot to me and he really has been amazing. The part I was nervous about was telling him about Gerald. I didn't know if he would run or if he would be mad at me or if he'd just refuse to be a part of his life.

"But he's been totally committed to being a father."

"Well, congratulations, girl. That had to be a relief," Cassandra said.

"I feel like a different person, you know? Like I've done something great for my son—and myself," Michele said.

"That's what men can do—the right man, the righteous man," Renita said. "When my husband and I are doing well, there's no better feeling. The trick that I haven't figured out is how to feel that way all the time."

"'Nita, *no one* has or ever will figure that one out," Angie said. "It would be the ninth Wonder of the World."

The ladies laughed.

"But let's get back to the original question," Angie said when the laughter subsided. "What's all this glow about? It can't be just because Solomon... That's his name, right?...has been a good father. Can it?"

All eyes shifted to Michele, who took a large gulp of her glass of Oya wine and decided she would share her good news with her friends. Their previous book club meetings had turned into complaint sessions about their jobs, finances, kids, men or the lack of quality men. She decided she would color that meeting with real talk about how her life had changed in five months.

"You asked for it." Michele smiled. "It was one thing to see Solomon and to learn that he wanted to be with me again. And it was another thing that he loves his son and is doing his part as his father.

"But…" Michele shook her head and looked off at nothing in particular, "…to consistently feel a man's hands on my body and to feel his passion…oh, my God, it has been something that changed how I feel about myself and about life."

"What?" Angie said.

"Angie, be quiet," Renita said. "Let her finish."

Michele continued. "It's just that—and I never felt like I needed a man to make me whole—having the passion we have is something that has stuck to me. The way he handles me and caresses me and kisses me and makes love to me…it's something that physically brings me pleasure all day long.

"It's like he's all over me. Even though we may have been together the night before, the next day I'm still carrying that intimacy with me. My body sometimes aches, but not like pain. It's like an intense yearning to feel him.

"But it really is more than that. It all starts with the physical; he knows what he's doing to me in bed. But—for me anyway—there's something really comforting about knowing you have good sex in your life.

"It gives me confidence and comfort. And it might seem like a little thing, but it makes me feel joyous. So, yeah, I'm glowing. I feel like an important part of my life is there and it brings that extra pep in my step. It makes me feel sexy and desired. It makes me more patient and understanding. It makes me feel better than happy. Happiness can come and go. Being joyous or joyful is a state of being, no matter what else is going on. That's how I feel. Joyous."

Her friends looked at her in amazement. They had never heard her talk so much at once and they were captivated by her thoughts. No one said anything, so Michele kept going.

"This is different from having somebody come over on a booty call—we've all had them—and, you know, basically provide a service. Feeling so strongly about him it makes the love-making so much more intense and so much more pleasurable.

"It was good before with him, but it is something incredible now. And you know what? It makes me understand why a woman would cheat on her husband. I don't condone it; don't get me wrong. If Solomon and I broke up—God forbid—and I had to move on to someone who didn't give me loving that stuck with me all the next day or I didn't crave his touch, it would be a disappointment.

"I probably would, eventually, seek that feeling that I have now. That's awful to say, I know. And I hope that, if it ever came to that, I'd be more committed than I'm sounding right now. But I've learned that sex is critical to a relationship. We must be honest enough to admit that. I know now that it changes my whole attitude about my everyday life.

"What woman doesn't want a man who is good to her and is a good provider and a good father? I'm convinced now that he could be all that, but if he isn't making you crave him sexually, well, it's not the same. Unbelievable sex can make up for a lot of flaws."

Her book club members nodded their heads knowingly.

"Girl, you sound like that man is putting it down," Angie said. "I joke around a lot, but I understand what you're saying. I almost married a guy once because that fool knew how to knock some boots. Damn, he was good."

"So why didn't you marry him?" Renita said.

"He was knocking boots with anyone he could, that's why," Angie answered. "Then he ended up in prison for selling drugs or something."

"He probably started getting *his* boots knocked in prison," Cassandra joked.

"Yeah, but you get her point, though?" Michele said. "He obviously had flaws. But he made her feel good."

"If you're so tied to the sex, aren't you giving him all the power?" Cassandra asked.

"I have two answers for that," Michele said. "Who cares about power if he's changing your outlook on life and the attitude you have going about your day? That's a fight for power that I don't even care to be involved in. He can have the power; as long as he doesn't abuse it.

"The other answer is it isn't a one-way street. You actually have power, too. If you're pleasing him as much as he's pleasing you, he's going through his day thinking about getting back to you to get what you're giving.

"Solomon and I talked about it, which is another residual of great sex. It opens you up. It makes you want to communicate with your man. He said to me before I said anything to him about all this that he has sat at his desk at work and stopped what he was doing and reminisced about us together.

"He said, 'I can feel your heat and your body right there.' And I was like, 'Wow, he's experiencing the same thing I am.'

"So, it is a two-way street. Neither one of us is thinking about who has power. We're not overthinking it. Truth be told, that's a real problem we have, as women. We are quick to analyze something up and down, around and around, back and forth.

"We do all that and we're missing the essence of what it is. If I spent time, Cassandra, trying to worry about or trying to figure out if he has the power over me, I would miss out on the pleasure. It would take away from it because I wouldn't be thinking about it.

"And, see, that's what this has also taught me. Relax. Enjoy the moment. We all want things to be perfect. It would've been perfect if Solomon had never left me and we'd stayed a couple and had a child and so forth. But if I stayed stuck on what I didn't have, I wouldn't have been able to fully embrace what I do have now.

"You understand what I'm saying? And, listen, this is all new to me. Five months ago I wasn't getting anything and I got to where I thought I wouldn't get any for a long time—if ever. I was fed up. We've all been there.

"But to be where I am now...I'm sorry if I'm preaching, y'all. I have a lot to say."

Angie said: "And to think, I thought this bitch was a prude. Turns out she's a little whore."

The women burst into laughter.

After several seconds, the noise died down.

"Girl, you make me want to go out and find Mr. Goodbar," Renita said.

"Don't you have a husband?" Michele said.

"And?" Renita responded.

"Ah, that's cold," Michele answered.

"It is what it is," Renita said. "I can't lie. You stay married long enough, it seems like maintaining what you're talking about is impossible. I love Steve. He's my husband. But he's not putting it down like he used to."

"Well, I'm no relationship expert," Michele said, "so I can't really sit here and try to offer you advice. But I'll tell you this: Solomon and I went twelve days straight making love."

"No wonder your ass is in pain," Angie blurted out, prompting more laughter.

"Whatever, crazy lady," Michele said. "My point is, in the middle of that time, we talked about how to maintain what we have as far as passion and desire and romance go. And he said, 'We can't let it get stale like everyone else does; that's the problem with many marriages. They get comfortable and let things go. We have to keep it sexy and fun.'

"We don't have years together to draw from. But we hope to, and we'll always draw from that idea that you have to continue to make the effort. This is the best I've felt in my entire life and I don't want to feel any other way. I just don't."

"Yeah, that sounds great in theory. But once you get years together and kids and work and other outside interests in the way, you're lucky to get any kind of sex once a week," Angie said. "If we do it twice a week, there has to be some holiday that week."

The other women chimed in with similar stories of being tired and unmotivated to maintain a relentless love life with the men in their lives. Michele wanted to tell them, "Clearly, he ain't hittin' it right. If he was, you'd understand what I'm saying and you'd make the time to get it." But she understood their experiences were different from hers. And if they did not get it from her lengthy open monologue on sex, then that was their loss.

"Well, I understand what you're saying," she said. "I'm just telling you my experience."

Her co-members continued the conversation and Michele receded to the background over the remainder of the meeting. She had opened up about herself and her love life like never before, and it felt good. Whether her friends truly understood her or not was really of little significance. She was glad to put into words how Solomon made her feel.

CHAPTER 16
IT GOES
BOTH WAYS

Solomon basked in the glow of their passion, too, which was pretty significant because before Michele, he had a rotation of four women he bedded at his whim. They all provided different levels of satisfaction, but none was enough to turn him into a one-woman man.

That fact was enough to let him know what he had with Michele was much more than physical. If it were just about sex, he could have settled down with Marie, Cathy, Cheryl or Evelyn.

They were all attractive women who were smart and stable…good women, the kind a man would be proud to introduce to family and his boys. And they all were committed to sexually pleasing him. Still, something was missing, and it was so indecipherable that Solomon could not articulate what it was.

But he knew this much: With them, it was mostly about satisfying an urge. There was not the emotional connection for him that one would think came with all the intimacy they shared.

In fact, after a while, being with them felt like a philanthropic act. The women had become dependent on Solomon—his presence, his mind, his confidence, his wit, his charm and, above all, his body. He made them feel like women.

For all they had to offer—and they had plenty—they found being single difficult to negotiate. They wanted and needed the attention and affection of a man. And yet, identifying one who could hold up his end was a challenge so many women had encountered.

Living as a single woman in Atlanta could be particularly daunting (and lonely) as there was a proliferation of African-American cute ladies with so much going on versus a collection of quality men whose numbers were decreased when you eliminated the married men, the men with women, the arrogant guys, the playas, the gay guys and the ignorant ones.

Left were a relatively few good men in a city full of promising female candidates. The ratio? A whole lot to a little.

So, combine the vast disparity of "quality" women to men with Solomon's personal baggage and it added up to a less-than-promising scenario for his four ladies; especially after his reconnection with Michele.

But they were aware of their plight, or at least the potential of their plight. Solomon did not hedge in explaining his position to them. Each of them accepted Solomon's terms—"I'm not doing the relationship thing," he had told them, one by one.

But they all believed their virtues would turn his mind and heart—a classic and misguided female position. Like usual, they were wrong.

In fact, he began to view his dealing with them as a community service. "What are you talking about?" his boy, Ray, asked.

"Let me explain," Solomon answered. They had been throwing down vodka and tonics while watching football, long before Michele reemerged. He had a nice buzz, which sometimes brought out some of the arrogance he usually tried to suppress.

"Here's the deal. These women, I don't have a problem with. But they can't hold me. And if I were a bad guy, I'd straight dump them. I care about them. I do. But I don't want to be bottled up by any of them. I don't want to sound cold, but it's like I have a duty/obligation to be there for them. That's a lot different from wanting to be with them.

"Ray, I'm only saying they deserve to feel good, too. Even though it's not all the time, they deserve to have a man pay attention to them, to make their bodies feel good.

"I treat them with respect. We have great conversation and I compliment them and we laugh. And I've been a true friend to them. They need that to feel like the women they are. I happen to be there to provide that service for them. That's community service; helping women feel like women should."

"Excuse me while I throw up," Ray said.

"You telling me, as a man, you don't understand that?" Solomon said.

"I understand you think you're the Messiah or something," he answered. "You think you're saving women's lives by halfway being there for them? Come on, man."

Solomon laughed. "I didn't say I'm 'saving their lives.' I said I'm adding to their lives. Look, they know the deal. I told them all I wasn't doing the relationship thing. I told them I liked being single—and that they could date other men. If they did, I didn't want to hear about it. And if I did hear about it, I'd be gone."

"Wait," Ray jumped in. "You want to do whatever you want, but you don't want them to do the same thing? How do you spell 'hypocrite'?"

"What can I say? I'm territorial," Solomon said. "What's mine is mine until I let it go… Still, if they want someone else, they can go get him. The thing is, I know they won't find someone else. I'm taking care of business."

"I'm a hen-pecked old married man at thirty-three, but how do you do all that juggling?" Ray asked. "I guess every man is not built the same. That would drive me crazy. Dealing with my wife is more than enough. To have three more…why put myself through that torture?"

After reconnecting with Michele, Solomon did not have an answer for that question. The value of the other women in his life rapidly diminished. Just seeing Michele cast a different feeling about them.

By the time he learned Gerald was his son, established a relationship with him and gained Michele's trust, his rotation of four women hit a standstill.

It got to where he stopped all communication. He wasn't

proud about that, but he wasn't sure what else to do.

"You're not sure what to do?" Ray said. "Here's an idea. Call them. Tell them. Matter of fact, tell them face-to-face."

"Yeah…yeah," Solomon said. "You're right. That's gonna be tough, but it's got to be done. You know how I know it has to be done? I came home Thursday from work and there was a note on my door from Evelyn."

"What?"

"Yes, man. She hadn't heard from me in a few weeks and was concerned; she wanted me to give her a call and let her know I'm okay," Solomon said.

"Well, did you?" Ray asked.

"I texted her that I was all right and would call her," he said.

"You sent the woman a text?"

"I know. I know," Solomon said. "Man, I've been busy with my son and Michele. That's all I've had time to do.

"But don't even say it. I'm going to make time to break it off with them, one-on-one, face-to-face."

Solomon said it, but he did not mean it. As detached and cold as he was, he did not want to face hurting anyone. He would rather fade away, knowing he hurt them but not having to deal with it.

He also knew that was not the manly thing to do. The manly thing would be to be straight up.

"How did I get to this point?" he said to himself that night after hanging with Ray.

He meant: How did he get to where he was actually,

truly, excitedly committed to one woman? It came down to one word.

Trust.

He trusted Michele. He believed in who she was and, most importantly, he believed in who she was to him. And so, he believed in their connection. And for him, "connection" was not about her finishing his sentences or them thinking the same thing at the same time.

It was more organic than that. It was a shared desire to experience life only with each other. It was a feeling of discomfort when they were not together. It was a feeling of exhilaration when they were, even if they were cooking dinner together or walking through Piedmont Park or sitting together at church.

It also was the inferno of passion they shared. Their attraction was "fire," the way Solomon described it.

"I don't know," he said to her as she lay in his arms one summer night. "I feel like I can consume all of you. Breathe you in and hold it. Hold you. By nature we are animalistic, but I think the connection we have is special.

"When I go home, I feel like I'm carrying you with me. It's crazy. I'm so attracted to ALL of you."

That was true, but some of it was purely physical, too. A lot of it, actually. He liked her look and her attitude and her body. Michele had a quiet confidence and a subtle sexiness that made Solomon desire her the way a fish does bait.

On top of that, Michele captured Solomon with her

daring. Midway through an evening of watching movies on the couch, he asked her about her favorite color. Instead of answering, she pulled the covers off of her, turned on the light and stood over Solomon.

She then slowly began to unbutton her blouse while staring into his eyes. Michele pulled off her top to reveal a black lace bra that fit snug around her 38C breasts.

"Oh, so black is your favorite color, huh?" Solomon said.

Michele did not answer; not with words. Instead, she loosened the tie of her drawstring pants and wiggled out of them, exposing matching black lace thongs that firmly hugged her body. She slowly spun around to give him a panoramic view.

"So," she said in a whisper, "what's *your* favorite color?"

Without hesitation, Solomon answered, "It's black now."

She asked him to stand up, which he did. She placed his arms on her shoulders and slowly, tantalizingly unbuckled his belt, unfastened his pants and let down his zipper.

His pants fell to the floor. They embraced and kissed and spent the next several minutes in a fury of passion.

Another time she did the classic move: drove to his house in a short raincoat and leopard-print pumps. He met her at the front door when she arrived that Friday evening.

"Look at you," he said. "What's under that?"

She was well aware of Solomon's affinity for lingerie

over nakedness, so she donned a leopard print bra with matching G-string. She asked him to untie the belt on the raincoat.

"Ummm, ummm, ummm," he muttered when the coat came open. "I'll be damned if you ain't sexy."

He then kissed her deeply and they lay on the floor, right there at his front door and made love.

"I was going to serve you dinner," he said as they rested on the carpet, trying to catch their breath.

"I don't know about you, but I just had dessert," Michele said. "So, I'm ready for dinner."

"And we got up and had a great dinner," Solomon told Ray. "That's what I'm talking about. That's how you keep things going in a relationship. That's my girl."

"Maybe I need to share your stories with my wife," Ray said. "I can't get her to even wear a gown to bed now. Now, it's big, ugly T-shirts. Not cool."

"Ah, man, that's a tough one, but you've got to say something," Solomon said. "I've had women who looked great while we were out. But as soon as we got home she takes off the makeup, wraps up her hair and jumps into bed looking like somebody from *Roots*. And then they want to be all romantic. I'm still looking fresh. She's looking like she's about to pick cotton. That's some messed-up stuff right there.

"But Michele gets it. I never said a word about anything like that to her. I've never seen her in anything other than some kind of lingerie when it's time to go to bed.

Some is sexier than others, but it's always appealing; never a big T-shirt or flannel pajamas."

"She's all right with me," Ray said. "I need to put her and my wife together. My folks need some lessons."

"Well, maybe you should give her the lessons," Solomon said. "You've got to let her know what you want to get what you want. I believe in that. Say what you want. That's your wife. If you can't talk to her, who can?"

"You'll be surprised," Ray said. "You've got to know my wife. She's super sensitive. If I tell her what I want, she'll go all overboard, thinking I don't like what she's doing."

"But you *don't*, Ray!" Solomon blurted out. "That's the whole point. How can you expect to be happy if you're not happy? Some things are pretty basic. Sounds like you want more than you're getting. If you don't tell her that you want more, how are you going to get more?

"That's how people end up cheating. Men and women. They are unhappy with what's not happening at home, so they seek what will make them happy somewhere else. And another thing: Is she unhappy with you? Would she tell you if she were not pleased?

"I'm not trying to be all in your business. I'm just saying that as messed up as I've been to women, I do know you can't get anything without communicating what you want. It could be that you both aren't pleased. So what do you do? Just be miserable?"

"I hear what you're saying, but I ain't miserable," Ray

said. "Wishing I had more in bed with my wife doesn't equate to being miserable. At least, not how I add things up."

"Well, you're a different guy from me," Solomon said. "I couldn't be happy—totally happy—with someone who didn't please me in bed. I'm sorry, but that's the truth. I don't care how sweet she is and how beautiful and how smart…if the sex isn't up to par, I'm having some real issues.

"And, quiet as it's kept, you aren't happy, either. If you were, we wouldn't be having this discussion. Ray, you're a man and I shouldn't have to explain this to you.

"Sex is the great equalizer. She can get on your nerves or disappoint you in some way or fall short in another. But if she's putting it down sexually, she has the pass marked 'access granted.' That's just how it is. And guess what? It goes both ways.

"That's the main reason why women cheat; because they ain't getting it the way they want it. You'd better be knocking the bottom out of that ass to please her. You do that and she generally will fly straight."

CHAPTER 17

TROUBLE
IN PARADISE

O n the way to work, while negotiating the per-
petual traffic on Interstate 20 West into Atlanta,
Solomon came to a dramatic conclusion: He
was at the most peaceful point of his adult life.

Things were going well at work. He and Michele
bonded so tightly it was scary. And his relationship with
Gerald was out of some storybook.

Then, as suddenly as a sneeze, a major part of that idyllic
life came crashing down like an imploded skyscraper.

With the return of school approaching, Solomon and
Michele agreed Gerald should begin going to bed earlier
to get into the routine that would take place once school
began.

The first night, Gerald abided by his mom's command
to turn in with no problem. Solomon walked with him
and chatted with him until he finished his prayers and
jumped into bed.

The next night, when nine o'clock arrived, Solomon
would not agree to another game of Trouble with Gerald.
"We can play tomorrow," he told his son. "It's time for
you to hit the hay."

"What's 'hit the hay'?" Gerald asked.

"Bed," his father told him.

"I don't want to go to bed now," Gerald said with defiance.

"It's time, Gerald," Solomon said. "We can play some more tomorrow."

"No," Gerald shot back. "I want to play Trouble."

Michele put down the *Essence* magazine she was reading. "Listen to your father."

"Michele," Solomon jumped in. He didn't say anything else; she understood that was his situation to handle and backed off.

"Gerald," Solomon said, "do not say 'no' to me again. Now, I told you to go to bed. So go before you're sorry."

"Mommy," he said, turning to Michele, "can I stay up and play Trouble?"

Solomon became incensed. "Don't ask your mother anything," he said, rising from his seat at the kitchen table. "I told you go to go bed. Don't say another word or I'm going to pull my belt off and beat your butt."

"Solomon," Michele interrupted.

"What?" he yelled at her. "Honey, let me deal with this."

Turning back to Gerald, he said, "You have five seconds to get to that room."

Gerald ran over to his mother's waiting arms.

If Solomon's anger could be measured, it would have to have been done in miles. He started unbuckling his belt as he stormed over to the living room to get Gerald.

"What are you doing?" Michele said, pulling Gerald away from Solomon's reach. "You can't beat him."

"What? Watch," Solomon said. "He's not going to disrespect me. No way."

"But you should talk about it," she said.

"This belt will do the talking."

He held the folded belt in one hand and pulled Gerald from Michele with the other. It was chaos. Mother and son were both screaming and crying. Solomon was seething.

He was quite aware of the new wave of parenting; more talking and less beating. He considered it a reason kids were more troublesome and just plain worse than older kids who were disciplined with a belt—or a switch or extension cord or anything within arm's reach of a parent.

One of the concerns he had with Michele that he did not share was how he would deal with having to discipline Gerald. It was bound to happen. Hardly were there any kids so angelic that a moment like that one would not occur—*especially if he has my blood running through his veins*, Solomon thought. *I got so many whippings I thought I was a slave.*

Gerald was about to get his first. Solomon did not want to be on that side of history with his son, but he insisted it had to be done. Making it worse was that Michele was not in agreement with him.

He didn't care. With Gerald locked in the death grip of his left hand, Solomon tattooed his butt with strikes of leather. The boy screamed. Michele could not take it;

she got up and ran to the bedroom, holding her ears.

Solomon actually smiled to himself as he was beating the boy. It amused him that he saw his father in himself. As he whaled on Gerald, he did just as his dad had done to him. That is, simultaneously he struck Gerald and ordered commands.

"Don't…(strike) you…(strike) ever…(strike) dis…(strike) re…(strike) spect… (strike) me…(strike)…again (strike)."

When he let Gerald's arm go, the boy lay on the floor writhing in pain. Solomon knew more than his feelings were hurt; he was mindful that he was beating a child and did not try to *really* hurt him. The idea was to let Gerald know he was in charge and that running to his mother was not a safe haven from his father, and that disrespect would not be tolerated.

"Now get up from there and go to bed," Solomon ordered.

Gerald scurried off the floor and ran down the hallway, holding his butt. Solomon laughed to himself, but not long. He was exhausted. "Damn," he said aloud. "That was a workout."

He heard Michele's bedroom door open. She was headed to Gerald's room when he interrupted.

"Michele, don't go in there," he said. "Leave him alone."

She stomped her way into the living room.

"I'm not having that," she said, looking up at Solomon. "You're not beating my baby. That's not acceptable."

"I know it's hard, but he has to be disciplined," Solomon said. "You think I'm going to stand for him disrespecting me and running to you like you're going to protect him from me? No. That's what's unacceptable."

"I don't believe in beatings," she said.

"Your parents didn't beat your ass when you messed up as a kid?"

"Yes, they did—"

"So why would you think now that it's unacceptable?" Solomon said. "That's the contradiction of today's parents. Your moms and pops whipped you, but you want to talk? Meanwhile, the kid has no fear of the parent and no respect. Michele, come on."

"Come on nothing," she barked. "You don't beat my child. Period. He and I have an understanding that bad behavior gets punishment. That's what we've done all this time."

"Well, it's a new time; I'm here now," Solomon said. "If he does something to you that you want to punish him on, then do that. But he *will not* disrespect me without me whipping his ass.

"It almost makes me laugh when I say this because it's the same stuff my parents said to me. But it's true. It does hurt me more than it hurt him. You think I liked doing that? That shit was painful. But a greater good will be served."

"You did like whipping him," Michele said. "Why else would you not try to talk to him first?"

"This isn't a democracy when it comes to parenting," Solomon answered. "The child does what the parent tells him to do. There's no gray area about that, Michele. And I'm a little pissed at you, too. He runs to you and you try to pull him away from me. That's not cool.

"We've been working together on raising Gerald and it's been going well. But it has to be a united front on discipline, too. Listen, I ain't stupid. I'll talk to him in the morning about all of this. But he needs to sleep on his behavior and what will happen if he disrespects me again."

"He's almost eight years old; he doesn't even know about disrespecting anyone," Michele said.

"Well, he does now," Solomon said. "And even simpler, he knows what telling me 'no' is, and I'm not having it. Not for one second, Michele. Next thing, he'll be telling you when you should go to bed.

"You've got to nip that crap in the bud right now. Why did he think it was okay to tell me he wasn't going to bed? I don't know where that came from, but it won't happen again. Watch."

"You're not going to beat him again, Solomon," Michele said.

"As his father, I'll discipline him as I see fit," he responded. "You do not and cannot control that. Now, I understand you've spoiled him and all that. I wasn't here. But I'm here now and he's not going to grow up thinking he's above getting his ass whipped. It's not happening."

"Well, we've got a serious problem because I don't agree with that," she said.

"You act like the boy is in Grady Hospital," Solomon said. "It's not about physically hurting him. I'm sure his butt might be a little sore, but he'll be fine in the morning. This is about the mental, letting him know who is in charge, letting him know that there are real ramifications for being disrespectful or disobedient.

"There has to be a fear in him that he knows I'll knock him silly if he gets out of line. You need to have that fear in him as well. Listen, my mother is seven inches shorter than me and getting up there in age, but if I got her really mad, she would grab the nearest thing and bust my head with it.

"She still commands fear and respect from me. If you don't have that in your child, then who's really in charge?"

"I don't think that way," Michele said. "Gerald is a sweet boy. He's respectful."

"Sweet, yes, but if you don't think he was disrespectful tonight, then you're right; we do have a problem."

Michele looked away for a few seconds. "What he did tonight did not deserve a beating, Solomon."

Solomon's heart dropped. He discovered in Michele something he detested. Weakness. "I'm leaving."

"Why? There's no need to go."

"Yes, there is," he said. "We're in this raising Gerald thing together. You told me it was important that he have a man in his life, his father. Well, I'm here. I've been here. And now you're basically telling me that it's okay for him to disrespect me and that I should handle that disrespect through a sit-down?

"We'll never agree on this, which makes this a real, true problem for us. If he gets out of line with me like that again, he's getting another whipping. You think I should sit down and have a summit with my seven-year-old son about him being rude to me. That's crazy and dangerous." He put his laptop in its case and zipped it up. "I'll be back in the morning so I can have that talk with him that we need to have."

"Fine," Michele said. "Go. You should go because you're not going to abuse my son. I'm not allowing that."

"You're not protecting him, Michele; you're handicapping him," Solomon said. "I know it was just you and him for a long time. But the moment you told me the deal, it all changed. I have a say in how he grows up, Michele. You can't stop that.

"And I resent that you think you can. You know him better than me, but you don't love him more than me. He's not untouchable. It could be that this was the one necessary time to send that message and he'll listen and do what he's told. But if it isn't, depending on the issue, he has more butt-whippings to come."

"I don't think so." Michele held the door open for Solomon.

"Well, you don't get to determine," he said. "I'm sure when I leave you'll get him a lollipop and lay down in bed with him and cuddle and wipe away his tears… Fine.

"But that's not helping him; it's making him soft and weak. You said you always wanted me in his life because you can't teach him how to be a man. And now I'm here and you still want to treat him like a baby. I don't know everything, but I know that's not good." He stepped outside Michele's front door. "Babying him is not giving him strength."

Michele's eyes were sad. She was scared. Her man was mad at her. Her son was upset. Her emotions were everywhere. When Solomon turned and walked away, she closed the door and burst into tears.

This was their first true test of the relationship. It had been fantasy-like to that point. Now they had seen each other at their worst. That's when love needed to kick in and hold it together.

But Solomon could not think about love just then. He thought about respect. Respect meant as much to him as anything. When he looked back on all the disappointments with women that had made him cold, he concluded it was their lack of respect for him that had caused it.

So when Michele told him that Gerald's actions did not merit a whipping, he took that as her disrespecting his role as a father. And that made him furious.

He called Ray, Gerald's godfather. "I'm telling Michele tomorrow, 'If you don't respect me enough to discipline my son, then a time will come when you'll disrespect me as your man, too. And I can't have that, either.'"

Ray, always a contrasting voice, said, "So, what's that mean? That you're breaking up with her?"

"Yeah," Solomon said. "It's like she thinks she's going to run things. I don't need to run them, but she's not going to run them, either."

"I understand no one should be in charge in a relationship," Ray said. "But you've got to calm down. You and Michele got back together and that's a miracle. You've been faithful to her, which is another miracle. Bigger than that, though, is that you didn't run from her because of what she might do.

"Now it sounds like that's what you're saying; that you want to break up because she might disrespect you."

"Nah, it's more than that," Solomon answered. "She *did* disrespect me. She tried to prevent me from disciplining Gerald. She told me that I couldn't whip him, like she's in charge of what I do."

"The second talk you have tomorrow needs to be with Michele," Ray said. "This shouldn't be the end of the relationship. You've got to talk it through."

"Yeah, well, I need to hear some stuff from her that shows me that she respects what I'm trying to do," Solomon said. "Otherwise, what's the point?"

"The point is you're a father and you need to be a father," Ray said. "The other point is that you love Michele. No way around that."

"Do you beat little Ray when he's out of line?" Solomon asked.

"Hell, yeah," Ray said.

"So you see my point?"

"But I also see this: It's been Michele and Gerald for almost eight years," Ray said. "She probably tried to compensate for you not being there by spoiling him and throwing her whole life into him. That's basically a woman's nature anyway.

"Then you come along and now you're trying to change what she built for eight years. It's hard for her."

"That may be true, but it's hard for me, too," Solomon said. "And I can't bend on discipline. Respect is everything. I was raised that way and that's what I believe in."

CHAPTER 18
ONE DOWN,
THREE TO GO

At home, Solomon felt strange, alone. He had an evening all mapped out with Michele. She was on her menstrual cycle, but he still planned to nestle up with her on the couch, eat popcorn and watch a funny movie they rented: *Somebodies* by a young filmmaker named Hadjii. And, he had thought, if he was lucky, Michele would give him a little "oral love" before they went to sleep.

It was fifteen after ten on a Friday night and he literally had nothing to do, except ponder the drama that had unfolded. In the past, when a woman disappointed him, he had a simple solution: move on to the next one.

Those feelings did not come over him on this occasion. Well, they did and they didn't. He did think of contacting another woman, but not for the same purposes of the past. Rather, it occurred to him that he should begin the inevitable conversations he had to have with the women who still, however barely, hung on to hope that he would be in their lives.

That thought let him know that Michele held a special, untapped place in his life. Even as he was disappointed in her, the pervasive feeling was that he loved her, which was an emotion he had never, truly experienced. He did, however, consider her position on him disciplining Gerald a real breach of their relationship.

Still, the more he thought about beating Gerald, the more of a funk he sank into. He loved his son, and he hoped that he would react as Solomon had as a child when his father (or mother) beat him. That is, in the morning it would all be forgotten.

The lesson was learned and, even at a young age, he understood that the beating came as a necessary evil of parenting. But would Michele's opposition to his method of discipline make the pain of it all linger with Gerald?

Solomon's mind became clouded with frightening thoughts. *What if he hates me now? What if Michele hates me? How do I overcome this?*

He started to call Michele to feel her out. He knew she was upset, but he did not want it to escalate into something really big. Before he could dial her number, his pride kicked in.

"Don't do it," it said to him. "Calling her would minimize all the points you made. Let her know you mean business."

And that was that. Solomon discarded the idea of calling Michele and, instead, called Evelyn, one of his stable of four women he "dated" before reconnecting with Michele. He called not to get with her, but to let her free.

"I know this must be a mistake," Evelyn said when she answered the phone. There was noise in the background, music.

"No mistake, E. How are you?" he said. "Where are you?"

"I'm at Hairston's. I felt like dancing. I'm just walking in," she said. "Come dance with me."

She had more than dancing on her mind. Other than running into her briefly at Target a few months before, he had not seen Evelyn in about seven months.

"I might do that," he said. "Be there in about thirty minutes."

Hairston's was a nightclub ten minutes or so from Solomon's house. It had been around in Stone Mountain, east of Atlanta, for at least fifteen years. It had staying power because it was a rarity: a nightclub for the over-thirty crowd.

The owners stopped investing money in the space—it had looked virtually the same for the last eight or ten years—but the music was good, the hot wings were tasty and the crowd was mature.

So, Solomon went upstairs and changed clothes and headed out to meet Evelyn. She got into his rotation one winter night when he pulled up at a Bank of America on North Druid Hills Road, right near Interstate 85, to go to the ATM.

Standing outside her car, shivering, was Evelyn. Her car was running. "You okay?" he asked. She was short and cute, brown-skinned with shoulder-length hair. Her coat was tied tight around her waist, offering a view of a hint that she had a shapely body. Solomon processed all that in a matter of seconds.

"I locked my keys in my car," she said.

"Ah, man," Solomon said. "Sorry to hear that. Do you have someone coming with a spare?"

"My phone is in my car," she said.

"Oh, hell. That's messed up," he said. "Listen, uh, I'm willing to help you, if you're comfortable with that. You have to be freezing. You can warm up in my car while I get some money out of the bank."

Evelyn pondered it for a few seconds. "Thank you. I really appreciate this."

He opened the door for her and she jumped in. He went to the other side of the car and turned up the heat.

When he returned from the ATM, he offered his cell phone. "Want to call a locksmith?"

"Well, my cousin has a set of my keys, but she's in Buckhead at work."

"I'm good with time, so I can take you to her, if you like, to pick up the key and bring you back."

"Really? You'd do that? Thank you," she said. "But do you think my car will be okay?"

"Well, someone would have to break in to get it," Solomon said. "I'm gonna say it will be all right. But don't hold me to that if we come back and it's gone."

Evelyn laughed.

"You warming up?" he asked. "How long you been standing out there?"

"Shoot, about ten, fifteen minutes," she answered.

"Are you serious? That's too bad. Here…" He handed over his BlackBerry. "Call your cousin."

She did. On the way to Buckhead, they got acquainted. "You know there are no such things as accidents," Evelyn said. "You were supposed to pull up when you did and meet me."

"I believe in that, too; to a degree," Solomon said. "You were out there for fifteen minutes and no one else pulled up?"

"A few people did, but only one person said something; this guy," she said. "I wasn't comfortable with how he was looking at me. I told him my boyfriend was almost there."

"Come to think of it, why isn't your boyfriend on the way?" That was his opening.

"You have to have a boyfriend to call a boyfriend," she said. "That's a sad story I don't even want to get into."

"I hear you," Solomon said. "I won't broach that subject."

They laughed.

"What are you up to? Where were you headed?" Evelyn said.

"I just came from Loehmann's, looking for a shirt or two and was going to meet a friend out for dinner," Solomon said. "But she cancelled while I was in the store. So I was going to go to Publix and go home and fix a meal."

"Well, after helping me like this, you should let me take you to dinner," she said. "Wait, wow, that *really* sounds forward. I'm sorry. I didn't mean to go there like that."

"It's cool," Solomon said. "I'd love to. You seem harmless. I'm safe with you."

Evelyn laughed. After retrieving the spare keys and getting her back to her car, she followed Solomon to Bluepointe, where they dined and had cocktails at the bar.

"And just think," she said, as a valet pulled up her car, "I had to lock my keys in my car to meet a nice man… The Lord works in mysterious ways."

They hugged and departed. That was the beginning. This was the end.

Solomon arrived at Hairston's around eleven and was instantly reminded of his days as a regular there. The place looked the same, smelled the same, felt the same. There was even this same corny guy wearing a box-cut hairstyle and cheap-looking suit still roaming the place.

Solomon took the scenic stroll around the club and ran into some guys he knew from golf, college and from around Atlanta. On the other side of the club, to the left of the entrance, beyond the second bar, was Evelyn.

High heels and short black dress; that was her party attire. She liked to show off her nice legs and small waist, despite having two children. A glass of Oya wine in her hand, she did not conceal her glee to see Solomon.

As he approached, she offered a smile that was as illuminating as the neon light that spun above the dance floor. "I miss seeing you," she said, hugging him tightly. "Who did you kick me to the curb for?"

That was Evelyn; an arrow-straight shooter.

"You haven't changed, I see," he said.

"Was I supposed to?"

"You wouldn't be you if you did."

Solomon ordered a French Connection—Grand Marnier and Courvoisier—and another Oya white zinfandel for Evelyn.

He raised his glass.

"What are we toasting to?" she asked.

"To truth, honesty and a good time."

"Uh-oh, sounds like a confession is coming."

"Not a confession," Solomon assured her. "A good, honest conversation, though."

"Can we dance a little first? Can I flirt with you before we have this talk? This wine is great and I feel good. I'd like to stay this way for a while."

"No doubt. We're here to have a good time… You're here by yourself?"

"Well, yeah," she said. "I finally got tired of hoping for a phone call from you. I came out, hoping to meet someone nice. And I end up here with you? How you like that?"

"I like it fine," Solomon said. He squinted his eyes some and leaned his head. She considered that flirting and he knew it. Maybe if he made her feel good, she wouldn't feel so bad when he gave her the news he wanted to share.

They found seats way in the back of the club and sipped

more drinks, shared some laughs and engaged in super-ficial conversation.

"Come on," he said, grabbing her hand. "Let's work up a sweat."

"Does it have to be on the dance floor? Can we work up a sweat in your bedroom?" She was serious.

Solomon did not answer, not with words. He continued to the dance floor. One of the biggest deterrents to outside sex for a man in a relationship was to not put himself in a position to get it. When Michele reemerged, Solomon shut it down, minimized communication with his quartet of women (and others he had flings with) and focused on what was in front of him.

But here was his first real, live test. Evelyn. Sexy Evelyn. They had a steamy past. Evelyn was ten years older than Solomon but had a youthful appearance and sexual drive. She credited Solomon for bringing out in her what the other men had not; an erotic nature.

Solomon smiled at Evelyn as they danced; she looked up at him as if he were some chocolate treat. For a moment, he let himself ponder one more intimate night with her. *What could it hurt?* one side of his brain questioned.

But cheating on Michele would not make him feel better, even if she never found out. It had been so long since he even had the option of "cheating" because he had not been committed to a woman for years.

And while he and Michele had never said the words, their commitment was ironclad.

Evelyn did not care what he was thinking. She moved in closer, grabbing his waist and pressing her body up against his as they moved to Jay-Z's and Alicia Keys' "Empire State of Mind." She grew up in Queens, NY, so that song was like an anthem to her.

And then something strange happened: Solomon felt awkward. He loved to feel a woman's body. On that same dance floor he had ridden women's booties many times before. Once, a woman, a particularly bold woman, had guided his hand under her dress and between her legs. *Right there, on the crowded dance floor.*

Evelyn was angling for something similar. The floor was packed, so there was no room for Solomon to retreat. She turned around and thrust her considerable ass on him. To avoid getting an erection, he started to think about baseball and math and C-SPAN. It didn't work.

When she felt his hardness, she smiled. And pressed harder. She understood a man with an erection was a man vulnerable to her desires. She also recalled the many times she would dance for Solomon at her house and what followed that erection she created.

Solomon remembered, too. They were fun memories. But they were memories, not his new reality. That was brought home when he felt his phone vibrate in the harness on his hip. He pulled it out on the dance floor. It was Michele.

And his erection deflated like a popped balloon. He leaned into Evelyn's ear.

"Let's go," he said, and she took it to mean to his house, so she gleefully maneuvered through the crowd, off the dance floor and straight toward the exit. At first, Solomon wanted to keep her in the club, but he decided it was too loud for the conversation he had in mind. He was not sure exactly what he would say, but he was ready to say it.

So, when they got outside, he walked her to her car.

"Where did you park?" she asked.

"Valet," he said. "But it doesn't matter. I have to tell you something."

He leaned on her car and folded his arms.

"I called you because I wanted to see you," he began. "I've been M.I.A. because I reconnected with a woman from several years ago that I really liked and cared about."

Evelyn looked at him like, "*And...*" She knew Solomon had at least one other woman in his life. So why was this such news?

"I'm in love with her," he added. "As much as I like you and care about you—and I hope you know that I do—I have to do right by her."

"I see," Evelyn said. "One question: What's wrong with me? I'm not mad about it and I'm trying to be happy for you. But all this time... What, more than a year? You never gave us a chance to really have something. You told me from the beginning that you didn't want a relationship. Now you're telling me that you're in one? What's that about?"

"I don't know," Solomon answered. "With this woman,

I left her eight years ago when I moved from D.C. to here. The—"

"Wait! Eight years ago?"

"Yes," Solomon said. "We dated back then and I abruptly ended it when I moved here. I ran into her several months ago and I realized right away that there was something special there."

"So all we had were good times and sex?" Evelyn said. "That's all it was to you."

"That's not a bad thing," he said. "All my memories and thoughts of you are good ones. How many people can say that about someone? I hope you know the kind of woman you are."

"The kind that's not good enough for you."

"I wanted to talk to you in person. It was important and I respect you. I'm sorry I didn't talk to you before now; instead of basically disappearing. It actually was—and still is, I guess—a complicated situation."

"Complicated? Why?" Evelyn asked. "Is she pregnant?"

"Actually, she's not," he answered. "But she has a seven-year-old son… And he's mine. I'm a father."

"Oh, come on, Solomon." She stepped back. They were standing in the parking lot, so she tried to keep her voice at a controlled pitch. "Are you serious?"

"I'm a daddy," he said with pride in his voice. "It's a long story. The short version is that when I left her in D.C., she was pregnant. I didn't tell her that I was moving; I just left. It sounds terrible, but that's who I was then. She had no way to reach me, so I never knew.

"So, here's the crazy part: She shows up out of the blue at my youth basketball banquet at the rec center. One of my players I coached actually was my son."

"Solomon, you'd better stop lying," Evelyn said.

"Seriously. That's exactly what happened. I'm not asking you to be happy for me. One day you will be since that's the kind of woman you are. You have a good heart. I do hope you understand."

Evelyn stared at him. He stepped to her and hugged her. "Thank you for being my friend."

She hugged him back. "It doesn't have to end. You can still let me dance for you."

Solomon smiled. "I wish I could; you're a good dancer."

"I'm going home; better yet, I'm going back in the club," she said. "I don't need a man to validate me. But I do, after this, need someone to make me feel wanted…"

They stared at each other. "I'm sorry, Evelyn," Solomon finally said.

She nodded her head. "Good luck…Daddy. And I mean that."

Evelyn smiled at Solomon, turned and headed back into the club. Solomon retrieved his cell phone as he watched her walk off. A sense of satisfaction came over him. Instead of being the cold Solomon who would vanish on a woman, he had a meaningful, heartfelt conversation to explain his actions. And while she wanted different results, she did respect Solomon for being upfront.

It reminded him of how he felt when he was a teenager after a classmate showed interest in him, but he rebuffed her because he already had a girlfriend. She thanked him for being honest. He was proud to do the right thing. This time, too.

CHAPTER 19

MORE TROUBLE
IN PARADISE

Solomon was surprised but happy that Michele had called him. He had never seen her so upset than after he had beaten Gerald. And when he thought about it, it actually scared him. He wondered how far her fury would take her.

But he was relieved when she called. He thought perhaps she had calmed down and wanted to talk rationally about the situation.

He was wrong.

He called her back while standing in the parking lot at Hairston's, eager to get on the proper page with the woman he connected with like no other. Turned out, she was as hostile and adamant about how her son would be disciplined by Solomon.

"I'm sorry I got so upset, Solomon, but I'm so serious about this," she started. "I don't believe in beatings. Kids have to be talked to and taught behavior. We're the adults and we have to be able to control ourselves and teach through means other than beatings. I can't take that."

"Clearly, this is something we should've talked about,

Michele," he said. "Like you, my parents beat me when I was out of line. Not every time, but when they thought I was outrageous, they beat my behind. And it was a deterrent for me.

"I believe in talking, too. I believe in both, actually. I want to talk to Gerald and let him understand why it happened and why he should be obedient. That's one of my roles as his father; to instill discipline in him. There's going to be a time when he's going to be as big and strong as me. But he should still fear and respect me. I can't have him thinking he can do or say whatever he wants to me. That has to be under control now to set the pattern for the rest of his life."

"You don't have to get that through a whipping," Michele said. "You—"

She stopped speaking because she could hear Solomon greeting someone. It was hard to make out exactly what they were saying, but she could hear particular words, like "jail" and "probation."

"Sorry about that, Michele," he said.

"Who was that? Where are you?" she asked.

"I'm standing in front of Hairston's, waiting on my car from the valet."

"Hairston's? So you left here and went to a club?"

"I didn't want to stay home and think about what happened. I needed to do something to occupy my mind."

"So being around a bunch of women was your choice?"

"Michele, it's not like that," he said. "Not at all. In fact…"

He contemplated telling her about his talk with Evelyn, but thought better of it.

"Anyway, can I come over, if that's okay with you? Can we talk about all this?"

"I was about to go to bed," she said.

"How can you sleep when this is hanging over us? You won't be able to sleep."

"You're right," Michele answered. "Are you coming now? Or do you need to get one last dance?"

He ignored her sarcasm. "I'm on my way."

En route, Solomon considered bending on his position for one reason; he believed his message had gotten through to Gerald and that he would not have to go there again. Then he thought about how his first beating did not prevent him from getting into more trouble that forced his dad to pull off his belt.

It was late, nearly 12:30, but he decided to call his father for some direction.

"You know how we raised you," his dad said. "But that's how *we* raised *you*. You have to do what you believe is best for your son as his father. I did tell you to make sure he grows up to be a man who respects you. Bottom line, it's a different time. You can't even yell at a kid anymore.

"Remember Ms. Shaw, your biology teacher at Douglass? I remember your hand being red from her spanking it with a stack of rulers because you talked in class. And she told us about it. And we gave her permission to do it. You can't do that today.

"So, it's different, son. But not so different that you shouldn't beat your child if you believe that's what he deserves."

"Would I be a punk if I told Michele, 'Okay, you win. I won't beat him again'?"

"You'd be a liar," he said. "You beat him because you believe in that form of discipline. From what you say, you didn't really hurt him; you were sending a message that he must respect you and what you tell him to do. So, while I appreciate you calling me for advice, I believe you will do what you think is necessary in that moment. If the little knucklehead gets out of line, you might have to physically put him back in place. He is, after all, his father's son.

"Maybe the thing to do is to do your best to assure Michele that you won't hurt him. He's your son and it's all about instilling respect in him. Tell her you're at a seven-year disadvantage and you're trying to make it up. But you can't make it up effectively by letting him think he can do whatever he wants."

"Dad, thanks," Solomon said. "I tried that, but maybe she was too angry to really hear me. We're going to sit down now and hopefully hash this out. I'll let you know how it turns out."

He arrived at Michele's threshold and immediately learned of how pissed she was. She opened the door and turned and walked away. Always, without fail, she greeted Solomon with a hug upon his entrance into her home. This was not good.

He entered the house and went directly to the kitchen and took a seat at the bar, facing the oven. This was a psychological move. The kitchen was Michele's haven, the place she felt most comfortable and was the most at-ease.

"You don't want to sit on the couch?" she asked.

"Nah, I'm good right here," Solomon said. "I like sitting up on the stool."

Michele came over and stood on the other side of the bar, next to the sink. Her arms were folded. Her facial expression and body language said she was uptight and upset.

Solomon noticed and tried to loosen her up with some levity.

He grinned. "You should unfold your arms before you give yourself a blood clot."

Michele did not budge—or smile.

Instead, she got right to it.

"So what are we going to do about this, Solomon? This is something I can't bend on."

The cold Solomon would have tried to impose his will on the matter. This Solomon, well, he tried to remain poised and non-committal.

"I'm not some maniac who wants to beat a child all the time; that's what you make me feel like when you get this upset and take this strong a stand," he said. "Are you telling me that there's nothing he can do that you think would warrant a whipping, beating, spanking? Nothing?"

"Nothing," she said without hesitation. "All conflicts can be resolved with words or some other form of punishment. That's what I believe."

"I'm not trying to be funny, but how did you come to this way of thinking?" His smile irritated Michele, who started to say something but Solomon did not allow the opening. "You told me your parents beat you growing up. You turned out fine, from what I can tell. The way I look at my youth, the things I experienced helped shape me into who I am.

"My mom made sure on Saturday morning I cleaned up my room and the bathroom. That's what I do now, as an adult. My point is you learn things as a kid that you carry over into your adult life. How is it you can go in the other direction now?"

"Because I didn't like getting beatings," she said. "I didn't understand it."

"Come on, you had to understand it," Solomon interjected. "Tell me you didn't like the pain, but don't tell me you didn't understand why you got a beating. Did you do something they thought you shouldn't have done, that you should have known not to do?"

"Yes, but I still didn't like it. And I do carry over things from my upbringing into my life now," Michele said. "But I don't bring the things I don't agree with. Like eating pork. We ate pork—bacon, ham, chitlins, whatever—growing up. But I don't now and I don't serve it to Gerald."

"I understand, Michele," Solomon said. "I want you to understand this. Please hear me on this: I wasn't trying to hurt him. I love that boy. If he were a girl, I would probably look at it differently on how to discipline him. And so would you. One of the things you told me was that you always wanted a man in his life to help teach him on how to be a man.

"Well, this is part of it. Respect. You give respect and you earn it. As his father, I cannot have him telling me 'no' about anything, ever. That can't happen. I believe if this was traumatic enough for him, I won't have this issue again.

"But I'm old school, Michele: Part of being a male growing into a young man is to handle whatever comes your way. That's why I got him in boxing. What's going to happen when he has to really engage in a fight or has to protect himself? He can't shy away from physical contact.

"Listen, that's a small part of it. I'm not trying to toughen him up through beating him. The bigger issue is respect. He's a kid. If we allow him to dismiss what I say—or even what you say—what are we teaching him? What will he do next? We've got to control that right now.

"He's a great kid, but he's a kid, and kids will test you to see how far they can go. And they'll go as far as you let them. It's human nature for them. I let him know that's not the way to be with his father."

Michele sighed. "Solomon, we're not getting anywhere with this."

"Well, what do you want me to say? That I'm not going to give him a whipping again? Well, I never thought I'd have to give him a whipping. I never wanted to give him a whipping," Solomon said. "But you can't have it both ways. You can't tell me about how glad you are his father is in his life but then try to handcuff me when I have to do the tough things that fathers do."

"You said you love him. You said you love me," Michele said. "If you do, then you'd do this for us. I don't want to see him resent you. And I don't want to resent you, either."

Before Solomon could answer, his cell phone rang. He had placed it on the counter, near where Michele stood.

"Who's calling you at this hour?"

"I don't know. Pick it up and see," Solomon said. He had never given a woman that option before; he did not want to create a precedent he could not uphold. But he was so into the moment that he spoke before he really gave any consideration.

"It says, 'Charles Gold, DeKalb County Jail.' What's that about?" Michele questioned.

"That's the guy I ran into tonight. Why the hell is he

calling me?" Solomon said. "He's going to have to leave me a message."

"Ah, what's this about jail? He works at the jail?"

"No."

"Is he in jail?"

"No."

"Then why does it say 'DeKalb County Jail,' Solomon?"

Solomon looked away. He said nothing.

"Were *you* in jail?"

"About four years ago I spent almost two days in jail. That guy, Charles, I met him there," he said after a lengthy delay. "He seemed like he had potential. A younger guy. I said that I would try to help him out."

Michele backed away from the bar until she backed into the counter behind her. The anger and resentment that dominated her face turned into confusion.

"Why were you in jail, Solomon?"

This was the one secret he had hoped to keep maximum security tight. Only Ray, among his vast collection of friends and associates, knew. He didn't even tell his parents. He sure as hell did not want to tell Michele.

"Are you a judgmental person?"

"What's there to judge? What did you do?"

"I had the worst split second of my life."

"What did you do, Solomon?"

He lifted his head up and looked into her eyes. He was good with words but he did not know how to cushion this news.

"What?" she asked again.

"This girl—woman—called the police on me."

"For what?"

"I slapped her."

The expression that covered her face changed to something indescribable. It expressed pain and confusion and even a little fear.

"You put your hands on a woman? You hit a woman? How could you do that? I was raised to believe that cowards beat women."

She paused and frowned.

"You're a woman-beater? I can't believe this. So, you get off on hurting people when you don't get your way?"

Solomon was conflicted in his emotions, too. He was embarrassed that she knew, confused that she would call him a "woman-beater" and angry that she would judge him off of one sentence.

"Hold on, now, don't let your mind take you crazy places," he said.

"Crazy places? You just told me you smacked a woman. That's a fact. That's not a crazy place."

"Calling me a woman-beater, saying I get off on hurting people…that's a crazy place."

Although he was not happy about having to defend his character, he was as calm as he had ever been in an intense situation.

Michele left the kitchen and walked to the living room and sat on the couch. Solomon followed her.

"Don't sit next to me; don't touch me." There was venom in how she spoke, which actually scared Solomon.

"Wait a minute, Michele. Don't you want to hear what I have to say before you jump to any more wild conclusions?"

"Go ahead. I want to hear this. I want you to convince me why it was all right for you to smack a woman."

"I can't do that because I'm not going to try to; there is no justification for it." He was sitting in a single chair, leaning forward with his forearms resting on his knees.

"Before I told you why I was in jail, I said it was my weakest moment, and it was," he went on. "I want to set the scene for you so you know why I had that moment; not to justify it in any way. The thing to do was to walk away. Even if I had cursed her out, that would've been a better option.

"But it didn't happen like that. We were at her house. We were kicking it, nothing serious. We had come in from dinner, where she had seen some guy she knew and had excused herself from the table to go speak to him at the bar.

"I wasn't cool with it, but I wasn't going to make a scene or trip on it, either. So she goes and stays for, like, fifteen minutes. Her food had come to the table by the time she got back, and it got cold. So she starts complaining.

"So, I'm livid, right? I wanted to do the right thing and wait for her before I started eating, but the more I waited, the more livid I got. Finally, I just ate.

"The manager had seen her at the bar and told her that the food was hot when it arrived but it just sat there for several minutes, untouched. She was drunk or getting drunk because she got indignant. I had to intervene to convince the guy to have her plate warmed up.

"Anyway, we get to her house and she pours some more wine and tells me I'm being a 'bitch' because I complained about her leaving me to go hang at the bar with another man. I'm ready to go off, but I realized she was drunk so I bit my tongue. But I was furious.

"So I say, 'You shouldn't use that word after the way you acted tonight.' She gets louder and more indignant. Spit is coming out of her mouth all over me.

"I said, 'Say it, don't spray it.' That makes her even more out of control. She's saying all kinds of stuff, yelling, acting a fool. I said, 'You know what? I'm gone.' She starts again with calling me a 'bitch' and saying stuff like, 'You're a punk' as she gets in my face.

"She's blocking my way from leaving and screaming nonsense at me and it was chaos. Then I snapped, for one second. I wanted to get out of there and for her to shut up. I slapped her. I'd had a few drinks, too, but I realized what I was doing. I didn't hit her hard, but it was hard enough for her to stumble back.

"She shut up then. I looked at her for a few seconds. I was shocked at myself. I apologized. 'Damn, I'm sorry,' I said. She felt her face and didn't say anything. I apologized again, walked by her and left the house. I got about a mile away and the cops pulled me over. She had called the police. I ended up getting a domestic violence charge."

"But you hit her," Michele said.

"I don't know what else you want me to say, Michele," Solomon said. "I let her foolishness get the best of me. I felt bad about it, like a coward. You don't hit women, period. That's how I was raised. If I was defending myself, that would be another thing. But she didn't hit me and didn't deserve to get slapped, no matter how belligerent she was or how drunk she was."

"So you spent two days in jail and you have a police record?" Michele asked.

"Yes, I did, but I don't have a record," he answered. "By the time the woman got me out on bail, she had sobered up and tried to have the charges dropped. But once domestic violence charges are filed against you in Georgia, that's it; you can't have the charges dropped. So, the state took up the case against me."

"So how is it you don't have a record?" she wanted to know.

"Well, I had no prior history of breaking the law and because the woman wanted the charges dropped, I was allowed to enter something called a diversion program. I had to complete twenty-four weeks of domestic violence/family classes. When I finished the class, I went back to court and the charges were expunged from my record. So I have no record."

"But you still have to live with the fact that you hit a woman," Michele said.

"And it's not easy to live with; I know better," he said.

"All I can say is it was a horrible moment for me. I regret it. I apologized. The woman I slapped said she's forgiven me and apologized to me because she recalled how crazy she was on all the alcohol."

"But you hit her," Michele repeated.

And Solomon's patience began to crumble.

"Why do you keep saying that? You're going to judge me on something that happened four years ago? Something the woman has moved past? Something I've gotten past? What's that about? How do you get to dump on me when we all have done stuff we regret, stuff we're embarrassed about?"

"I saw my college roommate go from her boyfriend slapping her to him beating her butt," Michele said.

And that was the fuse that set off the bomb in Solomon. "I don't give a shit about what happened to your friend; that has nothing to do with me," he said, his nose flaring. "You want to sit here and classify me as some sick bastard? You have some nerve. I could've told you that I was in jail for driving with a suspended license, or anything other than the truth.

"And instead of trying to open your mind to someone making a one-time mistake, you tell me about how a slap escalated with your roommate, like that's me or what would happen with me. Let me tell you something: I resent that crap. Don't sit here in judgment of me. And don't try to psychoanalyze me. You ain't qualified."

With that, he got up from his seat and stormed out of

the house. Michele was not sure what to do or how to respond. So she said nothing as he bolted.

She flopped back on her couch as the realization that all the wonderful notions she had for her life were splintered. Worse, she was unsure how to cement them—or if she even wanted to.

CHAPTER 20
BALL OF CONFUSION

For the second time in the same night, Solomon took a lonely drive home, confused about his feelings. This time, though, there was an added emotion: anger.

He resented Michele taking his incident with another woman from four years earlier as an indication of something sinister about him. Solomon believed he deserved the benefit of the doubt; especially from someone who had professed her love for him.

It was too late to call Ray or any of his friends or his dad. He had to deal with the turn of events by himself, which was dangerous.

A fragile mind like his could go to some dark places, and Solomon's anger guided him away from the light. By the time he reached Panola Road, near his house, he was practically sweating, he was so angry and so full of disdain.

Simply put, his feelings were hurt, which, to a man, was tantamount to challenging his pride. The idea that women were stronger than men was hardly something any man agreed with; but the reality that a man's emotions were more sensitive than a woman's was something few men would admit.

Solomon learned that men actually were as emotional as women, in different ways about different things. He told one of his fraternity brothers, Tony, "No, don't get me wrong; I'm not talking about men crying over a movie or because you break up with a woman," he said. "I'm talking about women always say, 'Men are so un-emotional,' and I'm saying think about how we are when we get together to watch a football game at a sports bar. We're jumping up and down and giving high-fives, ready to throw stuff at the TV.

"That's emotion; more emotion than you see a woman having about something she's passionate about. So, the idea that we're just stale with no emotions or we're afraid to show emotions is crazy. It's really about show-ing our emotions about *them*. We just aren't as excited about them as we are about our sports teams.

"And if we are as excited about them, that's when we get into heated arguments over something that really shouldn't matter that much. But we care, so we engage in it. Our emotions with women don't come out in shedding tears. They come out in how we respond to some of their nonsense, but only if we care enough."

Solomon came to this way of thinking in the most ironic way. Because of the "domestic violence" arrest, he was entered into a diversion program to have the charges dropped and his record cleared. It required him to take twenty-four counseling classes that addressed a number of areas around dealing with relationships and emotions.

Since he was too embarrassed to tell anyone about his arrest, he only shared what he learned when an opportunity arose. By the time he pulled into his garage that night, it occurred to him that he needed to find a way to temper his emotions, which were running on inferno.

So he did something he rarely did. He pulled out a notepad and pen and started writing. Something about the ink oozing out of the instrument soothed him. He had rather neat penmanship, for a man, and liked to see his handwriting on paper.

There were so many thoughts careening off his brain, so many raw emotions that he spent more than two hours at his kitchen table writing. He started by venting about Michele and how disappointed he was that she had misjudged him after he opened up to her.

"It would be one thing," he wrote, "if I had shown her some indication of being physically abusive. It actually was a relief to tell somebody about what happened. I chose her as that person, and she totally blew it. The sad thing is that I regret being honest with her. That's not something I, or anyone, should ever feel; regret telling the truth. But if I had not, maybe I would not feel as I do about her and us.

"And how do I feel about her and us? I'm not sure.

That alone is not good. Just a few days ago I was as sure about her as I had ever been about a woman. And that made me sure about us. Now...I'm confused."

About Gerald, he wrote: "I can't be mad at him; he did what he had been allowed to do. But I think I got my point across. Still, I must admit that I'm a little afraid that he will go into a shell and not feel the same about me as he did.

"If that happens, I don't know what I'd do. It'd be devastating. But I also know he's a kid and he wants his dad around. And if I'm around, we'll get past this and become even closer.

"But will we ever be as close as he and his mom are? I'm not jealous, but I am envious that she got those seven years while I had no idea he even existed. In some things you can't make up seven years. With this, I believe I can. I will."

He also wrote about the other women in his life. "Before I talked to Evelyn, I never was straight up with a woman before. Not in that way, at least. I was upfront about what I didn't want in the relationship, but I was never upfront about what I wanted. And there's a big difference.

"I also never told a woman that there was someone else I wanted to be with. But when I think about it, that was never the case before now. What does it say about me that I never had a woman that I really felt the need to be committed to? I trusted none of them. Then I trust

Michele and she basically betrays me in a different way from the others. But it's still betrayal and I know me: I don't get over that easily."

On and on his writing went, some thoughtful, some the ranting of a hurt and confused man.

By four-thirty in the morning, Solomon's eyes got so heavy he could not read his own writing or recall what he was trying to convey. He knew then it was time to put the pen down and lie down. But the mission was successful: penning his thoughts and feelings cleansed him of the anger that engulfed his body.

He mustered the energy to move to the couch in the den, where he stretched out fully clothed, curled up with the remote control in his hand and a sofa cushion under his head and fell into a deep sleep.

The dreams he had that early morning were related to his plight. He dreamed that Gerald defied him again, and when he didn't whip his son, the kid turned to leave the house. Before he exited, he turned to Solomon and said, "Bye…punk."

He dreamed of skydiving with Michele—and the parachute was stuck. As they plummeted toward the earth, Solomon pulled out an umbrella and they floated down, Mary Poppins-style to the beach of some indentified island.

Finally, Solomon awoke in a sweat; Michele had moved from her house and taken Gerald with her. He was afraid at first and when he realized it was a dream, he became more determined. He sat up on the couch and turned down the volume on the flat-screen.

"She can think what she wants and do what she wants," he said aloud of Michele. "But I'm going to do the same thing."

Translation: He was going to be the father to Gerald and the man to Michele he believed he should be.

To himself, he thought: *If I can't be true to who I am, then who am I?*

The sun could not have come up soon enough. Solomon was eager to confront the people in his life who caused him the most grief. "That's how it is," he said to himself. "It's hardly strangers who weigh on you. It's the people you care about who are heavy."

By seven-thirty in the morning, he was fully dressed and ready to go to Michele's house. He was not sure what he would say or if he should even go. But he knew he had to do something; his son was likely confused about getting a whipping and his woman confused about who he was.

Clarity is what he sought. What he got was more confusion.

Solomon waited three hours before heading back to Michele's house. He killed time watching news reports of the popular Bishop Eddie Long's homosexual sex scandal with teenage boys.

"Can you believe this guy?" he said to Ray over the phone.

"You shouldn't judge until you know all the facts," Ray responded. "For all he has done, he deserves the benefit of the doubt."

On another day, they would have had a serious debate, as Solomon had a much stronger stance and would have gone through great measures to express it. But his mind was on his issues, not anyone else's. So he let Ray off with this: "We'll finish this later."

He considered calling Michele before leaving home, but shunned that notion. He went over there and rang the doorbell.

Michele answered.

"You here again?" she asked. "Solomon, not today. I really don't have anything to say to you right now."

"Well, just listen to me," he said. "Can I come in?"

Michele stepped aside and let in Solomon. "Where's Gerald? I really need to talk to him."

"Talk to him about what?"

"About what happened, why it happened and what respect is. I want him to understand all that."

"Well, seems to me all that should have been discussed last night. Talking after the fact is a little late to me."

"Well, that's where we again disagree," he answered. "But I didn't come here to argue or get you upset. I came here to get things right with all of us. Two days ago we were great. I mean, fantastic. Now, there's too much between us. Let's get it back to where it was, where it is supposed to be."

Michele gave Solomon a look he could not quite decipher. And before she could say anything the doorbell rang. Solomon was closer to the door. "Want me to get it?"

"No, I got it," Michele said in a way that seemed uncomfortable to Solomon.

"What's wrong?"

"Nothing," she said, hurrying past Solomon to the door. She opened it and in came Gerald.

"Hey, man, I came here this morning to talk to you. Where you been?" Solomon said to Gerald.

The kid just looked at him. Then he turned behind him to see his mom let in someone else, a man.

Solomon's heart dropped. Who was this and why was Gerald with him?

A sheath of awkwardness covered the room. No one said anything for a few seconds. Finally, Michele spoke up.

"Gerald, honey, go to your room," she said.

"Hold on, I need to talk to him," Solomon said.

"Okay, but he needs to go to his room first," Michele said, looking at Solomon. Then she turned to her son. "Go ahead. Stay there until your...he comes back there."

Gerald did as he was told, leaving the adults in the living room by the front door.

Before awkwardness could set in again, Michele introduced the men. "Solomon, this is Gary. Gary, this is Solomon."

The men exchanged a reluctant handshake, both of them wondering who the other was.

"Good to meet you, Salamander," Gary said.

"Salamander? My name is Solomon. You got that, Barry?"

"Oh, my fault. Sorry," Gary said. "Sometimes you don't hear correctly, just like you didn't hear that my name is Gary with a 'g,' like in God."

"I got it now," Solomon said. "A 'g,' like in girl?"

Gary's arrogant smile disappeared and the men stared at each other as if they were about to draw weapons in a gunfight.

"Okay," Michele said. "Solomon, you wanted to talk to Gerald; he's back there."

It was clear to him that she wanted Solomon to leave the room, which was the reason he stayed. "So, Larry...I mean, Gary, why are you here?"

"Solomon..." Michele said.

"It's all right, it's okay, Michele," Gary said. "I was thinking the same thing about you, Sebastian... Anyway, this is my wife. What's your excuse?"

Solomon took a step back and turned to Michele.

She looked into his eyes and saw confusion and disappointment.

"Ex-wife, Gary. Ex-wife," she said, never turning away from Solomon. Her eyes were sorrowful; she'd had every opportunity to share with Solomon her past married life with Gary, but had not.

"Yes, ex-wife," he said. "But we have that connection. What's your story, Sinbad? I mean, Solomon?"

He stared at Michele a few seconds longer, searching

for something to prevent him from being devastated. And as much of a concern was it that she did share that bit of personal information, it was *really* a problem that he was standing in her living room after being out with his son.

"That's interesting, Girlie...I mean, Gary," Solomon said, turning to the man who was sort of a lighter-skinned version of him: tall and fit with closely cropped hair. Gary's face was shaven clean with thick eyebrows.

"I'm going to leave you here to be with your wife," Solomon added. "I need to go speak to my son. That's my excuse."

"Solomon!" Michele called out as he turned away. He stopped and looked at her in a way that she gathered meant that she had better let him go. She said nothing. He turned and headed to Gerald's bedroom.

He could hear Gary say to Michele: "That's Gerald's father? Really?"

Solomon turned his focus to Gerald so quickly that he had pushed Michele and Gary to the back of his mind by the time he arrived at his son's bedroom door. It was halfway open.

Solomon opened it slowly and found Gerald sitting at his computer, playing a videogame. He heard the door open but did not turn to see who was entering his room.

The confidence Solomon wore like a tattoo was not evident. He was somewhat timid and definitely unsure how to approach his son. So, he started slowly.

"How you doing, son?"

"I'm fine, Coach Money," Gerald responded without looking up. Calling him "Coach Money" was a serious blow to Solomon. It disappointed him and made him angry, too. It had not been long since he was so proud his son called him "Daddy." This let him know Gerald was not like he was as a kid.

When his dad beat him, it was over the next day. Solomon would go on and his dad would go on as if it did not happen, although they both remembered it clearly. But that type of discipline was a part of the culture created in the home.

Solomon, while shaken, did not panic. "Gerald, come over here for a minute. I need to talk to you."

The child did as asked and moved from the desk to the bed, all the while refusing to look at his father.

"Son, look at me."

Gerald looked up. Seeing his eyes and the anger that radiated from them scared Solomon. Did his son hate him? Could he recover from this?

"You're mad at me, Gerald. I know you are," he said. "And I wish you weren't, but I understand how you feel. You know why? I was in your position before. My dad gave me whippings when I was a kid, too. I hated when he did, but he did it to teach me something, to make me a better person.

"See, when you're your age, you might think you know everything. But even for someone as smart as you, you don't know much at all. Not yet. A parent's job—my job—is to help you grow up and be smart and respectful and a good, successful person.

"To get there is a long and sometimes hard road. But everything that happens to you in life—everything, the good and the bad—is supposed to make you better and stronger.

"As your father, the way it should work is simple: If I tell you to do something, you do it. Period. That's how it works with children and their parents. You don't question it and you certainly don't tell me you're not going to do it.

"You understand? That's very wrong, Gerald; very wrong, and disrespectful. You always, always must show your father and mother respect because they're your parents, the people who take care of you and who love you the most.

"Now, I wasn't around when you were really young, and I'm really sorry about that. If I were, then you would've been taught this a long time ago. You know what? You're going to get in trouble again for something. That's what happens when you're a kid. But you should never get in trouble again for telling me 'no' or being disrespectful. Okay?"

Gerald nodded his head.

"Gerald, you understand?" Solomon reiterated.

"Yes," he said.

"Yes what?"

"Yes sir," his son responded.

"Thank you," Solomon said. "I know you're going to be mad at me for a while, and that's all right. But that's not going to make me not love you and be here for you. And I'll tell you a secret, between me and you."

Gerald raised his head to look at his dad.

"It really made me sad to give you that whipping. I really wanted to cry."

"You did? Why?" Gerald asked.

"I love you so much, son. You mean everything to me. There's a saying, a cliché, that my father told me the first time be beat me. He said, 'This is going to hurt me more than it's going to hurt you.' And I said to myself, 'Well, let me beat you instead of you beating me, if that's the case.'"

Gerald flashed his illuminating smile.

"But I never really understood what he meant until now," Solomon continued. "He was right. It did hurt me a lot. You might've felt the pain of the belt, but I felt pain in my heart. I don't want to hurt you, Gerald. Ever. You still might not understand this, but being a parent sometimes is a tough job. You have to do some tough things.

"Like I said, you're going to get into trouble again; that's what happens as you grow up. Will you get another beating? I won't say that it won't happen again. But I can tell you that it won't happen because you didn't make up your bed or lost your watch.

"It has to be something I believe is really serious. I won't like it. It'll hurt me a lot. But I have to do my job, and that's to raise you right so that you become a young man that your mom and I—and God—will be proud of."

He reached over and put his hand on Gerald's shoulder. Tears filled his eyes. "You're my son and I love you."

"I love you, too, Daddy," Gerald said, and the tears streamed down Solomon's face like confetti at Times Square on New Year's Eve.

Father and son hugged a long hug. Solomon wiped the tears from his face as they did.

Finally, they let go.

"I love you, son," Solomon said.

"I love you, too, Daddy," Gerald said.

CHAPTER 21
TEMPERATURE DROPS

Once again, Solomon's emotions ran amok. He was relieved and thrilled he was able to hold together his fledgling relationship with his son. But he was disappointed and shocked to discover that Michele had been married and did not tell him. Worse, why was her ex-husband at her house?

"You can go ahead and finish your videogame, Gerald," Solomon said. "But only for thirty minutes. That's all for the day, right?"

"Right," Gerald said, and they bumped fists.

Solomon then headed for the living room. He was ready to confront Michele and Gary. But when he got there, he found Michele sitting alone on the couch, staring straight ahead.

"So, where's your husband?"

"Solomon, I'm sorry."

Her feelings were crossed, too. She was upset with learning Solomon had smacked a woman, even if it was four years earlier. And she had not gotten over him beating Gerald. At the same time she was sorry about the way he learned she had been married. That emotion took over.

"Sorry for what?" he said. "For not telling me you have an ex-husband? Could that be it?"

Michele did not answer for a few seconds.

"Solomon, I'm sorry," she said, finally.

It hit Solomon just then; there was a reversal of power. With the revelation that Michele was married, she lost her edge. Solomon's issues were pushed aside. He had the upper hand. And Solomon being Solomon, he did not waste the position of strength he suddenly held.

"So what else haven't you told me? Seems like you're good at holding back important information. First Gerald, now I find out that you were married? Damn."

"It's not fair to put Gerald in there; you left me, remember?" Michele said.

"Oh, so you have no shame about your stuff? You hold back info—important stuff—and it's okay?"

"No, it's not. I'm sorry, Solomon. I should've told you."

"So why didn't you?"

"Where's Gerald?" Michele asked, looking toward the rear of the house.

"You can talk," Solomon said. "I told him that he could have thirty minutes playing a videogame…I'm listening."

"It was so long ago that I didn't feel like it was something I needed to share with you," Michele said. "It was a mistake. Gary and I were married for fourteen months. That was about four years ago. A different life ago."

"Really?" Solomon's anger was misplaced; he was more

concerned with making her feel guilty about how she judged him than he was about her not sharing important personal information.

"Do you recall me telling you the same thing about my situation with that woman?" he added. "That was four years ago, too? So, if I take the position you took with me, I'd think you were full of it."

Michele looked at him.

"But I'm not going to be like you," Solomon said. "I'm going to do like you should do when you learn something; listen and not judge."

"I appreciate that."

Solomon, who had been standing over her, took a seat on the couch with her.

"The reality was that I was searching for someone, a man, to be there for Gerald," she said. "I met Gary and I knew in my heart we weren't supposed to be together. But he was good to me and to Gerald. So when he asked me to marry him, I looked at Gerald and did it for him."

"Michele, you're a smart woman," Solomon said. "You have to know marrying for something other than love is a bad idea. Even I know that."

She did not respond.

"Here's the problem with women that I'll never understand," Solomon went on. "You hope and pray that someone who's not right for you will magically become right for you. You know it's a mismatch, but you convince yourself that you can change him, or that the things he falls short on are not that bad.

"You know how many times I've heard this same story? 'He didn't please me in bed, but I figured it would get better after we were married.' Or 'He liked to go out every weekend, but I thought that would change when we got married.' And on and on.

"If you're forcing it, it won't work; simple as that. And here's the thing: I've heard the same crap from women of all levels of education, success, backgrounds, whatever. And that tells me one thing: You are all the same."

"There's some truth to that," Michele conceded. "But my reasons for marrying him were different. I realized that he wasn't right for me, but it wasn't about me. It was about my son."

"That's all well and good," Solomon said. "That's honorable, like the guy who marries the pregnant girl because she had or is having his baby. I get it. I don't understand how a thinking person can fool himself into believing a marriage will work when you basically are in it for the wrong reasons. But still it happens; a lot.

"Any woman I ever met who was divorced told me that she was divorced. Why not you? We talked about our lives in the eight years we were apart. You never even mentioned the guy, or marriage."

"I can't even explain why I did that, other than the fact that I was embarrassed. I knew better. Literally, about a month into it, I was like, 'This is such a big mistake.' I tried, though. And as much as I wanted it to work for Gerald, for him to have a man around, it was totally not right for me.

"I woke up early one morning, around four. I couldn't take it anymore. There was nothing there. So I woke him up and I told him, 'Gary, I'm sorry, but this isn't working for me.'

"He wasn't even surprised. He could tell long before I said something. I give him credit; he accepted it better than I would have if the positions were reversed. He said, 'I realized this was coming one day.' Two days later, he was gone. It wasn't easy, though; I really did like him and I respected how he was with Gerald, who was so young that he didn't really notice that he wasn't living with us anymore.

"Anyway, I'm sorry I didn't tell you about all this. It's really a part of my life that I wanted to forget. My friends and my family said I did it because I was depressed. We didn't have a wedding. We went downtown and saw a judge and got it done. It all was very unromantic. No one came. No one supported it.

"When we got divorced, it was like I regained my family and friends. They were still there for me, but they knew I was someplace I shouldn't have been."

Try as he might, Solomon knew that had he not vanished on Michele, there wouldn't have been a need for Gary to try to fill the role of father figure. So, in a sense, he blamed himself for Michele's decision.

"I respect the fact that he was there for Gerald," Solomon said. "That says a lot about him. But why was he here this morning?"

"He calls every so often to check on us," Michele said.

"He asked if he could take us to breakfast this morning. I told him that I wasn't going but that he could take Gerald. They were just getting back when you arrived."

"So where is he now?" Solomon asked.

"He left. He got mad at me because I didn't tell him about you, that you were Gerald's dad," she said. "Of course, he knew the entire story of us. And I think, even though it's been four years, that he still held out hope that we could get back together.

"So, finding out about you, well, he just left."

"Michele, what are you doing here?" Solomon said. "You didn't tell me about him and you didn't tell him about me. What's that about?"

"I don't know," she said, and then proceeded to reveal why. "With him, I knew he was still interested in me and I didn't want to hurt his feelings. I—"

"You didn't want to hurt his feelings?" Solomon jumped in. "What sense does that make? If you are not interested in him—"

"I'm not," Michele interjected.

"Then don't you understand that not telling him about me, about us, is unfair to him. I'm not trying to look out for the guy, but the reality is if you were not telling him about me, you were, in essence, telling him that you had no one, that you were available. This is the kind of…crap I've dealt with in the past with women.

"You have me, but you still want to keep this other thing at a distance, but not too far. That's why I became as cold as I did. That's why I was able to get up that morning and leave you and not look back; I knew something like this would happen."

"Something like what, Solomon?"

"Something like we're all good, but there's this other person lingering in the shadows, this other interest. That's why I went cold; I don't have time for the deceit. And when I told you about how many times I was disappointed by women, that was an ideal time to tell me your little secret.

"But you didn't. All these months later, you continued to communicate with him, obviously, and yet not tell either of us anything."

The more he talked, the more angry and disappointed he grew. Solomon was on the other end of her decisions; the worst place to be for him.

"So what I am I supposed to think about you, Michele? What other secrets do you have?"

He asked the question but he already knew the answer. She had made him wary of her, with how she reacted to him telling her about his arrest. This latest revelation added to his inner tumult.

"What secrets do you have?" Michele fired back. Playing the victim was not working, so she got on the offense. "You didn't tell me about your arrest until I forced it out of you.

"And I know you have women who you've been seeing. You ain't been with me every night."

"Oh, that's your response to all that has gone down?" Solomon said. "Turn the tables and put it on me? Well, as I said, I could've lied about why I was arrested. I didn't. I didn't because I thought I could share things with you. You're the only person I ever told about that and you tripped on me like I'm some abuser.

"And, yeah, I was dating when I ran into you. But I told you that I was dating other women. I didn't hide it. I may have done you wrong—no, I did do you wrong— but I don't lie or hold back information. But know this: I saw one of them recently and told her that I was in love with you and that I had a son and that we were done. That's how you handle situations."

"Really? How many women were you dating? Who you think you are, some Romeo?" Michele asked. "And what about the others? What have you told them?"

"Listen, Michele," Solomon said, sitting back down on the couch. His voice was calm. "Don't take this the wrong way. I told you that I don't trust women. And the women I dealt with understood the limitations in our relationships, if you want to call them that. I'm telling the other three why they haven't seen and hardly heard from me in months. At least I was."

"Three, huh? What's that mean?" Michele sighed. "So you don't feel like we're together anymore so you can do whatever you want?"

"What is it that you want, Michele?" he answered. "Let's cut out all the back and forth and really talk here.

I'm trying right now. Usually, in the past, I would roll out. But I'm trying to do something different here."

"You jump all over me but never addressed beating Gerald or you smacking a woman. I—"

"I DID address it; right then. What's wrong with you? You don't remember that? And I spoke to Gerald and he and I are great. I told him that I don't want to whip him again, but that as a boy, he probably would get in trouble again. That's how it is. He was all right with that. So, there is no issue there as it relates to him."

"Oh, yes it is an issue; I don't want you hitting him."

"Well, I'm not going to tell you something untrue. I don't plan to or even want to beat Gerald. Why would I? But I'm not going to promise you it's not going to happen again. That's a part of teaching discipline."

"We'll never get past this; or you smacking that woman," Michele said.

"I see." Solomon was remarkably calm, considering she had just sealed their fate. "That's too bad, Michele. I've tried; more than I ever have. But these last forty-eight hours have been exhausting. You think you'll be fine without me because that's exactly as it is. I've been all I could be to you and that's not enough. So, fine."

He did not even wait for a response from Michele. He got up off the couch and called for Gerald. He came running out and Solomon hugged him.

"Hey, man, I'm going to leave now."

"Where you going, Daddy?" he asked.

"Gotta go home and do some things. Want to go with me?"

Gerald turned to Michele. "Mommy, can I, please?"

"You don't want to stay here with me?"

"I'm always here with you. Please, can I go?"

"What time will you be back?" she asked.

"Why don't you pack a bag, Gerald, and spend the night? We can go to the gym and then cook dinner together tonight and watch a movie," Solomon said. "And I have this golf videogame I play online; I want you to check it out."

"Okay," Gerald said, and ran off to his room.

In the three minutes or so it took Gerald to throw his things together, Solomon did not even look at Michele. He stood by the door, playing with his BlackBerry or staring off in another direction.

Michele looked at him and forced herself to not say anything. *If he wants to be without me,* she thought, *then he should be. I don't want someone who doesn't want me. In fact, he's walking out on me again. This time I'm wide awake. Fine. Go.*

Gerald came out and Solomon took his bag. "Bye, Mommy."

"I don't get a hug?" she asked.

As Gerald headed over to embrace his mom, Solomon headed out the door. And he did not look back.

CHAPTER 22
SENSELESS
& SENSIBILITIES

Michele realized that she had a big problem, one she did not know how to solve.

She did not trust her instincts.

In fact, she was not sure if she had any instincts anymore, which ultimately meant she had no trust. And that scared her. She thought, *What kind of female is devoid of a woman's intuition?*

She believed Solomon was a keeper six months into their first go-round, but then he vanished. She reluctantly moved on and believed Gary would be the elixir to her problems. A year or so later, they were divorced. And Solomon's second time around seemingly ended as he walked out the door.

Sensations ran through her body to stop him from leaving, to tell him she really loved him, that she respected how he had embraced fatherhood and that their reconnection meant they were destined to be together. Those were real feelings. But she did not trust that was the right thing to do.

So, Michele kept her mouth shut and let him walk. She was left home alone, with her thoughts, insecurities and uncertainties; not exactly a comforting place. In the past she found clarity in skydiving. But she was unmotivated to use the certificate Solomon got her. She actually was saving it so they could jump together.

"What's wrong with me?" she asked her cousin, Sonya, whom she called. She had to speak with someone. Sonya had returned from a trip and was in her car near Atlanta's Hartsfield-Jackson Airport, headed home.

"I don't know what's wrong but you'd better figure it out, girl," Sonya said sharply. It was a different tone from what Michele was used to hearing from her.

"What's wrong with you?" Michele asked.

"Nothing," Sonya explained. "Maybe I'm too close to you; I've seen what your life was like before Solomon. To me, Solomon has been great. He's been there for you and for Gerald. He's great with his son. He's a gentleman. I don't get him dating four women at once, but that's beside the point; sort of. The point is you're in love with him but too scared to see it through."

"What? That's not true. Why would you say that? You act like him smacking a woman and beating Gerald is not a real concern."

"They can be concerns, but enough for you to not be with him? Come on, cousin," Sonya said. "Life is too short. And good men are too hard to find."

"I can't be worried about finding a good man," Michele shot back. "That's not how I'm living my life."

"Yeah, I saw how you lived your life without a good

man and it was a wreck. You married a nice guy you had no chemistry with, Michele. You dated other losers and finally stopped dating altogether. That was a great life, right?"

"How you—" Michele started. But Sonya cut in.

"No, I'm not finished. I also saw how you've been the last seven, eight months with Solomon. So don't tell me it's not a difference because it is. If you want someone to comfort you and make you feel like you're doing the right thing, then call someone else. I love you and I can't let you think that it's all right to try to control the father on how he disciplines his son. If he was hanging him by his fingernails or pulling his hair out, I could understand. But a whipping? Please. We basically grew up together. You got your butt whipped all the time, bad as you were. So how you gonna act like that's some act of the devil now?"

Michele was taken aback by her cousin's words. She didn't expect she would be so blunt, so hurtful.

"Well, I guess you told me, huh?" Michele said. "I'm sorry, but I look at those two things differently."

"What two things?" Sonya asked.

"Smacking a woman and beating a child," she answered. "That's too much violence."

"You can't be serious," Sonya said. "Girl, I should call your momma. What's wrong with you? You've got to get a grip. Listen, I would never condone a man smacking a woman. It's plain wrong. But he didn't have to tell you,

Michele. So, the fact that he did admit to something he's embarrassed about should tell you something other than he's a potential abuser.

"He lost his temper and smacked her. It is a big deal, but, to me, it's a bigger deal that he trusted you enough to share that with you. You're focusing on the wrong thing, Michele. What about the fact that a man who has had all kinds of trouble trusting women trusted you enough to tell something so personal?

"And as for Gerald, here is a man stepping up to raise his son the old school way. Look at this new generation of kids and how out of control many of them are. Almost everything goes back to how you were raised. There are a lot of exceptions. Look at my brother. We were raised together, the same way, but he took a different path of drugs and crime. So, it happens.

"But you whip Gerald into shape now—no pun intended—and maybe he understands discipline and doing the right thing now so he doesn't go bad as he gets older."

"You have all the answers, right?" Michele asked. "You've been on Solomon's side from the moment I met him. It's so transparent. Maybe you should be with him. Maybe that's what you really want."

"You can kiss my ass, Michele," Sonya said, and hung up.

She was angry that her cousin's mind was so messed up she would go there on her. Sonya also was concerned because Michele had always been levelheaded and rational.

But this was a different time. Michele was afraid of herself, and it manifested itself in sabotaging her relationship. At least that's what Solomon surmised.

"That's what women do," Solomon said to one of his fraternity brothers, William, who lived in Detroit. Gerald was in Solomon's driveway playing basketball with some neighbors, giving Solomon a chance to reach out to some of his friends.

"I've seen it so many times when a woman can't believe or even think she deserves the happiness she has, so she consciously or otherwise gets in the way of it," Solomon went on. "It's like 'this is too good to be true so I'm gonna create some drama to test it.' So, in the end, they end up sabotaging their own good thing."

"Yeah, I've experienced that, too," William said. "What we've got to understand, as men, is that most women need drama in the relationship. They need it for the same reason you just said: They need to test it. Every few months or so my girl says, 'Let's have a relationship check.' And I'm like, 'Why?'"

"Everything would be going great. No real arguments, no nothing. Everything's fine. Then the 'relationship check' comes and we end up arguing. How stupid is that? Can we just live our lives without all the constant evaluations of everything we do or say—and even shit we *don't* do. It drives me crazy."

"Right," Solomon said. "It's that or I used to get all the time: 'So, what are we doing? What do I call this? Are we in a relationship? Am I your woman or just some-body you see from time-to-time?' And I'm like, 'Well, I'm not sure we have to put a label on it, do we? I mean, we've been getting to know each other and having a great time in the process. Labeling it isn't going to make it any better, is it?'

"What I really wanted to say was, 'Listen, we've known each other for three months. Next week I might not even like your ass, so let's ride this out and see what happens. Relationship? Just be glad I'm making time to see you.' "

They shared a long laugh, which made Solomon realize he had not laughed in that way in a few days. And that told him things were not right in his life because he loved to laugh, even at himself.

"So what you gonna do about Michele?" William asked. "You obviously like her; I never heard you talk about a woman as much as you have about her. I know all about her putting off a career as a lawyer to start a catering business, her son, skydiving, everything. So you like her; a lot.

"You're my boy so I can say this to you: There have not been a lot of times you have really, really been excited about a woman. There have been chicks you've liked and chicks you've halfway liked. But I'm thinking she's a keeper because, unless you lied to me, you haven't been seeing anyone else."

"No, I didn't lie about that. That's true," Solomon said.

"That says more than a little bit right there, boy."

"What does it say?" Solomon knew the answer, but he wanted to see if William knew it, too.

"It says you didn't want to mess it up with Michele," he answered. "It says she's important to you. And here's the deep part: You gave out that signal before you learned you had a son with her.

"I ain't no psychic or psychologist, but I recognize when a man who keeps women at arm's length suddenly has one wrapped in his arms; that means a whole lot."

All that feedback did nothing to influence Solomon or Michele to reverse their course. Rather, their stubbornness resulted in each of them experiencing loneliness and frustration and regret.

Solomon spent that first day with Gerald, which was great because not only did they reinforce their bond, but it also kept his mind occupied. By the time they were done shopping, playing basketball in the driveway, eating dinner and playing a golf videogame, little Gerald was exhausted.

He fell asleep on his favorite movie, *Remember The Titans*. Solomon let him sleep on the couch; Gerald considered that somewhat of an adventure since his mom forbade him from doing so. He also let him have a Pepsi, which Michele did not allow, and a Whopper from Burger King. He was doing all that out of spite for Michele.

With Gerald asleep, Solomon had no other distractions and had to face the reality of his choice. Just as he was beginning to contemplate how to resolve the matter with Michele, he received a text message on his phone.

He hoped it was Michele. Instead, it was Cheryl, one of the women he had been seeing before Michele. Worse, Cheryl being Cheryl, it not only was a text, but a photo, too.

"You don't miss this?" was the text below a photo of her from the waist down in a G-string.

"Damn," Solomon said, observing her shapely physique. He met Cheryl after a night of partying in Buckhead about eighteen months earlier. He and a friend, Paul, sought food at Waffle House on Piedmont around 3 a.m. to soak up some of the alcohol they consumed at Tongue & Groove.

Paul started talking to a woman, Millie, among a group of three at the table next to them. The discussion was playful and lively. Solomon and Cheryl just observed and laughed. When the ladies were leaving, Cheryl said to Millie, "You need to give him your number. I've never seen a man who has time enough for you. But he does."

Millie said, "Well, you need to give your number to him," pointing to Solomon. Cheryl was more interested in getting her friend connected with Paul than she was in Solomon, but she gave up her phone number to get Millie to give up hers.

Solomon was insulted that Cheryl seemed unexcited about meeting him, which made him determined to turn around her feelings. So, he called her a few days later. They went out on several dates, and he could see how intrigued Cheryl grew. Still, he never made an attempt to so much as kiss her.

Finally, after about six weeks of dates that ended with him dropping her off, Cheryl had enough.

"Why won't you at least kiss me?" she asked.

"I didn't know you wanted me to," he said. "I can recall when we met that night, you didn't even want to give me your number. Your friend basically had to bargain for you to give it to me. So, I didn't think you were interested."

"What?" Cheryl said. "If I didn't want you to have my number, you wouldn't have gotten it. You've been thinking that all this time?"

Solomon did not answer her; not with words. He leaned over and kissed her deeply, and their adventurous sex life began. At the movies, in the parking lot, in the restaurant bathroom were just a few of the places Solomon and Cheryl expressed their sexual appetites.

So, he was hardly surprised to see a provocative photo from her.

He sent her a text message back that read: "Nice body. Who is this?"

"Don't be funny," she wrote back.

"No doubt. And I do miss it and u. But..." Solomon answered.

"But what?"

"But things have been different with me."

"Wanna talk about it?" she wrote.

Solomon made sure Gerald was nice and comfortable on the couch before he went upstairs and closed the door to his room. Then he called Cheryl.

"Wow, an actual phone call from Mr. Singletary. I can't believe it," she said upon answering. "You've been a ghost."

"I'm sorry, Cheryl. Nothing personal. Just a lot going on that I've had to deal with."

"I figured as much, since you couldn't even make time for me." She paused. "What's going on? A woman, right?"

"What else?"

"See, that's where you messed up," she said. "I'm not here to cause you any drama. I'm like you; let's just keep it moving. I could've made you feel better when she was making you feel bad."

That was Cheryl; always on the ready, never hung up about anything. Shortly after they met, Solomon told her he did not want a "relationship." She responded: "Who said I did? Relationships mean drama to me, and I don't want any of it. So let's just enjoy each other when we can. Deal?"

That deal was too good to be true, but Cheryl never gave Solomon any grief, only pleasure. She was five-foot-seven with a lean, strong body. No breasts to speak of, but hips and ass that looked to be child-bearing. Her innocent, slightly freckled face belied her freaky nature.

"So what's the problem with the woman?" she inquired.

It was such a good question that Solomon did not know how to answer. Then it came to him.

"I love her. That's the problem."

"Damn, that IS a problem," Cheryl said. "You're not the 'I love her' type. I know men. I've dealt with all kinds. You're the 'I love her and leave her' type. That's you.

"For you to say that is a big thing, Solomon. You don't know how to handle being in love, do you? It's not easy because human nature makes it that she will piss you off or disappoint you. Then what do you do?"

"Exactly," he said. "My instincts are to just say 'to hell with it.' But another part of me is against that. And I've never had two parts of me pulling against each other. It was always the whole me saying, 'I'm gone.'"

"Why don't you let me come over and take your mind off all this?" Cheryl was not serious; it was a test to see if Solomon really was about Michele.

"You know there was a time when I would've been all over that offer," Solomon said. "But, while I know physically that would make me feel great, inside it wouldn't be right. I'm pissed off at her right now, but I still can't go outside the relationship."

"If I were an egomaniac, I would be hurt," Cheryl said. "But I'm very confident in myself; and I'm proud of you. I wasn't serious about coming over there. I was seeing if you really, really were in love. Some men, whether in love or not, would still jump at the chance to get something extra.

"But you, Solomon, you've always been straight up. So, I knew if you were straight up with me before, you would be straight up with her. That's why I've barely heard from you; you've been building this relationship. Last thing you need is to be frolicking around—emphasis on licking—with me. We did some wild stuff, but they're merely good memories now.

"I wish you the best."

"Cheryl, you surprise me," Solomon said. "I wouldn't have expected you to be so…understanding and helpful. You're a good person. I just…in this case…thought you'd—"

"You thought I'd be upset that you told me you didn't want to be tied down, but now you're tied down? It's hard for me to be selfish when a man tells me that he's in love. I respect that and I wish you the best… If it doesn't work out, you know who to call."

"Before we go, I have something else to tell you about this situation," Solomon said. "I have a son. She—Michele—is the mother of my son."

He went on to explain the circumstances of how he learned of Gerald and how they developed a bond.

"I hope you don't think I'm some sort of kook, and I don't even know the woman, but you and her were destined to be together," Cheryl said. "Think about your history with her. There's something in me that tells me you and her will be all right. You have a family, Solomon."

"I can't go that far," he said. "We have a son together and some issues in a relationship. Other than that, I cannot say."

"I've got to go, Solomon, but let me ask you this one question: Do you want more? Answer that question and you can tell—and determine—your future."

No one asked Michele her thoughts on what she wanted with Solomon, but she had an answer: Everything.

Her cousin was right; her life had been far less than what she desired. She encountered men who lacked integrity, manners, depth…meaning they lacked overall appeal. Solomon, even with his borderline arrogance, still managed to be humble and chivalrous and thoughtful and passionate.

That last trait covered her like a rash that first night he left with Gerald. Suddenly, it came down on her, even amid her disappointment and confusion about him and their relationship, even after Sonya hung up on her in fury.

Michele lay in bed in total darkness and in heat. Her body craved his touch. She needed to feel his body, to smell his cologne, to hear his moans. All this was a first. A man had seldom pleased her to where the thought of him caused her the wetness she experienced that night.

It got worse as she could not stop her brain from revisiting their most recent encounter a few nights before. They went out to dinner at One Midtown Kitchen, near Piedmont Park. It was a slow Sunday night, and they posted up at the empty bar for cocktails and dinner and more cocktails.

That same sensation she had was over her at the bar. She asked Solomon to move his barstool closer to her, which he did. She leaned over and kissed him on his face, and he smiled, turned his head and kissed her on the lips.

"You're sexy," he said.

"I feel sexy," she said. "And horny."

"Really?" Solomon responded. He reached over and began rubbing her thighs. She pulled up her skirt so she could feel his hands on her skin. The more he rubbed, the higher she pulled her skirt up, until he had his hand deep between her legs. She wore no panties.

He could feel the heat coming from her insides. "You *are* horny, aren't you?"

Solomon turned from Michele to see where the bartender was; she was at the other end of the bar talking to a co-worker. The few people in the restaurant had no clear visual of them. So, Solomon eased his hands closer to the heat, and Michele spread her legs, inviting him to enter her with his finger.

He did, and the warm moisture in her covered his middle finger like lava. He slid his finger in deeper, rotating it, and Michele momentarily forgot where she was and threw her head back.

"Oh, God," she said.

She composed herself, but they were so lost in their pleasure moment that they did not see the bartender walk down to check on them. Before he could pull out, she was standing there, so he kept his finger in her and they acted, as best they could, as if everything was perfectly normal.

"No, we're fine right now," Solomon said to her.

"Maybe in a few minutes we'll have another drink," Michele managed to get out.

"Okay," the woman answered. "I'll check on you shortly." She went back to the end of the bar. And they went back to what they were doing. Finally, the awkward position caused Solomon's arm to ache, so he dislodged his finger from her hotness.

"Oh, my God," Michele said. "I need some water."

"You need to meet me in the bathroom."

"What?"

"They have individual bathrooms here. We can go in there. I can't wait to get home; I need to feel you now."

Michele did not offer any resistance. The suggestion actually excited her. They finished their drinks and some appetizers and paid the bill. Then they walked around the wall on the opposite side of the dining room to the bathroom.

"I'm going in first," Michele said. "Then I'll call you to come join me."

Solomon took a seat in the small waiting area; a minute later, he heard his name.

He entered the bathroom and locked the door behind

him. Michele leaned on the counter and pulled up her skirt, exposing her round ass. Solomon dropped his pants swiftly and pulled out what Michele affectionately called his pulsating "injection stick."

He slowly injected Michele, and her moans grew louder the deeper he got. She bounced back and forth, taking as much as she could, and he countered by thrusting forward to the same rhythm. They watched each other in the mirror making love and at one point laughed at the faces such pleasure produced.

She bent over lower, to receive more of him, and he widened his stance to get deeper. They were trying to be as quiet as possible, but Solomon could not resist the urge to smack Michele on her ass, which she loved.

After nearly ten minutes of nonstop stroking, Solomon was dripping in sweat—and ecstasy—and climaxed with a force that pushed Michele almost into the sink. Still, he continued to stroke her, even as his legs weakened.

"You're crazy," she said as they cleaned up. "Look at what you have me doing. I'm going to tell my momma."

They laughed.

"Tell your daddy," Solomon said. "I'm sure he'll be glad to hear about this."

They laughed some more. Solomon fixed his clothes and peeked out of the bathroom to make sure no one was there. Michele came out a few minutes later and they walked out of the restaurant into the warm night air, feeling exhilarated.

That recollection caused Michele a restless night. Not

only because it was so on fire, but also because it forced her to think about a man in ways she had not. She had told her book club members about how good, consistent sex had changed her life.

She wondered in the darkness if she could go back to living without it. And that fed right into her lack of confidence about her instincts. Was it shallow to build a relationship around amazing sex? Was she even doing that?

Michele had always thought of sex as a natural part of a relationship, not a necessity, which spoke to something significant: no one had ever really pleased her in bed. So, other things mattered more: financial security; honesty; ambition. But she made the hard admission to herself that if the sex was not banging, she'd be tempted to search for the bang.

I can't even believe I'm saying this, even if it is to myself, she thought. Then she thought, *If I can't be honest with myself, then who can I?*

The answer was her cousin, Sonya. That was another reason she was restless. Although it was nearly two in the morning, she called Sonya, who was more like a sister. Having her upset was something that did not digest well for Michele.

In a sleepy voice, Sonya answered her phone saying, "What's wrong?"

"I'm sorry, cousin," Michele said. "I know you love me and are looking out for me. I really didn't mean to offend you. Also, I'm not kissing your ass."

Sonya could not help but laugh.

"What are you doing up, girl? What time is it?"

"I'm tormented. Solomon is tormenting me," Michele said.

"How? What's he doing? He's there?" Sonya asked.

"No, he's home with Gerald," she answered. "But he's also here with me, in my bed; if you know what I mean."

Sonya was puzzled for a moment. "Oh... OH!!" she said finally. "Okay, I get it."

"I need it, Sonya," she said. "This isn't the first time in my life that I've been horny. But since I've been with him, it's the first time I specifically wanted a particular man. Before, it was just that I would like to have been touched and seduced by a man. Or maybe Denzel, but he doesn't count. With Solomon, I have these experiences I can draw from that are driving me crazy."

"Why don't you call the man?" Sonya suggested. "Simple solution."

"I know," Michele said. "But I can't do that. Not right now. Maybe I'm delaying the inevitable, but I'm not sure how I feel about all this stuff that has taken place.

"He's mad at me. I didn't tell him I was once married and he said I think he's an abuser. I'm mad at him because he beat my son, first and foremost, and he smacked this woman.

"He's not giving in and I'm not giving in. So I don't know where that leaves us."

Where that left her was home alone; a lot. Solomon was just as stubborn and just as adamant about his position. So, even though he missed Michele, he refused to call her or have any contact with her.

He put Gerald in the middle of communication with Michele, having his son tell his mom when his dad would pick him up from school and spend time with him on weekends. Their bond grew despite Solomon's absence from Michele's life.

The kid was too young to notice that his parents had not been in the same room together for nearly a month.

Every day, they both hoped the other one would crack; give in and make a phone call or send a text that would restart their relationship. But they were equally yoked when it came to stubbornness.

Solomon surprised himself; he did not go on a woman-chasing spree. Rather, he worked, played golf, spent time with Gerald and generally made himself available should Michele call him.

"Mexican standoff," he told one of his college friends, Kenny, who visited for a weekend from Charlotte.

"While you're standing off, you don't have to stand still, playa," he said to Solomon. "I ain't come here to listen to you moan about your girl. I came here to get in the mix, see what I can come up with. So, where the hell we going?"

It was a Friday night, so there were plenty of options. Solomon decided on The Lobby Bar at the 12 Hotel at Atlantic Station. It was a lively spot with a live band and a vast collection of fine women.

"This is what I'm talking about," Kenny said, heading

to the bar while observing all the beautiful available female talent. By the time Solomon returned from the bathroom, Kenny was holding court with four women. That was his way. He was shorter than six feet and plump, good-looking but not striking. He had a personality that drew people in. He was loud and inviting. You would either appreciate it or be offended by it. Kenny hardly cared, either way.

"Hey, you lucky I'm hanging out with you," he said to Solomon as they girl-watched. "I usually don't hang with tall, good-looking guys. What I need competition for?"

Solomon laughed. "You know you're stupid, right?"

"I'm just saying," Kenny added. "I'm short, going bald and fat. Just like big girls need love, so do guys like me."

One of four ladies he chatted up earlier waved for Kenny to come over to their table to the left of the bar and up against the floor-to-ceiling window. She did not have to wave twice.

"I love the A-T-L," Kenny said to Solomon. "I don't know how you live here, talking about you have a girl-friend. Gimme a break… Come on."

Kenny quickly headed over with Solomon reluctantly in tow. The woman thanked Kenny for the cocktail he paid for and he introduced Solomon to the gang. Solomon instantly caught the attention of one of the women—Wanda.

"What's your name again?" she inquired. "Solomon?"

Before he could answer, Wanda said, "King Solomon;

that's a character from an August Wilson play, 'The Gem of the Ocean.' Did you know that?"

"I know it's from The Bible," Solomon said. "I know that first. But as a matter of fact, I actually saw the play. The character was mostly called 'Solly Two Kings.'"

Wanda looked Solomon up and down. She thought: *A man who not only went to the theater, but he also appreciated the play enough to have paid attention.*

"Where's your drink?" she asked.

The women had made room for Kenny, who took an unoccupied chair from another table to sit at their table.

Clearly, the drinks had loosened Wanda's tongue.

"I don't see a wedding ring," she said to Solomon. "Does that mean you're single or just not wearing your ring?"

"Not married," he said, "but not single."

He surprised himself with that response. He had not talked to Michele in a month, but did not identify himself as available to an attractive woman who clearly had an interest in him.

Wanda, meanwhile, whose shiny lipgloss accentuated her lips to where they looked quite kissable, seemed to ignore Solomon's answer. Her complexion was just about the same as Michele's and she appeared to tote a desirable body from where she sat. For sure, her legs that stretched to the side of the table in front of her were long and shapely.

Solomon told himself to enjoy the moment, the adulation. A good-looking woman had interest. *Embrace it*, he thought.

And he tried. He offered a toast: "To new acquaintances."

They tapped glasses. "Yes," Wanda said. "I was going to go over to the Lowes tonight. My girls said it would be better here. They were right."

"So your man gave you a pass for tonight to hang with your girls?" Solomon asked.

"My husband doesn't give me passes," she said. "I'm grown and I can go where I please. I'm not disrespectful at all. But we all need a break from time-to-time."

"Husband? Is that what you said?"

Wanda nodded her head.

And therein was the problem that he had had with women all his life. Trust.

"So, your husband is all right with you having drinks with another man?" Solomon asked. "That can't be true."

"No, he probably wouldn't approve of it," Wanda said. "But I'm not going to tell. Are you?"

Solomon smiled, shook his head and took a sip of his drink.

"I don't get it," he said. He slid his chair closer and leaned in close to her ear. "Every day, women talk about how much men are dogs and can't be trusted. Every woman I know has the same thoughts about men. But what about you? What about women?

"No offense, but you're married and you're out here meeting men. I know I'm not the first one. So—"

"What are you calling me?"

"No, I'm not calling you anything. I'm not," Solomon said. "What I am saying is that women get really adamant about the shortcomings of men, but I don't ever hear them talking about how women are equally unfaithful."

"You can't seriously try to compare men to women?"

"I am, definitely," Solomon said. "Listen, who are men cheating with? Women. Most of the time they do so understanding the man already has someone else. I've been approached by or even had, uh, experiences with married women or women in relationships.

"The difference is that men might be more careless or even brag about their extra activities and some women won't tell anyone. Some will take it to their graves because they don't want their girl to think they're a slut."

"You calling me a slut," Wanda asked, and she was not joking.

Solomon leaned back. "What? No!"

"That's what it sounds like to me," she said, her voice rising so much that it caught Kenny's attention.

"Yo, what's up?" he said from across the table.

"Your boy is tripping, that's what's up," Wanda said.

Her girls then wanted to know what the problem was.

"The problem is the truth hurts," Solomon said, standing up. "All I did was speak the truth."

The four women started yelling mostly indecipherably at Solomon. Kenny controlled them. "Hey, wait, wait," he said. "Ladies, let's all calm down. We got more drinks coming. It's all good."

Then he grabbed Solomon by the arm and pulled him away from the table. "What's up, man? That honey is all over you. What did you say to her?"

"I told her she's a trick, like all women," Solomon said.

"What?" Kenny said.

"Man, I'm gone. That chick is married, out here flirting with me."

"And you're complaining? That's the best kind; a married chick. That means she only wants one thing: sex. You can't be mad about that."

"I'm just not dealing with it. I don't know; maybe I've actually grown up some. I'm tired of the chicks I don't have any connection to. I—"

"You want Michele. That's the deal, boy," Kenny said. "Hey, whatever works for you. But in the meantime, don't blow it for me. I've got two nights in Atlanta. This girl over there is about to make them great nights. But you can't be calling her friend a trick."

"Kenny, I'm gone. You can handle that crew without me," Solomon said. "Here's the ticket to the car. Call me when you're done. I'll take a cab over to the Lowes and chill there."

"Yo, don't go," he said. "Apologize to that chick and keep it moving. No need to leave."

"I'm not apologizing to her," he said. "I'll hang over here at the bar. Go ahead and close that deal."

"Nah, it's cool," Kenny said. "I got her number already. I'm just gonna say bye."

"You don't have to do that," Solomon said.

"Dog, we're together. If you're gone, I'm gone," he said.

Solomon went back to the bar as Kenny said his goodbyes. Solomon turned back toward Wanda, who had risen from her seat and walked toward him. He could not turn away from her; she was even more striking standing up. Elegant.

"Solomon," she said, extending her hand, "I'm sorry for getting out of hand. Sometimes a couple of drinks make me emotional. I just want you to know that I understand your point. And, yes, I'm married, but it's really not about being out here trying to find a man. It's been three years and we just don't have much going for us. Actually, it's really sad; I love him and I want us to work. But if he can't be home on the weekends, I need to do something other than sit around and wait on him.

"We all need attention and affection. So, sometimes I seek it from other men. But it hasn't gone beyond that; yet."

"Wanda, you don't have to explain anything to me," Solomon said. "I appreciate you sharing, but that's a situation you and your husband have to get right on. If you don't, what are you going to do? Continue to go out with your girls until you take that ultimate step? That's not a good look."

Kenny came over just then. "I'm ready, dog."

"I'm glad we met," Solomon said to Wanda. "Good luck."

"Wait," she said, digging into her purse that looked more like luxurious luggage. "Here's my card. You should call me. Maybe you can help me; one way or another."

All that and she still flirted with Solomon. "Thanks. I will reach out," he said, smiling.

When he and Kenny got into the car, his friend offered some advice.

"You know me; I'm the anti-relationship guy," Kenny said. "I don't even believe in relationships, so you know how I feel about marriage. But that's me. I know how you are; or how you were. The old Solomon would've scooped up that honey without hesitation.

"But this girl, Michele, she's got something on you, boy. I don't know what it is. I can't relate to it. I don't *want* to relate to it. But you need to get over yourself and get back with her. That's all I will say about it. You're my boy, so I can be frank. It's dumb to let her go when you don't want to; or have to."

Solomon looked straight ahead and offered no retort, other than, "I hear you."

They went on to the bar at the Lowes for an hour or so and then on to Atlanta's premier after-hours spot, Café Intermezzo, where Solomon liked to go for strong latte and tasty desserts.

"We don't have any place like this in Charlotte," Kenny said.

Solomon did not respond.

"Yo, what's up with you?"

"I don't know, man," he said. "I don't want to move

on from this girl, Michele, but I realize I have to. Too much drama."

"Well, you know me," Kenny said. "I don't do drama. But, to be honest and fair, some of the things you really want are the hardest to get. You've just got to put in the work."

"Yeah, but I don't want to do the work," Solomon said. "It shouldn't be that much work required if it is right."

"Man, you living in dream land," Kenny said. "You've got to work for what you want. If you don't want to do the work, then you don't really want it. Plus, I saw you tonight fail to close the deal on a fine honey. Never seen that before. That tells me something."

"What?"

"Tells me you don't know what you want."

CHAPTER 24
THE TRUTH
IS IN THE WINE

Solomon's dream about dancing with Michele was interrupted by the chiming of his cell phone. He was disoriented for a second. Finally, he answered it.

"Son, how's it going?" his dad said on the other end.

"Oh, hey, Pops. I'm good… What time is it?"

"It's a quarter to seven. You can't still be in bed. I thought you'd be up getting ready for work."

"Yeah, I will be; in fifteen minutes. I get up around seven… Everything all right?"

"Everything's good, actually," he said. "I wanted to tell you that I had dinner with your mother last night and—"

"Hold up. You had dinner with Ma?" Solomon said. "How did that happen? *Why* did that happen?"

"She called me and it turned out we were thinking the same thing," Mr. Singletary said.

"What was that?" the son asked.

"That we haven't seen our grandson yet," the father answered. "So, we met for dinner downtown and—"

"Wait," Solomon interrupted. "Downtown D.C.? Both of you hate to go downtown. I couldn't get you to go to a play with me in the city. But now you're meeting for dinner in D.C.? What's going on?"

"Nothing's *going on*," Mr. Singletary said. "We've been divorced for sixteen years. But we're still cordial."

"Since when?" Solomon said. "I didn't know you even talked."

"Well, we do…sometimes," he said. "Anyway, I called because we're coming to Atlanta in about four weeks to visit you and meet our grandson. It's time he meets us and we meet him."

"Ah, man, that's great. I've been telling him about you all and showing him photos," Solomon said, sitting up in the bed. "That's good stuff."

As his father continued, Solomon's attention was distracted. To his left, through his peripheral vision, he could see his sheets move. When he turned his head, he was shocked to see Marie, one of his old *reliables* he "dated" occasionally, stretching out.

"What the?" Solomon was confused.

"Hello," Mr. Singletary said into the phone.

"Hey, uh, Dad, can I, uh, can I, uh, call you back?"

"Yeah, sure. Everything okay?"

"I'm not sure, but I'll call you back in a few minutes."

Solomon made sure his phone call had ended before he addressed Marie.

"Marie, what's going on? What are you doing here?"

"Huh?" she responded. "You were drunk, yes, but you couldn't have been that drunk."

"What are you talking about?"

"You don't remember that I came over here last night, around midnight? You answered the door with a drink in your hand."

"What the hell? So, what happened?"

"Damn, nigga, you don't remember?" That was Marie's way; she was from Columbus, Ohio. Beautiful. Smart. Real.

Solomon placed his hands in his head.

"You got mad at me for coming over unannounced. You wouldn't even let me in."

"Good. You shouldn't come over here unless you're invited."

"Nigga, I came over here out of concern," she said. "Now, I'm a lady but you about to make me go somewhere with you I don't want to go. But I *can* go there."

"Where you need to go is home," Solomon said. "I can 'go there,' too, and you don't want to see it. Trust me."

"I'm trying to help your ass; that's why I didn't leave," Marie said.

"How did you get in the house if I kept you from coming in?" Solomon wanted to know.

"I just walked in…"

"You…how?"

"Boy, you were messed up," she said. "You were all indignant with me, kept me from coming in and told me to call you if I wanted to come over. Then you closed the door in my face.

"I stood there in shock for a few seconds. I came over because I hadn't heard from you in months and I was concerned. Then I see you and you're all bent, pissy drunk. So, anyway, you closed the door and I could see you through the side panel walking toward the kitchen.

"You were more like stumbling. I knocked on the door and it opened; you hadn't closed it all the way. So I came in. You got mad again at me; said you were going to have me arrested for breaking and entering.

"I can't believe you don't remember any of this."

"I sort of remember you being here; I made you a drink, right?"

"And you made yourself another one, too. I was like, 'Can we just sit down and talk?' You battled me on everything I said. I guess you're just an ornery drunk, huh? Anyway, you actually made me a good margarita. And you finished yours before I could even finish a fourth of mine.

"I asked you why you were so drunk and you went off."

"Ah, man. What did I say?" Solomon asked.

"What *didn't* you say?" Marie answered. "You were like, 'I'm a grown-ass man in my own house; you can't tell me what to do, whether I should drink or not. You have some nerve. You shouldn't even be here.'

"Then you called me 'Michele.' I said, 'Your ass might be drunk, but don't be calling me some other woman's name.'

"You said, 'I didn't call you Michele. I ain't thinking about that girl.' That told me you were thinking about her. And it wasn't hard to get to the bottom of why you went on a binge."

Solomon said, "Well, I remember coming home from work and feeling like I was going to stay in and get smashed. I can't remember ever really feeling like that.

"I didn't even eat. I stopped at Publix, picked up some limes and orange juice and came home and made it happen. I was watching *Law & Order*, I think. Seems like I fell asleep until you rang my doorbell."

"Well," Marie said, "you woke up in rare form. Just acting a fool. But when I got you to sit down and act like you had some sense, you told me a whole bunch of stuff."

"Like what?"

"Like you're in love with this Michele person," Marie began. "You didn't say the words, but it was what you didn't say, and what you said about me, which was not shocking but definitely a surprise.

"You told me that you were going to call to set up a meeting with me because you wanted to tell me face-to-face that you wouldn't see me anymore. You said you cared about me and appreciated me, but that you were trying to do something you hadn't really done before, which was be committed to one woman.

"Then you told me that you had trust issues about her because she didn't tell you she was married and that she wanted to control how you disciplined your son. Of course, I was stunned to hear you had a son. So you explained how you found that out and your history with, uh, Michele.

"You asked me what I thought and I told you that I sort of held out hope that we could really be a couple because I thought we got along great. I also told you I knew you were afraid of commitment; I just didn't know why. And then you told me about how girls disappointed you and basically made you the way you are—or were.

"You talked and talked. What I got from all of it, though, was that you really do want something with this woman. And I know that because in one breath you're telling me you can't see me. Then you immediately told me you weren't with her anymore because you had some problems. So if you're not with her, why wouldn't you want to see me?"

"What did I say to that?"

"You didn't say a damn thing," she said. "What you did was get up and stumble to the bathroom and throw up."

"Ah, come on. You're lying," Solomon said.

"Go in your bathroom and see for yourself," Marie said. "I was going to clean it up. Then I said, 'He ain't my man.' So, it's waiting for you; or Michele."

"Very funny," Solomon said and he slowly made his way off the bed. His legs were shaky and his head was pounding. His body was wrecked. "I feel like I got run over by a truck; then it backed up and ran over me again."

He got to the bathroom door and the odor and sight of his own vomit nearly made him hurl again. Marie could not watch him struggle, so she came over and helped him back to the bed.

"This is a first," she said. "I've never taken a man to bed so he could rest."

"Marie, I'm not drunk anymore, so believe me when I tell you that I'm glad you're my friend," he said when he got back to the bed. He pulled himself under the covers and clutched a pillow across his chest.

"I'm sorry about last night and I'm really sorry about never giving us a chance. As I told you last night, even though I don't remember saying it, I decided a while ago to deal with women from an emotional distance. It's a cold way to be, but it protected me from being…you know…"

"Hurt? Heartbroken?" Marie interjected. "You can say it, you know? Men. Always trying to hang on to that one last raggedy piece of manhood."

Solomon laughed. "You know what I mean. The point is that I respect and appreciate you and the friendship we have."

"Thanks for saying that," she said. "You actually are really good when you're sloppy drunk because you said something very similar to that last night. But I appreciate it more now since you seem to be aware of what you're saying.

"And since it seems like you're going to survive your alcohol poisoning, I want to say one thing before I leave: Many times a man's downfall is his pride. You told me, in so many words, that you loved that woman and you knew she loved you. So, what is the point of not being together? To prove you didn't give in first? That's really not cute or macho. It's dumb."

Solomon heard Marie, even agreed with her, but pride and principles overruled him. His pride, combined with his issues, made it a certainty he would not contact Michele.

He missed her. He wanted her back. He even, in a flash moment of truthfulness, admitted he needed her; he had no desires for anyone else. But his principles would only embrace her if she made all the concessions. She had to dismiss the notion of usurping his authority on how he disciplined his son. And she had to apologize for thinking he was a chronic abuser.

That same morning, Michele was less contemplative. She went on a date. A fellow caterer, Joseph Dancer, had been eyeing her for some time. They had met at Taste of Atlanta, and had stayed in touch on occasion via phone and e-mail.

Joseph's most recent contact included inviting her to a friend's 40th birthday party in Southwest Atlanta. His phone call came soon after Michele awoke that morning, feeling particularly grim about her prospects with Solomon. She, in fact, was mad at him.

She thought: *How could he go nearly six weeks without talking to me? He left me again, only this time he didn't sneak off. He just walked away. How could he be such an Ice Man? Didn't we really have something? He must not have loved me at all. And when is he going to disappear on Gerald?*

That last thought made her angry. He hadn't given any indication he would discard his son; he had been actually remarkable with him. But he was remarkably cold toward her, which left her feeling like he could dismiss them both at his whim.

While making breakfast with those thoughts swirling around her head, Joseph called. He had known Michele for more than a year and finally worked up the audacity to ask her out.

"Sure," she answered him. "Why not?"

"Why would you do that?" Sonya said that afternoon, when Michele told her of her plans.

"Because I can't sit around and wait on a man who might not ever come back."

"But you love Solomon and you don't have any interest in this other man. It's not fair to him."

"He's a nice guy," Michele said.

"Wow, really? That's ninety-nine percent of the men in the world. If that's the first and best thing you can say about him, then that tells you something."

"I've known him a long time, but I don't really know that much about him," Michele said. "So I'm going to find out if there's something more I like about him. What's wrong with that?"

Sonya did not answer. She knew her cousin—if her mind was made up, it was not to be altered.

"I'll pick up Gerald at about six," she said.

And at precisely seven o'clock, Joseph rang Michele's doorbell. It was if he was standing at her front door waiting for the hand to move to the twelve.

"Wow," Michele said. "Talk about being prompt."

She was ready, too. He came inside for a few moments and off they went to the party. But Solomon was all over her. First of all, she had heard of the restaurant before, but remembered when Joseph got there that Solomon had placed it on their list of spots to visit.

Then she measured everything about Joseph against Solomon. His looks: He was a subtly good-looking man. No really distinctive features, but he dressed neatly and carried himself with a self-assuredness that was attractive. He had the complexion of Terrence Howard with a slim frame.

His height: he was not as tall as Solomon and about equal to her in heels. His cologne: It was not flagrant; but not the intoxicating Cartier or John Varvatos Vintage of Solomon. His manners: He walked out of the house before her and only came over to open her door after she stood there waiting for him to do so.

Still, determined to have a good time, she tried to put Solomon out of her head and initiated a mindless conversation about the weather in Atlanta versus the weather in Texas, where he was from.

They arrived hungry at Marc and Deilah's beautifully decorated contemporary home off of Cascade. Joseph said he had been cooking all day and Michele's thoughts of Solomon ate at her appetite.

When they entered the house, Joseph morphed into a gregarious, life-of-the-party sort, which was opposite his calm, relaxed demeanor Michele had seen. He put his arm around her and introduced her to about a dozen others.

"If you think I can cook, wait until you taste this woman's cooking," he said.

Michele smiled and looked at him with a quizzical expression. He had no idea of her cooking talents. She was irritated. Why was he posing as if they knew each other beyond the initial meeting, phone calls and e-mails?

They went to the basement, where a bar was set up. He ran into three guys he knew and they immediately ordered shots of tequila. "Want one?" he asked Michele.

"No, thanks," she said. "I will have a glass of wine."

After he took the tequila shot, she asked him about complimenting her on her cooking. "Oh, I was just trying to do some marketing for you," he said. "These people like to do parties."

"But you don't know if I can cook or not."

"Someone who looks as good as you do *has* to be able to cook."

His attempt at flattery made no sense and augmented her irritation.

"Where's the food?" she asked.

A woman in the basement heard her and answered the question. "It's upstairs. I'm about to get some myself. You can go with me," she said.

She was Deilah, the hostess. "Beautiful home," Michele said. "Thanks for having me."

Joseph stayed at the bar, drinking. Upstairs, Deilah introduced Michele to more people and led her to the food. It was an elaborate spread of fish, chicken, rice, potatoes, broccoli salad, crab cakes and green beans.

It was awful. Bland. Overcooked. Disappointing.

Michele curbed her appetite by eating three cupcakes. But she was not fulfilled—or happy.

She went back downstairs to find Joseph, but he was not there. On her way upstairs, she ran into Deilah, who told her Joseph was on the deck at the back of the house.

When she stepped out there, she found Joseph and a few other guys smoking cigars.

"Hey, Michele, come on over," he said. He introduced her to the men and offered her a cigar, which reminded her of Solomon. He convinced her to try one with him and she actually enjoyed it; they would share one on occasion.

"No, thanks," she said. She could not bear the notion of getting that heavy cigar smoke on her clothes and in her hair. "I'm going to go back inside."

"I'm coming right in," Joseph said.

And just as he said, Joseph returned to the house to find Michele in the kitchen, listening to a few women discussing the awful treatment of President Barack Obama.

"Hey," Joseph said into her ear. She could smell a horrible combination of cigar and alcohol on his breath. "How's it going?"

"Fine. Fine," she said.

"Good. Did you get a chance to eat?" Joseph asked. She did not detect it at first, but he seemed eager, in hindsight, to hear Michele's answer.

"I did," she said, softly so no one else could hear her. "I hope it's all right to say this to you, but the food was terrible."

Joseph's face turned sour.

"What's wrong?" Michele said. "You hated it, too?"

"No, I didn't hate it," he said, anger evident in his voice. "You're the only person I know who doesn't love it."

"Why are you so angry?" she said. "You know the caterer or something?"

"*I'm* the caterer," he said, staring at her with eyes that, if they could burn, would disintegrate her.

A sheath of embarrassment covered Michele's body. Usually quick with a comeback, she had nothing.

"I'm so sorry, Joseph. I don't know what to say."

"You've said enough," he said, and walked away.

Michele was left standing there. She wanted to talk to Joseph, but there were no words to soothe her abrasive critique of his work. As a caterer herself, she understood how devastating and embarrassing it would be.

She searched the house for Joseph; she wanted to profusely apologize. She also wanted to tell him how subjective peoples' tastes were and as long as others enjoyed his food, he should dismiss her words as nothing more than a picky person venting.

But she could not find Joseph. She searched the basement, the living room, deck and kitchen. She asked the friends he had cigars with and Deilah, the hostess. No one knew where he was.

Finally, Michele decided to go outside, to the car, to see if he was there. And he was.

"Joseph, I've been trying to find you. Why did you just leave like that?"

"I didn't want to curse you out." He put his drink to his mouth and followed it with a tug off his cigar. He blew the smoke toward Michele's face.

"I guess you're the master chef, that you can go around telling me that my food sucks," he said. Anger seeped from every word. And embarrassment, too.

"I'm sorry, Joseph. You know almost everything is subjective. For every person who wasn't thrilled with my food, there were a dozen more to validate it. So, don't let what I said invalidate you. You know you're a good chef, and people have told you that."

"Yeah, but you didn't." He was almost pouting.

"I'm sorry I offended you. I wasn't trying to; I didn't even know you prepared the food."

"Why would my friends have an event and let some-one else cater? Of course, you knew I catered it. That's one reason I wanted you to come with me... That was a bad decision."

"I can't apologize enough, Joseph," Michele said. She was tired of apologizing and about ready to explode. "I don't know what to say."

She wanted to say, "Grow up and take criticism like a

man. Learn from it and get better." Instead, she held her tongue.

"So that's it? You don't have anything else to say?" Joseph asked.

"I don't know what I could say to make it better for you. I know you want the truth from people. That's how we know what to work on and what not to. Clearly, the guests are enjoying the food. You should focus on that," Michele answered.

"First you tell me my food is horrible and now you're telling me what to focus on. Let me tell you something: You can soak your clothes in gasoline and go to hell."

If he was looking to get a fiery response out of Michele, he succeeded.

"Can you take me home now? And maybe by the time you drop me off you will have grown up," she said.

"Now I'm a child; okay," Joseph said. "Well, I'm sure your mother told you to never ride with kids, so let's see if you can get an adult to take you home."

They stared at each other for a few seconds. He took the final bit of his drink and downed it, then took a puff of his cigar. He leaned over and blew the smoke in her face, and brushed past her and back into the party.

Michele was so livid she could have burst into tears. She was hurt, angry and fighting mad. She looked around the subdivision and had no idea where she was. She did not want to go back into the house, but she had no other recourse.

She entered and saw Joseph standing in the kitchen

with a few guys. They all turned toward her, laughing. She found Deilah and asked her to call a cab.

"What? Why?" she asked.

When Michele explained that Joseph would not take her home, Deilah was not happy.

"Between you and me, the food isn't great," she said. "But he's been a family friend for a long time, so we're in a real bind when it comes to looking at someone else to do the food.

"Whatever, I'm really disappointed he's being this way. My brother is here. He can take you home. You live all the way in DeKalb County, right? That's too long a drive for a taxi. Who knows how much that would cost?"

"If your brother doesn't mind—"

"Hold on," Deilah said. She caught her brother Anthony's attention and waved him over.

During the introduction, they checked each other out. *Cute*, Michele said to herself.

Anthony was quickly impressed. *Yeah, she can ride; I mean, get a ride anytime.*

"But you shouldn't leave now. We're about to sing 'Happy Birthday' and cut the cake; and Joseph did not make the cake," Deilah said, laughing.

"How well do you know Joseph?" Michele said. "I don't want to cause any drama. I came here with him and was going to leave with him. But he's acting like a child."

"I know him well, but we're not friends; he's my brother-in-law's friend," Anthony said. "So don't worry about that."

He led Michele back downstairs, to the bar where they got a glass of Shiraz and sang "Happy Birthday" and generally enjoyed each other's company. Before long, she saw Joseph staring at her in the distance.

"I actually have to get up relatively early, so I'm ready when you are," Anthony said.

"Let me thank your sister and I'm ready, too."

On the way out, Joseph came by. "You ready to go?"

"I'm gone," she answered. Anthony politely grabbed her by her elbow and led her out the door.

"I'm going to say you can charge his behavior to alcohol," Anthony said of Joseph.

Michele liked that. He could have tried to squash Joseph to elevate himself. Instead, he seemed to believe he would get where he wanted to go on his own merits. That was different from a few guys she encountered who did all they could to make themselves look better by making another man look bad.

On top of that, Anthony was handsome and a gentleman. They talked and laughed all the way up Interstate 20 to the Candler Road exit.

"Why do you have to get up so early on the weekend?" Michele asked.

"Well, I work at Coca-Cola and we have an event that I have to help coordinate."

And just like that, Solomon was back on her mind.

"Coca-Cola, huh? Do you know a guy there named Solomon?"

"I do," Anthony said. "Good people. We've hung out

a few times. He's definitely good people. How do you know him?"

Michele was confused on how to answer. Anthony had struck her attention, which was really good considering how the night had gone. Would telling him about her past with Solomon make a difference to him? Should it make a difference to her?

"Well, he's the father of my son," Michele said.

"Hold up," Anthony said, alternating between looking at her and the road as they drove along. "I've heard about you. This is crazy. I can't believe this."

"What have you heard?"

Anthony did not have it in him to lie. Although he was more than mildly interested in Michele, he was a strict adherer to "man codes."

"I heard that you all are not together now and that he's mad at you," he said. "But I also heard that he's pretty much miserable without you. Guess how I heard this?

"He used to date my cousin, Marie. She told me. He ended it with her and told her all about you and basically how much he loved you."

Michele's body warmed up. She knew Solomon to be ice cold, so, day by day, her hope of hearing from him diminished. This news gave her optimism, for she knew in the deepest recesses of her heart, she belonged to Solomon Singletary.

"Atlanta is too small," she said. "In five minutes, I learned you know two people I know here and I don't know that many people."

"Well, a woman once told me that if you play 'Negro Geography' long enough, two people will find common friends," he said. "And that's true."

They arrived at Michele's door.

"Can I give you some gas money, please?" she said. "This was very nice of you."

"I appreciate the offer; you'd be surprised how many women don't have that courtesy gene in their DNA. But I'm good. I'm really glad we met."

"Thanks for everything," Michele said.

"My pleasure," Anthony said. "And good luck with Solomon. I think you love him, too."

"Why do you say that?" Michele wanted to know.

"I can tell. You probably didn't even realize it," he said, "but when I told you what my cousin said, an expression came over your face."

"What are you, some kind of mind reader?"

"No, I just pay attention to detail," Anthony said. "I noticed you didn't say I'm wrong... Goodnight. Nice to meet you."

CHAPTER 25
ON
THE BRINK

For all the vibes Michele and Solomon had floated in the universe, they still did not come together. Their pride and stubbornness ruled.

It was silly because they both missed each other, wanted to be together, but refused to make the initial contact that would at least start a dialogue about a possible reconciliation. This was not foolish pride; it was masochistic pride. They only hurt themselves.

And the only point they proved was that they could not live without each other.

"I want you to invite Michele over for dinner," Solomon's friend, Ray, said.

"Not happening," Solomon said quickly. "I haven't spoken to her in two months. I pick up Gerald through him calling me and we work it out. I pull up at her house and he comes out and jumps in the car. Or I pick him up from school and drop him off at her house. That's it."

"That's crazy," Ray said. "You telling me that you love this woman but you don't want her enough to reach out to her? You can't be that simple."

Solomon laughed, but it wasn't funny. He didn't have an answer.

Another uneventful week went by and another, before drama invaded.

Solomon was interrupted during a meeting in a conference room at Coke. He excused himself from the long table to take a call from Sonya, Michele's cousin, who was reporting an emergency.

"Hello," he said into the phone.

She explained that during his lunch break Gerald had had a seizure in the school's cafeteria.

An ambulance was called—so was Michele, who frantically hurried to DeKalb Medical Center from a catering job she was setting up on the other side of town.

On the way, Michele called Sonya, who called Coca-Cola and tracked down Solomon. Michele did not ask her to; Sonya took it upon herself.

When she told him the severity of the situation with Gerald, he immediately addressed his manager and other representatives present.

"I'm sorry, but my son is in the hospital and I've got to get there now," he said. "I can't apologize enough, but I must go."

His manager understood his plight. "Solomon, go."

Dozens of things ran through his mind en route to the hospital, none of them comforting. Worst was the thought that he could lose Gerald after recently finding him.

That thought made him panic.

He called Sonya as he pulled into the hospital's parking lot.

"Have you heard anything else?"

"No. Michele was way out in Douglasville, so she's not there yet," Sonya said.

"I'm here," he said. "I'll call you back. And Sonya... thanks for calling me."

He ran into the emergency room with his head spinning.

"Ma'am," he said to the attendant at the desk, "I'm here about my son; Gerald Williams. He was brought in from school with seizures."

She looked at her computer and determined, "He's with the doctor now. You can take a seat over there. I'll let you know when the doctor is ready to see you."

The attendant gathered his name and other information and Solomon took a seat and waited. All he could do was think the worst. He was mad at himself for that, but he could not stop it.

He wondered, and worried, about Michele. She would never be able to recover from such a loss. It would be devastating to him, but Michele would never be the same.

It was then that he got on his knees right there in the waiting room and prayed.

"God, I'm desperate right now," he started. "I'm desperate for Your intervention and power to heal my son. Please bring him out of whatever trouble he is in. We need him to be all right. His mother needs him to be all right. God please spare us and make sure this boy is all right. In Jesus' precious name, I pray. Amen."

He heard someone else say "Amen" as he did and turned to see Michele. Her eyes were fire-engine red.

Solomon rose to his feet. Whatever foolish pride and stubborn position that existed before was discarded like so much trash. He hugged Michele and held her tightly.

"He's going to be okay," he said into her ear. "He's going to be okay."

Michele, at first, was too shaken to speak. The emotions of her son's condition were magnified with Solomon's presence and emotion at the hospital.

"Have you heard anything?" she finally said. They were still embracing.

"Not yet," he said. "Soon."

He felt her tears on his shoulder.

"Come on. Sit down," he said, and she obeyed.

He used his hand to wipe her face.

"Solomon, nothing can happen to him. I need him."

"I know, but he's going to be all right because we're here for him. Before you got here, I was scared. Now, the power of both us being here—and God's will—will make him better. He'll be all right."

The wait seemed interminable, when, in reality, Dr. Carter came out about ten minutes after Michele's arrival.

"Yes, we are the parents," Solomon said.

"Your son suffered a seizure from a violent allergic reaction to peanuts," the doc said. "Did you know he had that allergy?"

"No," they said in unison. "Peanuts?" Michele said.

"How serious is this?" Solomon asked.

"We have to consider it serious until we get him completely stable," the doctor said. "He had an anaphylactic reaction to the peanuts, which, in some cases, I'm sorry to say, have been fatal within minutes. We're beyond that point, so let's hope that he'll come around soon."

Michele sobbed and Solomon hugged her tighter.

"We treated him right away with epinephrine. But the reaction to the allergy could recur, so we must maintain ongoing observation. He's resting now, but we're monitoring him closely to make sure he doesn't slip into a coma."

"What? No," Michele said. "Please, no."

Solomon hugged her tightly. "Hey. Hey," he said softly but firmly into her ear. "Listen to me. He'll be all right. He's our son. He's strong. He'll be all right."

"Please stay here," Dr. Carter said. "I'll be back to update you as soon as I know something."

The doctor left and Solomon walked Michele back over to a seat. He held her as they sat, waiting. He was so consumed with comforting Michele that he did not have time to address his own worry or fears.

"How did you get here before me?" she asked Solomon.

"Sonya called me at work and I just left," he said. "I was so scared because I didn't know what to expect when I got here."

"I didn't expect to see you here," she said. "And I'm sorry I didn't call you. I didn't try to not call you. I was just in such a state of panic, all I could think about was my baby and if he was all right."

"I know; me, too."

"He has to be okay. Solomon, I couldn't take something happening to him. I've heard of how severe allergic reactions can be."

"Nothing's going to happen to Gerald," he said. "I believe the more positive energy we put out there for him to hold on to, that's what we're going to get back; positive results, because he'll be able to draw off of our will."

Michele did not respond. She wiped her tears and rested her head on Solomon's chest. He rubbed her arms and shoulders. She was quiet and still, and Solomon's thoughts began to carom off the hospital walls.

All the back-and-forth between him and Michele did not measure up to a bowl of rocks. It all seemed so pointless, so ridiculous. He loved her; loved a woman for the only time in his life, in fact. And to be without her because of a power struggle suddenly seemed shallow and stupid.

He learned in the family violence classes that it was more important to really hear someone else's point of view before trying to get his point of view across. Maybe if he understood the other's perspective his view might be altered, and drama could be averted. He questioned whether he really tried to understand her points.

And so, Solomon held Michele tighter, as if he was trying to extract the pain and worry from her and into him. He never allowed himself to care that much about a woman, to be that selfless, that, well, *righteous*.

But to see her so broken and so scared broke Solomon. The ice that coated his heart defrosted, quickly.

He was going to tell her his feelings, tell her he was wrong, that he missed her and that they had nothing between them that could not be fixed. But only after the positive news about Gerald would he empty his emotions on her.

"God," he began his silent prayer with Michele in his arms, "bring our child back to us, please. He's young and has his entire life to live as You order him to live it. Please don't take him away from us."

Shortly after his prayer, Dr. Carter approached him and Michele.

"Doctor," he said. He and Michele stood up, but held their collective breath.

"Gerald seems to be getting better," he said, and Solomon's grip around Michele's shoulder tightened. "He has reacted well to the medicine we administered. He's still sleeping, but his vital signs are very encouraging. We've moved him to a room on the third floor. He's resting and by tomorrow you should see a dramatic difference in his condition."

"Doctor, thank you," Solomon said.

Michele could only cry tears of relief.

"I'm sure you want to see him," Dr. Carter said. "The nurse here will take you up to his room."

Solomon hugged Michele and she hugged back. Then he leaned away from her and wiped the tears from her face.

"You can smile now; he's all right," he said.

He clutched her hand and they followed the nurse to the elevator and up to Gerald's Room 326.

Solomon let Michele go into the room first as he stopped the nurse outside the door.

"I can tell you right now that we're not leaving here tonight," he said. "We've got to be here for him. I hope there is no regulation against parents staying in the room with their child."

"No, you're fine," she said. "He needs to see you all as soon as he wakes up, so it's okay."

Solomon thanked her and went into the room to see Gerald sleeping with an IV in his left arm and his mom practically in bed with him.

"Michele, you're going to collapse the boy's chest," Solomon said.

His exaggeration worked; Michele laughed.

"I know, right?" she said. "Let me sit down and get myself together."

Solomon pulled over a chair next to the right side of the bed so Michele could sit and hold Gerald's hand at the same time. Then he moved a chair from the other side of the room to Michele's side.

She calmed down and collected her thoughts. She spoke softly, so as to not disturb Gerald.

"Thank you for being here," she said. "I couldn't have made it without you. I was so scared."

"I'm supposed to be here; that's my son."

"But how could you be so calm?"

"Calm? I'm glad it seemed that way," he answered. "In reality, I was petrified. I thought my heart was going to burst out of my chest. I couldn't get a positive thought to enter my mind, which is not like me at all. But…"

"But what?" Michele said, turning toward Solomon.

"But I saw how devastated and scared you were and I couldn't focus on me anymore," he said, looking at Gerald. Then he turned to her.

"All I could think about then was making it better for you, if that was possible," he added. "My fear didn't go away; it was pushed aside. I just felt like I had to be there for you, almost like if you were okay, Gerald would be okay.

"So my emotions shifted from worrying about Gerald to worrying about you."

"Really? But why?"

"Why? Because I love you. Simple as that."

"You do? I thought you hated me."

"I didn't like how things were going," Solomon said. "I didn't like what you thought about me. I didn't like feeling like I didn't trust you. But I never hated you. I always loved you."

He put his left arm around her shoulder. He was not looking for a response from Michele. He only wanted to tell her how he felt.

Something happened in that hospital waiting room. In that time of crisis, Solomon took inventory on himself and decided he could be better. His son was in danger and that forced him to understand the value of pulling his relationship with Michele out of danger.

"I went out on a date last weekend," Michele said.

Solomon did not move, but his heart rate climbed. Quickly.

"Really? Had fun?" he asked. It was a mistake to inquire. If she had said, "Yes, I did," it would have bothered Solomon more. But his position of not holding back was dominant.

"It was a disaster," she said. Solomon was not disappointed to hear that.

"The guy who took me to a house party got mad at me because I told him his food sucked, which it did, and told me I needed to get another ride home."

"What?" Solomon jumped in. "He told you to get another ride?"

"Yes, he was upset. I didn't know he was the caterer. And when I said the food was awful, he lost it," she recalled. "So the lady of the house hooks me up with her brother—"

"So you had two dates in one night?" Solomon jumped in.

"I didn't look at it that way. I got a ride from him. He was a nice guy, though. And it turned out that he knows you, works with you at Coke, and was singing your praises. I was like, 'Can I avoid this man?'"

"Who was it?" Solomon asked.

"Anthony. I didn't get his last name."

"I know Anthony; Anthony Richards. Good dude," Solomon said. "Glad to hear he wasn't one of those brothers who tries to squash you to advance his own agenda."

"I thought the same thing," she said.

"So, anyway, I tell you I love you; you tell me you went out on a date?" Solomon said, smiling. "Something seems wrong with that."

"I was trying to avoid telling you how much I love you."

"Why would you want to do that?"

"I almost think that if you know I love you, you know you can do things to hurt me. Like you would use it against me."

"That's not good," he said. "Or right. Listen, in the last months I've broken any ties I've had with women. Well, I still have one to tell, but she knows the deal, based on us not having any contact.

"There was nothing that happened where I was trying to hurt you. I was just trying to be a father; that's where it all started. You had your view on it, I had mine… And, to be honest, I really don't want to rehash all that stuff. I've rehashed it over and over for the last two months.

"You want to talk about it, fine," he added. "But if this situation has taught us anything, it's that we have to live."

As if he were listening, Gerald opened his eyes and moved his hand. The parents stood up.

"Hi, baby," Michele said. "Hi, baby."

"Hey, my man," Solomon said.

He looked at them with a confused expression on his face. Then he started crying, which made the floodgates open for Michele.

Solomon tried to comfort them both.

"Hey, hey, it's okay," he said in reassuring tones. "Your mom and dad are here. And we're going to stay here until you're ready to come home, okay?"

Gerald did not answer, not with words. The fear in his eyes, though, diminished, signaling he understood and, more importantly, found comfort in his father's words.

And so did Michele.

"I'm going to get the doctor to let him know you're awake now," Solomon said. "I'll be right back."

He rubbed Michele on her shoulder before stepping into the hallway. It was there that he released all the emotions that had engulfed him over the last several weeks; anger and disappointment, loneliness and regret, sadness and fear, relief and gratitude.

It all came rushing out, like water over a breached levee. For about thirty seconds he did not discard his own feelings or try to protect someone else's or put up a brave front. He let it all go and cried.

The release was pure and cleansing. Solomon could not recall the last time he had cried. This breakthrough felt as if he had disposed of untapped emotions that had weighed him down. He could breathe easier afterward. He felt free of himself.

CHAPTER 26
RELATIONSHIP ROUNDTABLE

Before long, Gerald was back to himself; active and joking and just being a kid. And Solomon and Michele were working their way beyond the troubles of the past. They were not altogether in unison, but they were open to something they were not before: compromise.

A week after the scare with their son, Solomon had them over his house for a cookout. It was just the three of them—and Ray, his wife, Cynthia, and son, Ray-Ray. After devouring Solomon's offering of grilled lamb chops, turkey burgers, corn on the cob and chicken wings, they tore through Michele's rum pound cake, and blueberry cobbler, with Blue Bell vanilla ice cream.

The boys played basketball in the driveway, leaving the parents available for some adult conversation.

"It's a shame we're just meeting, Cynthia," Michele said.

"I know, girl," Cynthia said. "I've heard a lot about you through Raymond. I'm glad we all slowed down long enough to get together."

"Me, too," Solomon said. "I can't even catch up with Ray anymore."

"Guess what?" Cynthia said. "Me, either."

She was not joking. There was an edge in how she spoke. Ray did not dare touch it.

"Anyway," he said, "it's good to see Gerald is back to normal."

"Why don't you want to address what I just said?" Cynthia insisted.

"Because we've already addressed it," he said. "I don't know why you're even bringing it up now. We're having a good time."

"You've been having a lot of good times lately," she added.

Solomon and Michele looked at each other. Clearly, there was drama in paradise, drama Ray had not shared with Solomon.

"Well, let's just ask the question then," Cynthia said. "Do you all think it is okay for your mate to go out pretty consistently without you?"

Solomon's mind started racing for a way to help his boy's cause. But Ray had not shared with him the circumstances of their discord, so he had to go on instinct.

"I'll go first, if that's okay, Michele," he began. "The one thing no relationship will overcome is a lack of trust. Trust me on this, I know. I won't even go into detail about my cases, but it matters a lot.

"So, if a man says, 'Honey, I'm going to go with the

fellas to watch Monday Night Football at the sports bar,' there shouldn't be any drama about that. Right? A man works, does his thing for his family, why can't he occasionally kick it with the boys?"

"Because it never happens that men don't have women around," Cynthia said.

"See what I'm dealing with?" Ray said.

"Don't even try it, Ray," she responded. "You have used the 'going out with the boys' story quite a bit. You must get tired of him calling you about it, don't you, Solomon?"

Solomon laughed to hide his surprise. Ray had not called Solomon about hanging out in months. And yet, when he tried to connect with him, Ray was frequently busy. So, he was getting the picture: Ray apparently had something going on outside of the house.

"I'm always up for hanging out," Solomon said. He focused on the answer and not Ray's predicament. "It's something that boggles a man's mind. If you ladies want to go to a book club meeting or have a girl's night out or just go shopping with a friend or two and a movie, we support you.

"Am I right, Michele? We don't have the length of history that they have, but we're coming up on a year and I've recommended places for you to hang out with your cousin or friends. I've encouraged you to go. It's a healthy thing.

"But I remember saying I was going to hang with some

guys from my job; you remember this, Michele? One night after work on a Friday, and she got quiet on me. Had nothing to say, which said a lot. It wasn't, 'Okay, where are you going? Have fun.' It was a smirk across her face and, 'Hmmmm.'

"I said, 'Excuse me?' She said, 'Well, I was thinking we would do something.' I said, 'I'm good with that, but we went out last night, both nights last weekend and the weekend before that. I sort of already committed to the guys. Let's hang out Saturday night.'

"She said, 'So, you weren't asking me, you were telling me?' Can you believe that? I'm a grown-ass man and she wanted me to *ask* her for permission to go out with some friends?

"So, what do you think happened, Ray?"

"I know what happened," he said. "Y'all got into an argument."

"Exactly," Solomon said, leaping from his seat in the family room to give Ray a high-five. "That's exactly what happened: a useless argument. And here's the thing: The argument wasn't really about me not asking her for permission. It was about her not wanting me to go out in the first place. She was just waiting for something to sink her teeth in and that was it."

"That's not fair, Solomon," Michele said. "You bring up the one case where I wasn't quite so comfortable with you going out. And that was only because there was an artist in town that I wanted to go see that night."

"What? This is news to me; you never said that, Michele," he countered. "On top of that, that wasn't the only case. What about when I had an alumni association event to go to. Gerald was with Sonya and you had a catering job. Instead of saying, 'Have fun,' you said, 'Why don't you stay home sometimes?' I said, 'I hardly go anywhere without you.' And your argument was that I shouldn't go to an event without you, even if it was important to my alumni association and even if you couldn't go. Sorry, but that's crazy. Isn't that crazy, Cynthia?"

"Of course, it's not crazy," Cynthia said. "It has to be more than her not wanting you to go."

"That's right, Cynthia," Michele said. "See, a woman understands a woman. As a matter of fact, the president of his alumni association is a woman he used to date."

"Oh, my goodness," Solomon said. "Where did you get that from?"

"I could tell by how you talked about her one day," Michele answered. "You talked about something you experienced together in a way that was more than a casual thing."

"Oh, yeah, you're right," he said sarcastically. "We were in a car accident together in college. She worked on the campus radio station with me and we were going to a remote event and a guy broadsided us. So, you're right, that was more than a casual thing. But how you made the leap to it being something romantic, well, I shouldn't even be surprised, no matter how outrageous it is.

"That's just where a woman's mind will go. Guys can't get together and enjoy each other's company, talk about sports, laugh at each other. I guess it's in our nature to always be on the prowl, huh?"

"Something like that," Cynthia said. "Are you denying that a man's primal instinct is to pursue women?"

"That might be true; in fact, it is true in most cases. No denying that," Solomon said. "But what about women? Are you denying that a woman's primal instinct is to lure a man with her attire, her perfume, her shoes, her attitude? *Please*. As much as men love chasing, women love to be chased."

"What are you trying to say?" Michele said.

"May I jump in, Solomon?" Ray said.

"Please do, my brother," Solomon answered.

"All the shopping, the lipgloss, the heels, the showing of the cleavage, the tight dress around your ass… What's that for? Who is that for?" Ray said. "So, okay, men have primal instincts. But when you all can't go anywhere without showing off every part of your body, what do you expect to happen? A man will, as you might say, attack, but only because you made it appealing for him to attack."

"Whatever, Ray," Cynthia said. "What about when you have a good woman who wears all that for you and you're still out seeking other prey? You get all that but still want more?"

"That does happen," Solomon said. "I can't really speak to that because I hadn't really had a girlfriend since sometime right after college. I let the women I dated know I dated other women."

"And they went for that?" Cynthia said. "Are you kidding me?"

"Let's make it very clear here," Michele said. "I was not a part of that."

"Michele is a different case altogether," Solomon said.

"Still, Solomon, if you dated more than one woman at the same time, you were doing what I'm talking about," Cynthia said. "Why can't one woman be enough?"

It was the universal question all men had to attempt to answer at one point or another. Here was Solomon's and Ray's opportunity.

"Honestly, some of it is a general thing where there is excitement in variety," Solomon said. "I don't know why. I can't explain it. Maybe it's primal.

"It also is about finding in one woman something not found in another. So, he basically puts together one ideal woman through multiple women."

"Do you know how fucking crazy that sounds, and how angry that makes me?" Cynthia said. "What you're saying is I'm not good enough so you need someone else to supplement me."

"Wait, I'm not trying to get you mad," Solomon said. "I thought we were having a candid conversation and that you wanted a man's view on this. You get mad, though, when you take it personally. This isn't a personal attack at you."

"But, see, that's how Cynthia is," Ray said. "I love my wife. But anything that's done that she can't comprehend means it's shady."

"Okay, now I'm dumb; I'm not smart enough to understand," Cynthia said sarcastically.

"Here she goes again, taking something to the next level," Ray said. "I wasn't saying that at all. Everyone here can see that but you."

"Well," Michele jumped in, "it sounds to me like there is a communication breakdown. I'm not a marriage counselor so don't get me wrong. I think some things are really basic. Your wife, Ray, is saying she's uncomfortable with your actions and some of the things you say to her. So it becomes really about you. What will you do to make her feel comfortable, or at least better about things?"

Ray looked down at his glass of Oya wine and finally took a sip of it.

"I love my wife," he said. "I don't want her feeling anything crazy about me. It bothers me when I hear her speak like that. But I'm not sure what to do, short of wearing an ankle bracelet with a GPS on it.

"Cynthia is an extremist; it's either all good or all bad. There's no in between, which is crazy because we mostly live in between good and bad. It doesn't matter what I do or what I say if she's dissecting every word or action, looking for the drama in it."

"Looking for the *truth* in it," Cynthia interjected. "The truth."

"Here's the thing, though," Ray said. "You don't recognize the truth. You identify what you think is *not* the truth and you pounce on that."

It got awkwardly quiet for a few seconds. Solomon broke it.

"To me, it all goes back to trust," he said. "Women always have issues with trust. And it's not about what I did to you. It's about what someone else did. So men get thrown into this category of being suspect simply because they're men. How is that fair?"

"Well, how can you talk?" Michele said. "You're the same man who refused to be in a relationship with a woman for years, according to you, because you believed the next one was just as untrustworthy as the previous one. You're being a hypocrite, acting like you don't understand what goes into having preconceived ideas about someone."

"I give you that; you're right," Solomon said. "It goes back to my original point several minutes ago. The idea that men are the devil in relationships and women are the angels is crazy. But women seem to hang on to that."

"If you're going to keep score, I think the men are way ahead of women," Michele said.

"That's right," Cynthia added. "You've already admitted there's this animalist thing going on."

"I have a question," Solomon said. "Who are the men doing all their dirt with? In my own life, married women have approached me. Women with so-called boyfriends have approached me. Worst of all, women who were so-called friends with the women I dated approached me. I don't know of many men that diabolical.

"And, of top of that, before Michele, I told women I didn't want a relationship and they accepted that. So, whatever is going on, women are making it happen because men aren't doing it alone."

"Right," Ray chimed in. "Nothing happens unless a woman wants it to happen. Men can pursue and desire and chase, but nothing goes down unless the woman says 'yes.' You all have all the power."

"But what about how men lie about their relationship status?" Cynthia asked. "I commend you, Solomon, for telling women you didn't want a relationship. They knew you were single and where you were coming from, so it was up to them to deal with you or not.

"But these men who go around trying to start relationships when they have someone they already call their woman, well, I don't get them."

"I don't, either," Ray said. "And I don't see why that concerns you; you're married."

"Well, I have a sister and two cousins and lots of single girlfriends, and I regularly hear the stories about men misleading women," Cynthia said.

"The bottom line is that we can't account for every man just as you all can't account for the scandalous women out here," Solomon said. "I tend to believe women are worse because all my experiences are with women. And when you think of all the women who constantly throw themselves at athletes or entertainers just because they are athletes or entertainers and that tells you something. You wonder why so many of those guys call women names or disrespect them? It's because so many of them throw themselves at men, knowing they are married or accounted for. And you expect the man to respect them after that?

"Men, on the other hand, don't chase women because they are so-called celebrities. We are interested in women who look good to us or who catch our attention in one way or another. She could be a schoolteacher or President of the U.S. It doesn't matter. But women throw themselves at guys they would have no interest in if they didn't see them on TV or have money."

"Well, if those guys are married, then what are they doing messing around with those women?" Michele said. "They have a bigger responsibility as a married man to do what's right. Just say no."

Everyone laughed, which was needed because the tension was mounting.

Then the boys came in, smelling like all outdoors, changing the subject entirely.

Solomon challenged them to one last game, and the men left the house to play basketball.

The women went to a window and watched from the inside. Cynthia looked on with skepticism. Michele looked on with gratitude. Her son and her man were playing ball together. A week before she had no indication she would ever have seen that.

I n the week that Gerald came home from the hospital, Solomon and Michele spent a lot of time together, but their focus was on their son and not their relationship. With his recovery complete, there was no escaping the concerns of the past.

So, the time came after Ray and his family left the cookout and after Gerald said goodnight to his parents and retired to his bedroom at Solomon's house.

Solomon returned downstairs to Michele, who was sitting in the family room, sipping on a cup of hot green tea.

"I made you some," she said.

"Thanks," he responded. "You must've read my mind."

"I wish I could read your mind, Solomon Singletary," Michele said. "You're an interesting man."

"Why do you say that?"

"You told me some really nice things in the hospital, but you would not even speak to me for two months before that," she said. "That's a long time. You have to either really hate someone or be really cold to totally go that long without contacting me. You said you don't hate me. So, I guess that means you're a cold man."

"I'm going to accept my responsibility, but what about you? You didn't contact me, either. So does that mean you either hate me or that you're cold?"

"As the man, I felt like the responsibility was on you to contact me," she said. "You walked out on me before, remember? It seemed to me like you would have done everything in your power to not make me feel that way again."

"Well, in that context, you're right and I'm sorry," Solomon said. "I really didn't even think about what happened all those years ago. I was focusing on what happened at that time and I was disappointed on two major things:

"One, you didn't really trust me enough to discipline Gerald as I saw fit, as his father and, two, you basically took the position that I was some woman beater, which was really disappointing because I trusted you enough to tell you about something very personal and painful.

"So, that was a lot for me. Please believe this: I wanted to call you every day. I'm just so anchored in—"

"In stubbornness?" Michele jumped in.

"I guess so," Solomon said, smiling. "When I think about it, I wish I had been smarter and not wasted all that time; we could've been building the relationship… I missed you."

"I missed you, too, Solomon," she said. "And I guess you can say the same about me. I'm stubborn. I take a position and I plant my feet and get ready to battle; especially when it comes to Gerald.

"As for your incident with that woman, I'm sorry it happened and I apologize for taking it to the extreme. I was lashing out because of our whole disagreement about Gerald. I'm sorry."

"I appreciate you saying that," Solomon said. "But we still have the issue of how to deal with Gerald when he gets out of line. He's a great kid; we know that. But he's a kid, so he'll get into more trouble and a decision will have to be made on how to deal with him."

"I know and I'm not going to worry about that," Michele said. "I still have concerns, but, in the end, you love our son and you have to be an authority over him. You're not trying to hurt him, but to teach him. So, I'm going to be okay...I think."

"And I'm going to be all right with knowing you've been married," Solomon said. "There's a part of me that's definitely jealous, to be honest. And I don't know why you wouldn't tell me. But I'm not going to sweat it, really.

"But I do have a question for you. Now, please don't get offended, but do you have a problem being alone?"

Michele was taken aback by the inquiry. She never saw herself as needy or needing a man around to validate her.

"Why would you ask me that?"

"Well, because you told me about a few guys you dated after me and you were married to another guy. Then, you told me that just a few days ago you went on a date with a guy to a house party. Maybe I'm reading too much into it. But I at least felt I should ask the question."

"I have to be honest and say that I prefer to be in a relationship. I prefer to be special to someone and to have someone special," she said. "It doesn't mean I settle for anything that comes along. I believe it's natural for someone to want companionship, someone to do things with, someone who is there to show they care. It's a comforting thing, I guess."

"I used to feel like it wasn't natural for anyone to be committed to one person," Solomon said. "It seemed unrealistic. I always thought that there wasn't anyone who could make me feel I should be committed. I'm being honest. But the ultimate truth is that before you, I didn't even have ambitions of being with one woman.

"Too many women disappointed me," he added, shaking his head. "I know how it feels to be hurt, to have your heart broken. I don't know. Maybe it's different for men. A man gets hurt and the pain is…is crippling. I will give it to women: You all are stronger than us. Maybe it's because men have been unfaithful for so long that women have been able to deal with it and keep on moving; even if they got knocked down pretty good.

"A hurt man…he takes it harder. If he gets over it, it takes a while, if he gets over it at all. I don't know why it's that way, but it is. So, for me, like I told you a while ago, I was all about protecting myself. I got hurt and decided I would do what I needed to do to prevent that from happening again."

"I understand what you're saying, but there are ways to go about it," Michele said. "But I'm not going to revisit that. I'll just say it's sort of like what I was trying to prevent with Gerald."

Solomon was confused. How did his disappointment in women relate to her not wanting him to whip Gerald? He wanted to pose the question, but not in a way that would put her on the defensive. They were getting along great and he was hoping to put the stamp on their reconciliation later that evening in the bedroom.

"Help me understand what you mean," he said.

"Well, I probably didn't put it the right way," she said. "The idea is that you were trying to protect yourself from being hurt and I was trying to protect Gerald from being hurt, too."

Solomon was not quite sure what to say. He didn't get the comparison—one was about emotional pain, another physical pain—but he skipped the subject until later.

He moved beside Michele on the couch and leaned in to kiss her face. She welcomed the feel of his lips. That one night of desiring him was not the only night. She craved him the way a pregnant woman would pickles or ice cream or some other treat.

Just the feel of the heat from his body and the scent of his cologne moved her. She closed her eyes as he kissed her face, and in those two seconds heat blanketed her body.

"Thank you," she said. "I need that."

"I would think you would need more than that," Solomon said. Michele smiled.

"A lot more," she said, turning her face toward his, without saying a word.

They pressed their lips together for a long kiss that was so passionate and erotic it seemed the room got darker and the music stopped. They were consumed with each other, two famished lovers reconnected after too long apart.

When their lips parted, Michele tossed the two decorative pillows on the couch across the room, onto the floor, and leaned back. Solomon followed her body's path, covering her body with his.

They kissed again, another emphatic, sensual kiss that actually caused Michele to get a little light-headed. She regained her composure when Solomon began kissing her on her neck.

She could feel the erection in his pants between her legs, causing her a sensation that made her body tremble. He pulled up to unbutton her blouse, and she lay defenseless to his kisses on her bare shoulders, neck and lips.

"I miss kissing you," he said in a whisper.

"Ohhhhh," she mumbled so softly should could not tell if it was audible.

Solomon leaned into her ear and declared, "I want to make love to you, Michele."

His breath on her ear excited her, but not as much as his words.

"Please, Solomon," Michele said. "Please."

They kissed deeply again and he pulled up to undress.

"I'll be right back," Michele said.

"Where you going?" a puzzled Solomon asked.

"To the bathroom, and to check on Gerald, make sure he's sleep," she said.

Solomon turned off the light in the kitchen and undressed down to his nakedness. It took Michele longer to return than he expected, but his desire for her had not diminished by the time she arrived.

"What took you so long?"

Michele wore a tank top and tight shorts and carried a comforter. The look on her face was indifferent.

"I'm sorry," she said. "You won't believe this."

"What is it?"

"My period came," Michele said. "I can't believe this."

"Ah, man, really?" Solomon said. Then he chuckled.

"What's funny?" Michele wanted to know.

"The real drama would be if it didn't come," he said. "This, this is all right... Come here."

Michelle plopped down on the couch next to Solomon.

"I wanted you so badly," she said. "I needed you so badly."

"Well, I'm here, baby," Solomon said. "I'm not going anywhere. I needed you, too. But the good news is that we actually do have each other. When you stop bleeding like a gutted cow, we'll do what we need to do."

Michele playfully pushed Solomon away. "You started so sweet and then you got jokes," she said, smiling. "A gutted cow? Wow, that's messed up."

"Seriously, it's all right," he said. "I'm okay."

"You don't look okay," she said, staring at his throbbing erection. "Damn. Looks like that thing needs to be tamed."

"Well, by all means, tame that damn thing," he said, and they both laughed.

"Let me reacquaint myself with my friend," she said.

Solomon fell back on the couch with his hands folded behind his head and his eyes closed. Michele placed one of the discarded pillows beneath her knees, providing a cushion from the floor.

"Since I can't have you like I want you," Michele said, "this is the next best thing. Enjoy it, baby."

Solomon liked the confidence she exuded about her sexual skills. Better than that, he liked her execution. Using her moist, soft tongue and wet mouth, she orally massaged Solomon until that erection spewed semen as if blasted from a shaken-up champagne bottle. She did not let any of it spill.

"Oh, my God," Solomon managed to get out. He was breathing heavily, like he would after a game of ball. "You're unbelievable."

Pleasing him like that turned Michele on in a big way. "Look at my nipples," she said. "They are so hard. And if I wasn't on my cycle, I'd be all wet down there in a different way from now."

Solomon, a man of many words, had few that were intelligible. "Come here, girl," he said. He moved over so they could rest on the couch together. Michele pulled the comforter over both of them. She lay with her back to Solomon, and he wrapped her in his arms as a running back would protect a football.

"I miss this as much as I miss anything," she said. "Simply laying here like this. We all love the big things. But the small things show more. And they last longer."

Solomon kissed her gently on her shoulder and said: "I feel like I'm where I'm supposed to be when I'm with you."

CHAPTER 28

THE TRUTH
OF THE MATTER

Michele jumped while sleeping and were it not for Solomon's firm grip, she would have been on the floor. It was 3:06 a.m.

"Hey, hey," he said in a comforting voice. "It's all right. I got you…You must've had a dream about skydiving because you jumped hard."

"Oh, wow, I'm sorry," she said.

"No, it must have been something else because I can feel how fast your heart is beating," Solomon said. "What did you dream?"

"I'm surprised this hasn't happened before," she said. "I have this one particular dream every so often."

"About what?"

Michele maneuvered so she and Solomon could switch positions. "Actually, I want to be honest with you about something."

"What is it?" Solomon said, holding his breath. Immediately he thought of her past truths that were bombshells: Gerald was his son and she had been married.

So, he braced himself for a punch in the gut.

"Well, I got upset about you beating Gerald and then learning you had smacked a woman because, in my household, that happened all the time, to the point of abuse," she began.

They were sitting up on the couch now, and Solomon put his arm around her.

"Really? Why didn't you say something?"

"Too much pride. Embarrassed. Stupid."

Solomon did not respond. He wanted to hear specifics, but only if she wanted to share them. Turns out, she did.

"My father was a salty drunk," she said. "When he had his drinks on the weekend, it was hell for my mother. He would find anything to beat on her about. And when there was nothing to complain about, he'd beat her anyway, saying, 'Oh, you did what you're supposed to do, now you think you're better than me?'

"It was awful. That's what I grew up with."

Solomon said, "I'm sorry to hear that. I had no idea."

"I know you didn't," she said. "He wasn't so bad with the kids. He would beat our butts good, but that was when we did something wrong. My mother just got it for no apparent reason.

"And she took it for a long time. I can remember as far back as four or five years old and hearing those beatings she took from him. When I got older and she got strong enough to leave, I asked her why she stayed, and she said, 'Because I loved your father and because I believe in family.'

"But at some point, after he hit her and she fell and

suffered a concussion, she had more than enough. She could've fallen and hit her head and died. She said before that concussion she never considered that he might kill her, intentionally or not."

Solomon rubbed Michele's back and shoulders. "Well, I'm glad you all made it out of there okay," he said. "I would've never guessed this about your father. I haven't met him but I've been around when you talk to him on the phone and it's a normal conversation."

"It is, but it took a long time to get to that point," she said. "He got help; he hasn't had a drink in fourteen years. It made all the difference in the world. Plus, I'm a girl and he's my daddy. You know how that relationship is.

"My brother, he's less forgiving than me. He deals with Daddy some, but there's clearly something between them. I mean, he could hear his mom getting beat up and couldn't do anything about it. You know how it is with mothers and sons."

"I do," he said. "Have you forgiven your mother for staying so long?"

"Wow, that's a deep question, Solomon." she said. "My therapist asked me that same exact question. I can't believe it. My answer is yes. My mom and I didn't really talk about it until I was about twenty-five.

"It was easy for me to forgive her because I knew she stayed for reasons she believed were good and unselfish reasons: love and her children. But she told me those were the same reasons she had to leave him, too."

"Your dad has to be remorseful now," Solomon said.

"He is. Every so often he'll say to me, 'Baby, I wish I was a better father to you and your brother as you grew up and a much better husband to your mother. I have a lot of regrets.'

"And I'll say, 'Daddy, you gotta keep focusing on the future and not the past. Mom is great. Your children are great. We went through the whole thing together, as a family. And we came out of it better people, all of us.'

"I know hearing that helps him. But because he has been healthy so long, it's hard to not look back with a clear head and feel bad. But he still goes to his AA meetings and he says he's still committed to living right. So, like him, I take it one day at a time with my daddy."

"How is your mom with him? What's their relationship like now?" Solomon asked.

"My mom still loves him," Michele said. "She knew it wasn't him. He committed the violence, but it was all alcohol-induced. When he wasn't drinking, he was the man she fell in love with.

"It struck me that you ended up in jail for smacking a woman and my mother never called the police on my dad. She said later that she didn't see how that would help, putting her husband in jail.

"I can remember weekends when my mom had stuff for us to do as a family to try to prevent him from going out and drinking with his buddies. We were probably overexposed to going out and doing things because she tried everything to get him to commit to being with us.

"See, here was the thing: my daddy didn't drink around

us. I never ever saw him put a glass of liquor to his mouth. And neither did my brother. And my mother knew that, so she tried to have us front and center with things to do to prevent him from drinking."

"Your mom is strong; that's where you get your strength," Solomon said.

"It's also why I'm so protective of Gerald," she said. "I know what it's like to be damaged as a child. It's my job to protect him from all the evils of the world, not that you're evil or anything."

She laughed and Solomon did, too.

"It's our job now," he said. "You have some help."

"I know and it's a real blessing," she said. "A single mom is the strongest creature on this earth. I don't know how single moms do it with two and three four kids. But if that were my situation, I would find the strength. That's what mothers do.

"And besides the concussion my mom got, the other reason she finally said, 'That's it' was something I said to her. When she hit her head, the same weekend I spent the night at my friend Jasmine's house. My parents knew their parents and it was great.

"So, my mom, unbeknownst to me, got hurt that Friday night, the night I was taken to Jasmine's house. My dad dropped me off and he was fine. Kissed me goodbye, gave me money and told me to be a good girl. Before he got home—my brother was away at a basketball camp— he stopped at a bar somewhere and started drinking.

"Meanwhile, I'm at Jasmine's house and we're having

a great time. Kind of late that night, she changed into her pajamas. We were playing in her room. She said, 'When are you going to put your pajamas on?' I was like, 'I am. Later.'

"The reality was my brother and I would sleep with our clothes on the weekends because we knew my dad was going to act up and my mother would come in rushing us out of the house. It was like we were firemen waiting for the call. To be ready to go quickly, we would go to bed with our clothes on Friday and Saturday nights.

"So I slept in my clothes at Jasmine's house. The next morning we were outside doing something and I asked her a very important question. I said, 'When is your dad going to beat your mom?'

"I thought it was the normal thing that happened in every household. She looked at me as if I were some kind of alien. 'What? What are you talking about?' she said. And in that instant I knew what was going on at our house was not normal.

"Even though I was about nine at that time, I was able to quickly recover. I said, 'I'm just playing. Let's go watch TV.' Jasmine said, 'Okay,' and that was that. But I remember it so clearly.

"And that was the last time I had to sleep in my clothes and the next-to-last time we ran away to a hotel. My mom would try to make leaving home a fun escape. She'd be battered, but she kept a stash of money in our room so we could have hotel and food money if we had to run. So we'd go check into a hotel and spend a night or two there. She would take us to the Monument and the Smithsonian and other landmarks. We would eat half-smokes on the street and play Frisbee on the Mall. A few times she was too sore to actually play with us. She'd sit on a bench or on the grass and watch us. But all that activity was designed to make us forget about what had happened.

"By Sunday evening we were back and my dad was sober and remorseful. He'd cook dinner and we'd go on like everything was normal. But that weekend I was at Jasmine's house my mom had the concussion. She was pretty much fed up. And when I told her what I asked Jasmine, she said that was it. My brother came back from camp that Sunday. Next thing I knew, we were in a hotel for about three days and then we moved into an apartment."

"Wow, Michele, that's a lot," Solomon said. "I'm sorry you had to go through all that."

"Well, I am too," she said. "But it's really hard to say because the things that happen in our lives, our experiences, make us who we are. So, I don't know who I would be if things didn't happen as they did.

"I'm scarred by it, but I don't think I'm damaged by it. I don't think my brother or mom are damaged. We went through therapy together for a while and my mom's therapy continued for a few years, I think.

"We don't even talk about it much anymore. My mom

was adamant about my brother not falling into the cycle of being abusive. And she was scared that I would be like her and accept abuse as a normal part of a relationship. That's what happens when you fall into that cycle."

"I see now how me telling you I smacked a girl would freak you out," Solomon said. "It makes sense now. But, just to reiterate, that's one of the biggest regrets of my life."

"Thanks for saying that," Michele said.

"So, what else do you have to tell me?" Solomon said. "You hold back stuff. And then when you come with it, it's earth-shattering."

Michele laughed. "One more thing."

"Oh, no. What now?" Solomon said, laughing. "You shot Kennedy? What?"

"I'm just kidding," she said. "That's it. I've bared my soul to you. There's nothing else left to reveal."

"You sure?" Solomon asked.

"Absolutely," Michele answered.

"Okay, then," he said. "How about some breakfast?"

"Solomon, it's like, four-thirty in the morning."

"Exactly. Breakfast time."

"Then do your thing," she said. "Wake me up when it's done."

Michele stretched across the couch and let out a sigh of relief. Solomon kissed her on the face and went to the bathroom to wash his hands.

"Sleep well, dear," he said. "Pleasant dreams this time."

CHAPTER 29
HERE COMES THE JUDGE

Solomon's and Michele's idyllic lives were interrupted by two elements of contrasting significance: the visit of his divorced parents and the court date for the carjacking.

The two were tied together; the night of the carjacking was minutes after Michele told Solomon he was Gerald's father. Solomon's mom and dad flew in from D.C. to finally meet their only grandchild.

And it so happened that their planned day of arrival was the Wednesday evening before the start of the Thursday court date. Solomon's car had been found almost three months after it was taken; the carjackers, both nineteen years old, were in it when Atlanta police pulled them over.

"I don't even want to relive that night... Well, that part of that night," Michele said. "That's the other nightmare I have sometimes, thinking about somebody with a gun to my head."

"I know," Solomon said. "It was so crazy. I remember it so well. It seemed like it was all in slow motion and then again it happened very quickly. Do you even want to go through a trial? I don't. I know it'll sound like I want to save the world, but I wonder if those kids are capable of being saved instead of being tossed into the prison system. We know what happens once they get there; nothing."

There were few witnesses to be called by the prosecution; Solomon and Michele and the arresting officers. The case could not be more clear-cut.

Meanwhile, Solomon had not told his parents of the events of that night. When he learned they would be in town during the start of the trial, he was compelled to share. He thought it better to tell them over the phone so they would not have to deal with it while dealing with meeting Gerald.

"How could you just be telling me this, boy?" Mr. Singletary said. "I understand not telling your mother; she's overly emotional. But you should've told me right away."

"My fault, Dad," Solomon said. "You're right. I'm sorry. You ever have anything like that happen to you?"

"I got robbed before," his father recalled. "I actually was in Chicago, hanging out with some friends a long time ago. I was at a liquor store on the Westside on my way to a party. When I came back out, two guys were waiting on me. Both of them had guns.

"I froze. Then I tried to talk them out of it."

"What? That's exactly what I did," Solomon said.

"Yeah, it was pure instinct," his dad said. "They still robbed me, but I think I convinced them to just take my money and not my wallet."

"Well, those guys acted like they wanted to shoot us, but I started talking and I think to just shut me up, they made us get out of the car," Solomon said. "Anyway, let me call Ma and tell her now, so hopefully you both can be over it when y'all get here next week."

"Oh, my God," Ms. Singletary said.

"Ma, calm down; it's over. We're fine," Solomon said.

"Why do you think it was okay to not tell me before now?" she said. "You're not too big to get your butt whipped."

"I know, I know," he said. "But you'll be here for the trial, so it kind of works out. But the focus should be on your grandson anyway."

Michele wanted to prepare her son for his grandparents.

"What are you going to tell him?" Solomon said. "He's already armed with everything he needs to know. We don't have to worry about him being ready for them. They'd better be ready for him."

Solomon left work early that Wednesday and picked up Gerald from school and then they headed to the airport. His son surprised him by having a sign that he made at school for Mr. and Ms. Singletary.

It was a large, colorful sign created with markers that read, simply: "Hi Grandma and Granddad."

"Ah, man, you're something else," he said to his son.

"They're going to really like that. In fact, they'll probably argue over who will get to keep it."

"Do you look like your father?" Gerald said.

"I do, a little bit," Solomon answered. "He's not as tall as me, but we have the same complexion and the same nose. I have my mother's eyes and mouth. So, I'm a mix; just like you are."

"I know. I look like you and Mommy," he said. "So I probably will look like Granddaddy or Grandma, too."

"You do," Solomon said. He was so proud. It made him think for the first time that seeing his father with his son would be three generations of Singletary men.

It made the conversation with his son that much more meaningful.

"You know what?" he said to Gerald as they parked the car. "We're going to go to a studio and have some photos taken this weekend."

Gerald smiled.

"Okay," Solomon said as they entered the airport terminal. "Can you figure out where we need to go?"

With his sign in hand, young Gerald was not intimidated. "I remember that we go this way," he said, pointing beyond the baggage claim. Solomon followed him.

"This way," he said, after reading a sign that directed them to flight arrivals.

Sure enough, Gerald got them to the proper place; the waiting area between the blue and red terminals at Hartsfield-Jackson. At the top of the steep escalator was where people gathered to wait on arriving family and friends. Gerald maneuvered his little body to the front and held up his sign, proudly.

After two large groups of passengers, up came Earl and Lorraine Singletary. Gerald spotted them from photos right away and held up his sign above his head.

His grandmother held her mouth and got teary-eyed. She hurried toward him and hugged him tightly. She was in love that quickly.

"Oh, how's my baby doing? Look at you," she said, tears rolling down her face.

"You look just like your daddy; and your granddaddy. So handsome. Give me a kiss."

Solomon and his father embraced while all that was going on. "Son, you look good."

"So do you, Dad. How was the flight?" Solomon cut his eyes at his mom, indicating he really wanted to know how they got along traveling together.

"We didn't crash, so it was fine," he said.

Then he turned to Gerald, who was just escaping the loving grasp of his grandmother.

"Hey there, buddy," he said.

"Hi, Grandpa," Gerald said as they shook hands, then hugged.

"We've got some catching up to do. I heard you're a pretty good basketball player," Mr. Singletary said.

"And football and boxing," Gerald eagerly added. "And Dad is teaching me golf next."

"Oh, I love it; another big-time athlete," his grandfather said.

Solomon hugged his mom. "How you doing, Ma?" he said. He glanced at his dad and said, "How was the flight?"

"Well, we didn't crash," she said.

Solomon laughed. "Come on, let's get your bags."

Gerald walked between his grandparents and welcomed all the adulation they poured on him. And they were enamored with him.

In the car ride home, Ms. Singletary asked about Michele. "Mommy is at work," Gerald interjected.

"Yeah, she was disappointed that she couldn't be with us to greet you," Solomon said. "But she said she wanted to cook dinner tonight."

When dinnertime came, Michele provided a delectable spread: fried chicken, mac and cheese, green beans, salad and salmon. She did not have time to bake dessert, so she picked up some treats from Cami Cakes in Buckhead.

"I like being here with all of Solomon's family," she said at the table, after Solomon recited grace. "Solomon didn't say it, but I could tell he was so excited you all were coming."

"This really does feel like family right now," Solomon said, looking at his mom and dad. "I can't remember the last time we all sat around a table together and had a meal. I think I was in the twelfth grade."

They ignored his observation and focused on Gerald. "When you get out of school tomorrow, we want to take you to the mall," his grandmother said. "We're going to shop and have dinner. Just the three of us."

"Thanks," he said.

"You're liking this grandparents thing, huh?" Michele said to Gerald. "Well, they can spoil you for a couple of days. That's what grandparents do."

They enjoyed the meal and the dinner conversation, but no one more than Gerald. He liked his grandparents and the feel of family. When it was time for bed, Mr. and Ms. Singletary walked him to his room.

"How you doing?" Solomon asked Michele. "You feeling all this?"

"I'm good," she said. "You seem so happy to see your parents together."

"It's weird. I like seeing them get along, but I'm almost waiting for an eruption, you know?" Solomon said. "But so far so good. Anyway, how do you feel about being around my entire family?"

"I'm fine," she said. "I'm comfortable. I can't even believe your parents aren't together. They get along so well. Maybe they started seeing each other again and didn't tell you."

"No way," Solomon said. "At the end, they didn't hate each other, but they hated to be around each other."

"You know better than me," she said. "I observed them and there was no tension in the air. But I could be wrong."

"I'm more focused on this court appearance tomorrow," Solomon said. "You ready?"

"All I can do is tell the truth," she said. "It was a long time ago now, but I still have dreams about it."

But then she felt like she was dreaming when the trial began. Ray, her cousin, Sonya, and Solomon's parents were in the courtroom. They heard the prosecuting attorney, Monique Bunch, deliver a strong opening statement that included: "These two defendants, a pair of young men with a history of crime and discord, robbed the two people at gunpoint on a night they should've remembered with fond and tender memories all their lives.

"Less than thirty minutes after Michele Williams informed her boyfriend, Solomon Singletary, that he was the father of her son, Gerald, these two men jumped in their car, put guns to their heads and threatened their lives.

"Only the grace of God prevented them from firing their weapons and killing these innocent people. They were that close to making a child parentless, and over what? Someone else's vehicle? Where does such lunacy come from, that these young men not only believe it is okay to forcefully take someone else's possessions, but threaten to kill them, too?

"Ladies and gentlemen of the jury, at the behest of the victims, we offered these defendants a plea deal that would've required a drug treatment program, and enrollment in a GED program so they could get their high school diplomas while serving three years in prison. I urge that this was the suggestion of the victims, the same people these young men threatened at gunpoint. Instead of accepting these generous terms, they arrogantly rebuffed the olive branch extended to them. That's why we're here today. As brazen as they were in carjacking this couple and threatening their lives, they are equally brash and arrogant in preferring a trial when they have been positively identified.

"Their position is that they are mistakenly identified and that they were sold Solomon Singletary's car by some friend who has since moved out of town. Amazing, right?

"Somehow, they expect you to believe these good people have misidentified them. Think about it: Someone puts a gun to your head, you don't forget their face, do you?"

It did not seem real to Michele or Solomon that they were sitting at the table at a felony trial, as if they were starring in an episode of *Law & Order*.

Michele was the first witness called to the stand. After a few preliminary questions, the lawyer got into the heart of the case:

Bunch: "That night started out as something special, didn't it?"

Michele: "It did. We were at Café Circa and I decided then to tell Solomon he was the father of my son, Gerald. Solomon and I had dated eight years before, but just as I got pregnant, he moved here and we lost contact. We reconnected several months ago. I was nervous that night, but I told him the news."

Bunch: "What was his reaction?"

Michele: "He was shocked at first, which was no surprise. We left the restaurant and sat in the car and talked about it. He was disappointed that he had missed seven years of Gerald's life, but he was so excited that he wanted to see him that night, even though he was in the bed sleep at my cousin Sonya's house. He insisted, so we headed to Sonya's house. When we got to the corner of Moreland Avenue and Hosea Williams Drive, those two young men jumped into the back of the car. It was chaos after that."

Bunch: "Can you describe the chaos?"

Michele could feel the emotion of it all coming back. She took a deep breath. "Well," she began, "they came in yelling and screaming. The one on the left there, he told Solomon to pull into the parking lot to our right."

Bunch: "You're identifying Quintavious Moss?"

Michele: "Yes."

Bunch: "Did you see his face?"

Michele: "Yes. I was in the passenger seat and he was sitting behind Solomon. I looked right into his eyes."

Bunch: "What happened next?"

Michele: "Well, there was a bunch of screaming between the two of them. Finally the one behind me pressed his gun up to the back of my head. He said he was going to shoot me. His friend told him to wait because he wanted to get our money first."

Solomon watched Michele testify and got angry. He

had been able to put the experience aside because there was so much going on with Gerald. Listening to her recount that night reminded him of how scared he was and how angry.

Michele finished and was then cross-examined by the defense lawyer, Manuel Proctor, a well-known civil rights attorney.

"So, Miss Williams, if you were sitting in the passenger seat and this defendant, Kenyan Parker, was behind you, as you testified, how could you see his face?"

Michele: "I didn't see his face when I was in the car. I saw the other young man's face."

Proctor: "So, as far as you know, he was not in the car."

Michele: "The police said he was in the car when they recovered it."

Proctor: "That wasn't my question."

Michele: "I didn't see his face at that—"

Proctor: "That will be all, Miss Williams... Wait, I'm sorry. Actually, I do have another question. You said you looked into the face of Quintavious Moss. For how long? A second? Two seconds?"

Michele: "I don't know, maybe two or three seconds. Could've been four or five?"

Proctor: "In that short amount of time, with all that fear and chaos, as you described it going on in the car, how can you say without question that the person you saw in the car was Quintavious Moss?"

Michele: "Because I saw him. He had on a baseball cap

turned to his left side. He was not clean-cut like he is now. He had braids or locs."

Proctor: "Which one was it? Locs or braids?"

Michele: "Locs."

Proctor: "You don't seem sure, Miss Williams. Anyway, let me ask you one last question. Have you ever had your purse snatched?"

Michele: "I did, about three or four years ago."

Proctor: "Who did it?"

Michele: "They—the police—never caught him."

Proctor: "What did he look like?"

Michele: "I didn't get to see his face; he came from behind me."

Proctor: "How did you describe him to the police?"

Michele: "I told them what I saw: a young black male wearing jeans and a white T-shirt with locs hanging under his cap."

Proctor: "Do you think all criminals wear locs, jeans and a baseball cap?"

Bunch: "Objection, your honor. Argumentative."

Judge Gore: "Sustained."

Proctor: "No more questions."

Bunch, standing at the prosecution table: "I would like to redirect, Your Honor."

Judge: "You may."

Bunch: "Ms. Williams, you said you didn't see Kenyan Parker's face when you were in the car. But did you see it after you got out of the car?"

Michele: "I did. We got out and stood there as they got in the front seats. The young man behind me got in the passenger seat. And he pointed his gun at us as they drove off. That's when I saw his face."

Bunch: "And are you sure it was the defendant, Kenyan Parker?"

Michele: "No doubt about it."

Bunch: "Thank you. No more questions."

Solomon was next on the stand.

Bunch: "Mr. Singletary, you heard the account of Michele Williams. How does yours differ from that night?"

Solomon: "It's very much the same. The only difference I can offer is that I not only looked into the eyes of both of those guys right there, I also had a conversation with them."

Bunch: "A conversation? With a gun to your head? What did you talk about?"

Solomon looked out into the courtroom at his parents. His dad was stoic; his mom was mortified. Michele wiped tears from her eyes.

"It was more of a back and forth," Solomon started. "I don't know where it came from. I didn't want to die, I didn't want to see Michele shot and I wanted to see my son. But as they were screaming for our money and talking about shooting us, I told them to stop. I can't sit here and act like I remember verbatim what we said to each other, but I told that one right there, Quintavious Moss, who had the gun pointed at my head, 'Get that gun off of my neck. You don't want to shoot me and you don't need to. We're giving you what you want.'

"He said, 'You think we playin'? Gimme your money. Then you'll see who's not gonna shoot somebody.'

"I told him I had just learned that I was a father. He said, 'What the eff that mean to me?'

"I don't know why I did, but I sensed something in him. I said, 'Look at me, man. You look like my cousin. We can't keep doing this to each other. Where's your father?'

"He said he didn't have a father. I said, 'So you want to put my son in that same position?'

"The other guy, Parker, who had the gun to Michele's head, he said, 'Man, eff what he talking about.'

"I just kept going. I said to him, 'Look at her. Doesn't she look like your sister or mother or aunt?'

"He grew angrier and said, 'Hell, no.'

"I said something else about being a father but he didn't want to hear it. He told Moss to shoot me.

"I said, 'Don't do it. You can take the car and the money. That ain't necessary. We're getting out the car and ya'll can go on. I got to be a father to this kid.'

"The guy behind me pulled his gun away from me. And it got quiet. We stared at each other for a few seconds. Then he said, 'Come on, man, let's go.'

"The other guy wasn't happy. He said they had to shoot us. But the young man behind me said, 'Let's just go.' Then he told us to get out. Kenyan Parker said, 'What? Man, we got to shoot these fools.'

"But I made some kind of connection with the other guy. He said, 'Let's just go.' Then he told us to get the eff out. And we did. And they drove off, with Parker pointing a gun at us as they pulled away in my car."

On cross-examination, Proctor asked Solomon: "What time of night did all this allegedly happen?"

Solomon: "Allegedly? It's not alleged. We were carjacked; by those guys. And it was after midnight."

Proctor: "Did you turn the lights on inside your car?"

Solomon: "No."

Proctor: "So how could you see the men if the light wasn't on in the car?"

Solomon: "It wasn't pitch-black. There were streetlights on. There was enough light because I saw them both clearly."

Proctor: "You must have the eyes of a bat... No more questions."

Solomon sat in the witness chair for a few seconds, staring at the defendants. Then his eyes shifted behind them, to their families. They looked defeated. Embarrassed. And they looked like they wanted more for those kids.

CHAPTER 30
MERCY, MERCY ME

When Solomon left the witness stand, the judge ordered a break for lunch. Solomon watched as the defendants turned to make eye contact with their families, as the marshals placed them in handcuffs.

A young woman whose eyes told of a hard life blew a kiss to Quintavious Moss. The young man looked remorseful that his family was involved in this drama.

The woman did not move until the defendants were ushered out of the courtroom, back to their cells. She shook her head, took a seat on the bench and pulled out some tissue to wipe her tears.

Solomon figured it was one of the kids' mothers. After they refused the plea deal, he declared he wanted them off the streets "where sane people live." Seeing Moss' mom so hurt turned his cold disposition warm.

He excused himself from the defense table with Michele and the prosecutor and made his way to the crying woman.

"Excuse me," he said.

She looked up and was shocked to see Solomon standing over her. She did not say anything.

"Can I sit down for a minute?" Solomon asked.

The woman nodded her head. Solomon sat. "Are you Quintavious' mother?"

She nodded her head again. "I'm sorry this is happening," he said.

The lady looked up at Solomon and turned away.

"What's your name?"

"Lucy," she said. Her voice was that of a broken woman.

"Lucy, what happened to your son?"

She shook her head. "I don't know. He's a good boy, a good big brother to his sister. But I believe it's my fault. I ran his father away from him. He was happy, normal when his dad was around. Three years ago, I couldn't take the cheating and I told him to leave for good this time. I didn't think he would go and leave his children behind. But he did.

"Q looked up to his dad. When he left, he kinda fell apart. He started being angry all the time. He stopped going to school and started hanging with that damned Kenyan and other bad apples. And now he's here."

"You think he wants to go to jail for a long time? I ask because we tried to get him to take a sentence that would help him," Solomon said.

"He's playing a fool to the streets," she said. "He thinks it makes him tough to not take a deal and to just do the time. I don't want this for him. And if his father knew this was going on, he would've made him take the deal. He loves me and respects me but he thinks I don't know what I'm talking about."

"Do you know where his father is?" Solomon asked.

"Maybe you could tell him to come down here and talk to your son."

"He's around. My sister said her girlfriend saw him yesterday at Greenbriar Mall," Lucy said.

"Could you call him and see if he would talk to your son? I'll talk to the lawyer. Maybe we can make the offer again," Solomon said.

"I can get a number and call his daddy," Lucy said. "But why are you doing this? Why are you being nice to someone who took you through something like that?"

"Because it's the right thing to do," Solomon said. "I was mad and bitter. But I saw you and I realize he has a family that cares about him. And, that night he really prevented something bad from happening. I could tell he didn't want to shoot me.

"And the other thing is, if we don't try to help these young men, who will? I ain't no saint, Miss Moss. But I believe you when you say he's a good kid doing bad things. Maybe we can save him. We should at least *try* to save him."

"Thank you," Lucy said. "I'm going to get my cell phone from security and see if I can convince his dad to come down here."

Solomon went to Ms. Bunch and Michele. "We should try a plea deal with them again," he said.

"Solomon, the trial has already started," Bunch said.

"But I watch TV; a deal can still be made," he said. "I don't want to see these kids get caught up in the prison system without giving them a chance to get better."

He looked at Michele. "We have a chance to help them. That was Moss' mother I was talking to. She's hurting. She doesn't want to see her son get convicted for fifteen years."

Michele smiled. "Look who isn't so cold anymore," she said. "I agree with you. Let's try to help them."

Bunch asked the judge for a continuance until the next day, while Lucy tried to reach and then convince Quintavious' dad, Quintin, to talk his son into taking a plea deal.

Late that afternoon, Quintin Moss, with baggy jeans hanging off his butt and smelling of a wretched combination of alcohol and weed, showed up at the Atlanta County Courthouse. Lucy met him on the steps.

"How my son gon' be on trial and you just calling a nigga?" Quintin asked.

"I didn't know if you cared or not," Lucy said. "Ain't nobody heard from you."

"You know I'm one hundred for my kids."

"Really? One hundred? One hundred what? One hundred proof. That's about it."

"Hey, I'm here, ain't I?" Quintin shot back.

"If you'd been here, none of this would've happened," she said.

Quintin looked away.

"The lawyer set it up to meet with Q," Lucy went on. "I need you to tell him to take the deal so he can get some drug counseling, get into an educational program and start getting his life together."

"He still gon' have to do three years," Quintin said.

"That's better than fifteen years, Quintin."

"Just take me to the place," he said, and she did.

They were directed into a small room with a table and chair on either side of it. Someone brought in a third chair. A minute or so later, Quintavious was led into the room.

When he saw his dad, he stopped walking. "What the hell he doing here?"

"Oh, now I'm 'he'?" Quintin said. "I can leave."

"Then leave; nobody want you here no way," Q said.

Quintin got up. Lucy grabbed his arm. "Please, Quintin sit down. Both of you sit down."

"Ma, I ain't siting down at no table across from him," the son said about the father.

"Yes, you are, Q," Lucy said. "I don't ever ask anything of you, which is part of the problem. But I'm asking now. Sit down and listen. If you don't want to talk, don't talk. But listen."

"Ma, listen to what?" Q said.

"Your father…" she said, "…wants to talk to you. The state wants to offer you the deal again."

The father and son stared at each other. Anger covered Q's eyes; embarrassment overtook Quintin's.

"Listen, son—" he started.

"Son? Man, you think I'm gonna sit here and listen to this crap…from you?" Q said.

"Son…" Lucy said, "…please, do it for me."

That softened Q's position. He leaned back in his seat and folded his arms as his father started again.

"Listen, I ain't been the best father; I know that," he said. "I got my problems. But don't make me having problems mess up your life. You ain't no thug, boy. You robbing people? Taking cars? Forget about me; I ain't been no good example. But I never wanted you to be like this.

"Remember when we used to play tackle football when you was four or five years old? It was good. We did good things, father/son things. You ran the ball just like I did. You were me... But the man I am now ain't what you should become. You better than me. That's what yo' momma wants and that's what I want, too.

"You ain't been to real prison before. You been locked up, and that ain't shit compared to what you got to go through in prison. You won't be 'round here so your momma can visit you. Those little girls you chasing ain't coming to Kansas or wherever they gon' send you. And for fifteen years. Shit, you ain't but eighteen."

"I'm nineteen," Q said.

"Either way, three years is a lot less than fifteen. You take this deal, get the help I ain't never got, get your GED and do your time like a man. Then you get out and be something. Fuck that bullshit, 'I ain't taking a deal.' That don't make you a man, not even on the streets. It makes you a fool everywhere.

"Don't be a fool. I don't know you like I used to but I remember that you ain't do much for yourself without thinking about yo' momma and yo' sister. You think they ain't hurting with you? You gon' hurt them more to go away for so long.

"One thing I know: I ain't done the best with my life, but I ain't bring no stupid ass nigga into the world. You'd have to be a stupid nigga to take fifteen years over three and a chance to get yourself better."

With that, Quintin Moss stood over the table, patted Lucy on the shoulder and walked out.

Mother and son sat there for several seconds in silence. Finally, Q rose from his chair.

He said, "I love you, Ma," and turned and walked toward the door to exit. Then he turned around to her. "Okay, Momma," he said. "Okay."

Lucy dropped her head in her hands and sobbed.

Not long after, Solomon and Michele got the news from Lucy.

"Thank you for being so nice," she said. "It means a lot to me and my son."

The lawyers ironed out the particulars and presented them to the judge the next morning. Defendant Kenyan Parker was not happy Q took the deal. But he accepted it, too.

After the process was finalized, Lucy brought over Michele and Solomon to her son before he was whisked away.

"You have something to say to them, don't you, Q?" Lucy said to her son.

Quintavious looked uncomfortable but sincere. "I'm

sorry about what happened," he said. "And thanks for trying to help me."

"Make your mother proud," Solomon said, and Q was pulled away.

Michele shook Lucy's hand. When Solomon extended his hand, she moved in for a hug. "Not too many people like you," she said. "I appreciate you so."

"You're welcome," Solomon said, holding her close. "Good luck. And keep us posted, please."

On the car ride home, Solomon told Michele, "This might sound strange, but maybe everything that happened that night—learning about Gerald being my son and us being carjacked—was supposed to happen to us. In different ways, they both had a big impact."

"You're probably right," Michele said. "I never told you this, but that night was the night I fell in love with you again. The way you handled that whole situation; learning about your son and then that craziness. I sat in the police car while you talked to them in such a controlled way. I felt like you saved my life twice that night."

"Saved your life? How?"

"The way you accepted the news I gave you; if you had been ugly or refused to believe me, it would've killed me," she said. "Not literally, but it definitely would've done something bad to my soul.

"Then you controlled that situation when we were being robbed. If you hadn't talked to them, made them think, no telling what would've happened to us. Basically, you made it happen. Nothing's sexier to a woman than a man being a man."

Solomon blushed, which was a rarity. "Since we're having confessions, I should tell you that us finding each other again was the chance I needed to save my soul," he said. "That might sound dramatic, but it's true. I had lost it. I did wrong to some good women who deserved more, either by not giving my all or not giving the relationship an honest try or just believing they would be the bastards other women were to me or just disappearing without a trace. It was selfish; I did it to protect myself, but it ate at me.

"Ray said I was a 'cold piece of work.' And he was right. I didn't care who was hurt as long as it wasn't me. But that wasn't who I really was. I wasn't sure how to get back to me or who I wanted to be; until I saw you. That's when it became clear that I needed to do right by you to be right with myself."

At his house, Solomon's parents and Gerald were watching a movie when he and Michele arrived from court. They were wrapped in blankets with all the lights out.

Mr. Singletary stopped the movie. "Maybe this is a time for full disclosure," he said to Michele and Solomon.

They knew what he meant; telling Gerald what had happened to them. And so, they did. Gerald was typically inquisitive but clearly not concerned because his parents were fine.

The grandparents interjected their views on the matter and Solomon concluded the talk by imparting a message his father had shared with him many years before: "Gerald, you're my son, a Singletary, and that means a whole lot of people expect a whole lot of good things out of you. That doesn't mean you have to discover a cure for cancer, although that would be great, or be President of the United States, which, with the way they've treated Barack Obama, I'm not sure I'd even want for you. But it does mean you can make your mark by being a good person, by standing up for what's right and by working for the things you want in life. That's how you honor your family."

"I like that, Daddy," Gerald said. "You should write that down so I won't forget any of it."

"I will," Solomon said.

He and Michele left the room and let them resume watching their movie. "This is freaking me out," he said.

"What?" Michele asked.

"My parents. I can't remember the last time they were this civil to each other. Not only are they civil, but they're actually nice to each other. What's going on? It can't be just Gerald, can it?"

"I don't know, but don't question it; embrace it," Michele said. "It might blow up. If it does, at least you have these moments to hold on to."

CHAPTER 31

A WARM
PIECE OF WORK

With live-in sitters in Gerald's grandparents, Solomon and Michele took to a night on the town. Michele called to invite Cynthia and Ray, but was told Ray was already out, running some errands.

So, it was just Solomon and Michele on Interstate 20 West, trying to decide where to go.

"Café Circa?" Michele suggested.

"They do have a new rooftop lounge," Solomon said. "But the last time we went there, a lot happened. You might tell me you're pregnant or something."

"Oh, no, I won't," Michele said, laughing.

"How about Serpas; great restaurant at Studioplex?" Solomon offered.

"I went there a few weeks ago. I kind of want something different," Michele said.

They decided on the lounge at the Mansion Hotel in Buckhead. They could get cocktails and eat there with live music. It was cool and fun, with a contemporary but warm feel. It was not too dark, but still romantic.

There, they sipped on margaritas and settled for wings and lobster bisque. Their conversation turned from a weekend destination with Cynthia and Ray to the direction of their relationship. Of course, it was Michele who wanted some clarity.

"So, Solomon, we've been through a lot and we're still here, together. What's next for us? I'm not trying to put any pressure on you, but I'd like to know what's on your mind."

"I've actually been thinking about that, too, Michele," he said. "You know me: I'm sort of cautious about marriage. When almost everyone you know who is married is complaining about being married, well, that tells you something."

"You can't go on other people's problems and think they'll be ours," Michele said. "We're not them. More important than that, they're not us. We've been through a lot that has tested if we should be together. And we *are* together. Do you want to be single all your life?"

"I'm not single; I'm with you," he answered.

"You know what I mean, Solomon."

"I want you. That's what I know. Last night, I had a conversation with this woman…a woman I'd been seeing. I hadn't seen or talked to her in a long time but she deserved to hear why. So I told her about us.

"She asked me if we were getting married. I told her that I didn't know. She told me that I needed to grow up and stop running from being a man. I was insulted at first. But when I thought about it later, I understood what she meant. Her position was that if I have the woman I say that I love, then why don't I know what I want to do with her?"

"Yeah," Michele said, "so what's your answer?"

"I love you and I love our son and I want us to be a family—that's my answer," he said. "The time will come when I'll light you up."

"Light me up?" she asked.

"Yeah, light you up—put a diamond on your finger," Solomon said. "Make it official that we're a family."

"Really?"

"Really. But you won't have a clue when it's going down. I love surprises," Solomon said. "It'll happen when you least expect it. The reality is we're a family. Gerald needs to see us together as a family."

They hugged. "I'm so happy right now," she said. "But I'm gonna know when you propose. No one can surprise me."

"Aren't we a surprise?" Solomon said. "You couldn't have expected this."

Michele did not answer.

"Ah, hello?" Solomon said. A look he had not seen covered Michele's face. "What's wrong?"

"Look over there," she said, nodding her head in the direction of two men engrossed in serious conversation. They were sitting side-by-side. One guy looked rather feminine, with a dangling earring and a tight-fitting, spandex T-shirt. He was overtly gay with the unmistakable gesturing and posturing.

The other guy was Solomon's friend, Ray.

"Isn't that Ray?" he said.

"It is," Michele said. "Cynthia told me he was out at IKEA. What is he doing with that man? Solomon, that man is obviously gay, right?"

"He looks gay to me; not to judge," Solomon said. "I'm tripping. Ray isn't gay. He can't be, could he, Michele?"

"I wouldn't have said so five minutes ago, but from what I'm seeing now…" She paused and sighed. "You tell me? Do straight men hang out with gay men?"

"No. Pure and simple. It never happens. No way. At least not knowingly," he answered.

They watched—stared, rather—as Ray and the man talked and laughed for another five minutes. Solomon and Michele ignored their drinks and food. They were engrossed in this unfolding drama.

Finally, the men rose from their seats and headed for the area outside the lounge. They walked left, toward the front lobby, past the bathroom and staircase. Michele and Solomon followed, an intrigued pair of voyeurs desperate to see as much as possible.

In the lobby, Ray looked at his watch and seemed alarmed by the time. He and the man hugged and Ray kissed him on the side of the face before heading through the rotunda and outside the hotel. The man turned and headed in the opposite direction.

"I don't believe this," Michele said. "Poor Cynthia. What are you going to do?"

"What am I going to do? What should I do? I don't know," Solomon said. "That was my man…"

"What do you mean, 'was' your man?"

"You just asked me if men hang out with gay men. I just told you 'no.' So I think you know what I need to do."

"But Solomon, that's your friend. You told me you all have traveled together, been there for each other. How can you just drop him now?" She gazed at him. "Don't tell me you're homophobic."

"No, I'm not," Solomon answered. "Or maybe I am. I don't know. They can do their thing as long as they stay away from me."

"Oh, they have to stay away from you?" Michele asked. "That's crazy. You can't be that way, Solomon."

"I don't mean it that way," he said. "I don't understand it. Just don't bring innocent women into it. He's married with a son. And I'm supposed to act like that's cool?"

"Yeah, right," Michele said. "You're concerned about Cynthia? No, this is about you and your insecurities."

Solomon shook his head and went back in to pay the tab. When he returned, Michele was waiting in the rotunda.

"Let's go," he said. When they got outside to valet parking, Ray was standing there looking out toward Peachtree Road.

Almost as if he sensed four eyes were zoomed in on him, he turned around. There was shock on his face.

"Hey, huh, what's up?" He smiled. Really, he was wondering how long they had been there and what they had seen.

"You're up, Ray," Solomon said. "What are you doing here? Cynthia told Michele you were running errands."

"I was," Ray said.

"Yeah, we saw," Solomon said, and Ray's heart dropped. The expression on his face was undeniable embarrassment.

"What's going on, Ray?" Solomon said. "Am I wrong or did that guy I saw you kiss look like a fag?"

"A fag?" Ray said. "That's real cave man talk right there."

"Oh, you offended by the word 'fag.' Since when?" Solomon asked. The tone of the conversation turned hostile.

"Since right now," Ray said loudly.

"Only fags are offended by that word," Solomon said.

"Solomon," Michele said. "Come on now; that's not right."

"Yo, I know you're not calling me out my name," Ray said.

"If the pink skirt fits, dance in it," Solomon shot back.

"You're lucky Michele is here," Ray said.

"She can leave," Solomon responded. "Michele, go ahead home. I want to see what this fag will do with you gone."

"I'm not going anywhere," she said. "You are not fighting."

The Mansion's valet workers and a security guard came over. "Do we have a problem here?" one of them said.

"No," Michele said. "We're leaving."

Just then, Ray's car pulled up.

"Sir, you should leave," the security guard said to Ray.

"Let's see what your wife has to say about this!" Solomon yelled as Ray got into the car.

Michele was livid. "What is wrong with you? How could you be that way? One minute we're talking about creating a family and the next you're acting like an ignorant child."

"First of all, I ain't no ignorant child, so don't call me that," he said. "Secondly, this man is married with a son and going around with men. I should be all right with that because we've been friends? I don't think so."

"You know what? Take me home," Michele said.

"What?" Solomon responded. "You're mad at me?"

"No, I'm disappointed in you," she said. "I expected a lot more from you. You're a sophisticated man. You don't go around calling someone, especially your friend, a fag."

The valet pulled up with the car. Solomon tried to open the door for her, but she did it herself; an indication of her anger. They drove through Buckhead and downtown on Peachtree Road without uttering a word.

Finally, Michele said, "What if Gerald grows up and you find out he's gay? You gonna call him a 'fag' and disown him?"

Solomon did not answer, but the mere thought scared

him. He continued to drive toward Interstate 20, both hands on the steering wheel.

"You told me he was the truest friend you had among all your huge group of guys," Michele said. "You told me he was the only one you confided in when you were arrested. You told me he was the first person you called after your parents when you learned Gerald was your son.

"You told me he would be the best man at your wedding, if you ever had one. You told me he is the godfather to Gerald. You told me you trusted him. You told me he was like the brother you never had.

"And now all that is gone, evaporated, because you think he's gay? I pray that's not the case. I pray you're the man I believe you are.

"This is a test for you, Solomon. You said you found your soul, but I don't know. If you judge your best friend based on what you think his sexuality is, then you're colder than Ray ever imagined."

Michele's words dug deep into Solomon's mind and heart. She was right about Ray and what he meant to Solomon. Men hardly ever expressed to each other the depth and importance of their friendship, but Ray actually did, when Gerald was in the hospital.

He said to Solomon while they sat in the waiting room: "I prayed for you because I believe you actually need Gerald more than he needs you. And I know if he's not all right, you won't be all right. And you're my boy, so I need you to be all right. It's a tough time for you. But I'm here for you. Always."

"You remember what Ray told you when Gerald was sick?" Michele asked, reading Solomon's thoughts.

Solomon's anger, disappointment and confusion subsided. Ray was his friend, unequivocally.

"Let's go to his house," Solomon said.

"Maybe you should call him first," she said.

Solomon agreed.

"Yeah," Ray said answering the phone.

"I wanted to come by your house and talk to you for a minute," Solomon said.

"About what?" he said.

"I want to apologize," Solomon said. "You're my man."

Ray agreed to let them come over. They stopped at the liquor store on Wesley Chapel and bought a bottle of champagne.

"Peace offering," Solomon said, raising the bottle of Vueve when Ray opened the door. Ray smiled.

"Hi, Michele," he said. "Come on in."

Cynthia emerged from the kitchen.

"Ray, uh, can we go out back for a minute?" Solomon said.

"No need; Cynthia knows everything," Ray said. "We can all talk right here."

Solomon looked at Michele, who gave him an indifferent look.

They took seats in the living room. Ray hit the mute button on the remote control.

"What's up?" Ray looked at Solomon.

"Listen, I, uh, I know a lot of people, and I then I have you," he said. "You've been a true friend. I was so surprised by what I saw that I forgot that and gave in to my fears and hang-ups.

"Michele reminded me of a lot of stuff that made me feel really good about our friendship and really bad about myself. No matter what, you're still Ray and we're still boys."

"The truth is," Ray said, "I wasn't really surprised by your reaction. I told Cynthia that. I know how you were with women; cold. Why wouldn't you be that way with me in this situation?

"Most men would be. *I* would be. The one thing I would've done differently is I would've asked you some questions instead of jumping the gun."

"You want to ask some question now, Solomon?" Cynthia said.

He was not sure what to say. He glanced at Michele, who gave him an expression that said, "Go ahead; ask."

Solomon kept his mouth shut. So Cynthia asked him, "You're okay with my husband being gay?"

Solomon did not hesitate. "I'm friends with Ray, not his sexuality," a mantra he adopted on his way there.

Then he asked Cynthia: "Are you all right with it?"

"No," she said.

Michele and Solomon tried to look as if they were not surprised. It didn't work.

"Well, that's not our business," Michele said.

"No, he asked the question; I'm just answering," Cynthia said. "And here's the rest of my answer: If he were gay, we'd have a real problem."

Then a smile creased her face and Ray laughed.

"You really think I'd be married to a gay man?" Cynthia said. "I have nothing against gay men. But I don't want to be married to one."

"And what does that say about me that you think I'm gay?" Ray asked, smiling.

"Wait a minute, wait a minute," Solomon said. "We saw you... I mean, the other guy was... We... What's going on?"

"The other guy," Ray said, "was my brother. My twin brother, Paul; he's gay."

An avalanche of relief fell down over Solomon. "Oh, man. I had no idea you even had a brother," he said. "I was serious about not caring about your sexuality. But it's better this way."

They all laughed.

"Yeah, that was Paul," Ray said. "It's been rough for him. My father and grandfather have disowned him and even my mother isn't what I think she could be to him.

"I watched my father have the same reaction you did, only a hundred times worse and directly at Paul. He tried to forbid me from communicating with him. But he's my brother; nothing can break that. We're twins— obviously not identical. But as twin brothers we have a special bond. I wasn't sure how Cynthia would feel about it, so when she thought I was out seeing someone else, I was with Paul. I explained that to her and, to my surprise, she has been supportive."

"Family is all we have," Cynthia said.

"I wasn't excited to learn about his preference about ten years ago," Ray added, "but it really does nothing to change who he is to me."

"That's such a mature approach," Michele said. "How can we judge other people when none of us are pure?"

Solomon felt pure in his heart, pure in his soul. He had overcome his distrust of women and opened up to Michele. She was going to be his wife. And he meant what he said about being Ray's friend no matter what, another sign of personal growth.

They popped the champagne and Cynthia poured some in the flutes. They had a toast just as the doorbell rang. Ray hurried to he door. When he opened it, his brother, Paul, stepped in.

They shook hands. Paul and Cynthia embraced and exchanged pleasantries.

Ray then introduced him to Solomon.

"This is my brother, Paul," he said. "Paul, this is—"

Solomon interrupted him. "I'm Solomon," he said, smiling, "your brother from another mother."

Everyone laughed.

He passed on a handshake and hugged Paul. During the embrace, his eyes met with Michele's, and his wife-to-be smiled the warmest smile.

ABOUT THE AUTHOR

Curtis Bunn is a national award-winning sports journalist who has evolved into one of the most critically acclaimed authors of contemporary fiction about relationships. His novel, *Baggage Check*, ascended to No. 1 on the *Essence* magazine and Cushcity.com bestseller lists. He has been featured in national magazines (including *Essence, Black Issues Book Review, Uptown, Black Enterprise, Rolling Out*) and local Atlanta media outlets (*The Atlanta Journal-Constitution*, Fox 5 Good Day Atlanta, Fox 5 Good Day Xtra!). He has written for *Black Enterprise, Honey* magazine, *ESPN The Magazine, Hoop* magazine and others. A native of Washington, D.C., Bunn covered the NBA, NFL, Olympics, college basketball, pro baseball, professional boxing and wrote columns for *The Washington Times, New York Newsday* and *New York Daily News* and *The Atlanta Journal-Constitution*.

In 2002, he founded the National Book Club Conference, which has developed into a premier annual literary event for readers and authors. This bolstered his connection to hundreds of reading groups around the country. His website is www.curtisbunn.com and he has more than 1,700 friends on Facebook.

READER DISCUSSION GUIDE

■ Are you surprised Solomon was so affected by his past relationships with women?

■ Could you forgive Solomon for the way he treated Michele early in the book?

■ What did you think of Michele's talk to her book club members about the importance of sex in her life? Do you agree or disagree with her?

■ Could you relate to Michele's struggle to trust Solomon and her reluctance to share news with him about her son, Gerald?

■ Did you ever find yourself pulling for Solomon and Michele to make it? To not make it?

■ How did you receive Michele's revelation to Solomon about Gerald? Did it surprise you? Did you think she should have kept it to herself?

■ Did Michele overreact to Solomon's indiscretion of the past and his disciplining of Gerald?

- Was the intimacy described in the book over the top, too mild or exciting?

- How does the potential of domestic violence impact your feeling/ interactions with a man? Was Michele's reaction to Solomon justified?

- Can a woman inspire a man to change? Can he go from cold to warm? Or is his core established and un-breakable?

To have Curtis Bunn's input on these questions and any others you may have, please e-mail him at curtisbunn@yahoo.com. He is available to attend book club meetings, participate in meetings via conference call or Skype and online chat sessions. Please visit www.curtisbunn.com for more information.

HOMECOMING WEEKEND

COMING SEPTEMBER 2012 FROM STREBOR BOOKS

CHAPTER 1
BUMPY ROAD

It was times like this when Jimmy resented his wife. He hated that she tainted his thoughts on marriage because he actually looked at the institution as something to savor. But his wife, well, she could create excruciating occasions that made him feel like getting into his car and driving off to no place in particular, just away from her, never bothering to look back.

Was it an overreaction? Maybe. Well, likely. But he was not a deadbeat husband, a bore or a louse. He, in fact, was the opposite, which, he believed, entitled him to some understanding and not the blow-torch heat his wife was known for spewing.

On this day in particular, it ate at Jimmy like a run-amok virus.

He had waited an entire decade for this weekend.

It was Homecoming.

Monica knew how excited he was about the trip—he talked incessantly about how much he looked forward to going back to his old college—but that did not stop her filling Jimmy's head with exactly what it did not welcome.

He had the trip all planned out. He was trying to get onto Interstate 95 South by noon so he could arrive before traffic built up at the tunnel between Hampton and Norfolk, Virginia around 3 o'clock. It was a solid three-hour, fifteen-minute drive from their home in Southeast Washington, D.C—and that included time for him to stop downtown to get his customary road food: a half-smoke with mustard and onions, a box of Boston Baked Beans candy, pumpkin seeds and a Welch's grape soda.

Monica, his wife, was sweet on occasion, needy on many and overbearing on too many. This was one of her patented meltdowns that bothered Jimmy like that sound of chalk screeching across a blackboard. When she acted as she did on this day—standing over him as he packed his bags, arms folded, mouth going, attitude funky—it was a miserable existence for Jimmy. He didn't do drama well, and Monica was in straight Queen Drama mode.

While she was dramatic and even over the top…she had a valid argument. She wondered why her husband was going back to Norfolk State University's homecoming without her?

Jimmy was so frustrated because of what he deemed her sinister objective: to pressure and nag him into not going or to bring her along, even as he was moments from departing. At worse, she wanted to put him in a foul mood so he would not enjoy himself. *Selfish*, he thought.

Why else would she go into her histrionics now? he surmised. *She knew I was going to homecoming for several months*. To act a fool just as he was about to leave frustrated him.

"I can't believe this is happening," he said. He had much more to say, but he worked hard on controlling his fly-off-the-handle temper, and the best way to handle that moment was to shut it down as best he could.

"Believe it," she said with much attitude.

Monica was not cute when she was this way. Ordinarily, she was a good-looking woman, not breathtaking but certainly attractive enough for Jimmy to be proud to call her his wife. When she was this way, though, she didn't look the same. In his eyes, she resembled something awkward and distorted, totally unappealing.

Her eyes seemed to darken and to fall back into the sockets, and she held a perceptible amount of saliva in her mouth. Some creature took over her physical being and the devil owned her mind, Jimmy thought.

Still, he loved his wife. She could be worse; their marriage could be worse. He could have been like one of his close friends, Lonnie, who simply had been emasculated by his spouse. She controlled everything from what he did (or didn't do) to with whom among his "friends" he communicated. He became a joke among their friends.

Monica was not *that* bad. This level of discord was not regular behavior; Jimmy would not have been able to take it if it were the norm. Other times she got on his nerves (what woman didn't?) for one thing or another, and he would often acquiesce, mumbling to himself: *Keep the peace.*

She figured that if she griped enough Jimmy would again look to keep the peace and give in. She was wrong. No amount of badgering was going to turn his position. For the most part, she was a responsible, fun wife and mother of their two kids. But something about him going back to his alma mater for homecoming turned her paranoid. Jimmy remained calm, but he would not budge.

"Baby," he said, trying his best to not sound condescending, "why must we go through this now? You knew about this trip for months. I'm about to leave. This makes no sense."

"Why is it that you *have* to go *and* that I can't go with you?" Monica said.

She went with Jimmy, a captain in the Army, a few places across the country. They moved back to D.C.

from California less than a year before, which was good and bad in this situation. It was good because he was back home and it was much easier to get to Norfolk from D.C. than the West Coast or the foreign stops they had. It was bad because he could not fall back on the excuse that it was not "cost-efficient" for both of them to make the cross-country trip for a two-day weekend, as he had in the past.

Jimmy's reality was that his wife did not go to Norfolk State. She did not go to an historically black college at all, which meant, to Jimmy, she didn't understand the value of the weekend—or that there was sort of a "no-spouse code" among most alumni, at least among those he knew well from school.

She went to the "University of Something or Other in Ohio," he liked to say, where the brothers and sisters there were in the vast minority. So, while homecoming there surely was fun, it did not include all the elements that make homecoming at an HBCU a special experience and sort of a family reunion.

Jimmy had been in touch with classmates who talked about how impressed and proud they were to see how much their school had grown. They talked about there being fifty-thousand people there, all black, all caught up in the pride and celebratory spirit that homecoming raises. At a non-HBCU, the homecoming weekend was about the football game mostly and a whole bunch of stuff that did not measure up to the cultural experience of an HBCU. At least that's what Jimmy—and many—thought.

"And there's nothing wrong with that," he told Monica. "It's just different. Our weekend is about us, the fellowshipping, the tailgate (before, during and after the game), the band, the parties and, above all, the pride of being at a place that essentially was home for us as teenagers. The place, really, where we were nurtured and grew up. That's what the black college experience gives you.

"Homecoming," he said, "is a celebration of all that."

"So what are you saying? Your homecoming means more to you than mine because you went to a black college?" Monica argued. "That's crazy."

"I'm not saying your homecoming isn't as important to you or that it isn't fun and great," Jimmy said. "But the mere fact that you have asked me to come with you to yours tells me you're not having that much fun.

"Listen, honey, it's not like I'm going there and meeting with some woman," he went on. "I feel funny about even having to say that. But that's what it comes down to, doesn't it?"

Jimmy lived mostly on the West Coast during the years after he graduated with honors as a commissioned officer. He had not made it back to a single homecoming since graduation. For the six years they had been married, Jimmy hardly even talked of homecoming because attending did not seem reasonable, as they lived on the West Coast on a wire-thin budget. He either could not take

TDY (leave) because had duty he could not abandon—or he was deployed to the Middle East. Surviving both Iraq and Afghanistan and moving back to D.C. allowed him to get excited about making homecoming, especially after he took Monica to campus during a summer visit to Virginia Beach.

"Monica, I told you on that trip that I was going to homecoming," he said, placing the last of his clothes in his luggage. "Don't act like you don't remember."

He lifted his zipped bag onto its wheels and headed to the garage door so he could dump it in the trunk and keep it moving.

"This is the only weekend I get all year to myself," he said. He was calm even though he was furious to have to go through such explanation. He somehow mastered the art—and it was an art—of composing himself in his most heated moments. Jimmy, in fact, smiled as he explained his position although he was percolating inside.

"I go hard as a husband and father," he said. "I don't golf, so I don't do golf trips. I don't run off to visit my family without you. I don't go the Super Bowl or NBA All-Star Weekend. I don't go visiting one of my boys for the weekend. This is it. I deserve this break."

The most important reason of all…he had to explain to her again just before he got into his car.

He said: "Even if I did take an occasional trip, this should not be a problem. I have earned it. Plus, you didn't go to school there. So, you'd be standing around bored, looking for me to entertain you. To be honest, I couldn't have the same kind of fun I normally would have with my fraternity brothers and friends. It's innocent fun, but we use harsh language and tell jokes that are not always, uh, politically correct. It's part of what we do. I'm not comfortable doing that around you and you'd be monitoring how much I drink, what I say, what I eat, who I hugged. I can hear you now: 'Who was that? An old girlfriend? Did you sleep with her?' That's not how it should be.

"Also, I would feel like I had to keep you from being miserable. I can hear you now complaining at the tailgate about needing to sit down and not wanting to go to the bathroom in the Porta Potty or not wanting the food. All that would not be fair to me at my homecoming.

"I have seen people—men and women—bring their spouses and have a miserable time because they were restricted. When you have your homecoming, I don't even think about going. I know you and your girlfriends want to talk freely and me being there would prevent that. And I don't know those people, so I don't want to be there, putting you in the awkward position of trying to keep me amused. It wouldn't be fair."

Monica was unfazed. "But that's the difference between you and me," she said. "I would enjoy my friends meeting my husband. But you'd prefer to run off like you're single."

Jimmy's patience was diminishing.

"You know, you're about to piss me off," he started. "All that I said and that's what you come back with? First of all, if they were really your friends, I would have met them by now. This isn't a family vacation. When you go on your book club trip to Atlanta, I know it's not a family trip. It's for you and your girls. I don't know what the hell y'all do down there and I don't really care. I trust that you understand you're married and will act like it. But you don't invite me on that trip and you shouldn't. That's how my homecoming is. It's not about acting like I'm single. Act like you know me."

With that, he knew he needed to leave before the scene turned ugly. He was a thirty-two-year-old man and she was making him feel like he was a kid asking for permission, which did not sit well with him—especially since it had been established long before that he was going alone.

"Monica," he said, hugging her; she did not hug him back, "I love you and I will call you when I get to Norfolk. Stop pouting and wish me a good time."

She just looked at him. They had a stare-down for a few seconds before Jimmy turned, opened the garage door, deposited his luggage and jumped into his car.

Monica stood there with her arms folded and a look of disgust on her face.

He honked his horn as he backed out. Jimmy did not like that his wife was being so sour about his homecoming trip. But he couldn't worry about it, either. If he did, it would put a cloud over his weekend. The forecast called for seventy-two degrees and lots of sun, meaning there was no room for clouds.

So instead of feeling awkward about leaving her there pissed at him, he felt reinvigorated, relieved and ready.

To really put that nonsense behind him, he called one of his boys, Carter, who was flying into Norfolk from New York. He was a fun and level-headed friend who graduated a year before Jimmy.

"Yo, I'm in a cab headed to LaGuardia," he said. "I can't wait to get down there. I got some work to do."

"Work to do" meant he had women to conquer. Homecoming was like a free-for-all for Carter.

"I don't think I'm going to make the parties," he said.

"What? How you gonna come to Homecoming and miss the parties?" Jimmy asked.

"Oh, that's right; we haven't really talked," he said. "Homecoming is a time for me and Barbara to reconnect. She's the love of my life, man. I should never have let her go back in the day. It's the biggest mistake of my life."

At least Carter was divorced, which allowed him to do whatever he liked.

"But hold up—isn't Barbara married?" Jimmy asked.

"With three kids, too," Carter said. It was strange the way he said it, like he was proud.

"I know that was your girl about a decade ago," Jimmy said. "But, man, she has a family now. And Barbara was a good girl. You think she's coming to Homecoming to get with you?"

"You don't understand, Jimbo," Carter said. "What she and I have is not ordinary. Why you think she's coming all the way from San Diego? We both tried to move on with our lives. And we have moved on, to a degree. But we still have that connection. Actually, it's even stronger now than ever. It's crazy."

"I wonder if she had the same issue I had—leaving her spouse husband behind," Jimmy said. "Monica gave me the business."

"Well, when hasn't she?" Carter said, laughing. "She's just being herself, I guess. I don't know if Barbara had any issues. I didn't ask. I just know she's coming.

"Listen, I'm not proud of this situation. And I've only told you and my brother about it. But I really understand what the power of love means because I would never imagine myself feeling this way about any woman, especially a married woman."

They chopped it up for a few more minutes before hanging up. Jimmy was headed to Norfolk to get the whole nostalgic feeling of seeing old friends and visiting the place that really made him—and really, to just get away from the daily grind at home.

Carter was headed there for love.

And there was little difference between the two reasons.